The Green Fairy Book

by
Ed. Andrew Lang

The Green Fairy Book
by Ed. Andrew Lang

Copyright © 2024

All Rights reserved.

No part of this publication may be reproduced, stored in a retrieval system, or transmitted in any form or by any means, electronic, mechanical, photocopying or Otherwise, without the written permission of the publisher.
The author/editor asserts the moral right to be identified as the author/editor of this work.

ISBN: 978-93-59329-75-8

Published by

DOUBLE 9 BOOKS
2/13-B, Ansari Road
Daryaganj, New Delhi – 110002
info@double9books.com
www.double9books.com
Tel. 011-40042856

This book is under public domain

ABOUT THE EDITOR

Andrew Lang FBA (31 March 1844 - 20 July 1912) was a Scottish poet, writer, literary critic, and anthropologist. He is primarily known for amassing folk and fairy stories. Andrew Lang lectures are named after him at the University of St Andrews. Lang was born in Selkirk, Scottish Borders, in 1844. He was the eldest of eight children born to John Lang, the Selkirk town clerk, and his wife Jane Plenderleath Sellar, the daughter of Patrick Sellar, the first Duke of Sutherland's factor. On April 17, 1875, he married Leonora Blanche Alleyne, the youngest daughter of Clifton and Barbados businessman C. T. Alleyne. Lang's Color/Rainbow Fairy Books, which he edited, were alternately credited to her as author, collaborator, or translator.

CONTENTS

THE BLUE BIRD 7
THE HALF-CHICK 27
THE STORY OF CALIPH STORK 31
THE ENCHANTED WATCH 40
ROSANELLA 44
SYLVAIN AND JOCOSA 49
FAIRY GIFTS 54
PRINCE NARCISSUS AND
THE PRINCESS POTENTILLA 58
PRINCE FEATHERHEAD AND THE PRINCESS CELANDINE 70
THE THREE LITTLE PIGS 81
HEART OF ICE 85
THE ENCHANTED RING 106
THE SNUFF-BOX 112
THE GOLDEN BLACKBIRD 116
THE LITTLE SOLDIER 121
THE MAGIC SWAN 135
THE DIRTY SHEPHERDESS 139
THE ENCHANTED SNAKE 143
THE BITER BIT 150
KING KOJATA (From the Russian) 157

PRINCE FICKLE AND FAIR HELENA (From the German) 167

PUDDOCKY (From the German) 172

THE STORY OF HOK LEE AND THE DWARFS 177

THE STORY OF THE THREE BEARS 181

PRINCE VIVIEN AND THE PRINCESS PLACIDA 184

LITTLE ONE-EYE, LITTLE TWO-EYES, AND
LITTLE THREE-EYES 202

JORINDE AND JORINGEL 208

ALLERLEIRAUH; OR, THE MANY-FURRED CREATURE 210

THE TWELVE HUNTSMEN 214

SPINDLE, SHUTTLE, AND NEEDLE 217

THE CRYSTAL COFFIN 220

THE THREE SNAKE-LEAVES 225

THE RIDDLE 228

JACK MY HEDGEHOG 231

THE GOLDEN LADS 236

THE WHITE SNAKE 241

THE STORY OF A CLEVER TAILOR 245

THE GOLDEN MERMAID 248

THE WAR OF THE WOLF AND THE FOX 255

THE STORY OF THE FISHERMAN AND HIS WIFE 259

THE THREE MUSICIANS 267

THE THREE DOGS 273

THE BLUE BIRD

Once upon a time there lived a King who was immensely rich. He had broad lands, and sacks overflowing with gold and silver; but he did not care a bit for all his riches, because the Queen, his wife, was dead. He shut himself up in a little room and knocked his head against the walls for grief, until his courtiers were really afraid that he would hurt himself. So they hung feather-beds between the tapestry and the walls, and then he could go on knocking his head as long as it was any consolation to him without coming to much harm. All his subjects came to see him, and said whatever they thought would comfort him: some were grave, even gloomy with him; and some agreeable, even gay; but not one could make the least impression upon him. Indeed, he hardly seemed to hear what they said. At last came a lady who was wrapped in a black mantle, and seemed to be in the deepest grief. She wept and sobbed until even the King's attention was attracted; and when she said that, far from coming to try and diminish his grief, she, who had just lost a good husband, was come to add her tears to his, since she knew what he must be feeling, the King redoubled his lamentations. Then he told the sorrowful lady long stories about the good qualities of his departed Queen, and she in her turn recounted all the virtues of her departed husband; and this passed the time so agreeably that the King quite forgot to thump his head against the feather-beds, and the lady did not need to wipe the tears from her great blue eyes as often as before. By degrees they came to talking about other things in which the King took an interest, and in a wonderfully short time the whole kingdom was astonished by the news that the King was married again to the sorrowful lady.

Now the King had one daughter, who was just fifteen years old. Her name was Fiordelisa, and she was the prettiest and most charming Princess imaginable, always gay and merry. The new Queen, who also had a daughter, very soon sent for her to come to the Palace. Turritella, for that was her name, had been brought up by her godmother, the Fairy Mazilla, but in spite of all the care bestowed upon her, she was neither beautiful nor gracious. Indeed, when the Queen saw how ill-tempered and ugly she appeared beside Fiordelisa she was in despair, and did everything in her power to turn the King against his own daughter, in the hope that he might take a fancy to Turritella. One day the King said that it was time Fiordelisa and Turritella were married, so he would give one of them to the first suitable Prince who visited his Court. The Queen answered:

'My daughter certainly ought to be the first to be married; she is older than yours, and a thousand times more charming!'

The King, who hated disputes, said, 'Very well, it's no affair of mine, settle it your own way.'

Very soon after came the news that King Charming, who was the most handsome and magnificent Prince in all the country round, was on his way to visit the King. As soon as the Queen heard this, she set all her jewellers, tailors, weavers, and embroiderers to work upon splendid dresses and ornaments for Turritella, but she told the King that Fiordelisa had no need of anything new, and the night before the King was to arrive, she bribed her waiting woman to steal away all the Princess's own dresses and jewels, so that when the day came, and Fiordelisa wished to adorn herself as became her high rank, not even a ribbon could she find.

However, as she easily guessed who had played her such a trick, she made no complaint, but sent to the merchants for some rich stuffs. But they said that the Queen had expressly forbidden them to supply her with any, and they dared not disobey. So the Princess had nothing left to put on but the little white frock she had been wearing the day before; and dressed in that, she went down when the time of the King's arrival came, and sat in a corner hoping to escape notice. The Queen received her guest with great ceremony, and presented him to her daughter, who was gorgeously attired, but so much splendour only made her ugliness more noticeable, and the King, after one glance at her, looked the other way. The Queen, however, only thought that he was bashful, and took pains to keep Turritella in full view. King Charming then asked it there was not another Princess, called Fiordelisa.

'Yes,' said Turritella, pointing with her finger, 'there she is, trying to keep out of sight because she is not smart.'

At this Fiordelisa blushed, and looked so shy and so lovely, that the King was fairly astonished. He rose, and bowing low before her, said—

'Madam, your incomparable beauty needs no adornment.'

'Sire,' answered the Princess, 'I assure you that I am not in the habit of wearing dresses as crumpled and untidy as this one, so I should have been better pleased if you had not seen me at all.'

'Impossible!' cried King Charming. 'Wherever such a marvellously beautiful Princess appears I can look at nothing else.'

Here the Queen broke in, saying sharply—

'I assure you, Sire, that Fiordelisa is vain enough already. Pray make her no more flattering speeches.'

The King quite understood that she was not pleased, but that did not matter to him, so he admired Fiordelisa to his heart's content, and talked to her for three hours without stopping.

The Queen was in despair, and so was Turritella, when they saw how much the King preferred Fiordelisa. They complained bitterly to the King, and begged and teased him, until he at last consented to have the Princess shut up somewhere out of sight while King Charming's visit lasted. So that night, as she went to her room, she was seized by four masked figures, and carried up into the topmost room of a high tower, where they left her in the deepest dejection. She easily guessed that she was to be kept out of sight for fear the King should fall in love with her; but then, how disappointing that was, for she already liked him very much, and would have been quite willing to be chosen for his bride! As King Charming did not know what had happened to the Princess, he looked forward impatiently to meeting her again, and he tried to talk about her with the courtiers who were placed in attendance on him. But by the Queen's orders they would say nothing good of her, but declared that she was vain, capricious, and bad-tempered; that she tormented her waiting-maids, and that, in spite of all the money that the King gave her, she was so mean that she preferred to go about dressed like a poor shepherdess, rather than spend any of it. All these things vexed the King very much, and he was silent.

'It is true,' thought he, 'that she was very poorly dressed, but then she was so ashamed that it proves that she was not accustomed to be so. I cannot believe that with that lovely face she can be as ill-tempered and contemptible as they say. No, no, the Queen must be jealous of her for the sake of that ugly daughter of hers, and so these evil reports are spread.'

The courtiers could not help seeing that what they had told the King did not please him, and one of them cunningly began to praise Fiordelisa, when he could talk to the King without being heard by the others.

King Charming thereupon became so cheerful, and interested in all he said, that it was easy to guess how much he admired the Princess. So when the Queen sent for the courtiers and questioned them about all they had found out, their report confirmed her worst fears. As to the poor Princess Fiordelisa, she cried all night without stopping.

'It would have been quite bad enough to be shut up in this gloomy tower before I had ever seen King Charming,' she said; 'but now when he is here, and they are all enjoying themselves with him, it is too unkind.'

The next day the Queen sent King Charming splendid presents of jewels and rich stuffs, and among other things an ornament made expressly in honour of the approaching wedding. It was a heart cut out of one huge ruby, and was surrounded by several diamond arrows, and pierced by one. A golden true-lover's knot above the heart bore the motto, 'But one can wound me,' and the whole jewel was hung upon a chain of immense pearls. Never, since the world has been a world, had such a thing been made, and the King was quite amazed when it was presented to him. The page who brought it begged him to accept it from the Princess, who chose him to be her knight.

'What!' cried he, 'does the lovely Princess Fiordelisa deign to think of me in this amiable and encouraging way?'

'You confuse the names, Sire,' said the page hastily. 'I come on behalf of the Princess Turritella.'

'Oh, it is Turritella who wishes me to be her knight,' said the King coldly. 'I am sorry that I cannot accept the honour.' And he sent the splendid gifts back to the Queen and Turritella, who were furiously angry at the contempt with which they were treated. As soon as he possibly could, King Charming went to see the King and Queen, and as he entered the hall he looked for Fiordelisa, and every time anyone came in he started round to see who it was, and was altogether so uneasy and dissatisfied that the Queen saw it plainly. But she would not take any notice, and talked of nothing but the entertainments she was planning. The Prince answered at random, and presently asked if he was not to have the pleasure of seeing the Princess Fiordelisa.

'Sire,' answered the Queen haughtily, 'her father has ordered that she shall not leave her own apartments until my daughter is married.'

'What can be the reason for keeping that lovely Princess a prisoner?' cried the King in great indignation.

'That I do not know,' answered the Queen; 'and even if I did, I might not feel bound to tell you.'

The King was terribly angry at being thwarted like this. He felt certain that Turritella was to blame for it, so casting a furious glance at her he abruptly took leave of the Queen, and returned to his own apartments. There he said to a young squire whom he had brought with him: 'I would give all I have in the world to gain the good will of one of the Princess's waiting-women, and obtain a moment's speech with Fiordelisa.'

'Nothing could be easier,' said the young squire; and he very soon made friends with one of the ladies, who told him that in the evening Fiordelisa would be at a little window which looked into the garden, where he could come and talk to her. Only, she said, he must take very great care not to be seen, as it would be as much as her place was worth to be caught helping King Charming to see the Princess. The squire was delighted, and promised all she asked; but the moment he had run off to announce his success to the King, the false waiting-woman went and told the Queen all that had passed. She at once determined that her own daughter should be at the little window; and she taught her so well all she was to say and do, that even the stupid Turritella could make no mistake.

The night was so dark that the King had not a chance of finding out the trick that was being played upon him, so he approached the window with the greatest delight, and said everything that he had been longing to say to Fiordelisa to persuade her of his love for her. Turritella answered as she had been taught, that she was very unhappy, and that there was no chance of her being better treated by the Queen until her daughter was married. And then the King entreated her to marry him; and thereupon he drew his ring from his finger and put it upon Turritella's, and she answered him as well as she could. The King could not help thinking that she did not say exactly what he would have expected from his darling Fiordelisa, but he persuaded himself that the fear of being surprised by the Queen was making her awkward and unnatural. He would not leave her until she had promised to see him again the next night, which Turritella did willingly enough. The Queen was overjoyed at the success of her stratagem, end promised herself that all would now be as she wished; and sure enough, as soon as it was dark the following night the King came, bringing with him a chariot which had been given him by an Enchanter who was his friend. This chariot was drawn by flying frogs, and the King easily persuaded Turritella to come out and let him put her into it, then mounting beside her he cried triumphantly—

'Now, my Princess, you are free; where will it please you that we shall hold our wedding?'

And Turritella, with her head muffled in her mantle, answered that the Fairy Mazilla was her godmother, and that she would like it to be at her castle. So the King told the Frogs, who had the map of the whole world in their heads, and very soon he and Turritella were set down at the castle of the Fairy Mazilla. The King would certainly have found out his mistake the moment they stepped into the brilliantly lighted castle, but Turritella held her mantle more closely round her, and asked to see the Fairy by herself, and quickly told her all that had happened, and how she had succeeded in deceiving King Charming.

'Oho! my daughter,' said the Fairy, 'I see we have no easy task before us. He loves Fiordelisa so much that he will not be easily pacified. I feel sure he will defy us!' Meanwhile the King was waiting in a splendid room with diamond walls, so clear that he could see the Fairy and Turritella as they stood whispering together, and he was very much puzzled.

'Who can have betrayed us?' he said to himself. 'How comes our enemy here? She must be plotting to prevent our marriage. Why doesn't my lovely Fiordelisa make haste and come hack to me?'

But it was worse than anything he had imagined when the Fairy Mazilla entered, leading Turritella by the hand, and said to him —

'King Charming, here is the Princess Turritella to whom you have plighted your faith. Let us have the wedding at once.'

'I!' cried the King. 'I marry that little creature! What do you take me for? I have promised her nothing!'

'Say no more. Have you no respect for a Fairy?' cried she angrily.

'Yes, madam,' answered the King, 'I am prepared to respect you as much as a Fairy can be respected, if you will give me back my Princess.'

'Am I not here?' interrupted Turritella. 'Here is the ring you gave me. With whom did you talk at the little window, if it was not with me?'

'What!' cried the King angrily, 'have I been altogether deceived and deluded? Where is my chariot? Not another moment will I stay here.'

'Oho,' said the Fairy, 'not so fast.' And she touched his feet, which instantly became as firmly fixed to the floor as if they had been nailed there.

'Oh! do whatever you like with me,' said the King; 'you may turn me to stone, but I will marry no one but Fiordelisa.'

And not another word would he say, though the Fairy scolded and threatened, and Turritella wept and raged for twenty days and twenty nights. At last the Fairy Mazilla said furiously (for she was quite tired out by his obstinacy), 'Choose whether you will marry my goddaughter, or do penance seven years for breaking your word to her.'

And then the King cried gaily: 'Pray do whatever you like with me, as long as you deliver me from this ugly scold!'

'Scold!' cried Turritella angrily. 'Who are you, I should like to know, that you dare to call me a scold? A miserable King who breaks his word, and goes about in a chariot drawn by croaking frogs out of a marsh!'

'Let us have no more of these insults,' cried the Fairy. 'Fly from that window, ungrateful King, and for seven years be a Blue Bird.' As she spoke the King's face altered, his arms turned to wings, his feet to little crooked black claws. In a moment he had a slender body like a bird, covered with shining blue feathers, his beak was like ivory, his eyes were bright as stars, and a crown of white feathers adorned his head.

As soon as the transformation was complete the King uttered a dolorous cry and fled through the open window, pursued by the mocking laughter of Turritella and the Fairy Mazilla. He flew on until he reached the thickest part of the wood, and there, perched upon a cypress tree, he bewailed his miserable fate. 'Alas! in seven years who knows what may happen to my darling Fiordelisa!' he said. 'Her cruel stepmother may have married her to someone else before I am myself again, and then what good will life be to me?'

In the meantime the Fairy Mazilla had sent Turritella back to the Queen, who was all anxiety to know how the wedding, had gone off. But when her daughter arrived and told her all that had happened she was terribly angry, and of course all her wrath fell upon Fiordelisa. 'She shall have cause to repent that the King admires her,' said the Queen, nodding her head meaningly, and then she and Turritella went up to the little room in the tower where the Princess was imprisoned. Fiordelisa was immensely surprised to see that Turritella was wearing a royal mantle and a diamond crown, and her heart sank when the Queen said: 'My daughter is come to show you some of her wedding presents, for she is King Charming's bride, and they are the happiest pair in the world, he loves her to distraction.' All this time Turritella was spreading out lace, and jewels, and rich brocades, and ribbons before Fiordelisa's unwilling eyes, and taking good care to display King Charming's ring, which she wore upon her thumb. The Princess recognised it as soon as her eyes fell upon it, and after that she could no longer doubt that he had indeed married Turritella. In despair she cried, 'Take away these miserable gauds! what pleasure has a wretched captive in the sight of them?' and then she fell insensible upon the floor, and the cruel Queen laughed maliciously, and went away with Turritella, leaving her there without comfort or aid. That night the Queen said to the King, that his daughter was so infatuated with King Charming, in spite of his never having shown any preference for her, that it was just as well she should stay in the tower until she came to her senses. To which he answered that it was her affair, and she could give what orders she pleased about the Princess.

When the unhappy Fiordelisa recovered, and remembered all she had just heard, she began to cry bitterly, believing that King Charming was lost to her for ever, and all night long she sat at her open window sighing and lamenting; but when it was dawn she crept away into the darkest corner of her little room and sat there, too unhappy to care about anything. As soon as night came again she once more leaned out into the darkness and bewailed her miserable lot.

Now it happened that King Charming, or rather the Blue Bird, had been flying round the palace in the hope of seeing his beloved Princess, but had not dared to go too near the windows for fear of being seen and recognised by Turritella. When night fell he had not succeeded in discovering where Fiordelisa was imprisoned, and, weary and sad, he perched upon a branch of a tall fir tree which grew close to the tower, and began to sing himself to sleep. But soon the sound of a soft voice lamenting attracted his attention, and listening intently he heard it say—

'Ah! cruel Queen! what have I ever done to be imprisoned like this? And was I not unhappy enough before, that you must needs come and taunt me with the happiness your daughter is enjoying now she is King Charming's bride?'

The Blue Bird, greatly surprised, waited impatiently for the dawn, and the moment it was light flew off to see who it could have been who spoke thus. But he found the window shut, and could see no one. The next night, however, he was on the watch, and by the clear moonlight he saw that the sorrowful lady at the window was Fiordelisa herself.

'My Princess! have I found you at last?' said he, alighting close to her.

'Who is speaking to me?' cried the Princess in great surprise.

'Only a moment since you mentioned my name, and now you do not know me, Fiordelisa,' said he sadly. 'But no wonder, since I am nothing but a Blue Bird, and must remain one for seven years.'

'What! Little Blue Bird, are you really the powerful King Charming?' said the Princess, caressing him.

'It is too true,' he answered. 'For being faithful to you I am thus punished. But believe me, if it were for twice as long I would bear it joyfully rather than give you up.'

'Oh! what are you telling me?' cried the Princess. 'Has not your bride, Turritella, just visited me, wearing the royal mantle and the diamond crown you gave her? I cannot be mistaken, for I saw your ring upon her thumb.'

Then the Blue Bird was furiously angry, and told the Princess all that had happened, how he had been deceived into carrying off Turritella, and how, for refusing to marry her, the Fairy Mazilla had condemned him to be a Blue Bird for seven years.

The Princess was very happy when she heard how faithful her lover was, and would never have tired of hearing his loving speeches and explanations, but too soon the sun rose, and they had to part lest the Blue Bird should be discovered. After promising to come again to the Princess's window as soon as it was dark, he flew away, and hid himself in a little hole in the fir-tree, while Fiordelisa remained devoured by anxiety lest he should be caught in a trap, or eaten up by an eagle.

But the Blue Bird did not long stay in his hiding-place. He flew away, and away, until he came to his own palace, and got into it through a broken window, and there he found the cabinet where his jewels were kept, and chose out a splendid diamond ring as a present for the Princess. By the time he got back, Fiordelisa was sitting waiting for him by the open window, and when he gave her the ring, she scolded him gently for having run such a risk to get it for her.

'Promise me that you will wear it always!' said the Blue Bird. And the Princess promised on condition that he should come and see her in the day as well as by night. They talked all night long, and the next morning the Blue Bird flew off to his kingdom, and crept into his palace through the broken window, and chose from his treasures two bracelets, each cut out of a single emerald. When he presented them to the Princess, she shook her head at him reproachfully, saying—

'Do you think I love you so little that I need all these gifts to remind me of you?'

And he answered—

'No, my Princess; but I love you so much that I feel I cannot express it, try as I may. I only bring you these worthless trifles to show that I have not ceased to think of you, though I have been obliged to leave you for a time.' The following night he gave Fiordelisa a watch set in a single pearl. The Princess laughed a little when she saw it, and said—

'You may well give me a watch, for since I have known you I have lost the power of measuring time. The hours you spend with me pass like minutes, and the hours that I drag through without you seem years to me.'

'Ah, Princess, they cannot seem so long to you as they do to me!' he answered. Day by day he brought more beautiful things for the Princess— diamonds, and rubies, and opals; and at night she decked herself with them to please him, but by day she hid them in her straw mattress. When the sun shone the Blue Bird, hidden in the tall fir-tree, sang to her so sweetly that all the passersby wondered, and said that the wood was inhabited by a spirit. And so two years slipped away, and still the Princess was a prisoner, and Turritella was not married. The Queen had offered her hand to all the neighbouring Princes, but they always answered that they would marry Fiordelisa with pleasure, but not Turritella on any account. This displeased the Queen terribly. 'Fiordelisa must be in league with them, to annoy me!' she said. 'Let us go and accuse her of it.'

So she and Turritella went up into the tower. Now it happened that it was nearly midnight, and Fiordelisa, all decked with jewels, was sitting at the window with the Blue Bird, and as the Queen paused outside the door to listen she heard the Princess and her lover singing together a little song he had just taught her. These were the words:—

'Oh! what a luckless pair are we,
One in a prison, and one in a tree.
All our trouble and anguish came
From our faithfulness spoiling our enemies' game.
But vainly they practice their cruel arts,
For nought can sever our two fond hearts.'

They sound melancholy perhaps, but the two voices sang them gaily enough, and the Queen burst open the door, crying, 'Ah! my Turritella, there is some treachery going on here!'

As soon as she saw her, Fiordelisa, with great presence of mind, hastily shut her little window, that the Blue Bird might have time to escape, and then turned to meet the Queen, who overwhelmed her with a torrent of reproaches.

'Your intrigues are discovered, Madam,' she said furiously; 'and you need not hope that your high rank will save you from the punishment you deserve.'

'And with whom do you accuse me of intriguing, Madam?' said the Princess. 'Have I not been your prisoner these two years, and who have I seen except the gaolers sent by you?'

While she spoke the Queen and Turritella were looking at her in the greatest surprise, perfectly dazzled by her beauty and the splendour of her jewels, and the Queen said:

'If one may ask, Madam, where did you get all these diamonds? Perhaps you mean to tell me that you have discovered a mine of them in the tower!'

'I certainly did find them here,' answered the Princess.

'And pray,' said the Queen, her wrath increasing every moment, 'for whose admiration are you decked out like this, since I have often seen you not half as fine on the most important occasions at Court?'

'For my own,' answered Fiordelisa. 'You must admit that I have had plenty of time on my hands, so you cannot be surprised at my spending some of it in making myself smart.'

'That's all very fine,' said the Queen suspiciously. 'I think I will look about, and see for myself.'

So she and Turritella began to search every corner of the little room, and when they came to the straw mattress out fell such a quantity of pearls, diamonds, rubies, opals, emeralds, and sapphires, that they were amazed, and could not tell what to think. But the Queen resolved to hide somewhere a packet of false letters to prove that the Princess had been conspiring with the King's enemies, and she chose the chimney as a good place. Fortunately for Fiordelisa this was exactly where the Blue Bird had perched himself, to keep an eye upon her proceedings, and try to avert danger from his beloved Princess, and now he cried:

'Beware, Fiordelisa! Your false enemy is plotting against you.'

This strange voice so frightened the Queen that she took the letter and went away hastily with Turritella, and they held a council to try and devise some means of finding out what Fairy or Enchanter was favouring the Princess. At last they sent one of the Queen's maids to wait upon Fiordelisa, and told her to pretend to be quite stupid, and to see and hear nothing, while she was really to watch the Princess day and night, and keep the Queen informed of all her doings.

Poor Fiordelisa, who guessed she was sent as a spy, was in despair, and cried bitterly that she dared not see her dear Blue Bird for fear that some evil might happen to him if he were discovered.

The days were so long, and the nights so dull, but for a whole month she never went near her little window lest he should fly to her as he used to do.

However, at last the spy, who had never taken her eyes off the Princess day or night, was so overcome with weariness that she fell into a deep sleep, and as son as the Princess saw that, she flew to open her window and cried softly:

'Blue Bird, blue as the sky,
Fly to me now, there's nobody by.'

And the Blue Bird, who had never ceased to flutter round within sight and hearing of her prison, came in an instant. They had so much to say, and were so overjoyed to meet once more, that it scarcely seemed to them five minutes before the sun rose, and the Blue Bird had to fly away.

But the next night the spy slept as soundly as before, so that the Blue Bird came, and he and the Princess began to think they were perfectly safe, and to make all sorts of plans for being happy as they were before the Queen's visit. But, alas! the third night the spy was not quite so sleepy, and when the Princess opened her window and cried as usual:

'Blue Bird, blue as the sky,
Fly to me now, there's nobody nigh,'

she was wide awake in a moment, though she was sly enough to keep her eyes shut at first. But presently she heard voices, and peeping cautiously, she saw by the moonlight the most lovely blue bird in the world, who was talking to the Princess, while she stroked and caressed it fondly.

The spy did not lose a single word of the conversation, and as soon as the day dawned, and the Blue Bird had reluctantly said good-bye to the Princess, she rushed off to the Queen, and told her all she had seen and heard.

Then the Queen sent for Turritella, and they talked it over, and very soon came to the conclusion than this Blue Bird was no other than King Charming himself.

'Ah! that insolent Princess!' cried the Queen. 'To think that when we supposed her to be so miserable, she was all the while as happy as possible with that false King. But I know how we can avenge ourselves!'

So the spy was ordered to go back and pretend to sleep as soundly as ever, and indeed she went to bed earlier than usual, and snored as naturally as possible, and the poor Princess ran to the window and cried:

'Blue Bird, blue as the sky,
Fly to me now, there's nobody by!'

But no bird came. All night long she called, and waited, and listened, but still there was no answer, for the cruel Queen had caused the fir tree to be hung all over with knives, swords, razors, shears, bill-hooks, and sickles, so that when the Blue Bird heard the Princess call, and flew towards her, his wings were cut, and his little black feet clipped off, and all pierced and stabbed in twenty places, he fell back bleeding into his hiding place in the tree, and lay there groaning and despairing, for he thought the Princess must have been persuaded to betray him, to regain her liberty.

'Ah! Fiordelisa, can you indeed be so lovely and so faithless?' he sighed, 'then I may as well die at once!' And he turned over on his side and began to die. But it happened that his friend the Enchanter had been very much alarmed at seeing the Frog chariot come back to him without

King Charming, and had been round the world eight times seeking him, but without success. At the very moment when the King gave himself up to despair, he was passing through the wood for the eighth time, and called, as he had done all over the world:

'Charming! King Charming! Are you here?'

The King at once recognised his friend's voice, and answered very faintly:

'I am here.'

The Enchanter looked all round him, but could see nothing, and then the King said again:

'I am a Blue Bird.'

Then the Enchanter found him in an instant, and seeing his pitiable condition, ran hither and thither without a word, until he had collected a handful of magic herbs, with which, and a few incantations, he speedily made the King whole and sound again.

'Now,' said he, 'let me hear all about it. There must be a Princess at the bottom of this.'

'There are two!' answered King Charming, with a wry smile.

And then he told the whole story, accusing Fiordelisa of having betrayed the secret of his visits to make her peace with the Queen, and indeed saying a great many hard things about her fickleness and her deceitful beauty, and so on. The Enchanter quite agreed with him, and even went further, declaring that all Princesses were alike, except perhaps in the matter of beauty, and advised him to have done with Fiordelisa, and forget all about her. But, somehow or other, this advice did not quite please the King.

'What is to be done next?' said the Enchanter, 'since you still have five years to remain a Blue Bird.'

'Take me to your palace,' answered the King; 'there you can at least keep me in a cage safe from cats and swords.'

'Well, that will be the best thing to do for the present,' said his friend. 'But I am not an Enchanter for nothing. I'm sure to have a brilliant idea for you before long.'

In the meantime Fiordelisa, quite in despair, sat at her window day and night calling her dear Blue Bird in vain, and imagining over and over again all the terrible things that could have happened to him, until she grew quite pale and thin. As for the Queen and Turritella, they were triumphant; but their triumph was short, for the King, Fiordelisa's father, fell ill and died, and all the people rebelled against the Queen and Turritella, and came in a body to the palace demanding Fiordelisa.

The Queen came out upon the balcony with threats and haughty words, so that at last they lost their patience, and broke open the doors of the palace, one of which fell back upon the Queen and killed her. Turritella fled to the Fairy Mazilla, and all the nobles of the kingdom fetched the Princess Fiordelisa from her prison in the tower, and made her Queen. Very soon, with all the care and attention they bestowed upon her, she recovered from the effects of her long captivity and looked more beautiful than ever, and was able to take counsel with her courtiers, and arrange for the governing of her kingdom during her absence. And then, taking a bagful of jewels, she set out all alone to look for the Blue Bird, without telling anyone where she was going.

Meanwhile, the Enchanter was taking care of King Charming, but as his power was not great enough to counteract the Fairy Mazilla's, he at last resolved to go and see if he could make any kind of terms with her for his friend; for you see, Fairies and Enchanters are cousins in a sort of way, after all; and after knowing one another for five or six hundred years and falling out, and making it up again pretty often, they understand one another well enough. So the Fairy Mazilla received him graciously. 'And what may you be wanting, Gossip?' said she.

'You can do a good turn for me if you will;' he answered. 'A King, who is a friend of mine, was unlucky enough to offend you—'

'Aha! I know who you mean,' interrupted the Fairy. 'I am sorry not to oblige you, Gossip, but he need expect no mercy from me unless he will marry my goddaughter, whom you see yonder looking so pretty and charming. Let him think over what I say.'

The Enchanter hadn't a word to say, for he thought Turritella really frightful, but he could not go away without making one more effort for his friend the King, who was really in great danger as long as he lived in a cage. Indeed, already he had met with several alarming accidents. Once the nail on which his cage was hung had given way, and his feathered Majesty had suffered much from the fall, while Madam Puss, who happened to be in the room at the time, had given him a scratch in the eye which came very near blinding him. Another time they had forgotten to give him any water to drink, so that he was nearly dead with thirst; and the worst thing of all was that he was in danger of losing his kingdom, for he had been absent so long that all his subjects believed him to be dead. So considering all these things the Enchanter agreed with the Fairy Mazilla that she should restore the King to his natural form, and should take Turritella to stay in his palace for several months, and if, after the time was over he still could not make up his mind to marry her, he should once more be changed into a Blue Bird.

Then the Fairy dressed Turritella in a magnificent gold and silver robe, and they mounted together upon a flying Dragon, and very soon reached King Charming's palace, where he, too, had just been brought by his faithful friend the Enchanter.

Three strokes of the Fairy's wand restored his natural form, and he was as handsome and delightful as ever, but he considered that he paid dearly for his restoration when he caught sight of Turritella, and the mere idea of marrying her made him shudder.

Meanwhile, Queen Fiordelisa, disguised as a poor peasant girl, wearing a great straw hat that concealed her face, and carrying an old sack over her shoulder, had set out upon her weary journey, and had travelled far, sometimes by sea and sometimes by land; sometimes on foot, and sometimes on horseback, but not knowing which way to go. She feared all the time that every step she took was leading her farther from her lover. One day as she sat, quite tired and sad, on the bank of a little brook, cooling her white feet in the clear running water, and combing her long hair that glittered like gold in the sunshine, a little bent old woman passed by, leaning on a stick. She stopped, and said to Fiordelisa:

'What, my pretty child, are you all alone?'

'Indeed, good mother, I am too sad to care for company,' she answered; and the tears ran down her cheeks.

'Don't cry,' said the old woman, 'but tell me truly what is the matter. Perhaps I can help you.'

The Queen told her willingly all that had happened, and how she was seeking the Blue Bird. Thereupon the little old woman suddenly stood up straight, and grew tall, and young, and beautiful, and said with a smile to the astonished Fiordelisa:

'Lovely Queen, the King whom you seek is no longer a bird. My sister Mazilla has given his own form back to him, and he is in his own kingdom. Do not be afraid, you will reach him, and will prosper. Take these four eggs; if you break one when you are in any great difficulty, you will find aid.'

So saying, she disappeared, and Fiordelisa, feeling much encouraged, put the eggs into her bag and turned her steps towards Charming's kingdom. After walking on and on for eight days and eight nights, she came at last to a tremendously high hill of polished ivory, so steep that it was impossible to get a foothold upon it. Fiordelisa tried a thousand times, and scrambled and slipped, but always in the end found herself exactly where she started from. At last she sat down at the foot of it in despair, and then suddenly bethought herself of the eggs. Breaking one quickly, she found in it some little gold hooks, and with these fastened to her feet and hands, she mounted the ivory hill without further trouble, for the little hooks saved her from slipping. As soon as she reached the top a new difficulty presented itself, for all the other side, and indeed the whole valley, was one polished mirror, in which thousands and thousands of people were admiring their reflections. For this was a magic mirror, in which people saw themselves just as they wished to appear, and pilgrims came to it from the four corners of the world. But nobody had ever been able to reach the top of the hill, and when they saw Fiordelisa standing there, they raised a terrible outcry, declaring that if she set foot upon their glass she would break it to pieces. The Queen, not knowing what to do, for she saw it would be dangerous to try to go down, broke the second egg, and out came a chariot, drawn by two white doves, and Fiordelisa got into it, and was floated softly away. After a night and a day the doves alighted outside the gate of King Charming's kingdom. Here the Queen got out of the chariot, and kissed the doves and thanked them, and then with a beating heart she walked into the town, asking the people she met where she could see the King. But they only laughed at her, crying:

'See the King? And pray, why do you want to see the King, my little kitchen-maid? You had better go and wash your face first, your eyes are not clear enough to see him!' For the Queen had disguised herself, and pulled her hair down about her eyes, that no one might know her. As they would not tell her, she went on farther, and presently asked again, and this time the people answered that to-morrow she might see the King driving through the streets with the Princess Turritella, as it was said that at last he had consented to marry her. This was indeed terrible news to Fiordelisa. Had she come all this weary way only to find Turritella had succeeded in making King Charming forget her?

She was too tired and miserable to walk another step, so she sat down in a doorway and cried bitterly all night long. As soon as it was light she hastened to the palace, and after being sent away fifty times by the guards, she got in at last, and saw the thrones set in the great hall for the King and Turritella, who was already looked upon as Queen.

Fiordelisa hid herself behind a marble pillar, and very soon saw Turritella make her appearance, richly dressed, but as ugly as ever, and with her came the King, more handsome and splendid even than Fiordelisa had remembered him. When Turritella had seated herself upon the throne, the Queen approached her.

'Who are you, and how dare you come near my high-mightiness, upon my golden throne?' said Turritella, frowning fiercely at her.

'They call me the little kitchen-maid,' she replied, 'and I come to offer some precious things for sale,' and with that she searched in her old sack, and drew out the emerald bracelets King Charming had given her.

'Ho, ho!' said Turritella, those are pretty bits of glass. I suppose you would like five silver pieces for them.'

'Show them to someone who understands such things, Madam,' answered the Queen; 'after that we can decide upon the price.'

Turritella, who really loved King Charming as much as she could love anybody, and was always delighted to get a chance of talking to him, now showed him the bracelets, asking how much he considered them worth. As soon as he saw them he remembered those he had given to Fiordelisa, and turned very pale and sighed deeply, and fell into such sad thought that he quite forgot to answer her. Presently she asked him again, and then he said, with a great effort:

'I believe these bracelets are worth as much as my kingdom. I thought there was only one such pair in the world; but here, it seems, is another.'

Then Turritella went back to the Queen, and asked her what was the lowest price she would take for them.

'More than you would find it easy to pay, Madam,' answered she; 'but if you will manage for me to sleep one night in the Chamber of Echoes, I will give you the emeralds.'

'By all means, my little kitchen-maid,' said Turritella, highly delighted.

The King did not try to find out where the bracelets had come from, not because he did not want to know, but because the only way would have been to ask Turritella, and he disliked her so much that he never spoke to her if he could possibly avoid it. It was he who had told Fiordelisa about the Chamber of Echoes, when he was a Blue Bird. It was a little room below the King's own bed-chamber, and was so ingeniously built that the softest whisper in it was plainly heard in the King's room. Fiordelisa wanted to reproach him for his faithlessness, and could not imagine a better way than this. So when, by Turritella's orders, she was left there she began to weep and lament, and never ceased until daybreak.

The King's pages told Turritella, when she asked them, what a sobbing and sighing they had heard, and she asked Fiordelisa what it was all about. The Queen answered that she often dreamed and talked aloud.

But by an unlucky chance the King heard nothing of all this, for he took a sleeping draught every night before he lay down, and did not wake up until the sun was high.

The Queen passed the day in great disquietude.

'If he did hear me,' she said, 'could he remain so cruelly indifferent? But if he did not hear me, what can I do to get another chance? I have plenty of jewels, it is true, but nothing remarkable enough to catch Turritella's fancy.'

Just then she thought of the eggs, and broke one, out of which came a little carriage of polished steel ornamented with gold, drawn by six green mice. The coachman was a rose-coloured rat, the postilion a grey one, and the carriage was occupied by the tiniest and most charming figures, who could dance and do wonderful tricks. Fiordelisa clapped her hands and danced for joy when she saw this triumph of magic art, and as soon as it was evening, went to a shady garden-path down which she knew Turritella would pass, and then she made the mice galop, and the tiny people show off their tricks, and sure enough Turritella came, and the moment she saw it all cried:

'Little kitchen-maid, little kitchen-maid, what will you take for your mouse-carriage?'

And the Queen answered:

'Let me sleep once more in the Chamber of Echoes.'

'I won't refuse your request, poor creature,' said Turritella condescendingly.

And then she turned to her ladies and whispered

'The silly creature does not know how to profit by her chances; so much the better for me.'

When night came Fiordelisa said all the loving words she could think of, but alas! with no better success than before, for the King slept heavily after his draught. One of the pages said:

'This peasant girl must be crazy;' but another answered:

'Yet what she says sounds very sad and touching.'

As for Fiordelisa, she thought the King must have a very hard heart if he could hear how she grieved and yet pay her no attention. She had but one more chance, and on breaking the last egg she found to her great delight that it contained a more marvellous thing than ever. It was a pie made of six birds, cooked to perfection, and yet they were all alive, and singing and talking, and they answered questions and told fortunes in the most amusing way. Taking this treasure Fiordelisa once more set herself to wait in the great hall through which Turritella was sure to pass, and as she sat there one of the King's pages came by, and said to her:

'Well, little kitchen-maid, it is a good thing that the King always takes a sleeping draught, for if not he would be kept awake all night by your sighing and lamenting.'

Then Fiordelisa knew why the King had not heeded her, and taking a handful of pearls and diamonds out of her sack, she said, 'If you can promise me that to-night the King shall not have his sleeping draught, I will give you all these jewels.'

'Oh! I promise that willingly,' said the page.

At this moment Turritella appeared, and at the first sight of the savoury pie, with the pretty little birds all singing and chattering, she cried:—

'That is an admirable pie, little kitchen-maid. Pray what will you take for it?'

'The usual price,' she answered. 'To sleep once more in the Chamber of Echoes.'

'By all means, only give me the pie,' said the greedy Turritella. And when night was come, Queen Fiordelisa waited until she thought everybody in the palace would be asleep, and then began to lament as before.

'Ah, Charming!' she said, 'what have I ever done that you should forsake me and marry Turritella? If you could only know all I have suffered, and what a weary way I have come to seek you.'

Now the page had faithfully kept his word, and given King Charming a glass of water instead of his usual sleeping draught, so there he lay wide awake, and heard every word Fiordelisa said, and even recognised her voice, though he could not tell where it came from.

'Ah, Princess!' he said, 'how could you betray me to our cruel enemies when I loved you so dearly?'

Fiordelisa heard him, and answered quickly:

'Find out the little kitchen-maid, and she will explain everything.'

Then the King in a great hurry sent for his pages and said:

'If you can find the little kitchen-maid, bring her to me at once.'

'Nothing could be easier, Sire,' they answered, 'for she is in the Chamber of Echoes.'

The King was very much puzzled when he heard this. How could the lovely Princess Fiordelisa be a little kitchen-maid? or how could a little kitchen-maid have Fiordelisa's own voice? So he dressed hastily, and ran down a little secret staircase which led to the Chamber of Echoes. There, upon a heap of soft cushions, sat his lovely Princess. She had laid aside all her ugly disguises and wore a white silken robe, and her golden hair shone in the soft lamp-light. The King was overjoyed at the sight, and rushed to throw himself at her feet, and asked her a thousand questions without giving her time to answer one. Fiordelisa was equally happy to be with him once more, and nothing troubled them but the remembrance of the Fairy Mazilla. But at this moment in came the Enchanter, and with him a famous Fairy, the same in fact who had given Fiordelisa the eggs. After greeting the King and Queen, they said that as they were united in wishing to help King Charming, the Fairy Mazilla had no longer any power against him, and he might marry Fiordelisa as soon as he pleased. The King's joy may be imagined, and as soon as it was day the news was spread through the palace, and everybody who saw Fiordelisa loved her directly. When Turritella heard what had happened she came running to the King, and when she saw Fiordelisa with him she was terribly angry, but before she could say a word the Enchanter and the Fairy changed her into a big brown owl, and she floated away out of one of the palace windows, hooting dismally. Then the wedding was held with great splendour, and King Charming and Queen Fiordelisa lived happily ever after.

L'Oiseau Bleu. Par Mme. d'Aulnoy.

THE HALF-CHICK

Once upon a time there was a handsome black Spanish hen, who had a large brood of chickens. They were all fine, plump little birds, except the youngest, who was quite unlike his brothers and sisters. Indeed, he was such a strange, queer-looking creature, that when he first chipped his shell his mother could scarcely believe her eyes, he was so different from the twelve other fluffy, downy, soft little chicks who nestled under her wings. This one looked just as if he had been cut in two. He had only one leg, and one wing, and one eye, and he had half a head and half a beak. His mother shook her head sadly as she looked at him and said:

'My youngest born is only a half-chick. He can never grow up a tall handsome cock like his brothers. They will go out into the world and rule over poultry yards of their own; but this poor little fellow will always have to stay at home with his mother.' And she called him Medio Pollito, which is Spanish for half-chick.

Now though Medio Pollito was such an odd, helpless-looking little thing, his mother soon found that he was not at all willing to remain under her wing and protection. Indeed, in character he was as unlike his brothers and sisters as he was in appearance. They were good, obedient chickens, and when the old hen chicked after them, they chirped and ran back to her side. But Medio Pollito had a roving spirit in spite of his one leg, and when his mother called to him to return to the coop, he pretended that he could not hear, because he had only one ear.

When she took the whole family out for a walk in the fields, Medio Pollito would hop away by himself, and hide among the Indian corn. Many an anxious minute his brothers and sisters had looking for him, while his mother ran to and fro cackling in fear and dismay.

As he grew older he became more self-willed and disobedient, and his manner to his mother was often very rude, and his temper to the other chickens very disagreeable.

One day he had been out for a longer expedition than usual in the fields. On his return he strutted up to his mother with the peculiar little hop and kick which was his way of walking, and cocking his one eye at her in a very bold way he said:

'Mother, I am tired of this life in a dull farmyard, with nothing but a dreary maize field to look at. I'm off to Madrid to see the King.'

'To Madrid, Medio Pollito!' exclaimed his mother; 'why, you silly chick, it would be a long journey for a grown-up cock, and a poor little thing like you would be tired out before you had gone half the distance. No, no, stay at home with your mother, and some day, when you are bigger, we will go a little journey together.'

But Medio Pollito had made up his mind, and he would not listen to his mother's advice, nor to the prayers and entreaties of his brothers and sisters.

'What is the use of our all crowding each other up in this poky little place?' he said. 'When I have a fine courtyard of my own at the King's palace, I shall perhaps ask some of you to come and pay me a short visit,' and scarcely waiting to say good-bye to his family, away he stumped down the high road that led to Madrid.

'Be sure that you are kind and civil to everyone you meet,' called his mother, running after him; but he was in such a hurry to be off, that he did not wait to answer her, or even to look back.

A little later in the day, as he was taking a short cut through a field, he passed a stream. Now the stream was all choked up, and overgrown with weeds and water-plants, so that its waters could not flow freely.

'Oh! Medio Pollito,' it cried, as the half-chick hopped along its banks, 'do come and help me by clearing away these weeds.'

'Help you, indeed!' exclaimed Medio Pollito, tossing his head, and shaking the few feathers in his tail. 'Do you think I have nothing to do but to waste my time on such trifles? Help yourself, and don't trouble busy travellers. I am off to Madrid to see the King,' and hoppity-kick, hoppity-kick, away stumped Medio Pollito.

A little later he came to a fire that had been left by some gipsies in a wood. It was burning very low, and would soon be out.

'Oh! Medio Pollito,' cried the fire, in a weak, wavering voice as the half-chick approached, 'in a few minutes I shall go quite out, unless you put some sticks and dry leaves upon me. Do help me, or I shall die!'

'Help you, indeed!' answered Medio Pollito. 'I have other things to do. Gather sticks for yourself, and don't trouble me. I am off to Madrid to see the King,' and hoppity-kick, hoppity-kick, away stumped Medio Pollito.

The next morning, as he was getting near Madrid, he passed a large chestnut tree, in whose branches the wind was caught and entangled. 'Oh! Medio Pollito,' called the wind, 'do hop up here, and help me to get free of these branches. I cannot come away, and it is so uncomfortable.'

'It is your own fault for going there,' answered Medio Pollito. 'I can't waste all my morning stopping here to help you. Just shake yourself off, and don't hinder me, for I am off to Madrid to see the King,' and hoppity-kick, hoppity-kick, away stumped Medio Pollito in great glee, for the towers and roofs of Madrid were now in sight. When he entered the town he saw before him a great splendid house, with soldiers standing before the gates. This he knew must be the King's palace, and he determined to hop up to the front gate and wait there until the King came out. But as he was hopping past one of the back windows the King's cook saw him:

'Here is the very thing I want,' he exclaimed, 'for the King has just sent a message to say that he must have chicken broth for his dinner,' and opening the window he stretched out his arm, caught Medio Pollito, and popped him into the broth-pot that was standing near the fire. Oh! how wet and clammy the water felt as it went over Medio Pollito's head, making his feathers cling to his side.

'Water, water!' he cried in his despair, 'do have pity upon me and do not wet me like this.'

'Ah! Medio Pollito,' replied the water, 'you would not help me when I was a little stream away on the fields, now you must be punished.'

Then the fire began to burn and scald Medio Pollito, and he danced and hopped from one side of the pot to the other, trying to get away from the heat, and crying out in pain:

Fire, fire! do not scorch me like this; you can't think how it hurts.'

'Ah! Medio Pollito,' answered the fire, 'you would not help me when I was dying away in the wood. You are being punished.'

At last, just when the pain was so great that Medio Pollito thought he must die, the cook lifted up the lid of the pot to see if the broth was ready for the King's dinner.

'Look here!' he cried in horror, 'this chicken is quite useless. It is burnt to a cinder. I can't send it up to the royal table;' and opening the window he threw Medio Pollito out into the street. But the wind caught him up, and whirled him through the air so quickly that Medio Pollito could scarcely breathe, and his heart beat against his side till he thought it would break.

'Oh, wind!' at last he gasped out, 'if you hurry me along like this you will kill me. Do let me rest a moment, or—' but he was so breathless that he could not finish his sentence.

'Ah! Medio Pollito,' replied the wind, 'when I was caught in the branches of the chestnut tree you would not help me; now you are punished.' And he swirled Medio Pollito over the roofs of the houses till they reached the highest church in the town, and there he left him fastened to the top of the steeple.

And there stands Medio Pollito to this day. And if you go to Madrid, and walk through the streets till you come to the highest church, you will see Medio Pollito perched on his one leg on the steeple, with his one wing drooping at his side, and gazing sadly out of his one eye over the town.

Spanish Tradition.

THE STORY OF CALIPH STORK

I.

Caliph Chasid, of Bagdad, was resting comfortably on his divan one fine afternoon. He was smoking a long pipe, and from time to time he sipped a little coffee which a slave handed to him, and after each sip he stroked his long beard with an air of enjoyment. In short, anyone could see that the Caliph was in an excellent humour. This was, in fact, the best time of day in which to approach him, for just now he was pretty sure to be both affable and in good spirits, and for this reason the Grand Vizier Mansor always chose this hour in which to pay his daily visit.

He arrived as usual this afternoon, but, contrary to his usual custom, with an anxious face. The Caliph withdrew his pipe for a moment from his lips and asked, 'Why do you look so anxious, Grand Vizier?'

The Grand Vizier crossed his arms on his breast and bent low before his master as he answered:

'Oh, my Lord! whether my countenance be anxious or not I know not, but down below, in the court of the palace, is a pedlar with such beautiful things that I cannot help feeling annoyed at having so little money to spare.'

The Caliph, who had wished for some time past to give his Grand Vizier a present, ordered his black slave to bring the pedlar before him at once. The slave soon returned, followed by the pedlar, a short stout man with a swarthy face, and dressed in very ragged clothes. He carried a box containing all manner of wares—strings of pearls, rings, richly mounted pistols, goblets, and combs. The Caliph and his Vizier inspected everything, and the Caliph chose some handsome pistols for himself and Mansor, and a jewelled comb for the Vizier's wife. Just as the pedlar was about to close his box, the Caliph noticed a small drawer, and asked if there was anything else in it for sale. The pedlar opened the drawer and showed them a box containing a black powder, and a scroll written in strange characters, which neither the Caliph nor the Mansor could read.

'I got these two articles from a merchant who had picked them up in the street at Mecca,' said the pedlar. 'I do not know what they may contain, but as they are of no use to me, you are welcome to have them for a trifle.'

The Caliph, who liked to have old manuscripts in his library, even though he could not read them, purchased the scroll and the box, and dismissed the pedlar. Then, being anxious to know what might be the contents of the scroll, he asked the Vizier if he did not know of anyone who might be able to decipher it.

'Most gracious Lord and master,' replied the Vizier, 'near the great Mosque lives a man called Selim the learned, who knows every language under the sun. Send for him; it may be that he will be able to interpret these mysterious characters.'

The learned Selim was summoned immediately.

'Selim,' said the Caliph, 'I hear you are a scholar. Look well at this scroll and see whether you can read it. If you can, I will give you a robe of honour; but if you fail, I will order you to receive twelve strokes on your cheeks, and five-and-twenty on the soles of your feet, because you have been falsely called Selim the learned.'

Selim prostrated himself and said, 'Be it according to your will, oh master!' Then he gazed long at the scroll. Suddenly he exclaimed: 'May I die, oh, my Lord, if this isn't Latin!'

'Well,' said the Caliph, 'if it is Latin, let us hear what it means.'

So Selim began to translate: 'Thou who mayest find this, praise Allah for his mercy. Whoever shall snuff the powder in this box, and at the same time shall pronounce the word "Mutabor!" can transform himself into any creature he likes, and will understand the language of all animals. When he wishes to resume the human form, he has only to bow three times towards the east, and to repeat the same word. Be careful, however, when wearing the shape of some beast or bird, not to laugh, or thou wilt certainly forget the magic word and remain an animal for ever.'

When Selim the learned had read this, the Caliph was delighted. He made the wise man swear not to tell the matter to anyone, gave him a splendid robe, and dismissed him. Then he said to his Vizier, 'That's what I call a good bargain, Mansor. I am longing for the moment when I can become some animal. To-morrow morning I shall expect you early; we will go into the country, take some snuff from my box, and then hear what is being said in air, earth, and water.'

II.

Next morning Caliph Chasid had barely finished dressing, and breakfasting, when the Grand Vizier arrived, according to orders, to accompany him in his expedition. The Caliph stuck the snuff-box in his girdle, and, having desired his servants to remain at home, started off with the Grand Vizier only in attendance. First they walked through the palace gardens, but they looked in vain for some creature which could tempt them to try their magic power. At length the Vizier suggested going further on to a pond which lay beyond the town, and where he had often seen a variety of creatures, especially storks, whose grave, dignified appearance and constant chatter had often attracted his attention.

The Caliph consented, and they went straight to the pond. As soon as they arrived they remarked a stork strutting up and down with a stately air, hunting for frogs, and now and then muttering something to itself. At the same time they saw another stork far above in the sky flying towards the same spot.

'I would wager my beard, most gracious master,' said the Grand Vizier, 'that these two long legs will have a good chat together. How would it be if we turned ourselves into storks?'

'Well said,' replied the Caliph; 'but first let us remember carefully how we are to become men once more. True! Bow three times towards the east and say "Mutabor!" and I shall be Caliph and you my Grand Vizier again. But for Heaven's sake don't laugh or we are lost!'

As the Caliph spoke he saw the second stork circling round his head and gradually flying towards the earth. Quickly he drew the box from his girdle, took a good pinch of the snuff, and offered one to Mansor, who also took one, and both cried together 'Mutabor!'

Instantly their legs shrivelled up and grew thin and red; their smart yellow slippers turned to clumsy stork's feet, their arms to wings; their necks began to sprout from between their shoulders and grew a yard long; their beards disappeared, and their bodies were covered with feathers.

'You've got a fine long bill, Sir Vizier,' cried the Caliph, after standing for some time lost in astonishment. 'By the beard of the Prophet I never saw such a thing in all my life!'

'My very humble thanks,' replied the Grand Vizier, as he bent his long neck; 'but, if I may venture to say so, your Highness is even handsomer as a stork than as a Caliph. But come, if it so pleases you, let us go near our comrades there and find out whether we really do understand the language of storks.'

Meantime the second stork had reached the ground. It first scraped its bill with its claw, stroked down its feathers, and then advanced towards the first stork. The two newly made storks lost no time in drawing near, and to their amazement overheard the following conversation:

'Good morning, Dame Longlegs. You are out early this morning!'

'Yes, indeed, dear Chatterbill! I am getting myself a morsel of breakfast. May I offer you a joint of lizard or a frog's thigh?'

'A thousand thanks, but I have really no appetite this morning. I am here for a very different purpose. I am to dance to-day before my father's guests, and I have come to the meadow for a little quiet practice.'

Thereupon the young stork began to move about with the most wonderful steps. The Caliph and Mansor looked on in surprise for some time; but when at last she balanced herself in a picturesque attitude on one leg, and flapped her wings gracefully up and down, they could hold out no longer; a prolonged peal burst from each of their bills, and it was some time before they could recover their composure. The Caliph was the first to collect himself. 'That was the best joke,' said he, 'I've ever seen. It's a pity the stupid creatures were scared away by our laughter, or no doubt they would have sung next!'

Suddenly, however, the Vizier remembered how strictly they had been warned not to laugh during their transformation. He at once communicated his fears to the Caliph, who exclaimed, 'By Mecca and Medina! it would indeed prove but a poor joke if I had to remain a stork for the remainder of my days! Do just try and remember the stupid word, it has slipped my memory.'

'We must bow three times eastwards and say "Mu...mu...mu..."'

They turned to the east and fell to bowing till their bills touched the ground, but, oh horror—the magic word was quite forgotten, and however often the Caliph bowed and however touchingly his Vizier cried 'Mu...mu...' they could not recall it, and the unhappy Chasid and Mansor remained storks as they were.

III.

The two enchanted birds wandered sadly on through the meadows. In their misery they could not think what to do next. They could not rid themselves of their new forms; there was no use in returning to the town and saying who they were; for who would believe a stork who announced that he was a Caliph; and even if they did believe him, would the people of Bagdad consent to let a stork rule over them?

So they lounged about for several days, supporting themselves on fruits, which, however, they found some difficulty in eating with their long bills. They did not much care to eat frogs or lizards. Their one comfort in their sad plight was the power of flying, and accordingly they often flew over the roofs of Bagdad to see what was going on there.

During the first few days they noticed signs of much disturbance and distress in the streets, but about the fourth day, as they sat on the roof of the palace, they perceived a splendid procession passing below them along the street. Drums and trumpets sounded, a man in a scarlet mantle, embroidered in gold, sat on a splendidly caparisoned horse surrounded by richly dressed slaves; half Bagdad crowded after him, and they all shouted, 'Hail, Mirza, the Lord of Bagdad!'

The two storks on the palace roof looked at each other, and Caliph Chasid said, 'Can you guess now, Grand Vizier, why I have been enchanted? This Mirza is the son of my deadly enemy, the mighty magician Kaschnur, who in an evil moment vowed vengeance on me. Still I will not despair! Come with me, my faithful friend; we will go to the grave of the Prophet, and perhaps at that sacred spot the spell may be loosed.'

They rose from the palace roof, and spread their wings toward Medina.

But flying was not quite an easy matter, for the two storks had had but little practice as yet.

'Oh, my Lord!' gasped the Vizier, after a couple of hours, 'I can get on no longer; you really fly too quick for me. Besides, it is nearly evening, and we should do well to find some place in which to spend the night.'

Chasid listened with favour to his servant's suggestion, and perceiving in the valley beneath them a ruin which seemed to promise shelter they flew towards it. The building in which they proposed to pass the night had apparently been formerly a castle. Some handsome pillars still stood amongst the heaps of ruins, and several rooms, which yet remained in fair preservation, gave evidence of former splendour. Chasid and his companion wandered along the passages seeking a dry spot, when suddenly Mansor stood still.

'My Lord and master,' he whispered, 'if it were not absurd for a Grand Vizier, and still more for a stork, to be afraid of ghosts, I should feel quite nervous, for someone, or something close by me, has sighed and moaned quite audibly.'

The Caliph stood still and distinctly heard a low weeping sound which seemed to proceed from a human being rather than from any animal. Full of curiosity he was about to rush towards the spot from whence the sounds of woe came, when the Vizier caught him by the wing with his bill, and implored him not to expose himself to fresh and unknown dangers. The Caliph, however, under whose stork's breast a brave heart beat, tore himself away with the loss of a few feathers, and hurried down a dark passage. He saw a door which stood ajar, and through which he distinctly heard sighs, mingled with sobs. He pushed open the door with his bill, but remained on the threshold, astonished at the sight which met his eyes. On the floor of the ruined chamber—which was but scantily lighted by a small barred window—sat a large screech owl. Big tears rolled from its large round eyes, and in a hoarse voice it uttered its complaints through its crooked beak. As soon as it saw the Caliph and his Vizier—who had crept up meanwhile—it gave vent to a joyful cry. It gently wiped the tears from its eyes with its spotted brown wings, and to the great amazement of the two visitors, addressed them in good human Arabic.

'Welcome, ye storks! You are a good sign of my deliverance, for it was foretold me that a piece of good fortune should befall me through a stork.'

When the Caliph had recovered from his surprise, he drew up his feet into a graceful position, bent his long neck, and said: 'Oh, screech owl! from your words I am led to believe that we see in you a companion in misfortune. But, alas! your hope that you may attain your deliverance through us is but a vain one. You will know our helplessness when you have heard our story.'

The screech owl begged him to relate it, and the Caliph accordingly told him what we already know.

IV.

When the Caliph had ended, the owl thanked him and said: 'You hear my story, and own that I am no less unfortunate than yourselves. My father is the King of the Indies. I, his only daughter, am named Lusa. That magician Kaschnur, who enchanted you, has been the cause of my misfortunes too. He came one day to my father and demanded my hand for his son Mirza. My father—who is rather hasty—ordered him to be thrown downstairs. The wretch not long after managed to approach me under another form, and one day, when I was in the garden, and asked for some refreshment, he brought me—in the disguise of a slave—a draught which changed me at once to this horrid shape. Whilst I was fainting with terror he transported me here, and cried to me with his awful voice: "There shall you remain, lonely and hideous, despised even by the brutes, till the end of your days, or till some one of his own free will asks you to be his wife. Thus do I avenge myself on you and your proud father."

'Since then many months have passed away. Sad and lonely do I live like any hermit within these walls, avoided by the world and a terror even to animals; the beauties of nature are hidden from me, for I am blind by day, and it is only when the moon sheds her pale light on this spot that the veil falls from my eyes and I can see.' The owl paused, and once more wiped her eyes with her wing, for the recital of her woes had drawn fresh tears from her.

The Caliph fell into deep thought on hearing this story of the Princess. 'If I am not much mistaken,' said he, 'there is some mysterious connection between our misfortunes, but how to find the key to the riddle is the question.'

The owl answered: 'Oh, my Lord! I too feel sure of this, for in my earliest youth a wise woman foretold that a stork would bring me some great happiness, and I think I could tell you how we might save ourselves.' The Caliph was much surprised, and asked her what she meant.

'The Magician who has made us both miserable,' said she, 'comes once a month to these ruins. Not far from this room is a large hall where he is in the habit of feasting with his companions. I have often watched them. They tell each other all about their evil deeds, and possibly the magic word which you have forgotten may be mentioned.'

'Oh, dearest Princess!' exclaimed the Caliph, 'say, when does he come, and where is the hall?'

The owl paused a moment and then said: 'Do not think me unkind, but I can only grant your request on one condition.'

'Speak, speak!' cried Chasid; 'command, I will gladly do whatever you wish!'

'Well,' replied the owl, 'you see I should like to be free too; but this can only be if one of you will offer me his hand in marriage.'

The storks seemed rather taken aback by this suggestion, and the Caliph beckoned to his Vizier to retire and consult with him.

When they were outside the door the Caliph said: 'Grand Vizier, this is a tiresome business. However, you can take her.'

'Indeed!' said the Vizier; 'so that when I go home my wife may scratch my eyes out! Besides, I am an old man, and your Highness is still young and unmarried, and a far more suitable match for a young and lovely Princess.'

'That's just where it is,' sighed the Caliph, whose wings drooped in a dejected manner; 'how do you know she is young and lovely? I call it buying a pig in a poke.'

They argued on for some time, but at length, when the Caliph saw plainly that his Vizier would rather remain a stork to the end of his days than marry the owl, he determined to fulfil the condition himself. The owl was delighted. She owned that they could not have arrived at a better time, as most probably the magicians would meet that very night.

She then proceeded to lead the two storks to the chamber. They passed through a long dark passage till at length a bright ray of light shone before them through the chinks of a half-ruined wall. When they reached it the owl advised them to keep very quiet. Through the gap near which they stood they could with ease survey the whole of the large hall. It was adorned with splendid carved pillars; a number of coloured lamps replaced the light of day. In the middle of the hall stood a round table covered with a variety of dishes, and about the table was a divan on which eight men were seated. In one of these bad men the two recognised the pedlar who had sold the magic powder. The man next him begged him to relate all his latest doings, and amongst them he told the story of the Caliph and his Vizier.

'And what kind of word did you give them?' asked another old sorcerer.

'A very difficult Latin word; it is "Mutabor."'

V.

As soon as the storks heard this they were nearly beside themselves with joy. They ran at such a pace to the door of the ruined castle that the owl could scarcely keep up with them. When they reached it the Caliph turned to the owl, and said with much feeling: 'Deliverer of my friend and myself, as a proof of my eternal gratitude, accept me as your husband.' Then he turned towards the east. Three times the storks bowed their long necks to the sun, which was just rising over the mountains. 'Mutabor!' they both cried, and in an instant they were once more transformed. In the rapture of their newly-given lives master and servant fell laughing and weeping into each other's arms. Who shall describe their surprise when they at last turned round and beheld standing before them a beautiful lady exquisitely dressed!

With a smile she held out her hand to the Caliph, and asked: 'Do you not recognise your screech owl?'

It was she! The Caliph was so enchanted by her grace and beauty, that he declared being turned into a stork had been the best piece of luck which had ever befallen him. The three set out at once for Bagdad. Fortunately, the Caliph found not only the box with the magic powder, but also his purse in his girdle; he was, therefore, able to buy in the nearest village all they required for their journey, and so at last they reached the gates of Bagdad.

Here the Caliph's arrival created the greatest sensation. He had been quite given up for dead, and the people were greatly rejoiced to see their beloved ruler again.

Their rage with the usurper Mirza, however, was great in proportion. They marched in force to the palace and took the old magician and his son prisoners. The Caliph sent the magician to the room where the Princess had lived as an owl, and there had him hanged. As the son, however, knew nothing of his father's acts, the Caliph gave him his choice between death and a pinch of the magic snuff. When he chose the latter, the Grand Vizier handed him the box. One good pinch, and the magic word transformed him to a stork. The Caliph ordered him to be confined in an iron cage, and placed in the palace gardens.

Caliph Chasid lived long and happily with his wife the Princess. His merriest time was when the Grand Vizier visited him in the afternoon; and when the Caliph was in particularly high spirits he would condescend to mimic the Vizier's appearance when he was a stork. He would strut gravely, and with well-stiffened legs, up and down the room, chattering, and showing how he had vainly bowed to the east and cried 'Mu...Mu...' The Caliphess and her children were always much entertained by this performance; but when the Caliph went on nodding and bowing, and calling 'Mu...mu...' too long, the Vizier would threaten laughingly to tell the Chaliphess the subject of the discussion carried on one night outside the door of Princess Screech Owl.

THE ENCHANTED WATCH

Once upon a time there lived a rich man who had three sons. When they grew up, he sent the eldest to travel and see the world, and three years passed before his family saw him again. Then he returned, magnificently dressed, and his father was so delighted with his behaviour, that he gave a great feast in his honour, to which all the relations and friends were invited.

When the rejoicings were ended, the second son begged leave of his father to go in his turn to travel and mix with the world. The father was enchanted at the request, and gave him plenty of money for his expenses, saying, 'If you behave as well as your brother, I will do honour to you as I did to him.' The young man promised to do his best, and his conduct during three years was all that it should be. Then he went home, and his father was so pleased with him that his feast of welcome was even more splendid than the one before.

The third brother, whose name was Jenik, or Johnnie, was considered the most foolish of the three. He never did anything at home except sit over the stove and dirty himself with the ashes; but he also begged his father's leave to travel for three years. 'Go if you like, you idiot; but what good will it do you?'

The youth paid no heed to his father's observations as long as he obtained permission to go. The father saw him depart with joy, glad to get rid of him, and gave him a handsome sum of money for his needs.

Once, as he was making one of his journeys, Jenik chanced to cross a meadow where some shepherds were just about to kill a dog. He entreated them to spare it, and to give it to him instead which they willingly did, and he went on his way, followed by the dog. A little further on he came upon a cat, which someone was going to put to death. He implored its life, and the cat followed him. Finally, in another place, he saved a serpent, which was also handed over to him and now they made a party of four—the dog behind Jenik, the cat behind the dog, and the serpent behind the cat.

Then the serpent said to Jenik, 'Go wherever you see me go,' for in the autumn, when all the serpents hide themselves in their holes, this serpent was going in search of his king, who was king of all the snakes.

Then he added: 'My king will scold me for my long absence, everyone else is housed for the winter, and I am very late. I shall have to tell him what danger I have been in, and how, without your help, I should certainly have lost my life. The king will ask what you would like in return, and be sure you beg for the watch which hangs on the wall. It has all sorts of wonderful properties, you only need to rub it to get whatever you like.'

No sooner said than done. Jenik became the master of the watch, and the moment he got out he wished to put its virtues to the proof. He was hungry, and thought it would be delightful to eat in the meadow a loaf of new bread and a steak of good beef washed down by a flask of wine, so he scratched the watch, and in an instant it was all before him. Imagine his joy!

Evening soon came, and Jenik rubbed his watch, and thought it would be very pleasant to have a room with a comfortable bed and a good supper. In an instant they were all before him. After supper he went to bed and slept till morning, as every honest man ought to do. Then he set forth for his father's house, his mind dwelling on the feast that would be awaiting him. But as he returned in the same old clothes in which he went away, his father flew into a great rage, and refused to do anything for him. Jenik went to his old place near the stove, and dirtied himself in the ashes without anybody minding.

The third day, feeling rather dull, he thought it would be nice to see a three-story house filled with beautiful furniture, and with vessels of silver and gold. So he rubbed the watch, and there it all was. Jenik went to look for his father, and said to him: 'You offered me no feast of welcome, but permit me to give one to you, and come and let me show you my plate.'

The father was much astonished, and longed to know where his son had got all this wealth. Jenik did not reply, but begged him to invite all their relations and friends to a grand banquet.

So the father invited all the world, and everyone was amazed to see such splendid things, so much plate, and so many fine dishes on the table. After the first course Jenik prayed his father to invite the King, and his daughter the Princess. He rubbed his watch and wished for a carriage ornamented with gold and silver, and drawn by six horses, with harness glittering with precious stones. The father did not dare to sit in this gorgeous coach, but went to the palace on foot. The King and his daughter were immensely surprised with the beauty of the carriage, and mounted the steps at once to go to Jenik's banquet. Then Jenik rubbed his watch afresh, and wished that for six miles the way to the house should be paved with marble. Who ever felt so astonished as the King? Never had he travelled over such a gorgeous road.

When Jenik heard the wheels of the carriage, he rubbed his watch and wished for a still more beautiful house, four stories high, and hung with gold, silver, and damask; filled with wonderful tables, covered with dishes such as no king had ever eaten before. The King, the Queen, and the Princess were speechless with surprise. Never had they seen such a splendid palace, nor such a high feast! At dessert the King asked Jenik's father to give him the young man for a son-in-law. No sooner said than done! The marriage took place at once, and the King returned to his own palace, and left Jenik with his wife in the enchanted house.

Now Jenik was not a very clever man, and at the end of a very short time he began to bore his wife. She inquired how he managed to build palaces and to get so many precious things. He told her all about the watch, and she never rested till she had stolen the precious talisman. One night she took the watch, rubbed it, and wished for a carriage drawn by four horses; and in this carriage she at once set out for her father's palace. There she called to her own attendants, bade them follow her into the carriage, and drove straight to the sea-side. Then she rubbed her watch, and wished that the sea might be crossed by a bridge, and that a magnificent palace might arise in the middle of the sea. No sooner said than done. The Princess entered the house, rubbed her watch, and in an instant the bridge was gone.

Left alone, Jenik felt very miserable. His father, mother, and brothers, and, indeed, everybody else, all laughed at him. Nothing remained to him but the cat and dog whose lives he had once saved. He took them with him and went far away, for he could no longer live with his family. He reached at last a great desert, and saw some crows flying towards a mountain. One of them was a long way behind, and when he arrived his brothers inquired what had made him so late. 'Winter is here,' they said, 'and it is time to fly to other countries.' He told them that he had seen in the middle of the sea the most wonderful house that ever was built.

On hearing this, Jenik at once concluded that this must be the hiding-place of his wife. So he proceeded directly to the shore with his dog and his cat. When he arrived on the beach, he said to the dog: 'You are an excellent swimmer, and you, little one, are very light; jump on the dog's back and he will take you to the palace. Once there, he will hide himself near the door, and you must steal secretly in and try to get hold of my watch.'

No sooner said than done. The two animals crossed the sea; the dog hid near the house, and the cat stole into the chamber. The Princess recognised him, and guessed why he had come; and she took the watch down to the cellar and locked it in a box. But the cat wriggled its way into the cellar, and the moment the Princess turned her back, he scratched and scratched till he had made a hole in the box. Then he took the watch between his teeth, and waited quietly till the Princess came back. Scarcely had she opened the door when the cat was outside, and the watch into the bargain.

The cat was no sooner beyond the gates than she said to the dog:

'We are going to cross the sea; be very careful not to speak to me.'

The dog laid this to heart and said nothing; but when they approached the shore he could not help asking, 'Have you got the watch?'

The cat did not answer—he was afraid that he might let the talisman fall. When they touched the shore the dog repeated his question.

'Yes,' said the cat.

And the watch fell into the sea. Then our two friends began each to accuse the other, and both looked sorrowfully at the place where their treasure had fallen in. Suddenly a fish appeared near the edge of the sea. The cat seized it, and thought it would make them a good supper.

'I have nine little children,' cried the fish. 'Spare the father of a family!'

'Granted,' replied the cat; 'but on condition that you find our watch.'

The fish executed his commission, and they brought the treasure back to their master. Jenik rubbed the watch and wished that the palace, with the Princess and all its inhabitants, should be swallowed up in the sea. No sooner said than done. Jenik returned to his parents, and he and his watch, his cat and his dog, lived together happily to the end of their days.

Deulin.

ROSANELLA

Everybody knows that though the fairies live hundreds of years they do sometimes die, and especially as they are obliged to pass one day in every week under the form of some animal, when of course they are liable to accident. It was in this way that death once overtook the Queen of the Fairies, and it became necessary to call a general assembly to elect a new sovereign. After much discussion, it appeared that the choice lay between two fairies, one called Surcantine and the other Paridamie; and their claims were so equal that it was impossible without injustice to prefer one to the other. Under these circumstances it was unanimously decided that whichever of the two could show to the world the greatest wonder should be Queen; but it was to be a special kind of wonder, no moving of mountains or any such common fairy tricks would do. Surcantine, therefore, resolved that she would bring up a Prince whom nothing could make constant. While Paridamie decided to display to admiring mortals a Princess so charming that no one could see her without falling in love with her. They were allowed to take their own time, and meanwhile the four oldest fairies were to attend to the affairs of the kingdom.

Now Paridamie had for a long time been very friendly with King Bardondon, who was a most accomplished Prince, and whose court was the model of what a court should be. His Queen, Balanice, was also charming; indeed it is rare to find a husband and wife so perfectly of one mind about everything. They had one little daughter, whom they had named 'Rosanella,' because she had a little pink rose printed upon her white throat. From her earliest infancy she had shown the most astonishing intelligence, and the courtiers knew her smart sayings by heart, and repeated them on all occasions. In the middle of the night following the assembly of fairies, Queen Balanice woke up with a shriek, and when her maids of honour ran to see what was the matter, they found she had had a frightful dream.

'I thought,' said she, 'that my little daughter had changed into a bouquet of roses, and that as I held it in my hand a bird swooped down suddenly and snatched it from me and carried it away.'

'Let some one run and see that all is well with the Princess,' she added.

So they ran; but what was their dismay when they found that the cradle was empty; and though they sought high and low, not a trace of Rosanella could they discover. The Queen was inconsolable, and so, indeed, was the King, only being a man he did not say quite so much about his feelings. He presently proposed to Balanice that they should spend a few days at one of their palaces in the country; and to this she willingly agreed, since her grief made the gaiety of the capital distasteful to her. One lovely summer evening, as they sat together on a shady lawn shaped like a star, from which radiated twelve splendid avenues of trees, the Queen looked round and saw a charming peasant-girl approaching by each path, and what was still more singular was that everyone carried something in a basket which appeared to occupy her whole attention. As each drew near she laid her basket at Balanice's feet, saying:

'Charming Queen, may this be some slight consolation to you in your unhappiness!'

The Queen hastily opened the baskets, and found in each a lovely baby-girl, about the same age as the little Princess for whom she sorrowed so deeply. At first the sight of them renewed her grief; but presently their charms so gained upon her that she forgot her melancholy in providing them with nursery-maids, cradle-rockers, and ladies-in-waiting, and in sending hither and thither for swings and dolls and tops, and bushels of the finest sweetmeats.

Oddly enough, every baby had upon its throat a tiny pink rose. The Queen found it so difficult to decide on suitable names for all of them, that until she could settle the matter she chose a special colour for everyone, by which it was known, so that when they were all together they looked like nothing so much as a nosegay of gay flowers. As they grew older it became evident that though they were all remarkably intelligent, and profited equally by the education they received, yet they differed one from another in disposition, so much so that they gradually ceased to be known as 'Pearl,' or 'Primrose,' or whatever might have been their colour, and the Queen instead would say:

'Where is my Sweet?' or 'my Beautiful,' or 'my Gay.'

Of course, with all these charms they had lovers by the dozen. Not only in their own court, but princes from afar, who were constantly arriving, attracted by the reports which were spread abroad; but these lovely girls, the first Maids of Honour, were as discreet as they were beautiful, and favoured no one.

But let us return to Surcantine. She had fixed upon the son of a king who was cousin to Bardondon, to bring up as her fickle Prince. She had before, at his christening, given him all the graces of mind and body that a prince could possibly require; but now she redoubled her efforts, and spared no pains in adding every imaginable charm and fascination. So that whether he happened to be cross or amiable, splendidly or simply attired, serious or frivolous, he was always perfectly irresistible! In truth, he was a charming young fellow, since the Fairy had given him the best heart in the world as well as the best head, and had left nothing to be desired but—constancy. For it cannot be denied that Prince Mirliflor was a desperate flirt, and as fickle as the wind; so much so, that by the time he arrived at his eighteenth birthday there was not a heart left for him to conquer in his father's kingdom—they were all his own, and he was tired of everyone! Things were in this state when he was invited to visit the court of his father's cousin, King Bardondon.

Imagine his feelings when he arrived and was presented at once to twelve of the loveliest creatures in the world, and his embarrassment was heightened by the fact that they all liked him as much as he liked each one of them, so that things came to such a pass that he was never happy a single instant without them. For could he not whisper soft speeches to Sweet, and laugh with Joy, while he looked at Beauty? And in his more serious moments what could be pleasanter than to talk to Grave upon some shady lawn, while he held the hand of Loving in his own, and all the others lingered near in sympathetic silence? For the first time in his life he really loved, though the object of his devotion was not one person, but twelve, to whom he was equally attached, and even Surcantine was deceived into thinking that this was indeed the height of inconstancy. But Paridamie said not a word.

In vain did Prince Mirliflor's father write commanding him to return, and proposing for him one good match after another. Nothing in the world could tear him from his twelve enchantresses.

One day the Queen gave a large garden-party, and just as the guests were all assembled, and Prince Mirliflor was as usual dividing his attentions between the twelve beauties, a humming of bees was heard. The Rose-maidens, fearing their stings, uttered little shrieks, and fled all together to a distance from the rest of the company. Immediately, to the horror of all who were looking on, the bees pursued them, and, growing suddenly to an enormous size, pounced each upon a maiden and carried her off into the air, and in an instant they were all lost to view. This amazing occurrence plunged the whole court into the deepest affliction, and Prince Mirliflor, after giving way to the most violent grief at first, fell gradually into a state of such deep dejection that it was feared if nothing could rouse him he would certainly die. Surcantine came in all haste to see what she could do for her darling, but he rejected with scorn all the portraits of lovely princesses which she offered him for his collection. In short, it was evident that he was in a bad way, and the Fairy was at her wits' end. One day, as he wandered about absorbed in melancholy reflections, he heard sudden shouts and exclamations of amazement, and if he had taken the trouble to look up he could not have helped being as astonished as everyone else, for through the air a chariot of crystal was slowly approaching which glittered in the sunshine. Six lovely maidens with shining wings drew it by rose-coloured ribbons, while a whole flight of others, equally beautiful, were holding long garlands of roses crossed above it, so as to form a complete canopy. In it sat the Fairy Paridamie, and by her side a Princess whose beauty positively dazzled all who saw her. At the foot of the great staircase they descended, and proceeded to the Queen's apartments, though everyone had run together to see this marvel, till it was quite difficult to make a way through the crowd; and exclamations of wonder rose on all sides at the loveliness of the strange Princess. 'Great Queen,' said Paridamie, 'permit me to restore to you your daughter Rosanella, whom I stole out of her cradle.'

After the first transports of joy were over the Queen said to Paridamie:

'But my twelve lovely ones, are they lost to me for ever? Shall I never see them again?'

But Paridamie only said:

'Very soon you will cease to miss them!' in a tone that evidently meant 'Don't ask me any more questions.' And then mounting again into her chariot she swiftly disappeared.

The news of his beautiful cousin's arrival was soon carried to the Prince, but he had hardly the heart to go and see her. However, it became absolutely necessary that he should pay his respects, and he had scarcely been five minutes in her presence before it seemed to him that she combined in her own charming person all the gifts and graces which had so attracted him in the twelve Rose-maidens whose loss he had so truly mourned; and after all it is really more satisfactory to make love to one person at a time. So it came to pass that before he knew where he was he was entreating his lovely cousin to marry him, and the moment the words had left his lips, Paridamie appeared, smiling and triumphant, in the chariot of the Queen of the Fairies, for by that time they had all heard of her success, and declared her to have earned the kingdom. She had to give a full account of how she had stolen Rosanella from her cradle, and divided her character into twelve parts, that each might charm Prince Mirliflor, and when once more united might cure him of his inconstancy once and for ever.

And as one more proof of the fascination of the whole Rosanella, I may tell you that even the defeated Surcantine sent her a wedding gift, and was present at the ceremony which took place as soon as the guests could arrive. Prince Mirliflor was constant for the rest of his life. And indeed who would not have been in his place? As for Rosanella, she loved him as much as all the twelve beauties put together, so they reigned in peace and happiness to the end of their long lives.

By the Comte de Caylus.

SYLVAIN AND JOCOSA

Once upon a time there lived in the same village two children, one called Sylvain and the other Jocosa, who were both remarkable for beauty and intelligence. It happened that their parents were not on terms of friendship with one another, on account of some old quarrel, which had, however, taken place so long ago, that they had quite forgotten what it was all about, and only kept up the feud from force of habit. Sylvain and Jocosa for their parts were far from sharing this enmity, and indeed were never happy when apart. Day after day they fed their flocks of sheep together, and spent the long sunshiny hours in playing, or resting upon some shady bank. It happened one day that the Fairy of the Meadows passed by and saw them, and was so much attracted by their pretty faces and gentle manners that she took them under her protection, and the older they grew the dearer they became to her. At first she showed her interest by leaving in their favourite haunts many little gifts such as they delighted to offer one to the other, for they loved each other so much that their first thought was always, 'What will Jocosa like?' or, 'What will please Sylvain?' And the Fairy took a great delight in their innocent enjoyment of the cakes and sweetmeats she gave them nearly every day. When they were grown up she resolved to make herself known to them, and chose a time when they were sheltering from the noonday sun in the deep shade of a flowery hedgerow. They were startled at first by the sudden apparition of a tall and slender lady, dressed all in green, and crowned with a garland of flowers. But when she spoke to them sweetly, and told them how she had always loved them, and that it was she who had given them all the pretty things which it had so surprised them to find, they thanked her gratefully, and took pleasure in answering the questions she put to them. When she presently bade them farewell, she told them never to tell anyone else that they had seen her. 'You will often see me again,' added she, 'and I shall be with you frequently, even when you do not see me.' So saying she vanished, leaving them in a state of great wonder and excitement. After this she came often, and taught them numbers of things, and showed them many of the marvels of her beautiful kingdom, and at last one day she said to them, 'You know that I have always been kind to you; now I think it is time you did something for me in your turn. You both remember the fountain I call my favourite? Promise me that every morning before the sun rises you will go to it and clear away every stone that impedes its course, and every dead leaf or broken twig that sullies its clear waters. I shall take it as a proof of your gratitude to me if you neither forget nor delay this duty, and I promise that so long as the sun's earliest rays find my favourite spring the clearest and sweetest in all my meadows, you two shall not be parted from one another.'

Sylvain and Jocosa willingly undertook this service, and indeed felt that it was but a very small thing in return for all that the fairy had given and promised to them. So for a long time the fountain was tended with the most scrupulous care, and was the clearest and prettiest in all the country round. But one morning in the spring, long before the sun rose, they were hastening towards it from opposite directions, when, tempted by the beauty of the myriads of gay flowers which grew thickly on all sides, they paused each to gather some for the other.

'I will make Sylvain a garland,' said Jocosa, and 'How pretty Jocosa will look in this crown!' thought Sylvain.

Hither and thither they strayed, led ever farther and farther, for the brightest flowers seemed always just beyond them, until at last they were startled by the first bright rays of the rising sun. With one accord they turned and ran towards the fountain, reaching it at the same moment, though from opposite sides. But what was their horror to see its usually tranquil waters seething and bubbling, and even as they looked down rushed a mighty stream, which entirely engulfed it, and Sylvain and Jocosa found themselves parted by a wide and swiftly-rushing river. All this had happened with such rapidity that they had only time to utter a cry, and each to hold up to the other the flowers they had gathered; but this was explanation enough. Twenty times did Sylvain throw himself into the turbulent waters, hoping to be able to swim to the other side, but each time an irresistible force drove him back upon the bank he had just quitted, while, as for Jocosa, she even essayed to cross the flood upon a tree which came floating down torn up by the roots, but her efforts were equally useless. Then with heavy hearts they set out to follow the course of the stream, which had now grown so wide that it was only with difficulty they could distinguish each other. Night and day, over mountains and through valleys, in cold or in heat, they struggled on, enduring fatigue and hunger and every hardship, and consoled only by the hope of meeting once more—until three years had passed, and at last they stood upon the cliffs where the river flowed into the mighty sea.

And now they seemed farther apart than ever, and in despair they tried once more to throw themselves into the foaming waves. But the Fairy of the Meadows, who had really never ceased to watch over them, did not intend that they should be drowned at last, so she hastily waved her wand, and immediately they found themselves standing side by side upon the golden sand. You may imagine their joy and delight when they realised that their weary struggle was ended, and their utter contentment as they clasped each other by the hand. They had so much to say that they hardly knew where to begin, but they agreed in blaming themselves bitterly for the negligence which had caused all their trouble; and when she heard this the Fairy immediately appeared to them. They threw themselves at her feet and implored her forgiveness, which she granted freely, and promised at the same time that now their punishment was ended she would always befriend them. Then she sent for her chariot of green rushes, ornamented with May dewdrops, which she particularly valued and always collected with great care; and ordered her six short-tailed moles to carry them all back to the well-known pastures, which they did in a remarkably short time; and Sylvain and Jocosa were overjoyed to see their dearly-loved home once more after all their toilful wanderings. The Fairy, who had set her mind upon securing their happiness, had in their absence quite made up the quarrel between their parents, and gained their consent to the marriage of the faithful lovers; and now she conducted them to the most charming little cottage that can be imagined, close to the fountain, which had once more resumed its peaceful aspect, and flowed gently down into the little brook which enclosed the garden and orchard and pasture which belonged to the cottage. Indeed, nothing more could have been thought of, either for Sylvain and Jocosa or for their flocks; and their delight satisfied even the Fairy who had planned it all to please them. When they had explored and admired until they were tired they sat down to rest under the rose-covered porch, and the Fairy said that to pass the time until the wedding guests whom she had invited could arrive she would tell them a story. This is it:

The Yellow Bird

Once upon a time a Fairy, who had somehow or other got into mischief, was condemned by the High Court of Fairyland to live for several years under the form of some creature, and at the moment of resuming her natural appearance once again to make the fortune of two men. It was left to her to choose what form she would take, and because she loved yellow she transformed herself into a lovely bird with shining golden feathers such as no one had ever seen before. When the time of her punishment was at an end the beautiful yellow bird flew to Bagdad, and let herself be caught by a Fowler at the precise moment when Badi-al-Zaman was walking up and down outside his magnificent summer palace. This Badi-al-Zaman— whose name means 'Wonder-of-the-World'—was looked upon in Bagdad as the most fortunate creature under the sun, because of his vast wealth. But really, what with anxiety about his riches and being weary of everything, and always desiring something he had not, he never knew a moment's real happiness. Even now he had come out of his palace, which was large and splendid enough for fifty kings, weary and cross because he could find nothing new to amuse him. The Fowler thought that this would be a favourable opportunity for offering him the marvellous bird, which he felt certain he would buy the instant he saw it. And he was not mistaken, for when Badi-al-Zaman took the lovely prisoner into his own hands, he saw written under its right wing the words, 'He who eats my head will become a king,' and under its left wing, 'He who eats my heart will find a hundred gold pieces under his pillow every morning.' In spite of all his wealth he at once began to desire the promised gold, and the bargain was soon completed. Then the difficulty arose as to how the bird was to be cooked; for among all his army of servants not one could Badi-al-Zaman trust. At last he asked the Fowler if he were married, and on hearing that he was he bade him take the bird home with him and tell his wife to cook it.

'Perhaps,' said he, 'this will give me an appetite, which I have not had for many a long day, and if so your wife shall have a hundred pieces of silver.'

The Fowler with great joy ran home to his wife, who speedily made a savoury stew of the Yellow Bird. But when Badi-al-Zaman reached the cottage and began eagerly to search in the dish for its head and its heart he could not find either of them, and turned to the Fowler's wife in a furious rage. She was so terrified that she fell upon her knees before him and confessed that her two children had come in just before he arrived, and had so teased her for some of the dish she was preparing that she had presently given the head to one and the heart to the other, since these morsels are not generally much esteemed; and Badi-al-Zaman rushed from the cottage vowing vengeance against the whole family. The wrath of a rich man is generally to be feared, so the Fowler and his wife resolved to send their children out of harm's way; but the wife, to console her husband, confided to him that she had purposely given them the head and heart of the bird because she had been able to read what was written under its wings. So, believing that their children's fortunes were made, they embraced them and sent them forth, bidding them get as far away as possible, to take different roads, and to send news of their welfare. For themselves, they remained hidden and disguised in the town, which was really rather clever of them; but very soon afterwards Badi-al-Zaman died of vexation and annoyance at the loss of the promised treasure, and then they went back to their cottage to wait for news of their children. The younger, who had eaten the heart of the Yellow Bird, very soon found out what it had done for him, for each morning when he awoke he found a purse containing a hundred gold pieces under his pillow. But, as all poor people may remember for their consolation, nothing in the world causes so much trouble or requires so much care as a great treasure. Consequently, the Fowler's son, who spent with reckless profusion and was supposed to be possessed of a great hoard of gold, was before very long attacked by robbers, and in trying to defend himself was so badly wounded that he died.

The elder brother, who had eaten the Yellow Bird's head, travelled a long way without meeting with any particular adventure, until at last he reached a large city in Asia, which was all in an uproar over the choosing of a new Emir. All the principal citizens had formed themselves into two parties, and it was not until after a prolonged squabble that they agreed that the person to whom the most singular thing happened should be Emir. Our young traveller entered the town at this juncture, with his agreeable face and jaunty air, and all at once felt something alight upon his head, which proved to be a snow-white pigeon. Thereupon all the people began to stare, and to run after him, so that he presently reached the palace with the pigeon upon his head and all the inhabitants of the city at his heels, and before he knew where he was they made him Emir, to his great astonishment.

As there is nothing more agreeable than to command, and nothing to which people get accustomed more quickly, the young Emir soon felt quite at his ease in his new position; but this did not prevent him from making every kind of mistake, and so misgoverning the kingdom that at last the whole city rose in revolt and deprived him at once of his authority and his life—a punishment which he richly deserved, for in the days of his prosperity he disowned the Fowler and his wife, and allowed them to die in poverty.

'I have told you this story, my dear Sylvain and Jocosa,' added the Fairy, 'to prove to you that this little cottage and all that belongs to it is a gift more likely to bring you happiness and contentment than many things that would at first seem grander and more desirable. If you will faithfully promise me to till your fields and feed your flocks, and will keep your word better than you did before, I will see that you never lack anything that is really for your good.'

Sylvain and Jocosa gave their faithful promise, and as they kept it they always enjoyed peace and prosperity. The Fairy had asked all their friends and neighbours to their wedding, which took place at once with great festivities and rejoicings, and they lived to a good old age, always loving one another with all their hearts.

By the Comte de Caylus.

FAIRY GIFTS

It generally happens that people's surroundings reflect more or less accurately their minds and dispositions, so perhaps that is why the Flower Fairy lived in a lovely palace, with the most delightful garden you can imagine, full of flowers, and trees, and fountains, and fish-ponds, and everything nice. For the Fairy herself was so kind and charming that everybody loved her, and all the young princes and princesses who formed her court, were as happy as the day was long, simply because they were near her. They came to her when they were quite tiny, and never left her until they were grown up and had to go away into the great world; and when that time came she gave to each whatever gift he asked of her. But it is chiefly of the Princess Sylvia that you are going to hear now. The Fairy loved her with all her heart, for she was at once original and gentle, and she had nearly reached the age at which the gifts were generally bestowed. However, the Fairy had a great wish to know how the other princesses who had grown up and left her, were prospering, and before the time came for Sylvia to go herself, she resolved to send her to some of them. So one day her chariot, drawn by butterflies, was made ready, and the Fairy said: 'Sylvia, I am going to send you to the court of Iris; she will receive you with pleasure for my sake as well as for your own. In two months you may come back to me again, and I shall expect you to tell me what you think of her.'

Sylvia was very unwilling to go away, but as the Fairy wished it she said nothing—only when the two months were over she stepped joyfully into the butterfly chariot, and could not get back quickly enough to the Flower-Fairy, who, for her part, was equally delighted to see her again.

'Now, child,' said she, 'tell me what impression you have received.'

'You sent me, madam,' answered Sylvia, 'to the Court of Iris, on whom you had bestowed the gift of beauty. She never tells anyone, however, that it was your gift, though she often speaks of your kindness in general. It seemed to me that her loveliness, which fairly dazzled me at first, had absolutely deprived her of the use of any of her other gifts or graces. In allowing herself to be seen, she appeared to think that she was doing all that could possibly be required of her. But, unfortunately, while I was still with her she became seriously ill, and though she presently recovered, her beauty is entirely gone, so that she hates the very sight of herself, and is in despair. She entreated me to tell you what had happened, and to beg you, in pity, to give her beauty back to her. And, indeed, she does need it terribly, for all the things in her that were tolerable, and even agreeable, when she was so pretty, seem quite different now she is ugly, and it is so long since she thought of using her mind or her natural cleverness, that I really don't think she has any left now. She is quite aware of all this herself, so you may imagine how unhappy she is, and how earnestly she begs for your aid.'

'You have told me what I wanted to know,' cried the Fairy, 'but alas! I cannot help her; my gifts can be given but once.'

Some time passed in all the usual delights of the Flower-Fairy's palace, and then she sent for Sylvia again, and told her she was to stay for a little while with the Princess Daphne, and accordingly the butterflies whisked her off, and set her down in quite a strange kingdom. But she had only been there a very little time before a wandering butterfly brought a message from her to the Fairy, begging that she might be sent for as soon as possible, and before very long she was allowed to return.

'Ah! madam,' cried she, 'what a place you sent me to that time!'

'Why, what was the matter?' asked the Fairy. 'Daphne was one of the princesses who asked for the gift of eloquence, if I remember rightly.'

'And very ill the gift of eloquence becomes a woman,' replied Sylvia, with an air of conviction. 'It is true that she speaks well, and her expressions are well chosen; but then she never leaves off talking, and though at first one may be amused, one ends by being wearied to death. Above all things she loves any assembly for settling the affairs of her kingdom, for on those occasions she can talk and talk without fear of interruption; but, even then, the moment it is over she is ready to begin again about anything or nothing, as the case may be. Oh! how glad I was to come away I cannot tell you.'

The Fairy smiled at Sylvia's unfeigned disgust at her late experience; but after allowing her a little time to recover she sent her to the Court of the Princess Cynthia, where she left her for three months. At the end of that time Sylvia came back to her with all the joy and contentment that one feels at being once more beside a dear friend. The Fairy, as usual, was anxious to hear what she thought of Cynthia, who had always been amiable, and to whom she had given the gift of pleasing.

'I thought at first,' said Sylvia, 'that she must be the happiest Princess in the world; she had a thousand lovers who vied with one another in their efforts to please and gratify her. Indeed, I had nearly decided that I would ask a similar gift.'

'Have you altered your mind, then?' interrupted the Fairy.

'Yes, indeed, madam,' replied Sylvia; 'and I will tell you why. The longer I stayed the more I saw that Cynthia was not really happy. In her desire to please everyone she ceased to be sincere, and degenerated into a mere coquette; and even her lovers felt that the charms and fascinations which were exercised upon all who approached her without distinction were valueless, so that in the end they ceased to care for them, and went away disdainfully.'

'I am pleased with you, child,' said the Fairy; 'enjoy yourself here for awhile and presently you shall go to Phyllida.'

Sylvia was glad to have leisure to think, for she could not make up her mind at all what she should ask for herself, and the time was drawing very near. However, before very long the Fairy sent her to Phyllida, and waited for her report with unabated interest.

'I reached her court safely,' said Sylvia, 'and she received me with much kindness, and immediately began to exercise upon me that brilliant wit which you had bestowed upon her. I confess that I was fascinated by it, and for a week thought that nothing could be more desirable; the time passed like magic, so great was the charm of her society. But I ended by ceasing to covet that gift more than any of the others I have seen, for, like the gift of pleasing, it cannot really give satisfaction. By degrees I wearied of what had so delighted me at first, especially as I perceived more and more plainly that it is impossible to be constantly smart and amusing without being frequently ill-natured, and too apt to turn all things, even the most serious, into mere occasions for a brilliant jest.'

The Fairy in her heart agreed with Sylvia's conclusions, and felt pleased with herself for having brought her up so well.

But now the time was come for Sylvia to receive her gift, and all her companions were assembled; the Fairy stood in the midst and in the usual manner asked what she would take with her into the great world.

Sylvia paused for a moment, and then answered: 'A quiet spirit.' And the Fairy granted her request.

This lovely gift makes life a constant happiness to its possessor, and to all who are brought into contact with her. She has all the beauty of gentleness and contentment in her sweet face; and if at times it seems less lovely through some chance grief or disquietude, the hardest thing that one ever hears said is:

'Sylvia's dear face is pale to-day. It grieves one to see her so.'

And when, on the contrary, she is gay and joyful, the sunshine of her presence rejoices all who have the happiness of being near her.

By the Comte de Caylus.

PRINCE NARCISSUS AND THE PRINCESS POTENTILLA

Once upon a time there lived a King and Queen who, though it is a very long while since they died, were much the same in their tastes and pursuits as people nowadays. The King, who was called Cloverleaf, liked hunting better than anything else; but he nevertheless bestowed as much care upon his kingdom as he felt equal to—that is to say, he never made an end of folding and unfolding the State documents. As to the Queen, she had once been very pretty, and she liked to believe that she was so still, which is, of course, always made quite easy for queens. Her name was Frivola, and her one occupation in life was the pursuit of amusement. Balls, masquerades, and picnics followed one another in rapid succession, as fast as she could arrange them, and you may imagine that under these circumstances the kingdom was somewhat neglected. As a matter of fact, if anyone had a fancy for a town, or a province, he helped himself to it; but as long as the King had his horses and dogs, and the Queen her musicians and her actors, they did not trouble themselves about the matter. King Cloverleaf and Queen Frivola had but one child, and this Princess had from her very babyhood been so beautiful, that by the time she was four years old the Queen was desperately jealous of her, and so fearful that when she was grown up she would be more admired than herself, that she resolved to keep her hidden away out of sight. To this end she caused a little house to be built not far beyond the Palace gardens, on the bank of a river. This was surrounded by a high wall, and in it the charming Potentilla was imprisoned. Her nurse, who was dumb, took care of her, and the necessaries of life were conveyed to her through a little window in the wall, while guards were always pacing to and fro outside, with orders to cut off the head of anyone who tried to approach, which they would certainly have done without thinking twice about it. The Queen told everyone, with much pretended sorrow, that the Princess was so ugly, and so troublesome, and altogether so impossible to love, that to keep her out of sight was the only thing that could be done for her. And this tale she repeated so often, that at last the whole court believed it. Things were in this state, and the Princess was about fifteen years old, when Prince Narcissus, attracted by the report of Queen Frivola's gay doings, presented himself at the court. He was not much older than the Princess, and was as handsome a Prince as you would see in a day's journey, and really, for his age, not so very scatter-brained. His parents were a King and Queen, whose story you will perhaps read some day. They died almost at the same time, leaving their kingdom to the eldest of their children, and commending their youngest son, Prince Narcissus, to the care of the Fairy Melinette. In this they did very well for him, for the Fairy was as kind as she was powerful, and she spared no pains in teaching the little Prince everything it was good for him to know, and even imparted to him some of her own Fairy lore. But as soon as he was grown up she sent him out to see the world for himself, though all the time she was secretly keeping watch over him, ready to help in any time of need. Before he started she gave him a ring which would render him invisible when he put it on his finger. These rings seem to be quite common; you must often have heard of them, even if you have never seen one. It was in the course of the Prince's wanderings, in search of experience of men and things, that he came to the court of Queen Frivola, where he was extremely well received. The Queen was delighted with him, so were all her ladies; and the King was very polite to him, though he did not quite see why the whole court was making such a fuss over him.

Prince Narcissus enjoyed all that went on, and found the time pass very pleasantly. Before long, of course, he heard the story about the Princess Potentilla, and, as it had by that time been repeated many times, and had been added to here and there, she was represented as such a monster of ugliness that he was really quite curious to see her, and resolved to avail himself of the magic power of his ring to accomplish his design. So he made himself invisible, and passed the guard without their so much as suspecting that anyone was near. Climbing the wall was rather a difficulty, but when he at length found himself inside it he was charmed with the peaceful beauty of the little domain it enclosed, and still more delighted when he perceived a slender, lovely maiden wandering among the flowers. It was not until he had sought vainly for the imaginary monster that he realised that this was the Princess herself, and by that time he was deeply in love with her, for indeed it would have been hard to find anyone prettier than Potentilla, as she sat by the brook, weaving a garland of blue forget-me-nots to crown her waving golden locks, or to imagine anything more gentle than the way she tended all the birds and beasts who inhabited her small kingdom, and who all loved and followed her. Prince Narcissus watched her every movement, and hovered near her in a dream of delight, not daring as yet to appear to her, so humble had he suddenly become in her presence. And when evening came, and the nurse fetched the Princess into her little house, he felt obliged to go back to Frivola's palace, for fear his absence should be noticed and someone should discover his new treasure. But he forgot that to go back absent, and dreamy, and indifferent, when he had before been gay and ardent about everything, was the surest way of awakening suspicion; and when, in response to the jesting questions which were put to him upon the subject, he only blushed and returned evasive answers, all the ladies were certain that he had lost his heart, and did their utmost to discover who was the happy possessor of it. As to the Prince, he was becoming day by day more attached to Potentilla, and his one thought was to attend her, always invisible, and help her in everything she did, and provide her with everything that could possibly amuse or please her. And the Princess, who had learnt to find diversion in very small things in her quiet life, was in a continual state of delight over the treasures which the Prince constantly laid where she must find them. Then Narcissus implored his faithful friend Melinette to send the Princess such dreams of him as should make her recognise him as a friend when he actually appeared before her eyes; and this device was so successful that the Princess quite dreaded the cessation of these amusing dreams, in which a certain Prince Narcissus was such a delightful lover and companion. After that he went a step further and began to have long talks with the Princess—still, however, keeping himself invisible, until she begged him so earnestly to appear to her that he could no longer resist, and after making her promise that, no matter what he was like, she would still love him, he drew the ring from his finger, and the Princess saw with delight that he was as handsome as he was agreeable. Now, indeed, they were perfectly happy, and they passed the whole long summer day in Potentilla's favourite place by the brook, and when at last Prince Narcissus had to leave her it seemed to them both that the hours had gone by with the most amazing swiftness. The Princess stayed where she was, dreaming of her delightful Prince, and nothing could have been further from her thoughts than any trouble or misfortune, when suddenly, in a cloud of dust and shavings, by came the enchanter Grumedan, and unluckily he chanced to catch sight of Potentilla. Down he came straightway and alighted at her feet, and one look at her charming blue eyes and smiling lips quite decided him that he must appear to her at once, though he was rather annoyed to remember that he had on only his second-best cloak. The Princess sprang to her feet with a cry of terror at this sudden apparition, for really the Enchanter was no beauty. To begin with, he was very big and clumsy, then he had but one eye, and his teeth were long, and he stammered badly; nevertheless, he had an excellent opinion of himself, and mistook the Princess's cry of terror for an exclamation of delighted surprise. After pausing a moment to give her time to admire him, the Enchanter made her the most complimentary speech he could invent, which, however, did not please her at all, though he was extremely delighted with it himself. Poor Potentilla only shuddered and cried:

'Oh! where is my Narcissus?'

To which he replied with a self-satisfied chuckle: 'You want a narcissus, madam? Well, they are not rare; you shall have as many as you like.'

Whereupon he waved his wand, and the Princess found herself surrounded and half buried in the fragrant flowers. She would certainly have betrayed that this was not the kind of narcissus she wanted, but for the Fairy Melinette, who had been anxiously watching the interview, and now thought it quite time to interfere. Assuming the Prince's voice, she whispered in Potentilla's ear:

'We are menaced by a great danger, but my only fear is for you, my Princess. Therefore I beg you to hide what you really feel, and we will hope that some way out of the difficulty may present itself.'

The Princess was much agitated by this speech, and feared lest the Enchanter should have overheard it; but he had been loudly calling her attention to the flowers, and chuckling over his own smartness in getting them for her; and it was rather a blow to him when she said very coldly that they were not the sort she preferred, and she would be glad if he would send them all away. This he did, but afterwards wished to kiss the Princess's hand as a reward for having been so obliging; but the Fairy Melinette was not going to allow anything of that kind. She appeared suddenly, in all her splendour, and cried:

'Stay, Grumedan; this Princess is under my protection, and the smallest impertinence will cost you a thousand years of captivity. If you can win Potentilla's heart by the ordinary methods I cannot oppose you, but I warn you that I will not put up with any of your usual tricks.'

This declaration was not at all to the Enchanter's taste; but he knew that there was no help for it, and that he would have to behave well, and pay the Princess all the delicate attentions he could think of; though they were not at all the sort of thing he was used to. However, he decided that to win such a beauty it was quite worth while; and Melinette, feeling that she could now leave the Princess in safety, hurried off to tell Prince Narcissus what was going forward. Of course, at the very mention of the Enchanter as a rival he was furious, and I don't know what foolish things he would not have done if Melinette had not been there to calm him down. She represented to him what a powerful enchanter Grumedan was, and how, if he were provoked, he might avenge himself upon the Princess, since he was the most unjust and churlish of all the enchanters, and had often before had to be punished by the Fairy Queen for some of his ill-deeds. Once he had been imprisoned in a tree, and was only released when it was blown down by a furious wind; another time he was condemned to stay under a big stone at the bottom of a river, until by some chance the stone should be turned over; but nothing could ever really improve him. The Fairy finally made Narcissus promise that he would remain invisible when he was with the Princess, since she felt sure that this would make things easier for all of them. Then began a struggle between Grumedan and the Prince, the latter under the name of Melinette, as to which could best delight and divert the Princess and win her approbation. Prince Narcissus first made friends with all the birds in Potentilla's little domain, and taught them to sing her name and her praises, with all their sweetest trills and most touching melodies, and all day long to tell her how dearly he loved her. Grumedan, thereupon, declared that there was nothing new about that, since the birds had sung since the world began, and all lovers had imagined that they sang for them alone. Therefore he said he would himself write an opera that should be absolutely a novelty and something worth hearing. When the time came for the performance (which lasted five weary hours) the Princess found to her dismay that the 'opera' consisted of this more than indifferent verse, chanted with all their might by ten thousand frogs:

'Admirable Potentilla, Do you think it kind or wise In this sudden way to kill a Poor Enchanter with your eyes?'

Really, if Narcissus had not been there to whisper in her ear and divert her attention, I don't know what would have become of poor Potentilla, for though the first repetition of this absurdity amused her faintly, she nearly died of weariness before the time was over. Luckily Grumedan did not perceive this, as he was too much occupied in whipping up the frogs, many of whom perished miserably from fatigue, since he did not allow them to rest for a moment. The Prince's next idea for Potentilla's amusement was to cause a fleet of boats exactly like those of Cleopatra, of which you have doubtless read in history, to come up the little river, and upon the most gorgeously decorated of these reclined the great Queen herself, who, as soon as she reached the place where Potentilla sat in rapt attention, stepped majestically on shore and presented the Princess with that celebrated pearl of which you have heard so much, saying:

'You are more beautiful than I ever was. Let my example warn you to make a better use of your beauty!'

And then the little fleet sailed on, until it was lost to view in the windings of the river. Grumedan was also looking on at the spectacle, and said very contemptuously:

'I cannot say I think these marionettes amusing. What a to-do to make over a single pearl! But if you like pearls, madam, why, I will soon gratify you.'

So saying, he drew a whistle from his pocket, and no sooner had he blown it than the Princess saw the water of the river bubble and grow muddy, and in another instant up came hundreds of thousands of great oysters, who climbed slowly and laboriously towards her and laid at her feet all the pearls they contained.

'Those are what I call pearls,' cried Grumedan in high glee. And truly there were enough of them to pave every path in Potentilla's garden and leave some to spare! The next day Prince Narcissus had prepared for the Princess's pleasure a charming arbour of leafy branches, with couches of moss and grassy floor and garlands everywhere, with her name written in different coloured blossoms. Here he caused a dainty little banquet to be set forth, while hidden musicians played softly, and the silvery fountains plashed down into their marble basins, and when presently the music stopped a single nightingale broke the stillness with his delicious chant.

'Ah!' cried the Princess, recognizing the voice of one of her favourites, 'Philomel, my sweet one, who taught you that new song?'

And he answered: 'Love, my Princess.'

Meanwhile the Enchanter was very ill-pleased with the entertainment, which he declared was dulness itself.

'You don't seem to have any idea in these parts beyond little squeaking birds!' said he. 'And fancy giving a banquet without so much as an ounce of plate!'

So the next day, when the Princess went out into her garden, there stood a summer-house built of solid gold, decorated within and without with her initials and the Enchanter's combined. And in it was spread an enormous repast, while the table so glittered with golden cups and plates, flagons and dishes, candlesticks and a hundred other things beside, that it was hardly possible to look steadily at it. The Enchanter ate like six ogres, but the Princess could not touch a morsel. Presently Grumedan remarked with a grin:

'I have provided neither musicians nor singers; but as you seem fond of music I will sing to you myself.'

Whereupon he began, with a voice like a screech-owl's, to chant the words of his 'opera,' only this time happily not at such a length, and without the frog accompaniment. After this the Prince again asked the aid of his friends the birds, and when they had assembled from all the country round he tied about the neck of each one a tiny lamp of some brilliant colour, and when darkness fell he made them go through a hundred pretty tricks before the delighted Potentilla, who clapped her little hands with delight when she saw her own name traced in points of light against the dark trees, or when the whole flock of sparks grouped themselves into bouquets of different colours, like living flowers. Grumedan leaning back in his armchair, with one knee crossed over the other and his nose in the air, looked on disdainfully.

'Oh! if you like fireworks, Princess,' said he; and the next night all the will-o'-the-wisps in the country came and danced on the plain, which could be seen from the Princess's windows, and as she was looking out, and rather enjoying the sight, up sprang a frightful volcano, pouring out smoke and flames which terrified her greatly, to the intense amusement of the Enchanter, who laughed like a pack of wolves quarrelling. After this, as many of the will-o'-the-wisps as could get in crowded into Potentilla's garden, and by their light the tall yew-trees danced minuets until the Princess was weary and begged to be excused from looking at anything more that night. But, in spite of Potentilla's efforts to behave politely to the tiresome old Enchanter, whom she detested, he could not help seeing that he failed to please her, and then he began to suspect very strongly that she must love someone else, and that somebody besides Melinette was responsible for all the festivities he had witnessed. So after much consideration he devised a plan for finding out the truth. He went to the Princess suddenly, and announced that he was most unwillingly forced to leave her, and had come to bid her farewell. Potentilla could scarcely hide her delight when she heard this, and his back was hardly turned before she was entreating Prince Narcissus to make himself visible once more. The poor Prince had been getting quite thin with anxiety and annoyance, and was only too delighted to comply with her request. They greeted one another rapturously, and were just sitting down to talk over everything cosily, and enjoy the Enchanter's discomfiture together, when out he burst in a fury from behind a bush. With his huge club he aimed a terrific blow at Narcissus, which must certainly have killed him but for the adroitness of the Fairy Melinette, who arrived upon the scene just in time to snatch him up and carry him off at lightning speed to her castle in the air. Poor Potentilla, however, had not the comfort of knowing this, for at the sight of the Enchanter threatening her beloved Prince she had given one shriek and fallen back insensible. When she recovered her senses she was more than ever convinced that he was dead, since even Melinette was no longer near her, and no one was left to defend her from the odious old Enchanter.

To make matters worse, he seemed to be in a very bad temper, and came blustering and raging at the poor Princess.

'I tell you what it is, madam,' said he: 'whether you love this whippersnapper Prince or not doesn't matter in the least. You are going to marry me, so you may as well make up your mind to it; and I am going away this very minute to make all the arrangements. But in case you should get into mischief in my absence, I think I had better put you to sleep.'

So saying, he waved his wand over her, and in spite of her utmost efforts to keep awake she sank into a profound and dreamless slumber.

As he wished to make what he considered a suitable entry into the King's palace, he stepped outside the Princess's little domain, and mounted upon an immense chariot with great solid wheels, and shafts like the trunk of an oak-tree, but all of solid gold. This was drawn with great difficulty by forty-eight strong oxen; and the Enchanter reclined at his ease, leaning upon his huge club, and holding carelessly upon his knee a tawny African lion, as if it had been a little lapdog. It was about seven o'clock in the morning when this extraordinary chariot reached the palace gates; the King was already astir, and about to set off on a hunting expedition; as for the Queen, she had only just gone off into her first sleep, and it would have been a bold person indeed who ventured to wake her.

The King was greatly annoyed at having to stay and see a visitor at such a time, and pulled off his hunting boots again with many grimaces. Meantime the Enchanter was stumping about in the hall, crying:

'Where is this King? Let him be told that I must see him and his wife also.'

The King, who was listening at the top of the staircase, thought this was not very polite; however, he took counsel with his favourite huntsman, and, following his advice, presently went down to see what was wanted of him. He was struck with astonishment at the sight of the chariot, and was gazing at it, when the Enchanter strode up to him, exclaiming:

'Shake hands, Cloverleaf, old fellow! Don't you know me?'

'No, I can't say I do,' replied the King, somewhat embarrassed.

'Why, I am Grumedan, the Enchanter,' said he, 'and I am come to make your fortune. Let us come in and talk things over a bit.'

Thereupon he ordered the oxen to go about their business, and they bounded off like stags, and were out of sight in a moment. Then, with one blow of his club, he changed the massive chariot into a perfect mountain of gold pieces.

'Those are for your lackeys,' said he to the King, 'that they may drink my health.'

Naturally a great scramble ensued, and at last the laughter and shouting awoke the Queen, who rang for her maids to ask the reason of such an unwonted hurry-burly. When they said that a visitor was asking for her, and then proceeded each one to tell breathlessly a different tale of wonder, in which she could only distinguish the words, 'oxen,' 'gold,' 'club,' 'giant,' 'lion,' she thought they were all out of their minds. Meanwhile the King was asking the Enchanter to what he was indebted for the honour of this visit, and on his replying that he would not say until the Queen was also present, messenger after messenger was dispatched to her to beg her immediate attendance. But Frivola was in a very bad humour at having been so unceremoniously awakened, and declared that she had a pain in her little finger, and that nothing should induce her to come.

When the Enchanter heard this he insisted that she must come.

'Take my club to her Majesty,' said he, 'and tell her that if she smells the end of it she will find it wonderfully reviving.'

So four of the King's strongest men-at-arms staggered off with it; and after some persuasion the Queen consented to try this novel remedy. She had hardly smelt it for an instant when she declared herself to be perfectly restored; but whether that was due to the scent of the wood or to the fact that as soon as she touched it out fell a perfect shower of magnificent jewels, I leave you to decide. At any rate, she was now all eagerness to see the mysterious stranger, and hastily throwing on her royal mantle, popped her second-best diamond crown over her night-cap, put a liberal dab of rouge upon each cheek, and holding up her largest fan before her nose—for she was not used to appearing in broad daylight—she went mincing into the great hall. The Enchanter waited until the King and Queen had seated themselves upon their throne, and then, taking his place between them, he began solemnly:

'My name is Grumedan. I am an extremely well-connected Enchanter; my power is immense. In spite of all this, the charms of your daughter Potentilla have so fascinated me that I cannot live without her. She fancies that she loves a certain contemptible puppy called Narcissus; but I have made very short work with him. I really do not care whether you consent to my marriage with your daughter or not, but I am bound to ask your consent, on account of a certain meddling Fairy called Melinette, with whom I have reason for wishing to keep on good terms.'

The King and Queen were somewhat embarrassed to know what answer to make to this terrible suitor, but at last they asked for time to talk over the matter: since, they said, their subjects might think that the heir to the throne should not be married with as little consideration as a dairymaid.

'Oh! take a day or two if you like,' said the Enchanter; 'but in the meantime, I am going to send for your daughter. Perhaps you will be able to induce her to be reasonable.'

So saying, he drew out his favourite whistle, and blew one ear-piercing note—whereupon the great lion, who had been dozing in the sunny courtyard, come bounding in on his soft, heavy feet. 'Orion,' said the Enchanter, 'go and fetch me the Princess, and bring her here at once. Be gentle now!'

At these words Orion went off at a great pace, and was soon at the other end of the King's gardens. Scattering the guards right and left, he cleared the wall at a bound, and seizing the sleeping Princess, he threw her on to his back, where he kept her by holding her robe in his teeth. Then he trotted gently back, and in less than five minutes stood in the great hall before the astonished King and Queen.

The Enchanter held his club close to the Princess's charming little nose, whereupon she woke up and shrieked with terror at finding herself in a strange place with the detested Grumedan. Frivola, who had stood by, stiff with displeasure at the sight of the lovely Princess, now stepped forward, and with much pretended concern proposed to carry off Potentilla to her own apartments that she might enjoy the quiet she seemed to need. Really her one idea was to let the Princess be seen by as few people as possible; so, throwing a veil over her head, she led her away and locked her up securely. All this time Prince Narcissus, gloomy and despairing, was kept a prisoner by Melinette in her castle in the air, and in spite of all the splendour by which he was surrounded, and all the pleasures which he might have enjoyed, his one thought was to get back to Potentilla. The Fairy, however, left him there, promising to do her very best for him, and commanding all her swallows and butterflies to wait upon him and do his bidding. One day, as he paced sadly to and fro, he thought he heard a voice he knew calling to him, and sure enough there was the faithful Philomel, Potentilla's favourite, who told him all that had passed, and how the sleeping Princess had been carried off by the Lion to the great grief of all her four-footed and feathered subjects, and how, not knowing what to do, he had wandered about until he heard the swallows telling one another of the Prince who was in their airy castle and had come to see if it could be Narcissus. The Prince was more distracted than ever, and tried vainly to escape from the castle, by leaping from the roof into the clouds; but every time they caught him, and rolling softly up, brought him back to the place from which he started, so at last he gave up the attempt and waited with desperate patience for the return of Melinette. Meanwhile matters were advancing rapidly in the court of King Cloverleaf, for the Queen quite made up her mind that such a beauty as Potentilla must be got out of the way as quickly as possible. So she sent for the Enchanter secretly, and after making him promise that he would never turn herself and King Cloverleaf out of their kingdom, and that he would take Potentilla far away, so that never again might she set eyes upon her, she arranged the wedding for the next day but one.

You may imagine how Potentilla lamented her sad fate, and entreated to be spared. All the comfort she could get out of Frivola was, that if she preferred a cup of poison to a rich husband she would certainly provide her with one.

When, then, the fatal day came the unhappy Potentilla was led into the great hall between the King and Queen, the latter wild with envy at the murmurs of admiration which rose on all sides at the loveliness of the Princess. An instant later in came Grumedan by the opposite door. His hair stood on end, and he wore a huge bag-purse and a cravat tied in a bow, his mantle was made of a shower of silver coins with a lining of rose colour, and his delight in his own appearance knew no bounds. That any Princess could prefer a cup of poison to himself never for an instant occurred to him. Nevertheless, that was what did happen, for when Queen Frivola in jest held out the fatal cup to the Princess, she took it eagerly, crying:

'Ah! beloved Narcissus, I come to thee!' and was just raising it to her lips when the window of the great hall burst open, and the Fairy Melinette floated in upon a glowing sunset cloud, followed by the Prince himself:

All the court looked on in dazzled surprise, while Potentilla, catching sight of her lover, dropped the cup and ran joyfully to meet him.

The Enchanter's first thought was to defend himself when he saw Melinette appear, but she slipped round his blind side, and catching him by the eyelashes dragged him off to the ceiling of the hall, where she held him kicking for a while just to give him a lesson, and then touching him with her wand she imprisoned him for a thousand years in a crystal ball which hung from the roof. 'Let this teach you to mind what I tell you another time,' she remarked severely. Then turning to the King and Queen, she begged them to proceed with the wedding, since she had provided a much more suitable bridegroom. She also deprived them of their kingdom, for they had really shown themselves unfit to manage it, and bestowed it upon the Prince and Princess, who, though they were unwilling to take it, had no choice but to obey the Fairy. However, they took care that the King and Queen were always supplied with everything they could wish for.

Prince Narcissus and Princess Potentilla lived long and happily, beloved by all their subjects. As for the Enchanter, I don't believe he has been let out yet.

La Princesse Pimprenella et Le Prince Romarin.

PRINCE FEATHERHEAD AND THE PRINCESS CELANDINE

Once upon a time there lived a King and Queen, who were the best creatures in the world, and so kind-hearted that they could not bear to see their subjects want for anything. The consequence was that they gradually gave away all their treasures, till they positively had nothing left to live upon; and this coming to the ears of their neighbour, King Bruin, he promptly raised a large army and marched into their country. The poor King, having no means of defending his kingdom, was forced to disguise himself with a false beard, and carrying his only son, the little Prince Featherhead, in his arms, and accompanied only by the Queen, to make the best of his way into the wild country. They were lucky enough to escape the soldiers of King Bruin, and at last, after unheard-of fatigues and adventures, they found themselves in a charming green valley, through which flowed a stream clear as crystal and overshadowed by beautiful trees. As they looked round them with delight, a voice said suddenly: 'Fish, and see what you will catch.' Now the King had always loved fishing, and never went anywhere without a fish-hook or two in his pocket, so he drew one out hastily, and the Queen lent him her girdle to fasten it to, and it had hardly touched the water before it caught a big fish, which made them an excellent meal—and not before they needed it, for they had found nothing until then but a few wild berries and roots. They thought that for the present they could not do better than stay in this delightful place, and the King set to work, and soon built a bower of branches to shelter them; and when it was finished the Queen was so charmed with it that she declared nothing was lacking to complete her happiness but a flock of sheep, which she and the little Prince might tend while the King fished. They soon found that the fish were not only abundant and easily caught, but also very beautiful, with glittering scales of every imaginable hue; and before long the King discovered that he could teach them to talk and whistle better than any parrot. Then he determined to carry some to the nearest town and try to sell them; and as no one had ever before seen any like them the people flocked about him eagerly and bought all he had caught, so that presently not a house in the city was considered complete without a crystal bowl full of fish, and the King's customers were very particular about having them to match the rest of the furniture, and gave him a vast amount of trouble in choosing them. However, the money he obtained in this way enabled him to buy the Queen her flock of sheep, as well as many of the other things which go to make life pleasant, so that they never once regretted their lost kingdom. Now it happened that the Fairy of the Beech-Woods lived in the lovely valley to which chance had led the poor fugitives, and it was she who had, in pity for their forlorn condition, sent the King such good luck to his fishing, and generally taken them under her protection. This she was all the more inclined to do as she loved children, and little Prince Featherhead, who never cried and grew prettier day by day, quite won her heart. She made the acquaintance of the King and the Queen without at first letting them know that she was a fairy, and they soon took a great fancy to her, and even trusted her with the precious Prince, whom she carried off to her palace, where she regaled him with cakes and tarts and every other good thing. This was the way she chose of making him fond of her; but afterwards, as he grew older, she spared no pains in educating and training him as a prince should be trained. But unfortunately, in spite of all her care, he grew so vain and frivolous that he quitted his peaceful country life in disgust, and rushed eagerly after all the foolish gaieties of the neighbouring town, where his handsome face and charming manners speedily made him popular. The King and Queen deeply regretted this alteration in their son, but did not know how to mend matters, since the good old Fairy had made him so self-willed.

Just at this time the Fairy of the Beech-Woods received a visit from an old friend of hers called Saradine, who rushed into her house so breathless with rage that she could hardly speak.

'Dear, dear! what is the matter?' said the Fairy of the Beech-Woods soothingly.

'The matter!' cried Saradine. 'You shall soon hear all about it. You know that, not content with endowing Celandine, Princess of the Summer Islands, with everything she could desire to make her charming, I actually took the trouble to bring her up myself; and now what does she do but come to me with more coaxings and caresses than usual to beg a favour. And what do you suppose this favour turns out to be—when I have been cajoled into promising to grant it? Nothing more nor less than a request that I will take back all my gifts—"since," says my young madam, "if I have the good fortune to please you, how am I to know that it is really I, myself? And that's how it will be all my life long, whenever I meet anybody. You see what a weariness my life will be to me under these circumstances, and yet I assure you I am not ungrateful to you for all your kindness!" I did all I could,' continued Saradine, 'to make her think better of it, but in vain; so after going through the usual ceremony for taking back my gifts, I'm come to you for a little peace and quietness. But, after all, I have not taken anything of consequence from this provoking Celandine. Nature had already made her so pretty, and given her such a ready wit of her own, that she will do perfectly well without me. However, I thought she deserved a little lesson, so to begin with I have whisked her off into the desert, and there left her!'

'What! all alone, and without any means of existence?' cried the kind-hearted old Fairy. 'You had better hand her over to me. I don't think so very badly of her after all. I'll just cure her vanity by making her love someone better than herself. Really, when I come to consider of it, I declare the little minx has shown more spirit and originality in the matter than one expects of a princess.'

Saradine willingly consented to this arrangement, and the old Fairy's first care was to smooth away all the difficulties which surrounded the Princess, and lead her by the mossy path overhung with trees to the bower of the King and Queen, who still pursued their peaceful life in the valley.

They were immensely surprised at her appearance, but her charming face, and the deplorably ragged condition to which the thorns and briers had reduced her once elegant attire, speedily won their compassion; they recognised her as a companion in misfortune, and the Queen welcomed her heartily, and begged her to share their simple repast. Celandine gracefully accepted their hospitality, and soon told them what had happened to her. The King was charmed with her spirit, while the Queen thought she had indeed been daring thus to go against the Fairy's wishes.

'Since it has ended in my meeting you,' said the Princess, 'I cannot regret the step I have taken, and if you will let me stay with you, I shall be perfectly happy.'

The King and Queen were only too delighted to have this charming Princess to supply the place of Prince Featherhead, whom they saw but seldom, since the Fairy had provided him with a palace in the neighbouring town, where he lived in the greatest luxury, and did nothing but amuse himself from morning to night. So Celandine stayed, and helped the Queen to keep house, and very soon they loved her dearly. When the Fairy of the Beech-Woods came to them, they presented the Princess to her, and told her story, little thinking that the Fairy knew more about Celandine than they did. The old Fairy was equally delighted with her, and often invited her to visit her Leafy Palace, which was the most enchanting place that could be imagined, and full of treasures. Often she would say to the Princess, when showing her some wonderful thing:

'This will do for a wedding gift some day.' And Celandine could not help thinking that it was to her that the Fairy meant to give the two blue wax-torches which burned without ever getting smaller, or the diamond from which more diamonds were continually growing, or the boat that sailed under water, or whatever beautiful or wonderful thing they might happen to be looking at. It is true that she never said so positively, but she certainly allowed the Princess to believe it, because she thought a little disappointment would be good for her. But the person she really relied upon for curing Celandine of her vanity was Prince Featherhead. The old Fairy was not at all pleased with the way he had been going on for some time, but her heart was so soft towards him that she was unwilling to take him away from the pleasures he loved, except by offering him something better, which is not the most effectual mode of correction, though it is without doubt the most agreeable.

However, she did not even hint to the Princess that Featherhead was anything but absolutely perfect, and talked of him so much that when at last she announced that he was coming to visit her, Celandine made up her mind that this delightful Prince would be certain to fall in love with her at once, and was quite pleased at the idea. The old Fairy thought so too, but as this was not at all what she wished, she took care to throw such an enchantment over the Princess that she appeared to Featherhead quite ugly and awkward, though to every one else she looked just as usual. So when he arrived at the Leafy Palace, more handsome and fascinating even than ever she had been led to expect, he hardly so much as glanced at the Princess, but bestowed all his attention upon the old Fairy, to whom he seemed to have a hundred things to say. The Princess was immensely astonished at his indifference, and put on a cold and offended air, which, however, he did not seem to observe. Then as a last resource she exerted all her wit and gaiety to amuse him, but with no better success, for he was of an age to be more attracted by beauty than by anything else, and though he responded politely enough, it was evident that his thoughts were elsewhere. Celandine was deeply mortified, since for her part the Prince pleased her very well, and for the first time she bitterly regretted the fairy gifts she had been anxious to get rid of. Prince Featherhead was almost equally puzzled, for he had heard nothing from the King and Queen but the praises of this charming Princess, and the fact that they had spoken of her as so very beautiful only confirmed his opinion that people who live in the country have no taste. He talked to them of his charming acquaintances in the town, the beauties he had admired, did admire, or thought he was going to admire, until Celandine, who heard it all, was ready to cry with vexation. The Fairy too was quite shocked at his conceit, and hit upon a plan for curing him of it. She sent to him by an unknown messenger a portrait of Princess Celandine as she really was, with this inscription: 'All this beauty and sweetness, with a loving heart and a great kingdom, might have been yours but for your well-known fickleness.'

This message made a great impression upon the Prince, but not so much as the portrait. He positively could not tear his eyes away from it, and exclaimed aloud that never, never had he seen anything so lovely and so graceful. Then he began to think that it was too absurd that he, the fascinating Featherhead, should fall in love with a portrait; and, to drive away the recollections of its haunting eyes, he rushed back to the town; but somehow everything seemed changed. The beauties no longer pleased him, their witty speeches had ceased to amuse; and indeed, for their parts, they found the Prince far less amiable than of yore, and were not sorry when he declared that, after all, a country life suited him best, and went back to the Leafy Palace. Meanwhile, the Princess Celandine had been finding the time pass but slowly with the King and Queen, and was only too pleased when Featherhead reappeared. She at once noticed the change in him, and was deeply curious to find the reason of it. Far from avoiding her, he now sought her company and seemed to take pleasure in talking to her, and yet the Princess did not for a moment flatter herself with the idea that he was in love with her, though it did not take her long to decide that he certainly loved someone. But one day the Princess, wandering sadly by the river, spied Prince Featherhead fast asleep in the shade of a tree, and stole nearer to enjoy the delight of gazing at his dear face unobserved. Judge of her astonishment when she saw that he was holding in his hand a portrait of herself! In vain did she puzzle over the apparent contradictoriness of his behaviour. Why did he cherish her portrait while he was so fatally indifferent to herself? At last she found an opportunity of asking him the name of the Princess whose picture he carried about with him always.

'Alas! how can I tell you?' replied he.

'Why should you not?' said the Princess timidly. 'Surely there is nothing to prevent you.'

'Nothing to prevent me!' repeated he, 'when my utmost efforts have failed to discover the lovely original. Should I be so sad if I could but find her? But I do not even know her name.'

More surprised than ever, the Princess asked to be allowed to see the portrait, and after examining it for a few minutes returned it, remarking shyly that at least the original had every cause to be satisfied with it.

'That means that you consider it flattered,' said the Prince severely. 'Really, Celandine, I thought better of you, and should have expected you to be above such contemptible jealousy. But all women are alike!'

'Indeed, I meant only that it was a good likeness,' said the Princess meekly.

'Then you know the original,' cried the Prince, throwing himself on his knees beside her. 'Pray tell me at once who it is, and don't keep me in suspense!'

'Oh! don't you see that it is meant for me?' cried Celandine.

The Prince sprang to his feet, hardly able to refrain from telling her that she must be blinded by vanity to suppose she resembled the lovely portrait even in the slightest degree; and after gazing at her for an instant with icy surprise, turned and left her without another word, and in a few hours quitted the Leafy Palace altogether.

Now the Princess was indeed unhappy, and could no longer bear to stay in a place where she had been so cruelly disdained. So, without even bidding farewell to the King and Queen, she left the valley behind her, and wandered sadly away, not caring whither. After walking until she was weary, she saw before her a tiny house, and turned her slow steps towards it. The nearer she approached the more miserable it appeared, and at length she saw a little old woman sitting upon the door-step, who said grimly:

'Here comes one of these fine beggars who are too idle to do anything but run about the country!'

'Alas! madam,' said Celandine, with tears in her pretty eyes, 'a sad fate forces me to ask you for shelter.'

'Didn't I tell you what it would be?' growled the old hag. 'From shelter we shall proceed to demand supper, and from supper money to take us on our way. Upon my word, if I could be sure of finding some one every day whose head was as soft as his heart, I wouldn't wish for a more agreeable life myself! But I have worked hard to build my house and secure a morsel to eat, and I suppose you think that I am to give away everything to the first passer-by who chooses to ask for it. Not at all! I wager that a fine lady like you has more money than I have. I must search her, and see if it is not so,' she added, hobbling towards Celandine with the aid of her stick.

'Alas! madam,' replied the Princess, 'I only wish I had. I would give it to you with all the pleasure in life.'

'But you are very smartly dressed for the kind of life you lead,' continued the old woman.

'What!' cried the Princess, 'do you think I am come to beg of you?'

'I don't know about that,' answered she; 'but at any rate you don't seem to have come to bring me anything. But what is it that you do want? Shelter?

Well, that does not cost much; but after that comes supper, and that I can't hear of. Oh dear no! Why, at your age one is always ready to eat; and now you have been walking, and I suppose you are ravenous?'

'Indeed no, madam,' answered the poor Princess, 'I am too sad to be hungry.'

'Oh, well! if you will promise to go on being sad, you may stay for the night,' said the old woman mockingly.

Thereupon she made the Princess sit down beside her, and began fingering her silken robe, while she muttered 'Lace on top, lace underneath! This must have cost you a pretty penny! It would have been better to save enough to feed yourself, and not come begging to those who want all they have for themselves. Pray, what may you have paid for these fine clothes?'

'Alas! madam,' answered the Princess, 'I did not buy them, and I know nothing about money.'

'What do you know, if I may ask?' said the old dame.

'Not much; but indeed I am very unhappy,' cried Celandine, bursting into tears, 'and if my services are any good to you—'

'Services!' interrupted the hag crossly. 'One has to pay for services, and I am not above doing my own work.'

'Madam, I will serve you for nothing,' said the poor Princess, whose spirits were sinking lower and lower. 'I will do anything you please; all I wish is to live quietly in this lonely spot.'

'Oh! I know you are only trying to take me in,' answered she; 'and if I do let you serve me, is it fitting that you should be so much better dressed I am? If I keep you, will you give me your clothes and wear some that I will provide you with? It is true that I am getting old and may want someone to take care of me some day.'

'Oh! for pity's sake, do what you please with my clothes,' cried poor Celandine miserably.

And the old woman hobbled off with great alacrity, and fetched a little bundle containing a wretched dress, such as the Princess had never even seen before, and nimbly skipped round, helping her to put it on instead of her own rich robe, with many exclamations of:

'Saints!—what a magnificent lining! And the width of it! It will make me four dresses at least. Why, child, I wonder you could walk under such a weight, and certainly in my house you would not have had room to turn round.'

So saying, she folded up the robe, and put it by with great care, while she remarked to Celandine:

'That dress of mine certainly suits you to a marvel; be sure you take great care of it.'

When supper-time came she went into the house, declining all the Princess's offers of assistance, and shortly afterwards brought out a very small dish, saying:

'Now let us sup.'

Whereupon she handed Celandine a small piece of black bread and uncovered the dish, which contained two dried plums.

'We will have one between us,' continued the old dame; 'and as you are the visitor, you shall have the half which contains the stone; but be very careful that you don't swallow it, for I keep them against the winter, and you have no idea what a good fire they make. Now, you take my advice—which won't cost you anything—and remember that it is always more economical to buy fruit with stones on this account.'

Celandine, absorbed in her own sad thoughts, did not even hear this prudent counsel, and quite forgot to eat her share of the plum, which delighted the old woman, who put it by carefully for her breakfast, saying:

'I am very much pleased with you, and if you go on as you have begun, we shall do very well, and I can teach you many useful things which people don't generally know. For instance, look at my house! It is built entirely of the seeds of all the pears I have eaten in my life. Now, most people throw them away, and that only shows what a number of things are wasted for want of a little patience and ingenuity.'

But Celandine did not find it possible to be interested in this and similar pieces of advice. And the old woman soon sent her to bed, for fear the night air might give her an appetite. She passed a sleepless night; but in the morning the old dame remarked:

'I heard how well you slept. After such a night you cannot want any breakfast; so while I do my household tasks you had better stay in bed, since the more one sleeps the less one need eat; and as it is market-day I will go to town and buy a pennyworth of bread for the week's eating.'

And so she chattered on, but poor Celandine did not hear or heed her; she wandered out into the desolate country to think over her sad fate. However, the good Fairy of the Beech-Woods did not want her to be starved, so she sent her an unlooked for relief in the shape of a beautiful white cow, which followed her back to the tiny house. When the old woman saw it her joy knew no bounds.

'Now we can have milk and cheese and butter!' cried she. 'Ah! how good milk is! What a pity it is so ruinously expensive!' So they made a little shelter of branches for the beautiful creature which was quite gentle, and followed Celandine about like a dog when she took it out every day to graze. One morning as she sat by a little brook, thinking sadly, she suddenly saw a young stranger approaching, and got up quickly, intending to avoid him. But Prince Featherhead, for it was he, perceiving her at the same moment, rushed towards her with every demonstration of joy: for he had recognised her, not as the Celandine whom he had slighted, but as the lovely Princess whom he had sought vainly for so long. The fact was that the Fairy of the Beech-Woods, thinking she had been punished enough, had withdrawn the enchantment from her, and transferred it to Featherhead, thereby in an instant depriving him of the good looks which had done so much towards making him the fickle creature he was. Throwing himself down at the Princess's feet, he implored her to stay, and at least speak to him, and she at last consented, but only because he seemed to wish it so very much. After that he came every day in the hope of meeting her again, and often expressed his delight at being with her. But one day, when he had been begging Celandine to love him, she confided to him that it was quite impossible, since her heart was already entirely occupied by another.

'I have,' said she, 'the unhappiness of loving a Prince who is fickle, frivolous, proud, incapable of caring for anyone but himself, who has been spoilt by flattery, and, to crown all, who does not love me.'

'But,' cried Prince Featherhead, 'surely you cannot care for so contemptible and worthless a creature as that.'

'Alas! but I do care,' answered the Princess, weeping.

'But where can his eyes be,' said the Prince, 'that your beauty makes no impression upon him? As for me, since I have possessed your portrait I have wandered over the whole world to find you, and, now we have met, I see that you are ten times lovelier than I could have imagined, and I would give all I own to win your love.'

'My portrait?' cried Celandine with sudden interest. 'Is it possible that Prince Featherhead can have parted with it?'

'He would part with his life sooner, lovely Princess,' answered he; 'I can assure you of that, for I am Prince Featherhead.'

At the same moment the Fairy of the Beech-Woods took away the enchantment, and the happy Princess recognised her lover, now truly hers, for the trials they had both undergone had so changed and improved them that they were capable of a real love for each other. You may imagine how perfectly happy they were, and how much they had to hear and to tell. But at length it was time to go back to the little house, and as they went along Celandine remembered for the first time what a ragged old dress she was wearing, and what an odd appearance she must present. But the Prince declared that it became her vastly, and that he thought it most picturesque. When they reached the house the old woman received them very crossly.

'I declare,' said she, 'that it's perfectly true: wherever there is a girl you may be sure that a young man will appear before long! But don't imagine that I'm going to have you here—not a bit of it, be off with you, my fine fellow!'

Prince Featherhead was inclined to be angry at this uncivil reception, but he was really too happy to care much, so he only demanded, on Celandine's behalf, that the old dame should give her back her own attire, that she might go away suitably dressed.

This request roused her to fury, since she had counted upon the Princess's fine robes to clothe her for the rest of her life, so that it was some time before the Prince could make himself heard to explain that he was willing to pay for them. The sight of a handful of gold pieces somewhat mollified her, however, and after making them both promise faithfully that on no consideration would they ask for the gold back again, she took the Princess into the house and grudgingly doled out to her just enough of her gay attire to make her presentable, while the rest she pretended to have lost. After this they found that they were very hungry, for one cannot live on love, any more than on air, and then the old woman's lamentations were louder than before. 'What!' she cried, 'feed people who were as happy as all that! Why, it was simply ruinous!'

But as the Prince began to look angry, she, with many sighs and mutterings, brought out a morsel of bread, a bowl of milk, and six plums, with which the lovers were well content: for as long as they could look at one another they really did not know what they were eating. It seemed as if they would go on for ever with their reminiscences, the Prince telling how he had wandered all over the world from beauty to beauty, always to be disappointed when he found that no one resembled the portrait; the Princess wondering how it was he could have been so long with her and yet never have recognised her, and over and over again pardoning him for his cold and haughty behaviour to her.

'For,' she said, 'you see, Featherhead, I love you, and love makes everything right! But we cannot stay here,' she added; 'what are we to do?'

The Prince thought they had better find their way to the Fairy of the Beech-Woods and put themselves once more under her protection, and they had hardly agreed upon this course when two little chariots wreathed with jasmine and honeysuckle suddenly appeared, and, stepping into them, they were whirled away to the Leafy Palace. Just before they lost sight of the little house they heard loud cries and lamentations from the miserly old dame, and, looking round, perceived that the beautiful cow was vanishing in spite of her frantic efforts to hold it fast. And they afterwards heard that she spent the rest of her life in trying to put the handful of gold the Prince had thrown to her into her money-bag. For the Fairy, as a punishment for her avarice, caused it to slip out again as fast as she dropped it in.

The Fairy of the Beech-Woods ran to welcome the Prince and Princess with open arms, only too delighted to find them so much improved that she could, with a clear conscience, begin to spoil them again. Very soon the Fairy Saradine also arrived, bringing the King and Queen with her. Princess Celandine implored her pardon, which she graciously gave; indeed the Princess was so charming she could refuse her nothing. She also restored to her the Summer Islands, and promised her protection in all things. The Fairy of the Beech-Woods then informed the King and Queen that their subjects had chased King Bruin from the throne, and were waiting to welcome them back again; but they at once abdicated in favour of Prince Featherhead, declaring that nothing could induce them to forsake their peaceful life, and the Fairies undertook to see the Prince and Princess established in their beautiful kingdoms. Their marriage took place the next day, and they lived happily ever afterwards, for Celandine was never vain and Featherhead was never fickle any more.

Le Prince Muguet et la Princesse Zaza.

THE THREE LITTLE PIGS

There was once upon a time a pig who lived with her three children on a large, comfortable, old-fashioned farmyard. The eldest of the little pigs was called Browny, the second Whitey, and the youngest and best looking Blacky. Now Browny was a very dirty little pig, and I am sorry to say spent most of his time rolling and wallowing about in the mud. He was never so happy as on a wet day, when the mud in the farmyard got soft, and thick, and slab. Then he would steal away from his mother's side, and finding the muddiest place in the yard, would roll about in it and thoroughly enjoy himself. His mother often found fault with him for this, and would shake her head sadly and say: 'Ah, Browny! some day you will be sorry that you did not obey your old mother.' But no words of advice or warning could cure Browny of his bad habits.

Whitey was quite a clever little pig, but she was greedy. She was always thinking of her food, and looking forward to her dinner; and when the farm girl was seen carrying the pails across the yard, she would rise up on her hind legs and dance and caper with excitement. As soon as the food was poured into the trough she jostled Blacky and Browny out of the way in her eagerness to get the best and biggest bits for herself. Her mother often scolded her for her selfishness, and told her that some day she would suffer for being so greedy and grabbing.

Blacky was a good, nice little pig, neither dirty nor greedy. He had nice dainty ways (for a pig), and his skin was always as smooth and shining as black satin. He was much cleverer than Browny and Whitey, and his mother's heart used to swell with pride when she heard the farmer's friends say to each other that some day the little black fellow would be a prize pig.

Now the time came when the mother pig felt old and feeble and near her end. One day she called the three little pigs round her and said:

'My children, I feel that I am growing odd and weak, and that I shall not live long. Before I die I should like to build a house for each of you, as this dear old sty in which we have lived so happily will be given to a new family of pigs, and you will have to turn out. Now, Browny, what sort of a house would you like to have?'

'A house of mud,' replied Browny, looking longingly at a wet puddle in the corner of the yard.

'And you, Whitey?' said the mother pig in rather a sad voice, for she was disappointed that Browny had made so foolish a choice.

'A house of cabbage,' answered Whitey, with a mouth full, and scarcely raising her snout out of the trough in which she was grubbing for some potato-parings.

'Foolish, foolish child!' said the mother pig, looking quite distressed. 'And you, Blacky?' turning to her youngest son, 'what sort of a house shall I order for you?'

'A house of brick, please mother, as it will be warm in winter, and cool in summer, and safe all the year round.'

'That is a sensible little pig,' replied his mother, looking fondly at him. 'I will see that the three houses are got ready at once. And now one last piece of advice. You have heard me talk of our old enemy the fox. When he hears that I am dead, he is sure to try and get hold of you, to carry you off to his den. He is very sly and will no doubt disguise himself, and pretend to be a friend, but you must promise me not to let him enter your houses on any pretext whatever.'

And the little pigs readily promised, for they had always had a great fear of the fox, of whom they had heard many terrible tales. A short time afterwards the old pig died, and the little pigs went to live in their own houses.

Browny was quite delighted with his soft mud walls and with the clay floor, which soon looked like nothing but a big mud pie. But that was what Browny enjoyed, and he was as happy as possible, rolling about all day and making himself in such a mess. One day, as he was lying half asleep in the mud, he heard a soft knock at his door, and a gentle voice said:

'May I come in, Master Browny? I want to see your beautiful new house.'

'Who are you?' said Browny, starting up in great fright, for though the voice sounded gentle, he felt sure it was a feigned voice, and he feared it was the fox.

'I am a friend come to call on you,' answered the voice.

'No, no,' replied Browny, 'I don't believe you are a friend. You are the wicked fox, against whom our mother warned us. I won't let you in.'

'Oho! is that the way you answer me?' said the fox, speaking very roughly in his natural voice. 'We shall soon see who is master here,' and with his paws he set to work and scraped a large hole in the soft mud walls. A moment later he had jumped through it, and catching Browny by the neck, flung him on his shoulders and trotted off with him to his den.

The next day, as Whitey was munching a few leaves of cabbage out of the corner of her house, the fox stole up to her door, determined to carry her off to join her brother in his den. He began speaking to her in the same feigned gentle voice in which he had spoken to Browny; but it frightened her very much when he said:

'I am a friend come to visit you, and to have some of your good cabbage for my dinner.'

'Please don't touch it,' cried Whitey in great distress. 'The cabbages are the walls of my house, and if you eat them you will make a hole, and the wind and rain will come in and give me a cold. Do go away; I am sure you are not a friend, but our wicked enemy the fox.' And poor Whitey began to whine and to whimper, and to wish that she had not been such a greedy little pig, and had chosen a more solid material than cabbages for her house. But it was too late now, and in another minute the fox had eaten his way through the cabbage walls, and had caught the trembling, shivering Whitey, and carried her off to his den.

The next day the fox started off for Blacky's house, because he had made up his mind that he would get the three little pigs together in his den, and then kill them, and invite all his friends to a feast. But when he reached the brick house, he found that the door was bolted and barred, so in his sly manner he began, 'Do let me in, dear Blacky. I have brought you a present of some eggs that I picked up in a farmyard on my way here.'

'No, no, Mister Fox,' replied Blacky, 'I am not going to open my door to you. I know your cunning ways. You have carried off poor Browny and Whitey, but you are not going to get me.'

At this the fox was so angry that he dashed with all his force against the wall, and tried to knock it down. But it was too strong and well-built; and though the fox scraped and tore at the bricks with his paws he only hurt himself, and at last he had to give it up, and limp away with his fore-paws all bleeding and sore.

'Never mind!' he cried angrily as he went off, 'I'll catch you another day, see if I don't, and won't I grind your bones to powder when I have got you in my den!' and he snarled fiercely and showed his teeth.

Next day Blacky had to go into the neighbouring town to do some marketing and to buy a big kettle. As he was walking home with it slung over his shoulder, he heard a sound of steps stealthily creeping after him.

For a moment his heart stood still with fear, and then a happy thought came to him. He had just reached the top of a hill, and could see his own little house nestling at the foot of it among the trees. In a moment he had snatched the lid off the kettle and had jumped in himself. Coiling himself round he lay quite snug in the bottom of the kettle, while with his fore-leg he managed to put the lid on, so that he was entirely hidden. With a little kick from the inside he started the kettle off, and down the hill it rolled full tilt; and when the fox came up, all that he saw was a large black kettle spinning over the ground at a great pace. Very much disappointed, he was just going to turn away, when he saw the kettle stop close to the little brick house, and in a moment later Blacky jumped out of it and escaped with the kettle into the house, when he barred and bolted the door, and put the shutter up over the window.

'Oho!' exclaimed the fox to himself, 'you think you will escape me that way, do you? We shall soon see about that, my friend,' and very quietly and stealthily he prowled round the house looking for some way to climb on to the roof.

In the meantime Blacky had filled the kettle with water, and having put it on the fire, sat down quietly waiting for it to boil. Just as the kettle was beginning to sing, and steam to come out of the spout, he heard a sound like a soft, muffled step, patter, patter, patter overhead, and the next moment the fox's head and fore-paws were seen coming down the chimney. But Blacky very wisely had not put the lid on the kettle, and, with a yelp of pain, the fox fell into the boiling water, and before he could escape, Blacky had popped the lid on, and the fox was scalded to death.

As soon as he was sure that their wicked enemy was really dead, and could do them no further harm, Blacky started off to rescue Browny and Whitey. As he approached the den he heard piteous grunts and squeals from his poor little brother and sister who lived in constant terror of the fox killing and eating them. But when they saw Blacky appear at the entrance to the den their joy knew no bounds. He quickly found a sharp stone and cut the cords by which they were tied to a stake in the ground, and then all three started off together for Blacky's house, where they lived happily ever after; and Browny quite gave up rolling in the mud, and Whitey ceased to be greedy, for they never forgot how nearly these faults had brought them to an untimely end.

HEART OF ICE

Once upon a time there lived a King and Queen who were foolish beyond all telling, but nevertheless they were vastly fond of one another. It is true that certain spiteful people were heard to say that this was only one proof the more of their exceeding foolishness, but of course you will understand that these were not their own courtiers, since, after all, they were a King and Queen, and up to this time all things had prospered with them. For in those days the one thing to be thought of in governing a kingdom was to keep well with all the Fairies and Enchanters, and on no account to stint them of the cakes, the ells of ribbon, and similar trifles which were their due, and, above all things, when there was a christening, to remember to invite every single one, good, bad, or indifferent, to the ceremony. Now, the foolish Queen had one little son who was just going to be christened, and for several months she had been hard at work preparing an enormous list of the names of those who were to be invited, but she quite forgot that it would take nearly as long to read it over as it had taken to write it out. So, when the moment of the christening arrived the King—to whom the task had been entrusted—had barely reached the end of the second page and his tongue was tripping with fatigue and haste as he repeated the usual formula: 'I conjure and pray you, Fairy so-and-so'—or 'Enchanter such-a-one'—'to honour me with a visit, and graciously bestow your gifts upon my son.'

To make matters worse, word was brought to him that the Fairies asked on the first page had already arrived and were waiting impatiently in the Great Hall, and grumbling that nobody was there to receive them. Thereupon he gave up the list in despair and hurried to greet those whom he had succeeded in asking, imploring their goodwill so humbly that most of them were touched, and promised that they would do his son no harm. But there happened to be among them a Fairy from a far country about whom they knew nothing, though her name had been written on the first page of the list. This Fairy was annoyed that after having taken the trouble to come so quickly, there had been no one to receive her, or help her to alight from the great ostrich on which she had travelled from her distant home, and now she began to mutter to herself in the most alarming way.

'Oh! prate away,' said she, 'your son will never be anything to boast of. Say what you will, he will be nothing but a Mannikin—'

No doubt she would have gone on longer in this strain, and given the unhappy little Prince half-a-dozen undesirable gifts, if it had not been for the good Fairy Genesta, who held the kingdom under her special protection, and who luckily hurried in just in time to prevent further mischief. When she had by compliments and entreaties pacified the unknown Fairy, and persuaded her to say no more, she gave the King a hint that now was the time to distribute the presents, after which ceremony they all took their departure, excepting the Fairy Genesta, who then went to see the Queen, and said to her:

'A nice mass you seem to have made of this business, madam. Why did you not condescend to consult me? But foolish people like you always think they can do without help or advice, and I observe that, in spite of all my goodness to you, you had not even the civility to invite me!'

'Ah! dear madam,' cried the King, throwing himself at her feet; 'did I ever have time to get as far as your name? See where I put in this mark when I abandoned the hopeless undertaking which I had but just begun!'

'There! there!' said the Fairy, 'I am not offended. I don't allow myself to be put out by trifles like that with people I really am fond of. But now about your son: I have saved him from a great many disagreeable things, but you must let me take him away and take care of him, and you will not see him again until he is all covered with fur!'

At these mysterious words the King and Queen burst into tears, for they lived in such a hot climate themselves that how or why the Prince should come to be covered with fur they could not imagine, and thought it must portend some great misfortune to him.

However, Genesta told them not to disquiet themselves.

'If I left him to you to bring up,' said she, 'you would be certain to make him as foolish as yourselves. I do not even intend to let him know that he is your son. As for you, you had better give your minds to governing your kingdom properly.' So saying, she opened the window, and catching up the little Prince, cradle and all, she glided away in the air as if she were skating upon ice, leaving the King and Queen in the greatest affliction. They consulted everyone who came near them as to what the Fairy could possibly have meant by saying that when they saw their son again he would be covered with fur. But nobody could offer any solution of the mystery, only they all seemed to agree that it must be something frightful, and the King and Queen made themselves more miserable than ever, and wandered about their palace in a way to make anyone pity them. Meantime the Fairy had carried off the little Prince to her own castle, and placed him under the care of a young peasant woman, whom she bewitched so as to make her think that this new baby was one of her own children. So the Prince grew up healthy and strong, leading the simple life of a young peasant, for the Fairy thought that he could have no better training; only as he grew older she kept him more and more with herself, that his mind might be cultivated and exercised as well as his body. But her care did not cease there: she resolved that he should be tried by hardships and disappointments and the knowledge of his fellowmen; for indeed she knew the Prince would need every advantage that she could give him, since, though he increased in years, he did not increase in height, but remained the tiniest of Princes. However, in spite of this he was exceedingly active and well formed, and altogether so handsome and agreeable that the smallness of his stature was of no real consequence. The Prince was perfectly aware that he was called by the ridiculous name of 'Mannikin,' but he consoled himself by vowing that, happen what might, he would make it illustrious.

In order to carry out her plans for his welfare the Fairy now began to send Prince Mannikin the most wonderful dreams of adventure by sea and land, and of these adventures he himself was always the hero. Sometimes he rescued a lovely Princess from some terrible danger, again he earned a kingdom by some brave deed, until at last he longed to go away and seek his fortune in a far country where his humble birth would not prevent his gaining honour and riches by his courage, and it was with a heart full of ambitious projects that he rode one day into a great city not far from the Fairy's castle. As he had set out intending to hunt in the surrounding forest he was quite simply dressed, and carried only a bow and arrows and a light spear; but even thus arrayed he looked graceful and distinguished. As he entered the city he saw that the inhabitants were all racing with one accord towards the market-place, and he also turned his horse in the same direction, curious to know what was going forward. When he reached the spot he found that certain foreigners of strange and outlandish appearance were about to make a proclamation to the assembled citizens, and he hastily pushed his way into the crowd until he was near enough to hear the words of the venerable old man who was their spokesman:

'Let the whole world know that he who can reach the summit of the Ice Mountain shall receive as his reward, not only the incomparable Sabella, fairest of the fair, but also all the realms of which she is Queen!' 'Here,' continued the old man after he had made this proclamation—'here is the list of all those Princes who, struck by the beauty of the Princess, have perished in the attempt to win her; and here is the list of these who have just entered upon the high emprise.'

Prince Mannikin was seized with a violent desire to inscribe his name among the others, but the remembrance of his dependent position and his lack of wealth held him back. But while he hesitated the old man, with many respectful ceremonies, unveiled a portrait of the lovely Sabella, which was carried by some of the attendants, and after one glance at it the Prince delayed no longer, but, rushing forward, demanded permission to add his name to the list. When they saw his tiny stature anti simple attire the strangers looked at each other doubtfully, not knowing whether to accept or refuse him. But the Prince said haughtily:

'Give me the paper that I may sign it,' and they obeyed. What between admiration for the Princess and annoyance at the hesitation shown by her ambassadors the Prince was too much agitated to choose any other name than the one by which he was always known. But when, after all the grand titles of the other Princes, he simply wrote 'Mannikin,' the ambassadors broke into shouts of laughter.

'Miserable wretches!' cried the Prince; 'but for the presence of that lovely portrait I would cut off your heads.'

But he suddenly remembered that, after all, it was a funny name, and that he had not yet had time to make it famous; so he was calm, and enquired the way to the Princess Sabella's country.

Though his heart did not fail him in the least, still he felt there were many difficulties before him, and he resolved to set out at once, without even taking leave of the Fairy, for fear she might try to stop him. Everybody in the town who knew him made great fun of the idea of Mannikin's undertaking such an expedition, and it even came to the ears of the foolish King and Queen, who laughed over it more than any of the others, without having an idea that the presumptuous Mannikin was their only son!

Meantime the Prince was travelling on, though the direction he had received for his journey were none of the clearest.

'Four hundred leagues north of Mount Caucasus you will receive your orders and instructions for the conquest of the Ice Mountain.'

Fine marching orders, those, for a man starting from a country near where Japan is nowadays!

However, he fared eastward, avoiding all towns, lest the people should laugh at his name, for, you see, he was not a very experienced traveller, and had not yet learned to enjoy a joke even if it were against himself. At night he slept in the woods, and at first he lived upon wild fruits; but the Fairy, who was keeping a benevolent eye upon him, thought that it would never do to let him be half-starved in that way, so she took to feeding him with all sorts of good things while he was asleep, and the Prince wondered very much that when he was awake he never felt hungry! True to her plan the Fairy sent him various adventures to prove his courage, and he came successfully through them all, only in his last fight with a furious monster rather like a tiger he had the ill luck to lose his horse. However, nothing daunted, he struggled on on foot, and at last reached a seaport. Here he found a boat sailing for the coast which he desired to reach, and, having just enough money to pay his passage, he went on board and they started. But after some days a fearful storm came on, which completely wrecked the little ship, and the Prince only saved his life by swimming a long, long way to the only land that was in sight, and which proved to be a desert island. Here he lived by fishing and hunting, always hoping that the good Fairy would presently rescue him. One day, as he was looking sadly out to sea, he became aware of a curious looking boat which was drifting slowly towards the shore, and which presently ran into a little creek and there stuck fast in the sand. Prince Mannikin rushed down eagerly to examine it, and saw with amazement that the masts and spars were all branched, and covered thickly with leaves until it looked like a little wood. Thinking from the stillness that there could be no one on board, the Prince pushed aside the branches and sprang over the side, and found himself surrounded by the crew, who lay motionless as dead men and in a most deplorable condition. They, too, had become almost like trees, and were growing to the deck, or to the masts, or to the sides of the vessel, or to whatever they had happened to be touching when the enchantment fell upon them. Mannikin was struck with pity for their miserable plight, and set to work with might and main to release them. With the sharp point of one of his arrows he gently detached their hands and feet from the wood which held them fast, and carried them on shore, one after another, where he rubbed their rigid limbs, and bathed them with infusions of various herbs with such success, that, after a few days, they recovered perfectly and were as fit to manage a boat as ever. You may be sure that the good Fairy Genesta had something to do with this marvellous cure, and she also put it into the Prince's head to rub the boat itself with the same magic herbs, which cleared it entirely, and not before it was time, for, at the rate at which it was growing before, it would very soon have become a forest! The gratitude of the sailors was extreme, and they willingly promised to land the Prince upon any coast he pleased; but, when he questioned them about the extraordinary thing that had happened to them and to their ship, they could in no way explain it, except that they said that, as they were passing along a thickly wooded coast, a sudden gust of wind had reached them from the land and enveloped them in a dense cloud of dust, after which everything in the boat that was not metal had sprouted and blossomed, as the Prince had seen, and that they themselves had grown gradually numb and heavy, and had finally lost all consciousness. Prince Mannikin was deeply interested in this curious story, and collected a quantity of the dust from the bottom of the boat, which he carefully preserved, thinking that its strange property might one day stand him in good stead.

Then they joyfully left the desert island, and after a long and prosperous voyage over calm seas they at length came in sight of land, and resolved to go on shore, not only to take in a fresh stock of water and provisions, but also to find out, if possible, where they were and in what direction to proceed.

As they neared the coast they wondered if this could be another uninhabited land, for no human beings could be distinguished, and yet that something was stirring became evident, for in the dust-clouds that moved near the ground small dark forms were dimly visible. These appeared to be assembling at the exact spot where they were preparing to run ashore, and what was their surprise to find they were nothing more nor less than large and beautiful spaniels, some mounted as sentries, others grouped in companies and regiments, all eagerly watching their disembarkation. When they found that Prince Mannikin, instead of saying, 'Shoot them,' as they had feared, said 'Hi, good dog!' in a thoroughly friendly and ingratiating way, they crowded round him with a great wagging of tails and giving of paws, and very soon made him understand that they wanted him to leave his men with the boat and follow them. The Prince was so curious to know more about them that he agreed willingly; so, after arranging with the sailors to wait for him fifteen days, and then, if he had not come back, to go on their way without him, he set out with his new friends. Their way lay inland, and Mannikin noticed with great surprise that the fields were well cultivated and that the carts and ploughs were drawn by horses or oxen, just as they might have been in any other country, and when they passed any village the cottages were trim and pretty, and an air of prosperity was everywhere. At one of the villages a dainty little repast was set before the Prince, and while he was eating, a chariot was brought, drawn by two splendid horses, which were driven with great skill by a large spaniel. In this carriage he continued his journey very comfortably, passing many similar equipages upon the road, and being always most courteously saluted by the spaniels who occupied them. At last they drove rapidly into a large town, which Prince Mannikin had no doubt was the capital of the kingdom. News of his approach had evidently been received, for all the inhabitants were at their doors and windows, and all the little spaniels had climbed upon the wall and gates to see him arrive. The Prince was delighted with the hearty welcome they gave him, and looked round him with the deepest interest. After passing through a few wide streets, well paved, and adorned with avenues of fine trees, they drove into the courtyard of a grand palace, which was full of spaniels who were evidently soldiers. 'The King's body-guard,' thought the Prince to himself as he returned their salutations, and then the carriage stopped, and he was shown into the presence of the King, who lay upon a rich Persian carpet surrounded by several little spaniels, who were occupied in chasing away the flies lest they should disturb his Majesty. He was the most beautiful of all spaniels, with a look of sadness in his large eyes, which, however, quite disappeared as he sprang up to welcome Prince Mannikin with every demonstration of delight; after which he made a sign to his courtiers, who came one by one to pay their respects to the visitor. The Prince thought that he would find himself puzzled as to how he should carry on a conversation, but as soon as he and the King were once more left alone, a Secretary of State was sent for, who wrote from his Majesty's dictation a most polite speech, in which he regretted much that they were unable to converse, except in writing, the language of dogs being difficult to understand. As for the writing, it had remained the same as the Prince's own.

Mannikin thereupon wrote a suitable reply, and then begged the King to satisfy his curiosity about all the strange things he had seen and heard since his landing. This appeared to awaken sad recollections in the King's mind, but he informed the Prince that he was called King Bayard, and that a Fairy, whose kingdom was next his own, had fallen violently in love with him, and had done all she could to persuade him to marry her; but that he could not do so as he himself was the devoted lover of the Queen of the Spice Islands. Finally, the Fairy, furious at the indifference with which her love was treated, had reduced him to the state in which the Prince found him, leaving him unchanged in mind, but deprived of the power of speech; and, not content with wreaking her vengeance upon the King alone, she had condemned all his subjects to a similar fate, saying:

'Bark, and run upon four feet, until the time comes when virtue shall be rewarded by love and fortune.'

Which, as the poor King remarked, was very much the same thing as if she had said, 'Remain a spaniel for ever and ever.'

Prince Mannikin was quite of the same opinion; nevertheless he said what we should all have said in the same circumstances:

'Your Majesty must have patience.'

He was indeed deeply sorry for poor King Bayard, and said all the consoling things he could think of, promising to aid him with all his might if there was anything to be done. In short they became firm friends, and the King proudly displayed to Mannikin the portrait of the Queen of the Spice Islands, and he quite agreed that it was worth while to go through anything for the sake of a creature so lovely. Prince Mannikin in his turn told his own history, and the great undertaking upon which he had set out, and King Bayard was able to give him some valuable instructions as to which would be the best way for him to proceed, and then they went together to the place where the boat had been left. The sailors were delighted to see the Prince again, though they had known that he was safe, and when they had taken on board all the supplies which the King had sent for them, they started once more. The King and Prince parted with much regret, and the former insisted that Mannikin should take with him one of his own pages, named Mousta, who was charged to attend to him everywhere, and serve him faithfully, which he promised to do.

The wind being favourable they were soon out of hearing of the general howl of regret from the whole army, which had been given by order of the King, as a great compliment, and it was not long before the land was entirely lost to view. They met with no further adventures worth speaking of, and presently found themselves within two leagues of the harbour for which they were making. The Prince, however, thought it would suit him better to land where he was, so as to avoid the town, since he had no money left and was very doubtful as to what he should do next. So the sailors set him and Mousta on shore, and then went back sorrowfully to their ship, while the Prince and his attendant walked off in what looked to them the most promising direction. They soon reached a lovely green meadow on the border of a wood, which seemed to them so pleasant after their long voyage that they sat down to rest in the shade and amused themselves by watching the gambols and antics of a pretty tiny monkey in the trees close by. The Prince presently became so fascinated by it that he sprang up and tried to catch it, but it eluded his grasp and kept just out of arm's reach, until it had made him promise to follow wherever it led him, and then it sprang upon his shoulder and whispered in his ear:

'We have no money, my poor Mannikin, and we are altogether badly off, and at a loss to know what to do next.'

'Yes, indeed,' answered the Prince ruefully, 'and I have nothing to give you, no sugar or biscuits, or anything that you like, my pretty one.'

'Since you are so thoughtful for me, and so patient about your own affairs,' said the little monkey, 'I will show you the way to the Golden Rock, only you must leave Mousta to wait for you here.'

Prince Mannikin agreed willingly, and then the little monkey sprang from his shoulder to the nearest tree, and began to run through the wood from branch to branch, crying, 'Follow me.'

This the Prince did not find quite so easy, but the little monkey waited for him and showed him the easiest places, until presently the wood grew thinner and they came out into a little clear grassy space at the foot of a mountain, in the midst of which stood a single rock, about ten feet high. When they were quite close to it the little monkey said:

'This stone looks pretty hard, but give it a blow with your spear and let us see what will happen.'

So the Prince took his spear and gave the rock a vigorous dig, which split off several pieces, and showed that, though the surface was thinly coated with stone, inside it was one solid mass of pure gold.

Thereupon the little monkey said, laughing at his astonishment:

'I make you a present of what you have broken off; take as much of it as you think proper.'

The Prince thanked her gratefully, and picked up one of the smallest of the lumps of gold; as he did so the little monkey was suddenly transformed into a tall and gracious lady, who said to him:

'If you are always as kind and persevering and easily contented as you are now you may hope to accomplish the most difficult tasks; go on your way and have no fear that you will be troubled any more for lack of gold, for that little piece which you modestly chose shall never grow less, use it as much as you will. But that you may see the danger you have escaped by your moderation, come with me.' So saying she led him back into the wood by a different path, and he saw that it was full of men and women; their faces were pale and haggard, and they ran hither and thither seeking madly upon the ground, or in the air, starting at every sound, pushing and trampling upon one another in their frantic eagerness to find the way to the Golden Rock.

'You see how they toil,' said the Fairy; 'but it is all of no avail: they will end by dying of despair, as hundreds have done before them.'

As soon as they had got back to the place where they had left Mousta the Fairy disappeared, and the Prince and his faithful Squire, who had greeted him with every demonstration of joy, took the nearest way to the city. Here they stayed several days, while the Prince provided himself with horses and attendants, and made many enquiries about the Princess Sabella, and the way to her kingdom, which was still so far away that he could hear but little, and that of the vaguest description, but when he presently reached Mount Caucasus it was quite a different matter. Here they seemed to talk of nothing but the Princess Sabella, and strangers from all parts of the world were travelling towards her father's Court.

The Prince heard plenty of assurances as to her beauty and her riches, but he also heard of the immense number of his rivals and their power. One brought an army at his back, another had vast treasures, a third was as handsome and accomplished as it was possible to be; while, as to poor Mannikin, he had nothing but his determination to succeed, his faithful spaniel, and his ridiculous name—which last was hardly likely to help him, but as he could not alter it he wisely determined not to think of it any more. After journeying for two whole months they came at last to Trelintin, the capital of the Princess Sabella's kingdom, and here he heard dismal stories about the Ice Mountain, and how none of those who had attempted to climb it had ever come back. He heard also the story of King Farda-Kinbras, Sabella's father. It appeared that he, being a rich and powerful monarch, had married a lovely Princess named Birbantine, and they were as happy as the day was long—so happy that as they were out sledging one day they were foolish enough to defy fate to spoil their happiness.

'We shall see about that,' grumbled an old hag who sat by the wayside blowing her fingers to keep them warm. The King thereupon was very angry, and wanted to punish the woman; but the Queen prevented him, saying:

'Alas! sire, do not let us make bad worse; no doubt this is a Fairy!'

'You are right there,' said the old woman, and immediately she stood up, and as they gazed at her in horror she grew gigantic and terrible, her staff turned to a fiery dragon with outstretched wings, her ragged cloak to a golden mantle, and her wooden shoes to two bundles of rockets. 'You are right there, and you will see what will come of your fine goings on, and remember the Fairy Gorgonzola!' So saying she mounted the dragon and flew off, the rockets shooting in all directions and leaving long trails of sparks.

In vain did Farda-Kinbras and Birbantine beg her to return, and endeavour by their humble apologies to pacify her; she never so much as looked at them, and was very soon out of sight, leaving them a prey to all kinds of dismal forebodings. Very soon after this the Queen had a little daughter, who was the most beautiful creature ever seen; all the Fairies of the North were invited to her christening, and warned against the malicious Gorgonzola. She also was invited, but she neither came to the banquet nor received her present; but as soon as all the others were seated at table, after bestowing their gifts upon the little Princess, she stole into the Palace, disguised as a black cat, and hid herself under the cradle until the nurses and the cradle-rockers had all turned their backs, and then she sprang out, and in an instant had stolen the little Princess's heart and made her escape, only being chased by a few dogs and scullions on her way across the courtyard. Once outside she mounted her chariot and flew straight away to the North Pole, where she shut up her stolen treasure on the summit of the Ice Mountain, and surrounded it with so many difficulties that she felt quite easy about its remaining there as long as the Princess lived, and then she went home, chuckling at her success. As to the other Fairies, they went home after the banquet without discovering that anything was amiss, and so the King and Queen were quite happy. Sabella grew prettier day by day. She learnt everything a Princess ought to know without the slightest trouble, and yet something always seemed lacking to make her perfectly charming. She had an exquisite voice, but whether her songs were grave or gay it did not matter, she did not seem to know what they meant; and everyone who heard her said:

'She certainly sings perfectly; but there is no tenderness, no heart in her voice.' Poor Sabella! how could there be when her heart was far away on the Ice Mountains? And it was just the same with all the other things that she did. As time went on, in spite of the admiration of the whole Court and the blind fondness of the King and Queen, it became more and more evident that something was fatally wrong: for those who love no one cannot long be loved; and at last the King called a general assembly, and invited the Fairies to attend, that they might, if possible, find out what was the matter. After explaining their grief as well as he could, he ended by begging them to see the Princess for themselves. 'It is certain,' said he, 'that something is wrong — what it is I don't know how to tell you, but in some way your work is imperfect.'

They all assured him that, so far as they knew, everything had been done for the Princess, and they had forgotten nothing that they could bestow on so good a neighbour as the King had been to them. After this they went to see Sabella; but they had no sooner entered her presence than they cried out with one accord:

'Oh! horror! — she has no heart!'

On hearing this frightful announcement, the King and Queen gave a cry of despair, and entreated the Fairies to find some remedy for such an unheard-of misfortune. Thereupon the eldest Fairy consulted her Book of Magic, which she always carried about with her, hung to her girdle by a thick silver chain, and there she found out at once that it was Gorgonzola who had stolen the Princess's heart, and also discovered what the wicked old Fairy had done with it.

'What shall we do? What shall we do?' cried the King and Queen in one breath.

'You must certainly suffer much annoyance from seeing and loving Sabella, who is nothing but a beautiful image,' replied the Fairy, 'and this must go on for a long time; but I think I see that, in the end, she will once more regain her heart. My advice is that you shall at once cause her portrait to be sent all over the world, and promise her hand and all her possessions to the Prince who is successful in reaching her heart. Her beauty alone is sufficient to engage all the Princes of the world in the quest.'

This was accordingly done, and Prince Mannikin heard that already five hundred Princes had perished in the snow and ice, not to mention their squires and pages, and that more continued to arrive daily, eager to try their fortune. After some consideration he determined to present himself at Court; but his arrival made no stir, as his retinue was as inconsiderable as his stature, and the splendour of his rivals was great enough to throw even Farda-Kinbras himself into the shade. However, he paid his respects to the King very gracefully, and asked permission to kiss the hand of the Princess in the usual manner; but when he said he was called 'Mannikin,' the King could hardly repress a smile, and the Princes who stood by openly shouted with laughter.

Turning to the King, Prince Mannikin said with great dignity:

'Pray laugh if it pleases your Majesty, I am glad that it is in my power to afford you any amusement; but I am not a plaything for these gentlemen, and I must beg them to dismiss any ideas of that kind from their minds at once,' and with that he turned upon the one who had laughed the loudest and proudly challenged him to a single combat. This Prince, who was called Fadasse, accepted the challenge very scornfully, mocking at Mannikin, whom he felt sure had no chance against himself; but the meeting was arranged for the next day. When Prince Mannikin quitted the King's presence he was conducted to the audience hall of the Princess Sabella. The sight of so much beauty and magnificence almost took his breath away for an instant, but, recovering himself with an effort, he said:

'Lovely Princess, irresistibly drawn by the beauty of your portrait, I come from the other end of the world to offer my services to you. My devotion knows no bounds, but my absurd name has already involved me in a quarrel with one of your courtiers. Tomorrow I am to fight this ugly, overgrown Prince, and I beg you to honour the combat with your presence, and prove to the world that there is nothing in a name, and that you deign to accept Mannikin as your knight.'

When it came to this the Princess could not help being amused, for, though she had no heart, she was not without humour. However, she answered graciously that she accepted with pleasure, which encouraged the Prince to entreat further that she would not show any favour to his adversary.

'Alas!' said she, 'I favour none of these foolish people, who weary me with their sentiment and their folly. I do very well as I am, and yet from one year's end to another they talk of nothing but delivering me from some imaginary affliction. Not a word do I understand of all their pratings about love, and who knows what dull things besides, which, I declare to you, I cannot even remember.'

Mannikin was quick enough to gather from this speech that to amuse and interest the Princess would be a far surer way of gaining her favour than to add himself to the list of those who continually teased her about that mysterious thing called 'love' which she was so incapable of comprehending. So he began to talk of his rivals, and found in each of them something to make merry over, in which diversion the Princess joined him heartily, and so well did he succeed in his attempt to amuse her that before very long she declared that of all the people at Court he was the one to whom she preferred to talk.

The following day, at the time appointed for the combat, when the King, the Queen, and the Princess had taken their places, and the whole Court and the whole town were assembled to see the show, Prince Fadasse rode into the lists magnificently armed and accoutred, followed by twenty-four squires and a hundred men-at-arms, each one leading, a splendid horse, while Prince Mannikin entered from the other side armed only with his spear and followed by the faithful Mousta. The contrast between the two champions was so great that there was a shout of laughter from the whole assembly; but when at the sounding of a trumpet the combatants rushed upon each other, and Mannikin, eluding the blow aimed at him, succeeded in thrusting Prince Fadasse from his horse and pinning him to the sand with his spear, it changed to a murmur of admiration.

So soon as he had him at his mercy, however, Mannikin, turning to the Princess, assured her that he had no desire to kill anyone who called himself her courtier, and then he bade the furious and humiliated Fadasse rise and thank the Princess to whom he owed his life. Then, amid the sounding of the trumpets and the shoutings of the people, he and Mousta retired gravely from the lists.

The King soon sent for him to congratulate him upon his success, and to offer him a lodging in the Palace, which he joyfully accepted. While the Princess expressed a wish to have Mousta brought to her, and, when the Prince sent for him, she was so delighted with his courtly manners and his marvellous intelligence that she entreated Mannikin to give him to her for her own. The Prince consented with alacrity, not only out of politeness, but because he foresaw that to have a faithful friend always near the Princess might some day be of great service to him. All these events made Prince Mannikin a person of much more consequence at the Court. Very soon after, there arrived upon the frontier the Ambassador of a very powerful King, who sent to Farda-Kinbras the following letter, at the same time demanding permission to enter the capital in state to receive the answer:

'I, Brandatimor, to Farda-Kinbras send greeting. If I had before this time seen the portrait of your beautiful daughter Sabella I should not have permitted all these adventurers and petty Princes to be dancing attendance and getting themselves frozen with the absurd idea of meriting her hand. For myself I am not afraid of any rivals, and, now I have declared my intention of marrying your daughter, no doubt they will at once withdraw their pretensions. My Ambassador has orders, therefore, to make arrangements for the Princess to come and be married to me without delay—for I attach no importance at all to the farrago of nonsense which you have caused to be published all over the world about this Ice Mountain. If the Princess really has no heart, be assured that I shall not concern myself about it, since, if anybody can help her to discover one, it is myself. My worthy father-in-law, farewell!'

The reading of this letter embarrassed and displeased Farda-Kinbras and Birbantine immensely, while the Princess was furious at the insolence of the demand. They all three resolved that its contents must be kept a profound secret until they could decide what reply should be sent, but Mousta contrived to send word of all that had passed to Prince Mannikin. He was naturally alarmed and indignant, and, after thinking it over a little, he begged an audience of the Princess, and led the conversation so cunningly up to the subject that was uppermost in her thoughts, as well as his own, that she presently told him all about the matter and asked his advice as to what it would be best to do. This was exactly what he had not been able to decide for himself; however, he replied that he should advise her to gain a little time by promising her answer after the grand entry of the Ambassador, and this was accordingly done.

The Ambassador did not at all like being put off after that fashion, but he was obliged to be content, and only said very arrogantly that so soon as his equipages arrived, as he expected they would do very shortly, he would give all the people of the city, and the stranger Princes with whom it was inundated, an idea of the power and the magnificence of his master. Mannikin, in despair, resolved that he would for once beg the assistance of the kind Fairy Genesta. He often thought of her and always with gratitude, but from the moment of his setting out he had determined to seek her aid only on the greatest occasions. That very night, when he had fallen asleep quite worn out with thinking over all the difficulties of the situation, he dreamed that the Fairy stood beside him, and said:

'Mannikin, you have done very well so far; continue to please me and you shall always find good friends when you need them most. As for this affair with the Ambassador, you can assure Sabella that she may look forward tranquilly to his triumphal entry, since it will all turn out well for her in the end.'

The Prince tried to throw himself at her feet to thank her, but woke to find it was all a dream; nevertheless he took fresh courage, and went next day to see the Princess, to whom he gave many mysterious assurances that all would yet be well. He even went so far as to ask her if she would not be very grateful to anyone who would rid her of the insolent Brandatimor. To which she replied that her gratitude would know no bounds. Then he wanted to know what would be her best wish for the person who was lucky enough to accomplish it. To which she said that she would wish them to be as insensible to the folly called 'love' as she was herself!

This was indeed a crushing speech to make to such a devoted lover as Prince Mannikin, but he concealed the pain it caused him with great courage.

And now the Ambassador sent to say that on the very next day he would come in state to receive his answer, and from the earliest dawn the inhabitants were astir, to secure the best places for the grand sight; but the good Fairy Genesta was providing them an amount of amusement they were far from expecting, for she so enchanted the eyes of all the spectators that when the Ambassador's gorgeous procession appeared, the splendid uniforms seemed to them miserable rags that a beggar would have been ashamed to wear, the prancing horses appeared as wretched skeletons hardly able to drag one leg after the other, while their trappings, which really sparkled with gold and jewels, looked like old sheepskins that would not have been good enough for a plough horse. The pages resembled the ugliest sweeps. The trumpets gave no more sound than whistles made of onion-stalks, or combs wrapped in paper; while the train of fifty carriages looked no better than fifty donkey carts. In the last of these sat the Ambassador with the haughty and scornful air which he considered becoming in the representative of so powerful a monarch: for this was the crowning point of the absurdity of the whole procession, that all who took part in it wore the expression of vanity and self-satisfaction and pride in their own appearance and all their surroundings which they believed their splendour amply justified.

The laughter and howls of derision from the whole crowd rose ever louder and louder as the extraordinary cortege advanced, and at last reached the ears of the King as he waited in the audience hall, and before the procession reached the palace he had been informed of its nature, and, supposing that it must be intended as an insult, he ordered the gates to be closed. You may imagine the fury of the Ambassador when, after all his pomp and pride, the King absolutely and unaccountably refused to receive him. He raved wildly both against King and people, and the cortege retired in great confusion, jeered at and pelted with stones and mud by the enraged crowd. It is needless to say that he left the country as fast as horses could carry him, but not before he had declared war, with the most terrible menaces, threatening to devastate the country with fire and sword.

Some days after this disastrous embassy King Bayard sent couriers to Prince Mannikin with a most friendly letter, offering his services in any difficulty, and enquiring with the deepest interest how he fared.

Mannikin at once replied, relating all that had happened since they parted, not forgetting to mention the event which had just involved Farda-Kinbras and Brandatimor in this deadly quarrel, and he ended by entreating his faithful friend to despatch a few thousands of his veteran spaniels to his assistance.

Neither the King, the Queen, nor the Princess could in the least understand the amazing conduct of Brandatimor's Ambassador; nevertheless the preparations for the war went forward briskly and all the Princes who had not gone on towards the Ice Mountain offered their services, at the same time demanding all the best appointments in the King's army. Mannikin was one of the first to volunteer, but he only asked to go as aide-de-camp to the Commander-in chief, who was a gallant soldier and celebrated for his victories. As soon as the army could be got together it was marched to the frontier, where it met the opposing force headed by Brandatimor himself, who was full of fury, determined to avenge the insult to his Ambassador and to possess himself of the Princess Sabella. All the army of Farda-Kinbras could do, being so heavily outnumbered, was to act upon the defensive, and before long Mannikin won the esteem of the officers for his ability, and of the soldiers for his courage, and care for their welfare, and in all the skirmishes which he conducted he had the good fortune to vanquish the enemy.

At last Brandatimor engaged the whole army in a terrific conflict, and though the troops of Farda-Kinbras fought with desperate courage, their general was killed, and they were defeated and forced to retreat with immense loss. Mannikin did wonders, and half-a-dozen times turned the retreating forces and beat back the enemy; and he afterwards collected t Prince Mannikin, of the hardships she fea[red], her anxiety for him, and all this with a hu[mour] put the finishing stroke to the Prince's de[light]. [Du]ring the congratulations of the King and Q[ueen on his] successful return, and there was even a gra[nd ball] herself. The Prince sent Mousta back to her [as a to]y, for was he not her lover's present?

[They] reached the capital, and were received with [joy. Far]da-Kinbras and Birbantine embraced Prince Mann[ikin, re]garded him as their heir and the future husband of [Sabella. He] replied that they did him too much honour. And t[hen, in] the presence of the Princess, who for the first tim[e] kissed her hand, and could not find a word to say. [He threw] himself on his knees beside her, held out the splen[did gift].

['The trea]sure is yours, since none of the dangers and difficulti[es I] have been sufficient to make me deserve it.'

[‘Nay,' sai]d she, 'if I take it, it is only that I may give it back to you [who give] to you already.'

[Just] in came the King and Queen, and interrupted them by [ques]tions imaginable, and not infrequently the same over and [over. It see]ms that there is always one thing that is sure to be said [by] everybody, and Prince Mannikin found that the question [a]sked by more than a thousand people on this particular [day was:]

['Did you find it very cold?'

[They] had come to request Prince Mannikin and the Princess to [come to] the Council Chamber, which they did, not knowing that he [me]nt the Prince to all the nobles assembled there as his son-in-[law and succe]ssor. But when Mannikin perceived his intention, he begged [to] speak first, and told his whole story, even to the fact that he [him]self to be a peasant's son. Scarcely had he finished speaking [when the sk]y grew black, the thunder growled, and the lightning flashed, [and in a bl]aze of light the good Fairy Genesta suddenly appeared. Turning [to M]annikin, she said:

['I am s]atisfied with you, since you have shown not only courage but [a good hea]rt.' Then she addressed King Farda-Kinbras, and informed him [of the true] history of the Prince, and how she had determined to give him [the educa]tion she knew would be best for a man who was to command

104 | The Green Fairy Book

---

troops enough to keep them in check until, the severe winter setting in, put an end to hostilities for a while.

He then returned to the Court, where consternation reigned. The King was in despair at the death of his trusty general, and ended by imploring Mannikin to take the command of the army, and his counsel was followed in all the affairs of the Court. He followed up his former plan of amusing the Princess, and on no account reminding her of that tedious thing called 'love,' so that she was always glad to see him, and the winter slipped by gaily for both of them.

The Prince was all the while secretly making plans for the next campaign; he received private intelligence of the arrival of a strong reinforcement of Spaniels, to whom he sent orders to post themselves along the frontier without attracting attention, and as soon as he possibly could he held a consultation with their Commander, who was an old and experienced warrior. Following his advice, he decided to have a pitched battle as soon as the enemy advanced, and this Brandatimor lost not a moment in doing, as he was perfectly persuaded that he was now going to make an end of the war and utterly vanquish Farda-Kinbras. But no sooner had he given the order to charge than the Spaniels, who had mingled with his troops unperceived, leaped each upon the horse nearest to him, and not only threw the whole squadron into confusion by the terror they caused, but, springing at the throats of the riders, unhorsed many of them by the suddenness of their attack; then turning the horses to the rear, they spread consternation everywhere, and made it easy for Prince Mannikin to gain a complete victory. He met Brandatimor in single combat, and succeeded in taking him prisoner; but he did not live to reach the Court, to which Mannikin had sent him: his pride killed him at the thought of appearing before Sabella under these altered circumstances. In the meantime Prince Fadasse and all the others who had remained behind were setting out with all speed for the conquest of the Ice Mountain, being afraid that Prince Mannikin might prove as successful in that as he seemed to be in everything else, and when Mannikin returned he heard of it with great annoyance. True he had been serving the Princess, but she only admired and praised him for his gallant deeds, and seemed no whit nearer bestowing on him the love he so ardently desired, and all the comfort Mousta could give him on the subject was that at least she loved no one else, and with that he had to content himself. But he determined that, come what might, he would delay no longer, but attempt the great undertaking for which he had come so far. When he went to take leave of the King and Queen they entreated him not to go, as they had just heard that Prince Fadasse, and all who accompanied him, had perished in the snow; but he persisted in his resolve. As for Sabella, she gave him

The Green Fairy Book | 101

her hand to kiss with precisely the same gracious indifference as she had given it to him the first time they met. It happened that this farewell took place before the whole Court, and so great a favourite had Prince Mannikin become that they were all indignant at the coldness with which the Princess treated him.

Finally the King said to him:

'Prince, you have constantly refilled all the gifts which, in my gratitude for your invaluable services, I have offered to you, but I wish the Princess to present you with her cloak of marten's fur, and that I hope you will not reject!' Now this was a splendid fur mantle which the Princess was very fond of wearing, not so much because she felt cold, as that its richness set off to perfection the delicate tints of her complexion and the brilliant gold of her hair. However, she took it off, and with graceful politeness begged Prince Mannikin to accept it, which you may be sure he was charmed to do, and, taking only this and a little bundle of all kinds of wood, and accompanied only by two spaniels out of the fifty who had stayed with him when the war was ended, he set forth, receiving many tokens of love and favour from the people in every town he passed through. At the last little village he left his horse behind him, to begin his toilful march through the snow, which extended, blank and terrible, in every direction as far as the eye could see. Here he had appointed to meet the other forty-eight spaniels, who received him joyfully, and assured him that, happen what might, they would follow and serve him faithfully. And so they started, full of heart and hope. At first there was a slight track, difficult, but not impossible to follow; but this was soon lost, and the Pole Star was their only guide. When the time came to call a halt, the Prince, who had after much consideration decided on his plan of action, caused a few twigs from the faggot he had brought with him to be planted in the snow, and then he sprinkled over them a pinch of the magic powder he had collected from the enchanted boat. To his great joy they instantly began to sprout and grow, and in a marvellously short time the camp was surrounded by a perfect grove of trees of all sorts, which blossomed and bore ripe fruit, so that all their wants were easily supplied, and they were able to make huge fires to warm themselves. The Prince then sent out several spaniels to reconnoitre, and they had the good luck to discover a horse laden with provisions stuck fast in the snow. They at once fetched their comrades, and brought the spoil triumphantly into the camp, and, as it consisted principally of biscuits, not a spaniel among them went supperless to sleep. In this way they journeyed by day and encamped safely at night, always remembering to take on a few branches to provide them with food and shelter. They passed by the way armies of those who had set out upon the perilous enterprise, who stood frozen stiffly, without sense others. 'You have already found the advantage of having a faithful friend,' she added to the Prince 'and now you will have the pleasure of seeing King Bayard and his subjects regain their natural forms as a reward for his kindness to you.'

Just then arrived a chariot drawn by eagles, which proved to contain the foolish King and Queen, who embraced their long-lost son with great joy, and were greatly struck with the fact that they did indeed find him covered with fur! While they were caressing Sabella and wringing her hands (which is a favourite form of endearment with foolish people) chariots were seen approaching from all points of the compass, containing numbers of Fairies.

'Sire,' said Genesta to Farda-Kinbras, 'I have taken the liberty of appointing your Court as a meeting-place for all the Fairies who could spare the time to come; and I hope you can arrange to hold the great ball, which we have once in a hundred years, on this occasion.'

The King having suitably acknowledged the honour done him, was next reconciled to Gorgonzola, and they two presently opened the ball together. The Fairy Marsontine restored their natural forms to King Bayard and all his subjects, and he appeared once more as handsome a king as you could wish to see. One of the Fairies immediately despatched her chariot for the Queen of the Spice Islands, and their wedding took place at the same time as that of Prince Mannikin and the lovely and gracious Sabella. They lived happily ever afterwards, and their vast kingdoms were presently divided between their children.

The Prince, out of grateful remembrance of the Princess Sabella's first gift to him bestowed the right of bearing her name upon the most beautiful of the martens, and that is why they are called sables to this day.

Comte de Caylus.

THE ENCHANTED RING

Once upon a time there lived a young man named Rosimond, who was as good and handsome as his elder brother Bramintho was ugly and wicked. Their mother detested her eldest son, and had only eyes for the youngest. This excited Bramintho's jealousy, and he invented a horrible story in order to ruin his brother. He told his father that Rosimond was in the habit of visiting a neighbour who was an enemy of the family, and betraying to him all that went on in the house, and was plotting with him to poison their father.

The father flew into a rage, and flogged his son till the blood came. Then he threw him into prison and kept him for three days without food, and after that he turned him out of the house, and threatened to kill him if he ever came back. The mother was miserable, and did nothing but weep, but she dared not say anything.

The youth left his home with tears in his eyes, not knowing where to go, and wandered about for many hours till he came to a thick wood. Night overtook him at the foot of a great rock, and he fell asleep on a bank of moss, lulled by the music of a little brook.

It was dawn when he woke, and he saw before him a beautiful woman seated on a grey horse, with trappings of gold, who looked as if she were preparing for the hunt.

'Have you seen a stag and some deerhounds go by?' she asked.

'No, madam,' he replied.

Then she added, 'You look unhappy; is there anything the matter? Take this ring, which will make you the happiest and most powerful of men, provided you never make a bad use of it. If you turn the diamond inside, you will become invisible. If you turn it outside, you will become visible again. If you place it on your little finger, you will take the shape of the King's son, followed by a splendid court. If you put it on your fourth finger, you will take your own shape.'

Then the young man understood that it was a Fairy who was speaking to him, and when she had finished she plunged into the woods. The youth was very impatient to try the ring, and returned home immediately. He found that the Fairy had spoken the truth, and that he could see and hear everything, while he himself was unseen. It lay with him to revenge himself, if he chose, on his brother, without the slightest danger to himself, and he told no one but his mother of all the strange things that had befallen him. He afterwards put the enchanted ring on his little finger, and appeared as the King's son, followed by a hundred fine horses, and a guard of officers all richly dressed.

His father was much surprised to see the King's son in his quiet little house, and he felt rather embarrassed, not knowing what was the proper way to behave on such a grand occasion. Then Rosimond asked him how many sons he had.

'Two,' replied he.

'I wish to see them,' said Rosimond. 'Send for them at once. I desire to take them both to Court, in order to make their fortunes.'

The father hesitated, then answered: 'Here is the eldest, whom I have the honour to present to your Highness.'

'But where is the youngest? I wish to see him too,' persisted Rosimond.

'He is not here,' said the father. 'I had to punish him for a fault, and he has run away.'

Then Rosimond replied, 'You should have shown him what was right, but not have punished him. However, let the elder come with me, and as for you, follow these two guards, who will escort you to a place that I will point out to them.'

Then the two guards led off the father, and the Fairy of whom you have heard found him in the forest, and beat him with a golden birch rod, and cast him into a cave that was very deep and dark, where he lay enchanted. 'Lie there,' she said, 'till your son comes to take you out again.'

Meanwhile the son went to the King's palace, and arrived just when the real prince was absent. He had sailed away to make war on a distant island, but the winds had been contrary, and he had been shipwrecked on unknown shores, and taken captive by a savage people. Rosimond made his appearance at Court in the character of the Prince, whom everyone wept for as lost, and told them that he had been rescued when at the point of death by some merchants. His return was the signal for great public rejoicings, and the King was so overcome that he became quite speechless, and did nothing but embrace his son. The Queen was even more delighted, and fetes were ordered over the whole kingdom.

One day the false Prince said to his real brother, 'Bramintho, you know that I brought you here from your native village in order to make your fortune; but I have found out that you are a liar, and that by your deceit you have been the cause of all the troubles of your brother Rosimond. He is in hiding here, and I desire that you shall speak to him, and listen to his reproaches.'

Bramintho trembled at these words, and, flinging himself at the Prince's feet, confessed his crime.

'That is not enough,' said Rosimond. 'It is to your brother that you must confess, and I desire that you shall ask his forgiveness. He will be very generous if he grants it, and it will be more than you deserve. He is in my ante-room, where you shall see him at once. I myself will retire into another apartment, so as to leave you alone with him.'

Bramintho entered, as he was told, into the anteroom. Then Rosimond changed the ring, and passed into the room by another door.

Bramintho was filled with shame as soon as he saw his brother's face. He implored his pardon, and promised to atone for all his faults. Rosimond embraced him with tears, and at once forgave him, adding, 'I am in great favour with the King. It rests with me to have your head cut off, or to condemn you to pass the remainder of your life in prison; but I desire to be as good to you as you have been wicked to me.' Bramintho, confused and ashamed, listened to his words without daring to lift his eyes or to remind Rosimond that he was his brother. After this, Rosimond gave out that he was going to make a secret voyage, to marry a Princess who lived in a neighbouring kingdom; but in reality he only went to see his mother, whom he told all that had happened at the Court, giving her at the same time some money that she needed, for the King allowed him to take exactly what he liked, though he was always careful not to abuse this permission. Just then a furious war broke out between the King his master and the Sovereign of the adjoining country, who was a bad man and one that never kept his word. Rosimond went straight to the palace of the wicked King, and by means of his ring was able to be present at all the councils, and learnt all their schemes, so that he was able to forestall them and bring them to naught. He took the command of the army which was brought against the wicked King, and defeated him in a glorious battle, so that peace was at once concluded on conditions that were just to everyone.

Henceforth the King's one idea was to marry the young man to a Princess who was the heiress to a neighbouring kingdom, and, besides that, was as lovely as the day. But one morning, while Rosimond was hunting in the forest where for the first time he had seen the Fairy, his benefactress suddenly appeared before him. 'Take heed,' she said to him in severe tones, 'that you do not marry anybody who believes you to be a Prince. You must never deceive anyone. The real Prince, whom the whole nation thinks you are, will have to succeed his father, for that is just and right. Go and seek him in some distant island, and I will send winds that will swell your sails and bring you to him. Hasten to render this service to your master, although it is against your own ambition, and prepare, like an honest man, to return to your natural state. If you do not do this, you will become wicked and unhappy, and I will abandon you to all your former troubles.'

Rosimond took these wise counsels to heart. He gave out that he had undertaken a secret mission to a neighbouring state, and embarked on board a vessel, the winds carrying him straight to the island where the Fairy had told him he would find the real Prince. This unfortunate youth had been taken captive by a savage people, who had kept him to guard their sheep. Rosimond, becoming invisible, went to seek him amongst the pastures, where he kept his flock, and, covering him with his mantle, he delivered him out of the hands of his cruel masters, and bore him back to the ship. Other winds sent by the Fairy swelled the sails, and together the two young men entered the King's presence.

Rosimond spoke first and said, 'You have believed me to be your son. I am not he, but I have brought him back to you.' The King, filled with astonishment, turned to his real son and asked, 'Was it not you, my son, who conquered my enemies and won such a glorious peace? Or is it true that you have been shipwrecked and taken captive, and that Rosimond has set you free?'

'Yes, my father,' replied the Prince. 'It is he who sought me out in my captivity and set me free, and to him I owe the happiness of seeing you once more. It was he, not I, who gained the victory.'

The King could hardly believe his ears; but Rosimond, turning the ring, appeared before him in the likeness of the Prince, and the King gazed distractedly at the two youths who seemed both to be his son. Then he offered Rosimond immense rewards for his services, which were refused, and the only favour the young man would accept was that one of his posts at Court should be conferred on his brother Bramintho. For he feared for himself the changes of fortune, the envy of mankind and his own weakness. His desire was to go back to his mother and his native village, and to spend his time in cultivating the land.

One day, when he was wandering through the woods, he met the Fairy, who showed him the cavern where his father was imprisoned, and told him what words he must use in order to set him free. He repeated them joyfully, for he had always longed to bring the old man back and to make his last days happy. Rosimond thus became the benefactor of all his family, and had the pleasure of doing good to those who had wished to do him evil. As for the Court, to whom he had rendered such services, all he asked was the freedom to live far from its corruption; and, to crown all, fearing that if he kept the ring he might be tempted to use it in order to regain his lost place in the world, he made up his mind to restore it to the Fairy. For many days he sought her up and down the woods and at last he found her. 'I want to give you back,' he said, holding out the ring, 'a gift as dangerous as it is powerful, and which I fear to use wrongfully. I shall never feel safe till I have made it impossible for me to leave my solitude and to satisfy my passions.'

While Rosimond was seeking to give back the ring to the Fairy, Bramintho, who had failed to learn any lessons from experience, gave way to all his desires, and tried to persuade the Prince, lately become King, to ill-treat Rosimond. But the Fairy, who knew all about everything, said to Rosimond, when he was imploring her to accept the ring:

'Your wicked brother is doing his best to poison the mind of the King towards you, and to ruin you. He deserves to be punished, and he must die; and in order that he may destroy himself, I shall give the ring to him.'

Rosimond wept at these words, and then asked:

'What do you mean by giving him the ring as a punishment? He will only use it to persecute everyone, and to become master.'

'The same things,' answered the Fairy, 'are often a healing medicine to one person and a deadly poison to another. Prosperity is the source of all evil to a naturally wicked man. If you wish to punish a scoundrel, the first thing to do is to give him power. You will see that with this rope he will soon hang himself.'

Having said this, she disappeared, and went straight to the Palace, where she showed herself to Bramintho under the disguise of an old woman covered with rags. She at once addressed him in these words:

'I have taken this ring from the hands of your brother, to whom I had lent it, and by its help he covered himself with glory. I now give it to you, and be careful what you do with it.'

Bramintho replied with a laugh:

'I shall certainly not imitate my brother, who was foolish enough to bring back the Prince instead of reigning in his place,' and he was as good as his word. The only use he made of the ring was to find out family secrets and betray them, to commit murders and every sort of wickedness, and to gain wealth for himself unlawfully. All these crimes, which could be traced to nobody, filled the people with astonishment. The King, seeing so many affairs, public and private, exposed, was at first as puzzled as anyone, till Bramintho's wonderful prosperity and amazing insolence made him suspect that the enchanted ring had become his property. In order to find out the truth he bribed a stranger just arrived at Court, one of a nation with whom the King was always at war, and arranged that he was to steal in the night to Bramintho and to offer him untold honours and rewards if he would betray the State secrets.

Bramintho promised everything, and accepted at once the first payment of his crime, boasting that he had a ring which rendered him invisible, and that by means of it he could penetrate into the most private places. But his triumph was short. Next day he was seized by order of the King, and his ring was taken from him. He was searched, and on him were found papers which proved his crimes; and, though Rosimond himself came back to the Court to entreat his pardon, it was refused. So Bramintho was put to death, and the ring had been even more fatal to him than it had been useful in the hands of his brother.

To console Rosimond for the fate of Bramintho, the King gave him back the enchanted ring, as a pearl without price. The unhappy Rosimond did not look upon it in the same light, and the first thing he did on his return home was to seek the Fairy in the woods.

'Here,' he said, 'is your ring. My brother's experience has made me understand many things that I did not know before. Keep it, it has only led to his destruction. Ah! without it he would be alive now, and my father and mother would not in their old age be bowed to the earth with shame and grief! Perhaps he might have been wise and happy if he had never had the chance of gratifying his wishes! Oh! how dangerous it is to have more power than the rest of the world! Take back your ring, and as ill fortune seems to follow all on whom you bestow it, I will implore you, as a favour to myself, that you will never give it to anyone who is dear to me.'

Fenelon.

THE SNUFF-BOX

As often happens in this world, there was once a young man who spent all his time in travelling. One day, as he was walking along, he picked up a snuff-box. He opened it, and the snuff-box said to him in the Spanish language, 'What do you want?' He was very much frightened, but, luckily, instead of throwing the box away, he only shut it tight, and put it in his pocket. Then he went on, away, away, away, and as he went he said to himself, 'If it says to me again "What do you want?" I shall know better what to say this time.' So he took out the snuff-box and opened it, and again it asked 'What do you want?' 'My hat full of gold,' answered the youth, and immediately it was full.

Our young man was enchanted. Henceforth he should never be in need of anything. So on he travelled, away, away, away, through thick forests, till at last he came to a beautiful castle. In the castle there lived a King. The young man walked round and round the castle, not caring who saw him, till the King noticed him, and asked what he was doing there. 'I was just looking at your castle.' 'You would like to have one like it, wouldn't you?' The young man did not reply, but when it grew dark he took his snuff-box and opened the lid. 'What do you want?' 'Build me a castle with laths of gold and tiles of diamond, and the furniture all of silver and gold.' He had scarcely finished speaking when there stood in front of him, exactly opposite the King's palace, a castle built precisely as he had ordered. When the King awoke he was struck dumb at the sight of the magnificent house shining in the rays of the sun. The servants could not do their work for stopping to stare at it. Then the King dressed himself, and went to see the young man. And he told him plainly that he was a very powerful Prince; and that he hoped that they might all live together in one house or the other, and that the King would give him his daughter to wife. So it all turned out just as the King wished. The young man married the Princess, and they lived happily in the palace of gold.

But the King's wife was jealous both of the young man and of her own daughter. The Princess had told her mother about the snuff-box, which gave them everything they wanted, and the Queen bribed a servant to steal the snuff-box. They noticed carefully where it was put away every night, and one evening, when the whole world was asleep, the woman stole it and brought it to her old mistress. Oh how happy the Queen was! She opened the lid, and the snuff-box said to her 'What do you want?' And she answered at once 'I want you to take me and my husband and my servants and this beautiful house and set us down on the other side of the Red Sea, but my daughter and her husband are to stay behind.'

When the young couple woke up, they found themselves back in the old castle, without their snuff-box. They hunted for it high and low, but quite vainly. The young man felt that no time was to be lost, and he mounted his horse and filled his pockets with as much gold as he could carry. On he went, away, away, away, but he sought the snuff-box in vain all up and down the neighbouring countries, and very soon he came to the end of all his money. But still he went on, as fast as the strength of his horse would let him, begging his way.

Someone told him that he ought to consult the moon, for the moon travelled far, and might be able to tell him something. So he went away, away, away, and ended, somehow or other, by reaching the land of the moon. There he found a little old woman who said to him 'What are you doing here? My son eats all living things he sees, and if you are wise, you will go away without coming any further.' But the young man told her all his sad tale, and how he possessed a wonderful snuff-box, and how it had been stolen from him, and how he had nothing left, now that he was parted from his wife and was in need of everything. And he said that perhaps her son, who travelled so far, might have seen a palace with laths of gold and tiles of diamond, and furnished all in silver and gold. As he spoke these last words, the moon came in and said he smelt mortal flesh and blood. But his mother told him that it was an unhappy man who had lost everything, and had come all this way to consult him, and bade the young man not to be afraid, but to come forward and show himself. So he went boldly up to the moon, and asked if by any accident he had seen a palace with the laths of gold and the tiles of diamond, and all the furniture of silver and gold. Once this house belonged to him, but now it was stolen. And the moon said no, but that the sun travelled farther than he did, and that the young man had better go and ask him.

So the young man departed, and went away, away, away, as well as his horse would take him, begging his living as he rode along, and, somehow or other, at last he got to the land of the sun. There he found a little old woman, who asked him, 'What are you doing here? Go away. Have you not heard that my son feeds upon Christians?' But he said no, and that he would not go, for he was so miserable that it was all one to him whether he died or not; that he had lost everything, and especially a splendid palace like none other in the whole world, for it had laths of gold and tiles of diamond, and all the furniture was of silver and gold. And that he had sought it far and long, and in all the earth there was no man more unhappy. So the old woman's heart melted, and she agreed to hide him.

When the Sun arrived, he declared that he smelt Christian flesh, and he meant to have it for his dinner. But his mother told him such a pitiful story of the miserable wretch who had lost everything, and had come from far to ask his help, that at last he promised to see him.

So the young man came out from his hiding-place and begged the sun to tell him if in the course of his travels he had not seen somewhere a palace that had not its like in the whole world, for its laths were of gold and its tiles of diamond, and all the furniture in silver and gold.

And the sun said no, but that perhaps the wind had seen it, for he entered everywhere, and saw things that no one else ever saw, and if anyone knew where it was, it was certainly the wind.

Then the poor young man again set forth as well as his horse could take him, begging his living as he went, and, somehow or other, he ended by reaching the home of the wind. He found there a little old woman busily occupied in filling great barrels with water. She asked him what had put it into his head to come there, for her son ate everything he saw, and that he would shortly arrive quite mad, and that the young man had better look out. But he answered that he was so unhappy that he had ceased to mind anything, even being eaten, and then he told her that he had been robbed of a palace that had not its equal in all the world, and of all that was in it, and that he had even left his wife, and was wandering over the world until he found it. And that it was the sun who had sent him to consult the wind. So she hid him under the staircase, and soon they heard the south wind arrive, shaking the house to its foundations. Thirsty as he was, he did not wait to drink, but he told his mother that he smelt the blood of a Christian man, and that she had better bring him out at once and make him ready to be eaten. But she bade her son eat and drink what was before him, and said that the poor young man was much to be pitied, and that the sun had granted him his life in order that he might consult the wind. Then she brought out the young man, who explained how he was seeking for his palace, and that no man had been able to tell him where it was, so he had come to the wind. And he added that he had been shamefully robbed, and that the laths were of gold and the tiles of diamond, and all the furniture in silver and gold, and he inquired if the wind had not seen such a palace during his wanderings.

And the wind said yes, and that all that day he had been blowing backwards and forwards over it without being able to move one single tile. 'Oh, do tell me where it is,' cried the you man. 'It is a long way off,' replied the wind, 'on the other side of the Red Sea.' But our traveller was not discouraged, he had already journeyed too far.

So he set forth at once, and, somehow or other, he managed to reach that distant land. And he enquired if anyone wanted a gardener. He was told that the head gardener at the castle had just left, and perhaps he might have a chance of getting the place. The young man lost no time, but walked up to the castle and asked if they were in want of a gardener; and how happy he was when they agreed to take him! Now he passed most of his day in gossiping with the servants about the wealth of their masters and the wonderful things in the house. He made friends with one of the maids, who told him the history of the snuff-box, and he coaxed her to let him see it. One evening she managed to get hold of it, and the young man watched carefully where she hid it away, in a secret place in the bedchamber of her mistress.

The following night, when everyone was fast asleep, he crept in and took the snuff-box. Think of his joy as he opened the lid! When it asked him, as of yore, 'What do you want?' he replied: 'What do I want? What do I want? Why, I want to go with my palace to the old place, and for the King and the Queen and all their servants to be drowned in the Red Sea.' He hardly finished speaking when he found himself back again with his wife, while all the other inhabitants of the palace were lying at the bottom of the Red Sea.

Sebillot.

THE GOLDEN BLACKBIRD

Once upon a time there was a great lord who had three sons. He fell very ill, sent for doctors of every kind, even bonesetters, but they, none of them, could find out what was the matter with him, or even give him any relief. At last there came a foreign doctor, who declared that the Golden Blackbird alone could cure the sick man.

So the old lord despatched his eldest son to look for the wonderful bird, and promised him great riches if he managed to find it and bring it back.

The young man began his journey, and soon arrived at a place where four roads met. He did not know which to choose, and tossed his cap in the air, determining that the direction of its fall should decide him. After travelling for two or three days, he grew tired of walking without knowing where or for how long, and he stopped at an inn which was filled with merrymakers and ordered something to eat and drink.

'My faith,' said he, 'it is sheer folly to waste more time hunting for this bird. My father is old, and if he dies I shall inherit his goods.'

The old man, after waiting patiently for some time, sent his second son to seek the Golden Blackbird. The youth took the same direction as his brother, and when he came to the cross roads, he too tossed up which road he should take. The cap fell in the same place as before, and he walked on till he came to the spot where his brother had halted. The latter, who was leaning out of the window of the inn, called to him to stay where he was and amuse himself.

'You are right,' replied the youth. 'Who knows if I should ever find the Golden Blackbird, even if I sought the whole world through for it. At the worst, if the old man dies, we shall have his property.'

He entered the inn and the two brothers made merry and feasted, till very soon their money was all spent. They even owed something to their landlord, who kept them as hostages till they could pay their debts.

The youngest son set forth in his turn, and he arrived at the place where his brothers were still prisoners. They called to him to stop, and did all they could to prevent his going further.

'No,' he replied, 'my father trusted me, and I will go all over the world till I find the Golden Blackbird.'

'Bah,' said his brothers, 'you will never succeed any better than we did. Let him die if he wants to; we will divide the property.'

As he went his way he met a little hare, who stopped to look at him, and asked:

'Where are you going, my friend?'

'I really don't quite know,' answered he. 'My father is ill, and he cannot be cured unless I bring him back the Golden Blackbird. It is a long time since I set out, but no one can tell me where to find it.'

'Ah,' said the hare, 'you have a long way to go yet. You will have to walk at least seven hundred miles before you get to it.'

'And how am I to travel such a distance?'

'Mount on my back,' said the little hare, 'and I will conduct you.'

The young man obeyed: at each bound the little hare went seven miles, and it was not long before they reached a castle that was as large and beautiful as a castle could be.

'The Golden Blackbird is in a little cabin near by,' said the little hare, 'and you will easily find it. It lives in a little cage, with another cage beside it made all of gold. But whatever you do, be sure not to put it in the beautiful cage, or everybody in the castle will know that you have stolen it.'

The youth found the Golden Blackbird standing on a wooden perch, but as stiff and rigid as if he was dead. And beside the beautiful cage was the cage of gold.

'Perhaps he would revive if I were to put him in that lovely cage,' thought the youth.

The moment that Golden Bird had touched the bars of the splendid cage he awoke, and began to whistle, so that all the servants of the castle ran to see what was the matter, saying that he was a thief and must be put in prison.

'No,' he answered, 'I am not a thief. If I have taken the Golden Blackbird, it is only that it may cure my father, who is ill, and I have travelled more than seven hundred miles in order to find it.'

'Well,' they replied, 'we will let you go, and will even give you the Golden Bird, if you are able to bring us the Porcelain Maiden.'

The youth departed, weeping, and met the little hare, who was munching wild thyme.

'What are you crying for, my friend?' asked the hare.

'It is because,' he answered, 'the castle people will not allow me to carry off the Golden Blackbird without giving them the Porcelain Maiden in exchange.'

'You have not followed my advice,' said the little hare. 'And you have put the Golden Bird into the fine cage.'

'Alas! yes!'

'Don't despair! the Porcelain Maiden is a young girl, beautiful as Venus, who dwells two hundred miles from here. Jump on my back and I will take you there.'

The little hare, who took seven miles in a stride, was there in no time at all, and he stopped on the borders of a lake.

'The Porcelain Maiden,' said the hare to the youth, 'will come here to bathe with her friends, while I just eat a mouthful of thyme to refresh me. When she is in the lake, be sure you hide her clothes, which are of dazzling whiteness, and do not give them back to her unless she consents to follow you.'

The little hare left him, and almost immediately the Porcelain Maiden arrived with her friends. She undressed herself and got into the water. Then the young man glided up noiselessly and laid hold of her clothes, which he hid under a rock at some distance.

When the Porcelain Maiden was tired of playing in the water she came out to dress herself, but, though she hunted for her clothes high and low, she could find them nowhere. Her friends helped her in the search, but, seeing at last that it was of no use, they left her, alone on the bank, weeping bitterly.

'Why do you cry?' said the young man, approaching her.

'Alas!' answered she, 'while I was bathing someone stole my clothes, and my friends have abandoned me.'

'I will find your clothes if you will only come with me.'

And the Porcelain Maiden agreed to follow him, and after having given up her clothes, the young man bought a small horse for her, which went like the wind. The little hare brought them both back to seek for the Golden Blackbird, and when they drew near to the castle where it lived the little hero said to the young man:

'Now, do be a little sharper than you were before, and you will manage to carry off both the Golden Blackbird and the Porcelain Maiden. Take the golden cage in one hand, and leave the bird in the old cage where he is, and bring that away too.'

The little hare then vanished; the youth did as he was bid, and the castle servants never noticed that he was carrying off the Golden Bird. When he reached the inn where his brothers were detained, he delivered them by paying their debt. They set out all together, but as the two elder brothers were jealous of the success of the youngest, they took the opportunity as they were passing by the shores of a lake to throw themselves upon him, seize the Golden Bird, and fling him in the water. Then they continued their journey, taking with them the Porcelain Maiden, in the firm belief that their brother was drowned. But, happily, he had snatched in falling at a tuft of rushes and called loudly for help. The little hare came running to him, and said 'Take hold of my leg and pull yourself out of the water.'

When he was safe on shore the little hare said to him:

'Now this is what you have to do: dress yourself like a Breton seeking a place as stable-boy, and go and offer your services to your father. Once there, you will easily be able to make him understand the truth.'

The young man did as the little hare bade him, and he went to his father's castle and enquired if they were not in want of a stable-boy.

'Yes,' replied his father, 'very much indeed. But it is not an easy place. There is a little horse in the stable which will not let anyone go near it, and it has already kicked to death several people who have tried to groom it.'

'I will undertake to groom it,' said the youth. 'I never saw the horse I was afraid of yet.' The little horse allowed itself to be rubbed down without a toss of its head and without a kick.

'Good gracious!' exclaimed the master; 'how is it that he lets you touch him, when no one else can go near him?'

'Perhaps he knows me,' answered the stable-boy.

Two or three days later the master said to him: 'The Porcelain Maiden is here: but, though she is as lovely as the dawn, she is so wicked that she scratches everyone that approaches her. Try if she will accept your services.'

When the youth entered the room where she was, the Golden Blackbird broke forth into a joyful song, and the Porcelain Maiden sang too, and jumped for joy.

'Good gracious!' cried the master. 'The Porcelain Maiden and the Golden Blackbird know you too?'

'Yes,' replied the youth, 'and the Porcelain Maiden can tell you the whole truth, if she only will.'

Then she told all that had happened, and how she had consented to follow the young man who had captured the Golden Blackbird.

'Yes,' added the youth, 'I delivered my brothers, who were kept prisoners in an inn, and, as a reward, they threw me into a lake. So I disguised myself and came here, in order to prove the truth to you.'

So the old lord embraced his son, and promised that he should inherit all his possessions, and he put to death the two elder ones, who had deceived him and had tried to slay their own brother.

The young man married the Porcelain Maiden, and had a splendid wedding-feast.

Sebillot.

THE LITTLE SOLDIER

I

Once upon a time there was a little soldier who had just come back from the war. He was a brave little fellow, but he had lost neither arms nor legs in battle. Still, the fighting was ended and the army disbanded, so he had to return to the village where he was born.

Now the soldier's name was really John, but for some reason or other his friends always called him the Kinglet; why, no one ever knew, but so it was.

As he had no father or mother to welcome him home, he did not hurry himself, but went quietly along, his knapsack on his back and his sword by his side, when suddenly one evening he was seized with a wish to light his pipe. He felt for his match-box to strike a light, but to his great disgust he found he had lost it.

He had only gone about a stone's throw after making this discovery when he noticed a light shining through the trees. He went towards it, and perceived before him an old castle, with the door standing open.

The little soldier entered the courtyard, and, peeping through a window, saw a large fire blazing at the end of a low hall. He put his pipe in his pocket and knocked gently, saying politely:

'Would you give me a light?'

But he got no answer.

After waiting for a moment John knocked again, this time more loudly. There was still no reply.

He raised the latch and entered; the hall was empty.

The little soldier made straight for the fireplace, seized the tongs, and was stooping down to look for a nice red hot coal with which to light his pipe, when clic! something went, like a spring giving way, and in the very midst of the flames an enormous serpent reared itself up close to his face.

And what was more strange still, this serpent had the head of a woman.

At such an unexpected sight many men would have turned and run for their lives; but the little soldier, though he was so small, had a true soldier's heart. He only made one step backwards, and grasped the hilt of his sword.

'Don't unsheath it,' said the serpent. 'I have been waiting for you, as it is you who must deliver me.'

'Who are you?'

'My name is Ludovine, and I am the daughter of the King of the Low Countries. Deliver me, and I will marry you and make you happy for ever after.'

Now, some people might not have liked the notion of being made happy by a serpent with the head of a woman, but the Kinglet had no such fears. And, besides, he felt the fascination of Ludovine's eyes, which looked at him as a snake looks at a little bird. They were beautiful green eyes, not round like those of a cat, but long and almond-shaped, and they shone with a strange light, and the golden hair which floated round them seemed all the brighter for their lustre. The face had the beauty of an angel, though the body was only that of a serpent.

'What must I do?' asked the Kinglet.

'Open that door. You will find yourself in a gallery with a room at the end just like this. Cross that, and you will see a closet, out of which you must take a tunic, and bring it back to me.'

The little soldier boldly prepared to do as he was told. He crossed the gallery in safety, but when he reached the room he saw by the light of the stars eight hands on a level with his face, which threatened to strike him. And, turn his eyes which way he would, he could discover no bodies belonging to them.

He lowered his head and rushed forward amidst a storm of blows, which he returned with his fists. When he got to the closet, he opened it, took down the tunic, and brought it to the first room.

'Here it is,' he panted, rather out of breath.

'Clic!' once more the flames parted. Ludovine was a woman down to her waist. She took the tunic and put it on.

It was a magnificent tunic of orange velvet, embroidered in pearls, but the pearls were not so white as her own neck.

'That is not all,' she said. 'Go to the gallery, take the staircase which is on the left, and in the second room on the first story you will find another closet with my skirt. Bring this to me.'

The Kinglet did as he was told, but in entering the room he saw, instead of merely hands, eight arms, each holding an enormous stick. He instantly unsheathed his sword and cut his way through with such vigour that he hardly received a scratch.

He brought back the skirt, which was made of silk as blue as the skies of Spain.

'Here it is,' said John, as the serpent appeared. She was now a woman as far as her knees.

'I only want my shoes and stockings now,' she said. 'Go and get them from the closet which is on the second story.'

The little soldier departed, and found himself in the presence of eight goblins armed with hammers, and flames darting from their eyes. This time he stopped short at the threshold. 'My sword is no use,' he thought to himself; 'these wretches will break it like glass, and if I can't think of anything else, I am a dead man.' At this moment his eyes fell on the door, which was made of oak, thick and heavy. He wrenched it off its hinges and held it over his head, and then went straight at the goblins, whom he crushed beneath it. After that he took the shoes and stockings out of the closet and brought them to Ludovine, who, directly she had put them on, became a woman all over.

When she was quite dressed in her white silk stockings and little blue slippers dotted over with carbuncles, she said to her deliverer, 'Now you must go away, and never come back here, whatever happens. Here is a purse with two hundred ducats. Sleep to-night at the inn which is at the edge of the wood, and awake early in the morning: for at nine o'clock I shall pass the door, and shall take you up in my carriage.' 'Why shouldn't we go now?' asked the little soldier. 'Because the time has not yet come,' said the Princess. 'But first you may drink my health in this glass of wine,' and as she spoke she filled a crystal goblet with a liquid that looked like melted gold.

John drank, then lit his pipe and went out.

II

When he arrived at the inn he ordered supper, but no sooner had he sat down to eat it than he felt that he was going sound asleep.

'I must be more tired than I thought,' he said to himself, and, after telling them to be sure to wake him next morning at eight o'clock, he went to bed.

All night long he slept like a dead man. At eight o'clock they came to wake him, and at half-past, and a quarter of an hour later, but it was no use; and at last they decided to leave him in peace.

The clocks were striking twelve when John awoke. He sprang out of bed, and, scarcely waiting to dress himself, hastened to ask if anyone had been to inquire for him.

'There came a lovely princess,' replied the landlady, 'in a coach of gold. She left you this bouquet, and a message to say that she would pass this way to-morrow morning at eight o'clock.'

The little soldier cursed his sleep, but tried to console himself by looking at his bouquet, which was of immortelles.

'It is the flower of remembrance,' thought he, forgetting that it is also the flower of the dead.

When the night came, he slept with one eye open, and jumped up twenty times an hour. When the birds began to sing he could lie still no longer, and climbed out of his window into the branches of one of the great lime-trees that stood before the door. There he sat, dreamily gazing at his bouquet till he ended by going fast asleep.

Once asleep, nothing was able to wake him; neither the brightness of the sun, nor the songs of the birds, nor the noise of Ludovine's golden coach, nor the cries of the landlady who sought him in every place she could think of.

As the clock struck twelve he woke, and his heart sank as he came down out of his tree and saw them laying the table for dinner.

'Did the Princess come?' he asked.

'Yes, indeed, she did. She left this flower-coloured scarf for you; said she would pass by to-morrow at seven o'clock, but it would be the last time.'

'I must have been bewitched,' thought the little soldier. Then he took the scarf, which had a strange kind of scent, and tied it round his left arm, thinking all the while that the best way to keep awake was not to go to bed at all. So he paid his bill, and bought a horse with the money that remained, and when the evening came he mounted his horse and stood in front of the inn door, determined to stay there all night.

Every now and then he stooped to smell the sweet perfume of the scarf round his arm; and gradually he smelt it so often that at last his head sank on to the horse's neck, and he and his horse snored in company.

When the Princess arrived, they shook him, and beat him, and screamed at him, but it was all no good. Neither man nor horse woke till the coach was seen vanishing away in the distance.

Then John put spurs to his horse, calling with all his might 'Stop! stop!' But the coach drove on as before, and though the little soldier rode after it for a day and a night, he never got one step nearer.

Thus they left many villages and towns behind them, till they came to the sea itself. Here John thought that at last the coach must stop, but, wonder of wonders! it went straight on, and rolled over the water as easily as it had done over the land. John's horse, which had carried him so well, sank down from fatigue, and the little soldier sat sadly on the shore, watching the coach which was fast disappearing on the horizon.

III

However, he soon plucked up his spirits again, and walked along the beach to try and find a boat in which he could sail after the Princess. But no boat was there, and at last, tired and hungry, he sat down to rest on the steps of a fisherman's hut.

In the hut was a young girl who was mending a net. She invited John to come in, and set before him some wine and fried fish, and John ate and drank and felt comforted, and he told his adventures to the little fisher-girl. But though she was very pretty, with a skin as white as a gull's breast, for which her neighbours gave her the name of the Seagull, he did not think about her at all, for he was dreaming of the green eyes of the Princess.

When he had finished his tale, she was filled with pity and said:

'Last week, when I was fishing, my net suddenly grew very heavy, and when I drew it in I found a great copper vase, fastened with lead. I brought it home and placed it on the fire. When the lead had melted a little, I opened the vase with my knife and drew out a mantle of red cloth and a purse containing fifty crowns. That is the mantle, covering my bed, and I have kept the money for my marriage-portion. But take it and go to the nearest seaport, where you will find a ship sailing for the Low Countries, and when you become King you will bring me back my fifty crowns.'

And the Kinglet answered: 'When I am King of the Low Countries, I will make you lady-in-waiting to the Queen, for you are as good as you are beautiful. So farewell,' said he, and as the Seagull went back to her fishing he rolled himself in the mantle and threw himself down on a heap of dried grass, thinking of the strange things that had befallen him, till he suddenly exclaimed:

'Oh, how I wish I was in the capital of the Low Countries!'

IV

In one moment the little soldier found himself standing before a splendid palace. He rubbed his eyes and pinched himself, and when he was quite sure he was not dreaming he said to a man who was smoking his pipe before the door, 'Where am I?'

'Where are you? Can't you see? Before the King's palace, of course.'

'What King?'

'Why the King of the Low Countries!' replied the man, laughing and supposing that he was mad.

Was there ever anything so strange? But as John was an honest fellow, he was troubled at the thought that the Seagull would think he had stolen her mantle and purse. And he began to wonder how he could restore them to her the soonest. Then he remembered that the mantle had some hidden charm that enabled the bearer to transport himself at will from place to place, and in order to make sure of this he wished himself in the best inn of the town. In an instant he was there.

Enchanted with this discovery, he ordered supper, and as it was too late to visit the King that night he went to bed.

The next day, when he got up, he saw that all the houses were wreathed with flowers and covered with flags, and all the church bells were ringing. The little soldier inquired the meaning of all this noise, and was told that the Princess Ludovine, the King's beautiful daughter, had been found, and was about to make her triumphal entry. 'That will just suit me,' thought the Kinglet; 'I will stand at the door and see if she knows me.'

He had scarcely time to dress himself when the golden coach of Ludovine went by. She had a crown of gold upon her head, and the King and Queen sat by her side. By accident her eyes fell upon the little soldier, and she grew pale and turned away her head.

'Didn't she know me?' the little soldier asked himself, 'or was she angry because I missed our meetings?' and he followed the crowd till he got to the palace. When the royal party entered he told the guards that it was he who had delivered the Princess, and wished to speak to the King. But the more he talked the more they believed him mad and refused to let him pass.

The little soldier was furious. He felt that he needed his pipe to calm him, and he entered a tavern and ordered a pint of beer. 'It is this miserable soldier's helmet,' said he to himself 'If I had only money enough I could look as splendid as the lords of the Court; but what is the good of thinking of that when I have only the remains of the Seagull's fifty crowns?'

He took out his purse to see what was left, and he found that there were still fifty crowns.

'The Seagull must have miscounted,' thought he, and he paid for his beer. Then he counted his money again, and there were still fifty crowns. He took away five and counted a third time, but there were still fifty. He emptied the purse altogether and then shut it; when he opened it the fifty crowns were still there!

Then a plan came into his head, and he determined to go at once to the Court tailor and coachbuilder.

He ordered the tailor to make him a mantle and vest of blue velvet embroidered with pearls, and the coachbuilder to make him a golden coach like the coach of the Princess Ludovine. If the tailor and the coachbuilder were quick he promised to pay them double.

A few days later the little soldier was driven through the city in his coach drawn by six white horses, and with four lacqueys richly dressed standing behind. Inside sat John, clad in blue velvet, with a bouquet of immortelles in his hand and a scarf bound round his arm. He drove twice round the city, throwing money to the right and left, and the third time, as he passed under the palace windows, he saw Ludovine lift a corner of the curtain and peep out.

V

The next day no one talked of anything but the rich lord who had distributed money as he drove along. The talk even reached the Court, and the Queen, who was very curious, had a great desire to see the wonderful Prince.

'Very well,' said the King; 'let him be asked to come and play cards with me.'

This time the Kinglet was not late for his appointment.

The King sent for the cards and they sat down to play. They had six games, and John always lost. The stake was fifty crowns, and each time he emptied his purse, which was full the next instant.

The sixth time the King exclaimed, 'It is amazing!'

The Queen cried, 'It is astonishing!'

The Princess said, 'It is bewildering!'

'Not so bewildering,' replied the little soldier, 'as your change into a serpent.'

'Hush!' interrupted the King, who did not like the subject.

'I only spoke of it,' said John, 'because you see in me the man who delivered the Princess from the goblins and whom she promised to marry.'

'Is that true?' asked the King of the Princess.

'Quite true,' answered Ludovine. 'But I told my deliverer to be ready to go with me when I passed by with my coach. I passed three times, but he slept so soundly that no one could wake him.'

'What is your name?' said the King, 'and who are you?'

'My name is John. I am a soldier, and my father is a boatman.'

'You are not a fit husband for my daughter. Still, if you will give us your purse, you shall have her for your wife.'

'My purse does not belong to me, and I cannot give it away.'

'But you can lend it to me till our wedding-day,' said the Princess with one of those glances the little soldier never could resist.

'And when will that be?'

'At Easter,' said the monarch.

'Or in a blue moon!' murmured the Princess; but the Kinglet did not hear her and let her take his purse.

Next evening he presented himself at the palace to play picquet with the King and to make his court to the Princess. But he was told that the King had gone into the country to receive his rents. He returned the following day, and had the same answer. Then he asked to see the Queen, but she had a headache. When this had happened five or six times, he began to understand that they were making fun of him.

'That is not the way for a King to behave,' thought John. 'Old scoundrel!' and then suddenly he remembered his red cloak.

'Ah, what an idiot I am!' said he. 'Of course I can get in whenever I like with the help of this.'

That evening he was in front of the palace, wrapped in his red cloak.

On the first story one window was lighted, and John saw on the curtains the shadow of the Princess.

'I wish myself in the room of the Princess Ludovine,' said he, and in a second he was there.

The King's daughter was sitting before a table counting the money that she emptied from the inexhaustible purse.

'Eight hundred and fifty, nine hundred, nine hundred and fifty—'

'A thousand,' finished John. 'Good evening everybody!'

The Princess jumped and gave a little cry. 'You here! What business have you to do it? Leave at once, or I shall call—'

'I have come,' said the Kinglet, 'to remind you of your promise. The day after to-morrow is Easter Day, and it is high time to think of our marriage.'

Ludovine burst out into a fit of laughter. 'Our marriage! Have you really been foolish enough to believe that the daughter of the King of the Low Countries would ever marry the son of a boatman?'

'Then give me back the purse,' said John.

'Never,' said the Princess, and put it calmly in her pocket.

'As you like,' said the little soldier. 'He laughs best who laughs the last;' and he took the Princess in his arms. 'I wish,' he cried, 'that we were at the ends of the earth;' and in one second he was there, still clasping the Princess tightly in his arms.

'Ouf,' said John, laying her gently at the foot of a tree. 'I never took such a long journey before. What do you say, madam?' The Princess understood that it was no time for jesting, and did not answer. Besides she was still feeling giddy from her rapid flight, and had not yet collected her senses.

VI

The King of the Low Countries was not a very scrupulous person, and his daughter took after him. This was why she had been changed into a serpent. It had been prophesied that she should be delivered by a little soldier, and that she must marry him, unless he failed to appear at the meeting-place three times running. The cunning Princess then laid her plans accordingly.

The wine that she had given to John in the castle of the goblins, the bouquet of immortelles, and the scarf, all had the power of producing sleep like death. And we know how they had acted on John.

However, even in this critical moment, Ludovine did not lose her head.

'I thought you were simply a street vagabond,' said she, in her most coaxing voice; 'and I find you are more powerful than any king. Here is your purse. Have you got my scarf and my bouquet?'

'Here they are,' said the Kinglet, delighted with this change of tone, and he drew them from his bosom. Ludovine fastened one in his buttonhole and the other round his arm. 'Now,' she said, 'you are my lord and master, and I will marry you at your good pleasure.'

'You are kinder than I thought,' said John; 'and you shall never be unhappy, for I love you.'

'Then, my little husband, tell me how you managed to carry me so quickly to the ends of the world.'

The little soldier scratched his head. 'Does she really mean to marry me,' he thought to himself, 'or is she only trying to deceive me again?'

But Ludovine repeated, 'Won't you tell me?' in such a tender voice he did not know how to resist her.

'After all,' he said to himself, 'what does it matter telling her the secret, as long as I don't give her the cloak.'

And he told her the virtue of the red mantle.

'Oh dear, how tired I am!' sighed Ludovine. 'Don't you think we had better take a nap? And then we can talk over our plans.'

She stretched herself on the grass, and the Kinglet did the same. He laid his head on his left arm, round which the scarf was tied, and was soon fast asleep.

Ludovine was watching him out of one eye, and no sooner did she hear him snore than she unfastened the mantle, drew it gently from under him and wrapped it round her, took the purse from his pocket, and put it in hers, and said: 'I wish I was back in my own room.' In another moment she was there.

VII

Who felt foolish but John, when he awoke, twenty-four hours after, and found himself without purse, without mantle, and without Princess? He tore his hair, he beat his breast, he trampled on the bouquet, and tore the scarf of the traitress to atoms.

Besides this he was very hungry, and he had nothing to eat.

He thought of all the wonderful things his grandmother had told him when he was a child, but none of them helped him now. He was in despair, when suddenly he looked up and saw that the tree under which he had been sleeping was a superb plum, covered with fruit as yellow as gold.

'Here goes for the plums,' he said to himself, 'all is fair in war.'

He climbed the tree and began to eat steadily. But he had hardly swallowed two plums when, to his horror, he felt as if something was growing on his forehead. He put up his hand and found that he had two horns!

He leapt down from the tree and rushed to a stream that flowed close by. Alas! there was no escape: two charming little horns, that would not have disgraced the head of a goat.

Then his courage failed him.

'As if it was not enough,' said he, 'that a woman should trick me, but the devil must mix himself up in it and lend me his horns. What a pretty figure I should cut if I went back into the world!'

But as he was still hungry, and the mischief was done, he climbed boldly up another tree, and plucked two plums of a lovely green colour. No sooner had he swallowed two than the horns disappeared. The little soldier was enchanted, though greatly surprised, and came to the conclusion that it was no good to despair too quickly. When he had done eating an idea suddenly occurred to him.

'Perhaps,' thought he, 'these pretty little plums may help me to recover my purse, my cloak, and my heart from the hands of this wicked Princess. She has the eyes of a deer already; let her have the horns of one. If I can manage to set her up with a pair, I will bet any money that I shall cease to want her for my wife. A horned maiden is by no means lovely to look at.' So he plaited a basket out of the long willows, and placed in it carefully both sorts of plums. Then he walked bravely on for many days, having no food but the berries by the wayside, and was in great danger from wild beasts and savage men. But he feared nothing, except that his plums should decay, and this never happened.

At last he came to a civilised country, and with the sale of some jewels that he had about him on the evening of his flight he took passage on board a vessel for the Low Countries. So, at the end of a year and a day, he arrived at the capital of the kingdom.

VIII

The next day he put on a false beard and the dress of a date merchant, and, taking a little table, he placed himself before the door of the church.

He spread carefully out on a fine white cloth his Mirabelle plums, which looked for all the world as if they had been freshly gathered, and when he saw the Princess coming out of church he began to call out in a feigned voice: 'Fine plums! lovely plums!'

'How much are they?' said the Princess.

'Fifty crowns each.'

'Fifty crowns! But what is there so very precious about them? Do they give one wit, or will they increase one's beauty?'

'They could not increase what is perfect already, fair Princess, but still they might add something.'

Rolling stones gather no moss, but they sometimes gain polish; and the months which John had spent in roaming about the world had not been wasted. Such a neatly turned compliment flattered Ludovine.

'What will they add?' she smilingly asked.

'You will see, fair Princess, when you taste them. It will be a surprise for you.'

Ludovine's curiosity was roused. She drew out the purse and shook out as many little heaps of fifty crowns as there were plums in the basket. The little soldier was seized with a wild desire to snatch the purse from her and proclaim her a thief, but he managed to control himself.

His plums all sold, he shut up shop, took off his disguise, changed his inn, and kept quiet, waiting to see what would happen.

No sooner had she reached her room than the Princess exclaimed, 'Now let us see what these fine plums can add to my beauty,' and throwing off her hood, she picked up a couple and ate them.

Imagine with what surprise and horror she felt all of a sudden that something was growing out of her forehead. She flew to her mirror and uttered a piercing cry.

'Horns! so that was what he promised me! Let someone find the plum-seller at once and bring him to me! Let his nose and ears be cut off! Let him be flayed alive, or burnt at a slow fire and his ashes scattered to the winds! Oh, I shall die of shame and despair!'

Her women ran at the sound of her screams, and tried to wrench off the horns, but it was of no use, and they only gave her a violent headache.

The King then sent round a herald to proclaim that he would give the hand of the Princess to anyone who would rid her of her strange ornaments. So all the doctors and sorcerers and surgeons in the Low Countries and the neighbouring kingdoms thronged to the palace, each with a remedy of his own. But it was all no good, and the Princess suffered so much from their remedies that the King was obliged to send out a second proclamation that anyone who undertook to cure the Princess, and who failed to do it, should be hanged up to the nearest tree.

But the prize was too great for any proclamation to put a stop to the efforts of the crowd of suitors, and that year the orchards of the Low Countries all bore a harvest of dead men.

IX

The King had given orders that they should seek high and low for the plum-seller, but in spite of all their pains, he was nowhere to be found.

When the little soldier discovered that their patience was worn out, he pressed the juice of the green Queen Claude plums into a small phial, bought a doctor's robe, put on a wig and spectacles, and presented himself before the King of the Low Countries. He gave himself out as a famous physician who had come from distant lands, and he promised that he would cure the Princess if only he might be left alone with her.

'Another madman determined to be hanged,' said the King. 'Very well, do as he asks; one should refuse nothing to a man with a rope round his neck.'

As soon as the little soldier was in the presence of the Princess he poured some drops of the liquid into a glass. The Princess had scarcely tasted it, when the tip of the horns disappeared.

'They would have disappeared completely,' said the pretended doctor, 'if there did not exist something to counteract the effect. It is only possible to cure people whose souls are as clean as the palm of my hand. Are you sure you have not committed some little sin? Examine yourself well.'

Ludovine had no need to think over it long, but she was torn in pieces between the shame of a humiliating confession, and the desire to be unhorned. At last she made answer with downcast eyes,

'I have stolen a leather purse from a little soldier.'

'Give it to me. The remedy will not act till I hold the purse in my hands.'

It cost Ludovine a great pang to give up the purse, but she remembered that riches would not benefit her if she was still to keep the horns.

With a sigh, she handed the purse to the doctor, who poured more of the liquid into the glass, and when the Princess had drunk it, she found that the horns had diminished by one half.

'You must really have another little sin on your conscience. Did you steal nothing from this soldier but his purse?'

'I also stole from him his cloak.'

'Give it me.'

'Here it is.'

This time Ludovine thought to herself that when once the horns had departed, she would call her attendants and take the things from the doctor by force.

She was greatly pleased with this idea, when suddenly the pretended physician wrapped himself in the cloak, flung away the wig and spectacles, and showed to the traitress the face of the Little Soldier.

She stood before him dumb with fright.

'I might,' said John, 'have left you horned to the end of your days, but I am a good fellow and I once loved you, and besides—you are too like the devil to have any need of his horns.'

X

John had wished himself in the house of the Seagull. Now the Seagull was seated at the window, mending her net, and from time to time her eyes wandered to the sea as if she was expecting someone. At the noise made by the little soldier, she looked up and blushed.

'So it is you!' she said. 'How did you get here?' And then she added in a low voice, 'And have you married your Princess?'

Then John told her all his adventures, and when he had finished, he restored to her the purse and the mantle.

'What can I do with them?' said she. 'You have proved to me that happiness does not lie in the possession of treasures.'

'It lies in work and in the love of an honest woman,' replied the little soldier, who noticed for the first time what pretty eyes she had. 'Dear Seagull, will you have me for a husband?' and he held out his hand.

'Yes, I will,' answered the fisher maiden, blushing very red, 'but only on condition that we seal up the purse and the mantle in the copper vessel and throw them into the sea.'

And this they did.

Charles Deulin.

THE MAGIC SWAN

There were once upon a time three brothers, of whom the eldest was called Jacob, the second Frederick, and the youngest Peter. This youngest brother was made a regular butt of by the other two, and they treated him shamefully. If anything went wrong with their affairs, Peter had to bear the blame and put things right for them, and he had to endure all this ill-treatment because he was weak and delicate and couldn't defend himself against his stronger brothers. The poor creature had a most trying life of it in every way, and day and night he pondered how he could make it better. One day, when he was in the wood gathering sticks and crying bitterly, a little old woman came up to him and asked him what was the matter; and he told her all his troubles.

'Come, my good youth,' said the old dame, when he had finished his tale of woe, 'isn't the world wide enough? Why don't you set out and try your fortune somewhere else?'

Peter took her words to heart, and left his father's house early one morning to try his fortune in the wide world, as the old woman had advised him. But he felt very bitterly parting from the home where he had been born, and where he had at least passed a short but happy childhood, and sitting down on a hill he gazed once more fondly on his native place.

Suddenly the little old woman stood before him, and, tapping him on the shoulder, said, 'So far good, my boy; but what do you mean to do now?'

Peter was at a loss what to answer, for so far he had always thought that fortune would drop into his mouth like a ripe cherry. The old woman, who guessed his thoughts, laughed kindly and said, 'I'll tell you what you must do, for I've taken a fancy to you, and I'm sure you won't forget me when you've made your fortune.'

Peter promised faithfully he wouldn't, and the old woman continued:

'This evening at sunset go to yonder pear-tree which you see growing at the cross roads. Underneath it you will find a man lying asleep, and a beautiful large swan will be fastened to the tree close to him. You must be careful not to waken the man, but you must unfasten the swan and take it away with you. You will find that everyone will fall in love with its beautiful plumage, and you must allow anyone who likes to pull out a feather. But as soon as the swan feels as much as a finger on it, it will scream out, and then you must say, "Swan, hold fast." Then the hand of the person who has touched the bird will be held as in a vice, and nothing will set it free, unless you touch it with this little stick which I will make you a present of. When you have captured a whole lot of people in this way, lead your train straight on with you; you will come to a big town where a Princess lives who has never been known to laugh. If you can only make her laugh your fortune is made; then I beg you won't forget your old friend.'

Peter promised again that he wouldn't, and at sunset he went to the tree the old woman had mentioned. The man lay there fast asleep, and a large beautiful swan was fastened to the tree beside him by a red cord. Peter loosed the bird, and led it away with him without disturbing the bird's master.

He walked on with the swan for some time, and came at last to a building-yard where some men were busily at work. They were all lost in admiration of the bird's beautiful plumage, and one forward youth, who was covered with clay from head to foot, called out, 'Oh, if I'd only one of those feathers how happy I should be!'

'Pull one out then,' said Peter kindly, and the youth seized one from the bird's tail; instantly the swan screamed, and Peter called out, 'Swan, hold fast,' and do what he could the poor youth couldn't get his hand away. The more he howled the more the others laughed, till a girl who had been washing clothes in the neighbouring stream hurried up to see what was the matter. When she saw the poor boy fastened to the swan she felt so sorry for him that she stretched out her hand to free him. The bird screamed.

'Swan, hold fast,' called out Peter, and the girl was caught also.

When Peter had gone on for a bit with his captives, they met a chimney sweep, who laughed loudly over the extraordinary troop, and asked the girl what she was doing.

'Oh, dearest John,' replied the girl, 'give me your hand and set me free from this cursed young man.'

'Most certainly I will, if that's all you want,' replied the sweep, and gave the girl his hand. The bird screamed.

'Swan, hold fast,' said Peter, and the black man was added to their number.

They soon came to a village where a fair was being held. A travelling circus was giving a performance, and the clown was just doing his tricks.

He opened his eyes wide with amazement when he saw the remarkable trio fastened on to the swan's tail.

'Have you gone raving mad, Blackie?' he asked as well as he could for laughing.

'It's no laughing matter,' the sweep replied. 'This wench has got so tight hold of me that I feel as if I were glued to her. Do set me free, like a good clown, and I'll do you a good turn some day.'

Without a moment's hesitation the clown grasped the black outstretched hand. The bird screamed.

'Swan, hold fast,' called out Peter, and the clown became the fourth of the party.

Now in the front row of the spectators sat the respected and popular Mayor of the village, who was much put out by what he considered nothing but a foolish trick. So much annoyed was he that he seized the clown by the hand and tried to tear him away, in order to hand him over to the police.

Then the bird screamed, and Peter called out, 'Swan, hold fast,' and the dignified Mayor shared the fate of his predecessors.

The Mayoress, a long thin stick of a woman, enraged at the insult done to her husband, seized his free arm and tore at it with all her might, with the only result that she too was forced to swell the procession. After this no one else had any wish to join them.

Soon Peter saw the towers of the capital in front of him. Just before entering it, a glittering carriage came out to meet him, in which was seated a young lady as beautiful as the day, but with a very solemn and serious expression. But no sooner had she perceived the motley crowd fastened to the swan's tail than she burst into a loud fit of laughter, in which she was joined by all her servants and ladies in waiting.

'The Princess has laughed at last,' they all cried with joy.

She stepped out of her carriage to look more closely at the wonderful sight, and laughed again over the capers the poor captives cut. She ordered her carriage to be turned round and drove slowly back into the town, never taking her eyes off Peter and his procession.

When the King heard the news that his daughter had actually laughed, he was more than delighted, and had Peter and his marvellous train brought before him. He laughed himself when he saw them till the tears rolled down his cheeks.

'My good friend,' he said to Peter, 'do you know what I promised the person who succeeded in making the Princess laugh?'

'No, I don't,' said Peter.

'Then I'll tell you,' answered the King; 'a thousand gold crowns or a piece of land. Which will you choose?'

Peter decided in favour of the land. Then he touched the youth, the girl, the sweep, the clown, the Mayor, and the Mayoress with his little stick, and they were all free again, and ran away home as if a fire were burning behind them; and their flight, as you may imagine, gave rise to renewed merriment.

Then the Princess felt moved to stroke the swan, at the same time admiring its plumage. The bird screamed.

'Swan, hold fast,' called out Peter, and so he won the Princess for his bride. But the swan flew up into the air, and vanished in the blue horizon. Peter now received a duchy as a present, and became a very great man indeed; but he did not forget the little old woman who had been the cause of all his good fortune, and appointed her as head housekeeper to him and his royal bride in their magnificent castle.

Kletke.

THE DIRTY SHEPHERDESS

Once upon a time there lived a King who had two daughters, and he loved them with all his heart. When they grew up, he was suddenly seized with a wish to know if they, on their part, truly loved him, and he made up his mind that he would give his kingdom to whichever best proved her devotion.

So he called the elder Princess and said to her, 'How much do you love me?'

'As the apple of my eye!' answered she.

'Ah!' exclaimed the King, kissing her tenderly as he spoke, 'you are indeed a good daughter.'

Then he sent for the younger, and asked her how much she loved him.

'I look upon you, my father,' she answered, 'as I look upon salt in my food.'

But the King did not like her words, and ordered her to quit the court, and never again to appear before him. The poor Princess went sadly up to her room and began to cry, but when she was reminded of her father's commands, she dried her eyes, and made a bundle of her jewels and her best dresses and hurriedly left the castle where she was born.

She walked straight along the road in front of her, without knowing very well where she was going or what was to become of her, for she had never been shown how to work, and all she had learnt consisted of a few household rules, and receipts of dishes which her mother had taught her long ago. And as she was afraid that no housewife would want to engage a girl with such a pretty face, she determined to make herself as ugly as she could.

She therefore took off the dress that she was wearing and put on some horrible old rags belonging to a beggar, all torn and covered with mud. After that she smeared mud all over her hands and face, and shook her hair into a great tangle. Having thus changed her appearance, she went about offering herself as a goose-girl or shepherdess. But the farmers' wives would have nothing to say to such a dirty maiden, and sent her away with a morsel of bread for charity's sake.

After walking for a great many days without being able to find any work, she came to a large farm where they were in want of a shepherdess, and engaged her gladly.

One day when she was keeping her sheep in a lonely tract of land, she suddenly felt a wish to dress herself in her robes of splendour. She washed herself carefully in the stream, and as she always carried her bundle with her, it was easy to shake off her rags, and transform herself in a few moments into a great lady.

The King's son, who had lost his way out hunting, perceived this lovely damsel a long way off, and wished to look at her closer. But as soon as the girl saw what he was at, she fled into the wood as swiftly as a bird. The Prince ran after her, but as he was running he caught his foot in the root of a tree and fell, and when he got up again, she was nowhere to be seen.

When she was quite safe, she put on her rags again, and smeared over her face and hands. However the young Prince, who was both hot and thirsty, found his way to the farm, to ask for a drink of cider, and he inquired the name of the beautiful lady that kept the sheep. At this everyone began to laugh, for they said that the shepherdess was one of the ugliest and dirtiest creatures under the sun.

The Prince thought some witchcraft must be at work, and he hastened away before the return of the shepherdess, who became that evening the butt of everybody's jests.

But the King's son thought often of the lovely maiden whom he had only seen for a moment, though she seemed to him much more fascinating than any lady of the Court. At last he dreamed of nothing else, and grew thinner day by day till his parents inquired what was the matter, promising to do all they could to make him as happy as he once was. He dared not tell them the truth, lest they should laugh at him, so he only said that he should like some bread baked by the kitchen girl in the distant farm.

Although the wish appeared rather odd, they hastened to fulfil it, and the farmer was told the request of the King's son. The maiden showed no surprise at receiving such an order, but merely asked for some flour, salt, and water, and also that she might be left alone in a little room adjoining the oven, where the kneading-trough stood. Before beginning her work she washed herself carefully, and even put on her rings; but, while she was baking, one of her rings slid into the dough. When she had finished she dirtied herself again, and let the lumps of the dough stick to her fingers, so that she became as ugly as before.

The loaf, which was a very little one, was brought to the King's son, who ate it with pleasure. But in cutting it he found the ring of the Princess, and declared to his parents that he would marry the girl whom that ring fitted.

So the King made a proclamation through his whole kingdom and ladies came from afar to lay claim to the honour. But the ring was so tiny that even those who had the smallest hands could only get it on their little fingers. In a short time all the maidens of the kingdom, including the peasant girls, had tried on the ring, and the King was just about to announce that their efforts had been in vain, when the Prince observed that he had not yet seen the shepherdess.

They sent to fetch her, and she arrived covered with rags, but with her hands cleaner than usual, so that she could easily slip on the ring. The King's son declared that he would fulfil his promise, and when his parents mildly remarked that the girl was only a keeper of sheep, and a very ugly one too, the maiden boldly said that she was born a princess, and that, if they would only give her some water and leave her alone in a room for a few minutes, she would show that she could look as well as anyone in fine clothes.

They did what she asked, and when she entered in a magnificent dress, she looked so beautiful that all saw she must be a princess in disguise. The King's son recognized the charming damsel of whom he had once caught a glimpse, and, flinging himself at her feet, asked if she would marry him. The Princess then told her story, and said that it would be necessary to send an ambassador to her father to ask his consent and to invite him to the wedding.

The Princess's father, who had never ceased to repent his harshness towards his daughter, had sought her through the land, but as no one could tell him anything of her, he supposed her dead. Therefore it was with great joy he heard that she was living and that a king's son asked her in marriage, and he quitted his kingdom with his elder daughter so as to be present at the ceremony.

By the orders of the bride, they only served her father at the wedding breakfast bread without salt, and meat without seasoning. Seeing him make faces, and eat very little, his daughter, who sat beside him, inquired if his dinner was not to his taste.

'No,' he replied, 'the dishes are carefully cooked and sent up, but they are all so dreadfully tasteless.'

'Did not I tell you, my father, that salt was the best thing in life? And yet, when I compared you to salt, to show how much I loved you, you thought slightingly of me and you chased me from your presence.'

The King embraced his daughter, and allowed that he had been wrong to misinterpret her words. Then, for the rest of the wedding feast they gave him bread made with salt, and dishes with seasoning, and he said they were the very best he had ever eaten.

Sebillot.

THE ENCHANTED SNAKE

There was once upon a time a poor woman who would have given all she possessed for a child, but she hadn't one.

Now it happened one day that her husband went to the wood to collect brushwood, and when he had brought it home, he discovered a pretty little snake among the twigs.

When Sabatella, for that was the name of the peasant's wife, saw the little beast, she sighed deeply and said, 'Even the snakes have their brood; I alone am unfortunate and have no children.' No sooner had she said these words than, to her intense surprise, the little snake looked up into her face and spoke: 'Since you have no children, be a mother to me instead, and I promise you will never repent it, for I will love you as if I were your own son.'

At first Sabatella was frightened to death at hearing a snake speak, but plucking up her courage, she replied, 'If it weren't for any other reason than your kindly thought, I would agree to what you say, and I will love you and look after you like a mother.'

So she gave the snake a little hole in the house for its bed, fed it with all the nicest food she could think of, and seemed as if she never could show it enough kindness. Day by day it grew bigger and fatter, and at last one morning it said to Cola-Mattheo, the peasant, whom it always regarded as its father, 'Dear papa, I am now of a suitable age and wish to marry.'

'I'm quite agreeable,' answered Mattheo, 'and I'll do my best to find another snake like yourself and arrange a match between you.'

'Why, if you do that,' replied the snake, 'we shall be no better than the vipers and reptiles, and that's not what I want at all. No; I'd much prefer to marry the King's daughter; therefore I pray you go without further delay, and demand an audience of the King, and tell him a snake wishes to marry his daughter.'

Cola-Mattheo, who was rather a simpleton, went as he was desired to the King, and having obtained an audience, he said, 'Your Majesty, I have often heard that people lose nothing by asking, so I have come to inform you that a snake wants to marry your daughter, and I'd be glad to know if you are willing to mate a dove with a serpent?'

The King, who saw at once that the man was a fool, said, in order to get quit of him, 'Go home and tell your friend the snake that if he can turn this palace into ivory, inlaid with gold and silver, before to-morrow at noon, I will let him marry my daughter.' And with a hearty laugh he dismissed the peasant.

When Cola-Mattheo brought this answer back to the snake, the little creature didn't seem the least put out, but said, 'To-morrow morning, before sunrise, you must go to the wood and gather a bunch of green herbs, and then rub the threshold of the palace with them, and you'll see what will happen.'

Cola-Mattheo, who was, as I have said before, a great simpleton, made no reply; but before sunrise next morning he went to the wood and gathered a bunch of St. John's Wort, and rosemary, and suchlike herbs, and rubbed them, as he had been told, on the floor of the palace. Hardly had he done so than the walls immediately turned into ivory, so richly inlaid with gold and silver that they dazzled the eyes of all beholders. The King, when he rose and saw the miracle that had been performed, was beside himself with amazement, and didn't know what in the world he was to do.

But when Cola-Mattheo came next day, and, in the name of the snake, demanded the hand of the Princess, the King replied, 'Don't be in such a hurry; if the snake really wants to marry my daughter, he must do some more things first, and one of these is to turn all the paths and walls of my garden into pure gold before noon to-morrow.'

When the snake was told of this new condition, he replied, 'To-morrow morning, early, you must go and collect all the odds and ends of rubbish you can find in the streets, and then take them and throw them on the paths and walls of the garden, and you'll see then if we won't be more than a match for the old King.'

So Cola-Mattheo rose at cock-crow, took a large basket under his arm, and carefully collected all the broken fragments of pots and pans, and jugs and lamps, and other trash of that sort. No sooner had he scattered them over the paths and walls of the King's garden than they became one blaze of glittering gold, so that everyone's eyes were dazzled with the brilliancy, and everyone's soul was filled with wonder. The King, too, was amazed at the sight, but still he couldn't make up his mind to part with his daughter, so when Cola-Mattheo came to remind him of his promise he replied, 'I have still a third demand to make. If the snake can turn all the trees and fruit of my garden into precious stones, then I promise him my daughter in marriage.'

When the peasant informed the snake what the King had said, he replied, 'To-morrow morning, early, you must go to the market and buy all the fruit you see there, and then sow all the stones and seeds in the palace garden, and, if I'm not mistaken, the King will be satisfied with the result.'

Cola-Mattheo rose at dawn, and taking a basket on his arm, he went to the market, and bought all the pomegranates, apricots, cherries, and other fruit he could find there, and sowed the seeds and stones in the palace garden. In one moment, the trees were all ablaze with rubies, emeralds, diamonds, and every other precious stone you can think of.

This time the King felt obliged to keep his promise, and calling his daughter to him, he said, 'My dear Grannonia,' for that was the Princess's name, 'more as a joke than anything else, I demanded what seemed to me impossibilities from your bridegroom, but now that he has done all I required, I am bound to stick to my part of the bargain. Be a good child, and as you love me, do not force me to break my word, but give yourself up with as good grace as you can to a most unhappy fate.'

'Do with me what you like, my lord and father, for your will is my law,' answered Grannonia.

When the King heard this, he told Cola-Mattheo to bring the snake to the palace, and said that he was prepared to receive the creature as his son-in-law.

The snake arrived at court in a carriage made of gold and drawn by six white elephants; but wherever it appeared on the way, the people fled in terror at the sight of the fearful reptile.

When the snake reached the palace, all the courtiers shook and trembled with fear down to the very scullion, and the King and Queen were in such a state of nervous collapse that they hid themselves in a far-away turret. Grannonia alone kept her presence of mind, and although both her father and mother implored her to fly for her life, she wouldn't move a step, saying, 'I'm certainly not going to fly from the man you have chosen for my husband.'

As soon as the snake saw Grannonia, it wound its tail round her and kissed her. Then, leading her into a room, it shut the door, and throwing off its skin, it changed into a beautiful young man with golden locks, and flashing eyes, who embraced Grannonia tenderly, and said all sorts of pretty things to her.

When the King saw the snake shut itself into a room with his daughter, he said to his wife, 'Heaven be merciful to our child, for I fear it is all over with her now. This cursed snake has most likely swallowed her up.' Then they put their eyes to the keyhole to see what had happened.

Their amazement knew no bounds when they saw a beautiful youth standing before their daughter with the snake's skin lying on the floor beside him. In their excitement they burst open the door, and seizing the skin they threw it into the fire. But no sooner had they done this than the young man called out, 'Oh, wretched people! what have you done?' and before they had time to look round he had changed himself into a dove, and dashing against the window he broke a pane of glass, and flew away from their sight.

But Grannonia, who in one and the same moment saw herself merry and sad, cheerful and despairing, rich and beggared, complained bitterly over this robbery of her happiness, this poisoning of her cup of joy, this unlucky stroke of fortune, and laid all the blame on her parents, though they assured her that they had meant no harm. But the Princess refused to be comforted, and at night, when all the inhabitants of the palace were asleep, she stole out by a back door, disguised as a peasant woman, determined to seek for her lost happiness till she found it. When she got to the outskirts of the town, led by the light of the moon, she met a fox, who offered to accompany her, an offer which Grannonia gladly accepted, saying 'You are most heartily welcome, for I don't know my way at all about the neighbourhood.'

So they went on their way together, and came at last to a wood, where, being tired with walking, they paused to rest under the shade of a tree, where a spring of water sported with the tender grass, refreshing it with its crystal spray.

They laid themselves down on the green carpet and soon fell fast asleep, and did not waken again till the sun was high in the heavens. They rose up and stood for some time listening to the birds singing, because Grannonia delighted in their songs.

When the fox perceived this, he said: 'If you only understood, as I do, what these little birds are saying, your pleasure would be even greater.'

Provoked by his words—for we all know that curiosity is as deeply inborn in every woman as even the love of talking—Grannonia implored the fox to tell her what the birds had said.

At first the wily fox refused to tell her what he had gathered from the conversation of the birds, but at last he gave way to her entreaties, and told her that they had spoken of the misfortunes of a beautiful young Prince, whom a wicked enchantress had turned into a snake for the period of seven years. At the end of this time he had fallen in love with a charming Princess, but that when he had shut himself up into a room with her, and had thrown off his snake's skin, her parents had forced their way into the room and had burnt the skin, whereupon the Prince, changed into the likeness of a dove, had broken a pane of glass in trying to fly out of the window, and had wounded himself so badly that the doctors despaired of his life.

Grannonia, when she learnt that they were talking of her lover, asked at once whose son he was, and if there was any hope of his recovery; to which the fox made answer that the birds had said he was the son of the King of Vallone Grosso, and that the only thing that could cure him was to rub the wounds on his head with the blood of the very birds who had told the tale.

Then Grannonia knelt down before the fox, and begged him in her sweetest way to catch the birds for her and procure their blood, promising at the same time to reward him richly.

'All right,' said the fox, 'only don't be in such a hurry; let's wait till night, when the little birds have gone to roost, then I'll climb up and catch them all for you.'

So they passed the day, talking now of the beauty of the Prince, now of the father of the Princess, and then of the misfortune that had happened. At last the night arrived, and all the little birds were asleep high up on the branches of a big tree. The fox climbed up stealthily and caught the little creatures with his paws one after the other; and when he had killed them all he put their blood into a little bottle which he wore at his side and returned with it to Grannonia, who was beside herself with joy at the result of the fox's raid. But the fox said, 'My dear daughter, your joy is in vain, because, let me tell you, this blood is of no earthly use to you unless you add some of mine to it,' and with these words he took to his heels.

Grannonia, who saw her hopes dashed to the ground in this cruel way, had recourse to flattery and cunning, weapons which have often stood the sex in good stead, and called out after the fox, 'Father Fox, you would be quite right to save your skin, if, in the first place, I didn't feel I owed so much to you, and if, in the second, there weren't other foxes in the world; but as you know how grateful I feel to you, and as there are heaps of other foxes about, you can trust yourself to me. Don't behave like the cow that kicks the pail over after it has filled it with milk, but continue your journey with me, and when we get to the capital you can sell me to the King as a servant girl.'

It never entered the fox's head that even foxes can be outwitted, so after a bit he consented to go with her; but he hadn't gone far before the cunning girl seized a stick, and gave him such a blow with it on the head, that he dropped down dead on the spot. Then Grannonia took some of his blood and poured it into her little bottle; and went on her way as fast as she could to Vallone Grosso.

When she arrived there she went straight to the Royal palace, and let the King be told she had come to cure the young Prince.

The King commanded her to be brought before him at once, and was much astonished when he saw that it was a girl who undertook to do what all the cleverest doctors of his kingdom had failed in. As an attempt hurts no one, he willingly consented that she should do what she could.

'All I ask,' said Grannonia, 'is that, should I succeed in what you desire, you will give me your son in marriage.'

The King, who had given up all hopes of his son's recovery, replied: 'Only restore him to life and health and he shall be yours. It is only fair to give her a husband who gives me a son.'

And so they went into the Prince's room. The moment Grannonia had rubbed the blood on his wounds the illness left him, and he was as sound and well as ever. When the King saw his son thus marvellously restored to life and health, he turned to him and said: 'My dear son, I thought of you as dead, and now, to my great joy and amazement, you are alive again. I promised this young woman that if she should cure you, to bestow your hand and heart on her, and seeing that Heaven has been gracious, you must fulfil the promise I made her; for gratitude alone forces me to pay this debt.'

But the Prince answered: 'My lord and father, I would that my will were as free as my love for you is great. But as I have plighted my word to another maiden, you will see yourself, and so will this young woman, that I cannot go back from my word, and be faithless to her whom I love.'

When Grannonia heard these words, and saw how deeply rooted the Prince's love for her was, she felt very happy, and blushing rosy red, she said: 'But should I get the other lady to give up her rights, would you then consent to marry me?'

'Far be it from me,' replied the Prince, 'to banish the beautiful picture of my love from my heart. Whatever she may say, my heart and desire will remain the same, and though I were to lose my life for it, I couldn't consent to this exchange.'

Grannonia could keep silence no longer, and throwing off her peasant's disguise, she discovered herself to the Prince, who was nearly beside himself with joy when he recognised his fair lady-love. He then told his father at once who she was, and what she had done and suffered for his sake.

Then they invited the King and Queen of Starza-Longa to their Court, and had a great wedding feast, and proved once more that there is no better seasoning for the joys of true love than a few pangs of grief.

THE BITER BIT

Once upon a time there lived a man called Simon, who was very rich, but at the same time as stingy and miserly as he could be. He had a housekeeper called Nina, a clever capable woman, and as she did her work carefully and conscientiously, her master had the greatest respect for her.

In his young days Simon had been one of the gayest and most active youths of the neighbourhood, but as he grew old and stiff he found it very difficult to walk, and his faithful servant urged him to get a horse so as to save his poor old bones. At last Simon gave way to the request and persuasive eloquence of his housekeeper, and betook himself one day to the market where he had seen a mule, which he thought would just suit him, and which he bought for seven gold pieces.

Now it happened that there were three merry rascals hanging about the market-place, who much preferred living on other people's goods to working for their own living. As soon as they saw that Simon had bought a mule, one of them said to his two boon companions, 'My friends, this mule must be ours before we are many hours older.'

'But how shall we manage it,' asked one of them.

'We must all three station ourselves at different intervals along the old man's homeward way, and must each in his turn declare that the mule he has bought is a donkey. If we only stick to it you'll see the mule will soon be ours.' This proposal quite satisfied the others, and they all separated as they had agreed.

Now when Simon came by, the first rogue said to him, 'God bless you, my fine gentleman.'

'Thanks for your courtesy,' replied Simon.

'Where have you been?' asked the thief.

'To the market,' was the reply.

'And what did you buy there?' continued the rogue.

'This mule.'

'Which mule?'

'The one I'm sitting upon, to be sure,' replied Simon.

'Are you in earnest, or only joking?'

'What do you mean?'

'Because it seems to me you've got hold of a donkey, and not of a mule.'

'A donkey? Rubbish!' screamed Simon, and without another word he rode on his way. After a few hundred yards he met the second confederate, who addressed him, 'Good day, dear sir, where are you coming from?'

'From the market,' answered Simon.

'Did things go pretty cheap?' asked the other.

'I should just think so,' said Simon.

'And did you make any good bargain yourself?'

'I bought this mule on which you see me.'

'Is it possible that you really bought that beast for a mule?'

'Why certainly.'

'But, good heavens, it's nothing but a donkey!'

'A donkey!' repeated Simon, 'you don't mean to say so; if a single other person tells me that, I'll make him a present of the wretched animal.'

With these words he continued his way, and very soon met the third knave, who said to him, 'God bless you, sir; are you by any chance coming from the market?'

'Yes, I am,' replied Simon.

'And what bargain did you drive there?' asked the cunning fellow.

'I bought this mule on which I am riding.'

'A mule! Are you speaking seriously, or do you wish to make a fool of me?'

'I'm speaking in sober earnest,' said Simon; 'it wouldn't occur to me to make a joke of it.'

'Oh, my poor friend,' cried the rascal, 'don't you see that is a donkey and not a mule? you have been taken in by some wretched cheats.'

'You are the third person in the last two hours who has told me the same thing,' said Simon, 'but I couldn't believe it,' and dismounting from the mule he spoke: 'Keep the animal, I make you a present of it.' The rascal took the beast, thanked him kindly, and rode on to join his comrades, while Simon continued his journey on foot.

As soon as the old man got home, he told his housekeeper that he had bought a beast under the belief that it was a mule, but that it had turned out to be a donkey—at least, so he had been assured by several people he had met on the road, and that in disgust he had at last given it away.

'Oh, you simpleton!' cried Nina; 'didn't you see that they were only playing you a trick? Really, I thought you'd have had more gumption than that; they wouldn't have taken me in in that way.'

'Never mind,' replied Simon, 'I'll play them one worth two of that; for depend upon it they won't be contented with having got the donkey out of me, but they'll try by some new dodge to get something more, or I'm much mistaken.'

Now there lived in the village not far from Simon's house, a peasant who had two goats, so alike in every respect that it was impossible to distinguish one from the other. Simon bought them both, paid as small a price as he could for them, and leading them home with him, he told Nina to prepare a good meal, as he was going to invite some friends to dinner. He ordered her to roast some veal, and to boil a pair of chickens, and gave her some herbs to make a good savoury, and told her to bake the best tart she could make. Then he took one of the goats and tied it to a post in the courtyard, and gave it some grass to eat; but he bound a cord round the neck of the other goat and led it to the market.

Hardly had he arrived there, than the three gentlemen who had got his mule perceived him, and coming up to him said: 'Welcome, Mr. Simon, what brings you here; are you on the look out for a bargain?'

'I've come to get some provisions,' he answered, 'because some friends are coming to dine with me today, and it would give me much pleasure if you were to honour me with your company also.'

The accomplices willingly accepted this invitation; and after Simon had made all his purchases, he tied them on to the goat's back, and said to it, in the presence of the three cheats, 'Go home now, and tell Nina to roast the veal, and boil the chickens, and tell her to prepare a savoury with herbs, and to bake the best tart she can make. Have you followed me? Then go, and Heaven's blessing go with you.'

As soon as it felt itself free, the laden goat trotted off as quickly as it could, and to this day nobody knows what became of it. But Simon, after wandering about the market for some time with his three friends and some others he had picked up, returned home to his house.

When he and his guests entered the courtyard, they noticed the goat tied to the post quietly chewing the cud. They were not a little astonished at this, for of course they thought it was the same goat that Simon had sent home laden with provisions. As soon as they reached the house Mr. Simon said to his housekeeper, 'Well, Nina, have you done what I told the goat to tell you to do?' The artful woman, who at once understood her master, answered, 'Certainly I have. The veal is roasted, and the chickens boiled.'

'That's all right,' said Simon.

When the three rogues saw the cooked meats, and the tart in the oven, and heard Nina's words, they were nearly beside themselves with amazement, and began to consult at once how they were to get the goat into their own possession. At last, towards the end of the meal, having sought in vain for some cunning dodge to get the goat away from Mr. Simon, one of them said to him, 'My worthy host, you must sell your goat to us.'

Simon replied that he was most unwilling to part with the creature, as no amount of money would make up to him for its loss; still, if they were quite set on it, he would let them have the goat for fifty gold pieces.

The knaves, who thought they were doing a capital piece of business, paid down the fifty gold pieces at once, and left the house quite happily, leading the goat with them. When they got home they said to their wives, 'You needn't begin to cook the dinner to-morrow till we send the provisions home.'

The following day they went to the market and bought chickens and other eatables, and after they had packed them on the back of the goat (which they had brought with them), they told it all the dishes they wished their wives to prepare. As soon as the goat felt itself free, it ran as quickly as it could, and was very soon lost to sight, and, as far as I know, was never heard of again.

When the dinner hour approached all three went home and asked their wives if the goat had returned with the necessary provisions, and had told them what they wished prepared for their meal.

'Oh, you fools and blockheads!' cried their wives, 'how could you ever believe for a moment that a goat would do the work of a servant-maid? You have been finely deceived for once in a way. Of course, if you are always taking in other people, your turn to be taken in comes too, and this time you've been made to look pretty foolish.'

When the three comrades saw that Mr. Simon had got the better of them, and done them out of fifty gold pieces, they flew into such a rage that they made up their minds to kill him, and, seizing their weapons for this purpose, went to his house.

But the sly old man, who was terrified for his life that the three rogues might do him some harm, was on his guard, and said to his housekeeper, 'Nina, take this bladder, which is filled with blood, and hide it under your cloak; then when these thieves come I'll lay all the blame on you, and will pretend to be so angry with you that I will run at you with my knife, and pierce the bladder with it; then you must fall on the ground as if you were dead, and leave the rest to me.'

Hardly had Simon said these words when the three rogues appeared and fell on him to kill him.

'My friends,' called out Simon to then, 'what do you accuse me of? I am in no way to blame; perhaps my housekeeper has done you some injury of which I know nothing.' And with these words, he turned on Nina with his knife, and stuck it right into her, so that he pierced the bladder filled with blood. Instantly the housekeeper fell down as if she were dead, and the blood streamed all over the ground.

Simon then pretended to be seized with remorse at the sight of this dreadful catastrophe, and cried out in a loud voice, 'Unhappy wretch that I am! What have I done? Like a madman I have killed the woman who is the prop and stay of my old age. How could I ever go on living without her?' Then he seized a pipe, and when he had blown into it for some time Nina sprang up alive and well.

The rogues were more amazed than ever; they forgot their anger, and buying the pipe for two hundred gold pieces, they went joyfully home.

Not long after this one of them quarrelled with his wife, and in his rage he thrust his knife into her breast so that she fell dead on the ground. Then he took Simon's pipe and blew into it with all his might, in the hopes of calling his wife back to life. But he blew in vain, for the poor soul was as dead as a door-nail.

When one of his comrades heard what had happened, he said, 'You blockhead, you can't have done it properly; just let me have a try,' and with these words he seized his wife by the roots of her hair, cut her throat with a razor, and then took the pipe and blew into it with all his might but he couldn't bring her back to life. The same thing happened to the third rogue, so that they were now all three without wives.

Full of wrath they ran to Simon's house, and, refusing to listen to a word of explanation or excuse, they seized the old man and put him into a sack, meaning to drown him in the neighbouring river. On their way there, however, a sudden noise threw them into such a panic that they dropped the sack with Simon in it and ran for their lives.

Soon after this a shepherd happened to pass by with his flock, and while he was slowly following the sheep, who paused here and there by the wayside to browse on the tender grass, he heard a pitiful voice wailing, 'They insist on my taking her, and I don't want her, for I am too old, and I really can't have her.' The shepherd was much startled, for he couldn't make out where these words, which were repeated more than once, came from, and looked about him to the right and left; at last he perceived the sack in which Simon was hidden, and going up to it he opened it and discovered Simon repeating his dismal complaint. The shepherd asked him why he had been left there tied up in a sack.

Simon replied that the king of the country had insisted on giving him one of his daughters as a wife, but that he had refused the honour because he was too old and too frail. The simple-minded shepherd, who believed his story implicitly, asked him, 'Do you think the king of the country would give his daughter to me?'

'Yes, certainly, I know he would,' answered Simon, 'if you were tied up in this sack instead of me.' Then getting out of the sack, he tied the confiding shepherd up in it instead, and at his request fastened it securely and drove the sheep on himself.

An hour had scarcely passed when the three rogues returned to the place where they had left Simon in the sack, and without opening it, one of them seized it and threw it into the river. And so the poor shepherd was drowned instead of Mr. Simon!

The three rogues, having wreaked their vengeance, set out, for home. On their way they noticed a flock of sheep grazing not far from the road. They longed to steal a few of the lambs, and approached the flock, and were more than startled to recognise Mr. Simon, whom they had drowned in the river, as the shepherd who was looking after the sheep. They asked him how he had managed to get out of the river, to which he replied:

'Get along with you—you are no better than silly donkeys without any sense; if you had only drowned me in deeper water I would have returned with three times as many sheep.'

When the three rogues heard this, they said to him: 'Oh, dear Mr. Simon, do us the favour to tie us up in sacks and throw us into the river that we may give up our thieving ways and become the owners of flocks.'

'I am ready,' answered Simon, 'to do what you please; there's nothing in the world I wouldn't do for you.'

So he took three strong sacks and put a man in each of them, and fastened them up so tightly that they couldn't get out, and then he threw them all into the river; and that was the end of the three rogues. But Mr. Simon returned home to his faithful Nina rich in flocks and gold, and lived for many a year in health and happiness.

Kletke.

KING KOJATA (From the Russian)

There was once upon a time a king called Kojata, whose beard was so long that it reached below his knees. Three years had passed since his marriage, and he lived very happily with his wife, but Heaven granted him no heir, which grieved the King greatly. One day he set forth from his capital, in order to make a journey through his kingdom. He travelled for nearly a year through the different parts of his territory, and then, having seen all there was to be seen, he set forth on his homeward way. As the day was very hot and sultry he commanded his servants to pitch tents in the open field, and there await the cool of the evening. Suddenly a frightful thirst seized the King, and as he saw no water near, he mounted his horse, and rode through the neighbourhood looking for a spring. Before long he came to a well filled to the brim with water clear as crystal, and on the bosom of which a golden jug was floating. King Kojata at once tried to seize the vessel, but though he endeavoured to grasp it with his right hand, and then with his left, the wretched thing always eluded his efforts and refused to let itself be caught. First with one hand, and then with two, did the King try to seize it, but like a fish the goblet always slipped through his fingers and bobbed to the ground only to reappear at some other place, and mock the King.

'Plague on you!' said King Kojata. 'I can quench my thirst without you,' and bending over the well he lapped up the water so greedily that he plunged his face, beard and all, right into the crystal mirror. But when he had satisfied his thirst, and wished to raise himself up, he couldn't lift his head, because someone held his beard fast in the water. 'Who's there? let me go!' cried King Kojata, but there was no answer; only an awful face looked up from the bottom of the well with two great green eyes, glowing like emeralds, and a wide mouth reaching from ear to ear showing two rows of gleaming white teeth, and the King's beard was held, not by mortal hands, but by two claws. At last a hoarse voice sounded from the depths. 'Your trouble is all in vain, King Kojata; I will only let you go on condition that you give me something you know nothing about, and which you will find on your return home.'

The King didn't pause to ponder long, 'for what,' thought he, 'could be in my palace without my knowing about it—the thing is absurd;' so he answered quickly:

'Yes, I promise that you shall have it.'

The voice replied, 'Very well; but it will go ill with you if you fail to keep your promise.' Then the claws relaxed their hold, and the face disappeared in the depths. The King drew his chin out of the water, and shook himself like a dog; then he mounted his horse and rode thoughtfully home with his retinue. When they approached the capital, all the people came out to meet them with great joy and acclamation, and when the King reached his palace the Queen met him on the threshold; beside her stood the Prime Minister, holding a little cradle in his hands, in which lay a new-born child as beautiful as the day. Then the whole thing dawned on the King, and groaning deeply he muttered to himself 'So this is what I did not know about,' and the tears rolled down his cheeks. All the courtiers standing round were much amazed at the King's grief, but no one dared to ask him the cause of it. He took the child in his arms and kissed it tenderly; then laying it in its cradle, he determined to control his emotion and began to reign again as before.

The secret of the King remained a secret, though his grave, careworn expression escaped no one's notice. In the constant dread that his child would be taken from him, poor Kojata knew no rest night or day. However, time went on and nothing happened. Days and months and years passed, and the Prince grew up into a beautiful youth, and at last the King himself forgot all about the incident that had happened so long ago.

One day the Prince went out hunting, and going in pursuit of a wild boar he soon lost the other huntsmen, and found himself quite alone in the middle of a dark wood. The trees grew so thick and near together that it was almost impossible to see through them, only straight in front of him lay a little patch of meadowland. Overgrown with thistles and rank weeds, in the centre of which a leafy lime tree reared itself. Suddenly a rustling sound was heard in the hollow of the tree, and an extraordinary old man with green eyes and chin crept out of it.

'A fine day, Prince Milan,' he said; 'you've kept me waiting a good number of years; it was high time for you to come and pay me a visit.'

'Who are you, in the name of wonder?' demanded the astonished Prince.

'You'll find out soon enough, but in the meantime do as I bid you. Greet your father King Kojata from me, and don't forget to remind him of his debt;

the time has long passed since it was due, but now he will have to pay it. Farewell for the present; we shall meet again.'

With these words the old man disappeared into the tree, and the Prince returned home rather startled, and told his father all that he had seen and heard.

The King grew as white as a sheet when he heard the Prince's story, and said, 'Woe is me, my son! The time has come when we must part,' and with a heavy heart he told the Prince what had happened at the time of his birth.

'Don't worry or distress yourself, dear father,' answered Prince Milan. 'Things are never as bad as they look. Only give me a horse for my journey, and I wager you'll soon see me back again.'

The King gave him a beautiful charger, with golden stirrups, and a sword. The Queen hung a little cross round his neck, and after much weeping and lamentation the Prince bade them all farewell and set forth on his journey.

He rode straight on for two days, and on the third he came to a lake as smooth as glass and as clear as crystal. Not a breath of wind moved, not a leaf stirred, all was silent as the grave, only on the still bosom of the lake thirty ducks, with brilliant plumage, swam about in the water. Not far from the shore Prince Milan noticed thirty little white garments lying on the grass, and dismounting from his horse, he crept down under the high bulrushes, took one of the garments and hid himself with it behind the bushes which grew round the lake. The ducks swam about all over the place, dived down into the depths and rose again and glided through the waves. At last, tired of disporting themselves, they swam to the shore, and twenty-nine of them put on their little white garments and instantly turned into so many beautiful maidens. Then they finished dressing and disappeared. Only the thirtieth little duck couldn't come to the land; it swam about close to the shore, and, giving out a piercing cry, it stretched its neck up timidly, gazed wildly around, and then dived under again. Prince Milan's heart was so moved with pity for the poor little creature that he came out from behind the bulrushes, to see if he could be of any help. As soon as the duck perceived him, it cried in a human voice, 'Oh, dear Prince Milan, for the love of Heaven give me back my garment, and I will be so grateful to you.' The Prince lay the little garment on the bank beside her, and stepped back into the bushes. In a few seconds a beautiful girl in a white robe stood before him, so fair and sweet and young that no pen could describe her. She gave the Prince her hand and spoke.

'Many thanks, Prince Milan, for your courtesy. I am the daughter of a wicked magician, and my name is Hyacinthia. My father has thirty young daughters, and is a mighty ruler in the underworld, with many castles and great riches. He has been expecting you for ages, but you need have no fear if you will only follow my advice. As soon as you come into the presence of my father, throw yourself at once on the ground and approach him on your knees. Don't mind if he stamps furiously with his feet and curses and swears. I'll attend to the rest, and in the meantime we had better be off.'

With these words the beautiful Hyacinthia stamped on the ground with her little foot, and the earth opened and they both sank down into the lower world.

The palace of the Magician was all hewn out of a single carbuncle, lighting up the whole surrounding region, and Prince Milan walked into it gaily.

The Magician sat on a throne, a sparkling crown on his head; his eyes blazed like a green fire, and instead of hands he had claws. As soon as Prince Milan entered he flung himself on his knees. The Magician stamped loudly with his feet, glared frightfully out of his green eyes, and cursed so loudly that the whole underworld shook. But the Prince, mindful of the counsel he had been given, wasn't the least afraid, and approached the throne still on his knees. At last the Magician laughed aloud and said, 'You rogue, you have been well advised to make me laugh; I won't be your enemy any more. Welcome to the underworld! All the same, for your delay in coming here, we must demand three services from you. For to-day you may go, but to-morrow I shall have something more to say to you.'

Then two servants led Prince Milan to a beautiful apartment, and he lay down fearlessly on the soft bed that had been prepared for him, and was soon fast asleep.

Early the next morning the Magician sent for him, and said, 'Let's see now what you've learnt. In the first place you must build me a palace to-night, the roof of purest gold, the walls of marble, and the windows of crystal; all round you must lay out a beautiful garden, with fish-ponds and artistic waterfalls. If you do all this, I will reward you richly; but if you don't, you shall lose your head.'

'Oh, you wicked monster!' thought Prince Milan, 'you might as well have put me to death at once.' Sadly he returned to his room, and with bent head sat brooding over his cruel fate till evening. When it grew dark, a little bee flew by, and knocking at the window, it said, 'Open, and let me in.'

Milan opened the window quickly, and as soon as the bee had entered, it changed into the beautiful Hyacinthia.

'Good evening, Prince Milan. Why are you so sad?'

'How can I help being sad? Your father threatens me with death, and I see myself already without a head.'

'And what have you made up your mind to do?'

'There's nothing to be done, and after all I suppose one can only die once.'

'Now, don't be so foolish, my dear Prince; but keep up your spirits, for there is no need to despair. Go to bed, and when you wake up to-morrow morning the palace will be finished. Then you must go all round it, giving a tap here and there on the walls to look as if you had just finished it.'

And so it all turned out just as she had said. As soon as it was daylight Prince Milan stepped out of his room, and found a palace which was quite a work of art down to the very smallest detail. The Magician himself was not a little astonished at its beauty, and could hardly believe his eyes.

'Well, you certainly are a splendid workman,' he said to the Prince. 'I see you are very clever with your hands, now I must see if you are equally accomplished with your head. I have thirty daughters in my house, all beautiful princesses. To-morrow I will place the whole thirty in a row. You must walk past them three times, and the third time you must show me which is my youngest daughter Hyacinthia. If you don't guess rightly, you shall lose your head.'

'This time you've made a mistake,' thought Prince Milan, and going to his room he sat down at the window. Just fancy my not recognising the beautiful Hyacinthia! Why, that is the easiest thing in the world.'

'Not so easy as you think,' cried the little bee, who was flying past. 'If I weren't to help you, you'd never guess. We are thirty sisters so exactly alike that our own father can hardly distinguish us apart.'

'Then what am I to do?' asked Prince Milan.

'Listen,' answered Hyacinthia. 'You will recognise me by a tiny fly I shall have on my left cheek, but be careful for you might easily make a mistake.'

The next day the Magician again commanded Prince Milan to be led before him. His daughters were all arranged in a straight row in front of him, dressed exactly alike, and with their eyes bent on the ground.

'Now, you genius,' said the Magician, 'look at these beauties three times, and then tell us which is the Princess Hyacinthia.'

Prince Milan went past them and looked at them closely. But they were all so precisely alike that they looked like one face reflected in thirty mirrors, and the fly was nowhere to be seen; the second time he passed them he still saw nothing; but the third time he perceived a little fly stealing down one cheek, causing it to blush a faint pink. Then the Prince seized the girl's hand and cried out, 'This is the Princess Hyacinthia!'

'You're right again,' said the Magician in amazement; 'but I've still another task for you to do. Before this candle, which I shall light, burns to the socket, you must have made me a pair of boots reaching to my knees. If they aren't finished in that time, off comes your head.'

The Prince returned to his room in despair; then the Princess Hyacinthia came to him once more changed into the likeness of a bee, and asked him, 'Why so sad, Prince Milan?'

'How can I help being sad? Your father has set me this time an impossible task. Before a candle which he has lit burns to the socket, I am to make a pair of boots. But what does a prince know of shoemaking? If I can't do it, I lose my head.'

'And what do you mean to do?' asked Hyacinthia.

'Well, what is there to be done? What he demands I can't and won't do, so he must just make an end of me.'

'Not so, dearest. I love you dearly, and you shall marry me, and I'll either save your life or die with you. We must fly now as quickly as we can, for there is no other way of escape.'

With these words she breathed on the window, and her breath froze on the pane. Then she led Milan out of the room with her, shut the door, and threw the key away. Hand in hand, they hurried to the spot where they had descended into the lower world, and at last reached the banks of the lake. Prince Milan's charger was still grazing on the grass which grew near the water. The horse no sooner recognized his master, than it neighed loudly with joy, and springing towards him, it stood as if rooted to the ground, while Prince Milan and Hyacinthia jumped on its back. Then it sped onwards like an arrow from a bow.

In the meantime the Magician was waiting impatiently for the Prince. Enraged by the delay, he sent his servants to fetch him, for the appointed time was past.

The servants came to the door, and finding it locked, they knocked; but the frozen breath on the window replied in Prince Milan's voice, 'I am coming directly.' With this answer they returned to the Magician. But when the Prince still did not appear, after a time he sent his servants a second time to bring him. The frozen breath always gave the same answer, but the

Prince never came. At last the Magician lost all patience, and commanded the door to be burst open. But when his servants did so, they found the room empty, and the frozen breath laughed aloud. Out of his mind with rage, the Magician ordered the Prince to be pursued.

Then a wild chase began. 'I hear horses' hoofs behind us,' said Hyacinthia to the Prince. Milan sprang from the saddle, put his ear to the ground and listened. 'Yes,' he answered, 'they are pursuing us, and are quite close.' 'Then no time must be lost,' said Hyacinthia, and she immediately turned herself into a river, Prince Milan into an iron bridge, and the charger into a blackbird. Behind the bridge the road branched off into three ways.

The Magician's servants hurried after the fresh tracks, but when they came to the bridge, they stood, not knowing which road to take, as the footprints stopped suddenly, and there were three paths for them to choose from. In fear and trembling they returned to tell the Magician what had happened. He flew into a dreadful rage when he saw them, and screamed out, 'Oh, you fools! the river and bridge were they! Go back and bring them to me at once, or it will be the worse for you.'

Then the pursuit began afresh. 'I hear horses' hoofs,' sighed Hyacinthia. The Prince dismounted and put his ear to the ground. 'They are hurrying after us, and are already quite near.' In a moment the Princess Hyacinthia had changed herself, the Prince, and his charger into a thick wood where a thousand paths and roads crossed each other. Their pursuers entered the forest, but searched in vain for Prince Milan and his bride. At last they found themselves back at the same spot they had started from, and in despair they returned once more with empty hands to the Magician.

'Then I'll go after the wretches myself,' he shouted. 'Bring a horse at once; they shan't escape me.'

Once more the beautiful Hyacinthia murmured, 'I hear horses' hoofs quite near.' And the Prince answered, 'They are pursuing us hotly and are quite close.'

'We are lost now, for that is my father himself. But at the first church we come to his power ceases; he may chase us no further. Hand me your cross.'

Prince Milan loosened from his neck the little gold cross his mother had given him, and as soon as Hyacinthia grasped it, she had changed herself into a church, Milan into a monk, and the horse into a belfry. They had hardly done this when the magician and his servants rode up.

'Did you see no one pass by on horseback, reverend father?' he asked the monk.

'Prince Milan and Princess Hyacinthia have just gone on this minute; they stopped for a few minutes in the church to say their prayers, and bade me light this wax candle for you, and give you their love.'

'I'd like to wring their necks,' said the magician, and made all haste home, where he had every one of his servants beaten to within an inch of their lives.

Prince Milan rode on slowly with his bride without fearing any further pursuit. The sun was just setting, and its last rays lit up a large city they were approaching. Prince Milan was suddenly seized with an ardent desire to enter the town.

'Oh my beloved,' implored Hyacinthia, 'please don't go; for I am frightened and fear some evil.'

'What are you afraid of?' asked the Prince. 'We'll only go and look at what's to be seen in the town for about an hour, and then we'll continue our journey to my father's kingdom.'

'The town is easy to get into, but more difficult to get out of,' sighed Hyacinthia. 'But let it be as you wish. Go, and I will await you here, but I will first change myself into a white milestone; only I pray you be very careful. The King and Queen of the town will come out to meet you, leading a little child with them. Whatever you do, don't kiss the child, or you will forget me and all that has happened to us. I will wait for you here for three days.'

The Prince hurried to the town, but Hyacinthia remained behind disguised as a white milestone on the road. The first day passed, and then the second, and at last the third also, but Prince Milan did not return, for he had not taken Hyacinthia's advice. The King and Queen came out to meet him as she had said, leading with them a lovely fair-haired little girl, whose eyes shone like two clear stars. The child at once caressed the Prince, who, carried away by its beauty, bent down and kissed it on the cheek. From that moment his memory became a blank, and he forgot all about the beautiful Hyacinthia.

When the Prince did not return, poor Hyacinthia wept bitterly and changing herself from a milestone into a little blue field flower, she said, 'I will grow here on the wayside till some passer-by tramples me under foot.' And one of her tears remained as a dewdrop and sparkled on the little blue flower.

Now it happened shortly after this that an old man passed by, and seeing the flower, he was delighted with its beauty. He pulled it up carefully by the roots and carried it home. Here he planted it in a pot, and watered and tended the little plant carefully. And now the most extraordinary thing happened, for from this moment everything in the old man's house was changed. When he awoke in the morning he always found his room tidied and put into such beautiful order that not a speck of dust was to be found anywhere. When he came home at midday, he found a table laid out with the most dainty food, and he had only to sit down and enjoy himself to his heart's content. At first he was so surprised he didn't know what to think, but after a time he grew a little uncomfortable, and went to an old witch to ask for advice.

The witch said, 'Get up before the cock crows, and watch carefully till you see something move, and then throw this cloth quickly over it, and you'll see what will happen.'

All night the old man never closed an eye. When the first ray of light entered the room, he noticed that the little blue flower began to tremble, and at last it rose out of the pot and flew about the room, put everything in order, swept away the dust, and lit the fire. In great haste the old man sprang from his bed, and covered the flower with the cloth the old witch had given him, and in a moment the beautiful Princess Hyacinthia stood before him.

'What have you done?' she cried. 'Why have you called me back to life? For I have no desire to live since my bridegroom, the beautiful Prince Milan, has deserted me.'

'Prince Milan is just going to be married,' replied the old man. 'Everything is being got ready for the feast, and all the invited guests are flocking to the palace from all sides.'

The beautiful Hyacinthia cried bitterly when she heard this; then she dried her tears, and went into the town dressed as a peasant woman. She went straight to the King's kitchen, where the white-aproned cooks were running about in great confusion. The Princess went up to the head cook, and said, 'Dear cook, please listen to my request, and let me make a wedding-cake for Prince Milan.'

The busy cook was just going to refuse her demand and order her out of the kitchen, but the words died on his lips when he turned and beheld the beautiful Hyacinthia, and he answered politely, 'You have just come in the nick of time, fair maiden. Bake your cake, and I myself will lay it before Prince Milan.'

The cake was soon made. The invited guests were already thronging round the table, when the head cook entered the room, bearing a beautiful wedding cake on a silver dish, and laid it before Prince Milan. The guests were all lost in admiration, for the cake was quite a work of art. Prince Milan at once proceeded to cut it open, when to his surprise two white doves sprang out of it, and one of them said to the other: 'My dear mate, do not fly away and leave me, and forget me as Prince Milan forgot his beloved Hyacinthia.'

Milan sighed deeply when he heard what the little dove said. Then he jumped up suddenly from the table and ran to the door, where he found the beautiful Hyacinthia waiting for him. Outside stood his faithful charger, pawing the ground. Without pausing for a moment, Milan and Hyacinthia mounted him and galloped as fast as they could into the country of King Kojata. The King and Queen received them with such joy and gladness as had never been heard of before, and they all lived happily for the rest of their lives.

PRINCE FICKLE AND FAIR HELENA (From the German)

There was once upon a time a beautiful girl called Helena. Her own mother had died when she was quite a child, and her stepmother was as cruel and unkind to her as she could be. Helena did all she could to gain her love, and performed the heavy work given her to do cheerfully and well; but her stepmother's heart wasn't in the least touched, and the more the poor girl did the more she asked her to do.

One day she gave Helena twelve pounds of mixed feathers and bade her separate them all before evening, threatening her with heavy punishment if she failed to do so.

The poor child sat down to her task with her eyes so full of tears that she could hardly see to begin. And when she had made one little heap of feathers, she sighed so deeply that they all blew apart again. And so it went on, and the poor girl grew more and more miserable. She bowed her head in her hands and cried, 'Is there no one under heaven who will take pity on me?'

Suddenly a soft voice replied, 'Be comforted, my child: I have come to help you.'

Terrified to death, Helena looked up and saw a Fairy standing in front of her, who asked in the kindest way possible, 'Why are you crying, my dear?'

Helena, who for long had heard no friendly voice, confided her sad tale of woe to the Fairy, and told her what the new task she had been given to do was, and how she despaired of ever accomplishing it.

'Don't worry yourself about it any more,' said the kind Fairy; 'lie down and go to sleep, and I'll see that your work is done all right.' So Helena lay down, and when she awoke all the feathers were sorted into little bundles; but when she turned to thank the good Fairy she had vanished.

In the evening her stepmother returned and was much amazed to find Helena sitting quietly with her work all finished before her.

She praised her diligence, but at the same time racked her brain as to what harder task she could set her to do.

The next day she told Helena to empty a pond near the house with a spoon which was full of holes. Helena set to work at once, but she very soon found that what her stepmother had told her to do was an impossibility. Full of despair and misery, she was in the act of throwing the spoon away, when suddenly the kind Fairy stood before her again, and asked her why she was so unhappy?

When Helena told her of her stepmother's new demand she said, 'Trust to me and I will do your task for you. Lie down and have a sleep in the meantime.'

Helena was comforted and lay down, and before you would have believed it possible the Fairy roused her gently and told her the pond was empty. Full of joy and gratitude, Helena hurried to her stepmother, hoping that now at last her heart would be softened towards her. But the wicked woman was furious at the frustration of her own evil designs, and only thought of what harder thing she could set the girl to do.

Next morning she ordered her to build before evening a beautiful castle, and to furnish it all from garret to basement. Helena sat down on the rocks which had been pointed out to her as the site of the castle, feeling very depressed, but at the same time with the lurking hope that the kind Fairy would come once more to her aid.

And so it turned out. The Fairy appeared, promised to build the castle, and told Helena to lie down and go to sleep in the meantime. At the word of the Fairy the rocks and stones rose and built themselves into a beautiful castle, and before sunset it was all furnished inside, and left nothing to be desired. You may think how grateful Helena was when she awoke and found her task all finished.

But her stepmother was anything but pleased, and went through the whole castle from top to bottom, to see if she couldn't find some fault for which she could punish Helena. At last she went down into one of the cellars, but it was so dark that she fell down the steep stairs and was killed on the spot.

So Helena was now mistress of the beautiful castle, and lived there in peace and happiness. And soon the noise of her beauty spread abroad, and many wooers came to try and gain her hand.

Among them came one Prince Fickle by name, who very quickly won the love of fair Helena. One day, as they were sitting happily together under a lime-tree in front of the castle, Prince Fickle broke the sad news to Helena that he must return to his parents to get their consent to his marriage. He promised faithfully to come back to her as soon as he could and begged her to await his return under the lime-tree where they had spent so many happy hours.

Helena kissed him tenderly at parting on his left cheek, and begged him not to let anyone else kiss him there while they were parted, and she promised to sit and wait for him under the lime-tree, for she never doubted that the Prince would be faithful to her and would return as quickly as he could.

And so she sat for three days and three nights under the tree without moving. But when her lover never returned, she grew very unhappy, and determined to set out to look for him. She took as many of her jewels as she could carry, and three of her most beautiful dresses, one embroidered with stars, one with moons, and the third with suns, all of pure gold. Far and wide she wandered through the world, but nowhere did she find any trace of her bridegroom. At last she gave up the search in despair. She could not bear to return to her own castle where she had been so happy with her lover, but determined rather to endure her loneliness and desolation in a strange land. She took a place as herd-girl with a peasant, and buried her jewels and beautiful dresses in a safe and hidden spot.

Every day she drove the cattle to pasture, and all the time she thought of nothing but her faithless bridegroom. She was very devoted to a certain little calf in the herd, and made a great pet of it, feeding it out of her own hands. She taught it to kneel before her, and then she whispered in its ear:

'Kneel, little calf, kneel; Be faithful and leal, Not like Prince Fickle, Who once on a time Left his fair Helena Under the lime.'

After some years passed in this way, she heard that the daughter of the king of the country she was living in was going to marry a Prince called 'Fickle.' Everybody rejoiced at the news except poor Helena, to whom it was a fearful blow, for at the bottom of her heart she had always believed her lover to be true.

Now it chanced that the way to the capital led right past the village where Helena was, and often when she was leading her cattle forth to the meadows Prince Fickle rode past her, without ever noticing the poor herd-girl, so engrossed was he in thoughts of his new bride. Then it occurred to

Helena to put his heart to the test and to see if it weren't possible to recall herself to him. So one day as Prince Fickle rode by she said to her little calf:

'Kneel, little calf, kneel; Be faithful and leal, Not like Prince Fickle, Who once on a time Left his poor Helena Under the lime.'

When Prince Fickle heard her voice it seemed to him to remind him of something, but of what he couldn't remember, for he hadn't heard the words distinctly, as Helena had only spoken them very low and with a shaky voice. Helena herself had been far too moved to let her see what impression her words had made on the Prince, and when she looked round he was already far away. But she noticed how slowly he was riding, and how deeply sunk he was in thought, so she didn't quite give herself up as lost.

In honour of the approaching wedding a feast lasting many nights was to be given in the capital. Helena placed all her hopes on this, and determined to go to the feast and there to seek out her bridegroom.

When evening drew near she stole out of the peasant's cottage secretly, and, going to her hiding-place, she put on her dress embroidered with the gold suns, and all her jewels, and loosed her beautiful golden hair, which up to now she had always worn under a kerchief, and, adorned thus, she set out for the town.

When she entered the ball-room all eyes were turned on her, and everyone marvelled at her beauty, but no one knew who she was. Prince Fickle, too, was quite dazzled by the charms of the beautiful maiden, and never guessed that she had once been his own ladylove. He never left her side all night, and it was with great difficulty that Helena escaped from him in the crowd when it was time to return home. Prince Fickle searched for her everywhere, and longed eagerly for the next night, when the beautiful lady had promised to come again.

The following evening the fair Helena started early for the feast.

This time she wore her dress embroidered with silver moons, and in her hair she placed a silver crescent. Prince Fickle was enchanted to see her again, and she seemed to him even more beautiful than she had been the night before. He never left her side, and refused to dance with anyone else. He begged her to tell him who she was, but this she refused to do. Then he implored her to return again next evening, and this she promised him she would.

On the third evening Prince Fickle was so impatient to see his fair enchantress again, that he arrived at the feast hours before it began, and never took his eyes from the door. At last Helena arrived in a dress all covered with gold and silver stars, and with a girdle of stars round her waist, and a band of stars in her hair. Prince Fickle was more in love with her than ever, and begged her once again to tell him her name.

Then Helena kissed him silently on the left cheek, and in one moment Prince Fickle recognized his old love. Full of remorse and sorrow, he begged for her forgiveness, and Helena, only too pleased to have got him back again, did not, you may be sure, keep him waiting very long for her pardon, and so they were married and returned to Helena's castle, where they are no doubt still sitting happily together under the lime-tree.

PUDDOCKY (From the German)

There was once upon a time a poor woman who had one little daughter called 'Parsley.' She was so called because she liked eating parsley better than any other food, indeed she would hardly eat anything else. Her poor mother hadn't enough money always to be buying parsley for her, but the child was so beautiful that she could refuse her nothing, and so she went every night to the garden of an old witch who lived near and stole great branches of the coveted vegetable, in order to satisfy her daughter.

This remarkable taste of the fair Parsley soon became known, and the theft was discovered. The witch called the girl's mother to her, and proposed that she should let her daughter come and live with her, and then she could eat as much parsley as she liked. The mother was quite pleased with this suggestion, and so the beautiful Parsley took up her abode with the old witch.

One day three Princes, whom their father had sent abroad to travel, came to the town where Parsley lived and perceived the beautiful girl combing and plaiting her long black hair at the window. In one moment they all fell hopelessly in love with her, and longed ardently to have the girl for their wife; but hardly had they with one breath expressed their desire than, mad with jealousy, they drew their swords and all three set upon each other. The struggle was so violent and the noise so loud that the old witch heard it, and said at once 'Of course Parsley is at the bottom of all this.'

And when she had convinced herself that this was so, she stepped forward, and, full of wrath over the quarrels and feuds Parsley's beauty gave rise to, she cursed the girl and said, 'I wish you were an ugly toad, sitting under a bridge at the other end of the world.'

Hardly were the words out of her mouth than Parsley was changed into a toad and vanished from their sight. The Princes, now that the cause of their dispute was removed, put up their swords, kissed each other affectionately, and returned to their father.

The King was growing old and feeble, and wished to yield his sceptre and crown in favour of one of his sons, but he couldn't make up his mind which of the three he should appoint as his successor. He determined that fate should decide for him. So he called his three children to him and said,

'My dear sons, I am growing old, and am weary of reigning, but I can't make up my mind to which of you three I should yield my crown, for I love you all equally. At the same time I would like the best and cleverest of you to rule over my people. I have, therefore, determined to set you three tasks to do, and the one that performs them best shall be my heir. The first thing I shall ask you to do is to bring me a piece of linen a hundred yards long, so fine that it will go through a gold ring.' The sons bowed low, and, promising to do their best, they started on their journey without further delay.

The two elder brothers took many servants and carriages with them, but the youngest set out quite alone. In a short time they came to three cross roads; two of them were gay and crowded, but the third was dark and lonely.

The two elder brothers chose the more frequented ways, but the youngest, bidding them farewell, set out on the dreary road.

Wherever linen was to be bought, there the two elder brothers hastened. They loaded their carriages with bales of the finest linen they could find and then returned home.

The youngest brother, on the other hand, went on his weary way for many days, and nowhere did he come across any linen that would have done. So he journeyed on, and his spirits sank with every step. At last he came to a bridge which stretched over a deep river flowing through a flat and marshy land. Before crossing the bridge he sat down on the banks of the stream and sighed dismally over his sad fate. Suddenly a misshapen toad crawled out of the swamp, and, sitting down opposite him, asked: 'What's the matter with you, my dear Prince?'

The Prince answered impatiently, 'There's not much good my telling you, Puddocky, for you couldn't help me if I did.'

'Don't be too sure of that,' replied the toad; 'tell me your trouble and we'll see.'

Then the Prince became most confidential and told the little creature why he had been sent out of his father's kingdom.

'Prince, I will certainly help you,' said the toad, and, crawling back into her swamp, she returned dragging after her a piece of linen not bigger than a finger, which she lay before the Prince, saying, 'Take this home, and you'll see it will help you.'

The Prince had no wish to take such an insignificant bundle with him; but he didn't like to hurt Puddocky's feelings by refusing it, so he took up the little packet, put it in his pocket, and bade the little toad farewell.

Puddocky watched the Prince till he was out of sight and then crept back into the water.

The further the Prince went the more he noticed that the pocket in which the little roll of linen lay became heavier, and in proportion his heart grew lighter. And so, greatly comforted, he returned to the Court of his father, and arrived home just at the same time as his brothers with their caravans. The King was delighted to see them all again, and at once drew the ring from his finger and the trial began. In all the waggon-loads there was not one piece of linen the tenth part of which would go through the ring, and the two elder brothers, who had at first sneered at their youngest brother for returning with no baggage, began to feel rather small. But what were their feelings when he drew a bale of linen out of his pocket which in fineness, softness, and purity of colour was unsurpassable! The threads were hardly visible, and it went through the ring without the smallest difficulty, at the same time measuring a hundred yards quite correctly.

The father embraced his fortunate son, and commanded the rest of the linen to be thrown into the water; then, turning to his children he said, 'Now, dear Princes, prepare yourselves for the second task. You must bring me back a little dog that will go comfortably into a walnut-shell.'

The sons were all in despair over this demand, but as they each wished to win the crown, they determined to do their best, and after a very few days set out on their travels again.

At the cross roads they separated once more. The youngest went by himself along his lonely way, but this time he felt much more cheerful. Hardly had he sat down under the bridge and heaved a sigh, than Puddocky came out; and, sitting down opposite him, asked, 'What's wrong with you now, dear Prince?'

The Prince, who this time never doubted the little toad's power to help him, told her his difficulty at once. 'Prince, I will help you,' said the toad again, and crawled back into her swamp as fast as her short little legs would carry her. She returned, dragging a hazel nut behind her, which she laid at the Prince's feet and said, 'Take this nut home with you and tell your father to crack it very carefully, and you'll see then what will happen.' The Prince thanked her heartily and went on his way in the best of spirits, while the little puddock crept slowly back into the water.

When the Prince got home he found his brothers had just arrived with great waggon-loads of little dogs of all sorts. The King had a walnut shell ready, and the trial began; but not one of the dogs the two eldest sons had brought with them would in the least fit into the shell. When they had tried all their little dogs, the youngest son handed his father the hazel-nut, with a modest bow, and begged him to crack it carefully. Hardly had the old King done so than a lovely tiny dog sprang out of the nutshell, and ran about on the King's hand, wagging its tail and barking lustily at all the other little dogs. The joy of the Court was great. The father again embraced his fortunate son, commanded the rest of the small dogs to be thrown into the water and drowned, and once more addressed his sons. 'The two most difficult tasks have been performed. Now listen to the third and last: whoever brings the fairest wife home with him shall be my heir.'

This demand seemed so easy and agreeable and the reward was so great, that the Princes lost no time in setting forth on their travels. At the cross roads the two elder brothers debated if they should go the same way as the youngest, but when they saw how dreary and deserted it looked they made up their minds that it would be impossible to find what they sought in these wilds, and so they stuck to their former paths.

The youngest was very depressed this time and said to himself, 'Anything else Puddocky could have helped me in, but this task is quite beyond her power. How could she ever find a beautiful wife for me? Her swamps are wide and empty, and no human beings dwell there; only frogs and toads and other creatures of that sort.' However, he sat down as usual under the bridge, and this time he sighed from the bottom of his heart.

In a few minutes the toad stood in front of him and asked, 'What's the matter with you now, my dear Prince?'

'Oh, Puddocky, this time you can't help me, for the task is beyond even your power,' replied the Prince.

'Still,' answered the toad, 'you may as well tell me your difficulty, for who knows but I mayn't be able to help you this time also.'

The Prince then told her the task they had been set to do. 'I'll help you right enough, my dear Prince,' said the little toad; 'just you go home, and I'll soon follow you.' With these words, Puddocky, with a spring quite unlike her usual slow movements, jumped into the water and disappeared.

The Prince rose up and went sadly on his way, for he didn't believe it possible that the little toad could really help him in his present difficulty. He had hardly gone a few steps when he heard a sound behind him, and, looking round, he saw a carriage made of cardboard, drawn by six big rats, coming towards him. Two hedgehogs rode in front as outriders, and on the box sat a fat mouse as coachman, and behind stood two little frogs as footmen. In the carriage itself sat Puddocky, who kissed her hand to the Prince out of the window as she passed by.

Sunk deep in thought over the fickleness of fortune that had granted him two of his wishes and now seemed about to deny him the last and best, the Prince hardly noticed the absurd equipage, and still less did he feel inclined to laugh at its comic appearance.

The carriage drove on in front of him for some time and then turned a corner. But what was his joy and surprise when suddenly, round the same corner, but coming towards him, there appeared a beautiful coach drawn by six splendid horses, with outriders, coachmen, footmen and other servants all in the most gorgeous liveries, and seated in the carriage was the most beautiful woman the Prince had ever seen, and in whom he at once recognised the beautiful Parsley, for whom his heart had formerly burned. The carriage stopped when it reached him, and the footmen sprang down and opened the door for him. He got in and sat down beside the beautiful Parsley, and thanked her heartily for her help, and told her how much he loved her.

And so he arrived at his father's capital, at the same moment as his brothers who had returned with many carriage-loads of beautiful women. But when they were all led before the King, the whole Court with one consent awarded the prize of beauty to the fair Parsley.

The old King was delighted, and embraced his thrice fortunate son and his new daughter-in-law tenderly, and appointed them as his successors to the throne. But he commanded the other women to be thrown into the water and drowned, like the bales of linen and the little dogs. The Prince married Puddocky and reigned long and happily with her, and if they aren't dead I suppose they are living still.

THE STORY OF HOK LEE AND THE DWARFS

There once lived in a small town in China a man named Hok Lee. He was a steady industrious man, who not only worked hard at his trade, but did all his own house-work as well, for he had no wife to do it for him. 'What an excellent industrious man is this Hok Lee!' said his neighbours; 'how hard he works: he never leaves his house to amuse himself or to take a holiday as others do!'

But Hok Lee was by no means the virtuous person his neighbours thought him. True, he worked hard enough by day, but at night, when all respectable folk were fast asleep, he used to steal out and join a dangerous band of robbers, who broke into rich people's houses and carried off all they could lay hands on.

This state of things went on for some time, and, though a thief was caught now and then and punished, no suspicion ever fell on Hok Lee, he was such a very respectable, hard-working man.

Hok Lee had already amassed a good store of money as his share of the proceeds of these robberies when it happened one morning on going to market that a neighbour said to him:

'Why, Hok Lee, what is the matter with your face? One side of it is all swelled up.'

True enough, Hok Lee's right cheek was twice the size of his left, and it soon began to feel very uncomfortable.

'I will bind up my face,' said Hok Lee; 'doubtless the warmth will cure the swelling.' But no such thing. Next day it was worse, and day by day it grew bigger and bigger till it was nearly as large as his head and became very painful.

Hok Lee was at his wits' ends what to do. Not only was his cheek unsightly and painful, but his neighbours began to jeer and make fun of him, which hurt his feelings very much indeed.

One day, as luck would have it, a travelling doctor came to the town. He sold not only all kinds of medicine, but also dealt in many strange charms against witches and evil spirits.

Hok Lee determined to consult him, and asked him into his house.

After the doctor had examined him carefully, he spoke thus: 'This, O Hok Lee, is no ordinary swelled face. I strongly suspect you have been doing some wrong deed which has called down the anger of the spirits on you. None of my drugs will avail to cure you, but, if you are willing to pay me handsomely, I can tell you how you may be cured.'

Then Hok Lee and the doctor began to bargain together, and it was a long time before they could come to terms. However, the doctor got the better of it in the end, for he was determined not to part with his secret under a certain price, and Hok Lee had no mind to carry his huge cheek about with him to the end of his days. So he was obliged to part with the greater portion of his ill-gotten gains.

When the Doctor had pocketed the money, he told Hok Lee to go on the first night of the full moon to a certain wood and there to watch by a particular tree. After a time he would see the dwarfs and little sprites who live underground come out to dance. When they saw him they would be sure to make him dance too. 'And mind you dance your very best,' added the doctor. 'If you dance well and please them they will grant you a petition and you can then beg to be cured; but if you dance badly they will most likely do you some mischief out of spite.' With that he took leave and departed.

Happily the first night of the full moon was near, and at the proper time Hok Lee set out for the wood. With a little trouble he found the tree the doctor had described, and, feeling nervous, he climbed up into it.

He had hardly settled himself on a branch when he saw the little dwarfs assembling in the moonlight. They came from all sides, till at length there appeared to be hundreds of them. They seemed in high glee, and danced and skipped and capered about, whilst Hok Lee grew so eager watching them that he crept further and further along his branch till at length it gave a loud crack. All the dwarfs stood still, and Hok Lee felt as if his heart stood still also.

Then one of the dwarfs called out, 'Someone is up in that tree. Come down at once, whoever you are, or we must come and fetch you.'

In great terror, Hok Lee proceeded to come down; but he was so nervous that he tripped near the ground and came rolling down in the most absurd manner. When he had picked himself up, he came forward with a low bow, and the dwarf who had first spoken and who appeared to be the leader, said, 'Now, then, who art thou, and what brings thee here?'

So Hok Lee told him the sad story of his swelled cheek, and how he had been advised to come to the forest and beg the dwarfs to cure him.

'It is well,' replied the dwarf. 'We will see about that. First, however, thou must dance before us. Should thy dancing please us, perhaps we may be able to do something; but shouldst thou dance badly, we shall assuredly punish thee, so now take warning and dance away.'

With that, he and all the other dwarfs sat down in a large ring, leaving Hok Lee to dance alone in the middle. He felt half frightened to death, and besides was a good deal shaken by his fall from the tree and did not feel at all inclined to dance. But the dwarfs were not to be trifled with.

'Begin!' cried their leader, and 'Begin!' shouted the rest in chorus.

So in despair Hok Lee began. First he hopped on one foot and then on the other, but he was so stiff and so nervous that he made but a poor attempt, and after a time sank down on the ground and vowed he could dance no more.

The dwarfs were very angry. They crowded round Hok Lee and abused him. 'Thou to come here to be cured, indeed!' they cried, 'thou hast brought one big cheek with thee, but thou shalt take away two.' And with that they ran off and disappeared, leaving Hok Lee to find his way home as best he might.

He hobbled away, weary and depressed, and not a little anxious on account of the dwarfs' threat.

Nor were his fears unfounded, for when he rose next morning his left cheek was swelled up as big as his right, and he could hardly see out of his eyes. Hok Lee felt in despair, and his neighbours jeered at him more than ever. The doctor, too, had disappeared, so there was nothing for it but to try the dwarfs once more.

He waited a month till the first night of the full moon came round again, and then he trudged back to the forest, and sat down under the tree from which he had fallen. He had not long to wait. Ere long the dwarfs came trooping out till all were assembled.

'I don't feel quite easy,' said one; 'I feel as if some horrid human being were near us.'

When Hok Lee heard this he came forward and bent down to the ground before the dwarfs, who came crowding round, and laughed heartily at his comical appearance with his two big cheeks.

'What dost thou want?' they asked; and Hok Lee proceeded to tell them of his fresh misfortunes, and begged so hard to be allowed one more trial at dancing that the dwarfs consented, for there is nothing they love so much as being amused.

Now, Hok Lee knew how much depended on his dancing well, so he plucked up a good spirit and began, first quite slowly, and faster by degrees, and he danced so well and gracefully, and made such new and wonderful steps, that the dwarfs were quite delighted with him.

They clapped their tiny hands, and shouted, 'Well done, Hok Lee, well done, go on, dance more, for we are pleased.'

And Hok Lee danced on and on, till he really could dance no more, and was obliged to stop.

Then the leader of the dwarfs said, 'We are well pleased, Hok Lee, and as a recompense for thy dancing thy face shall be cured. Farewell.'

With these words he and the other dwarfs vanished, and Hok Lee, putting his hands to his face, found to his great joy that his cheeks were reduced to their natural size. The way home seemed short and easy to him, and he went to bed happy, and resolved never to go out robbing again.

Next day the whole town was full of the news of Hok's sudden cure. His neighbours questioned him, but could get nothing from him, except the fact that he had discovered a wonderful cure for all kinds of diseases.

After a time a rich neighbour, who had been ill for some years, came, and offered to give Hok Lee a large sum of money if he would tell him how he might get cured. Hok Lee consented on condition that he swore to keep the secret. He did so, and Hok Lee told him of the dwarfs and their dances.

The neighbour went off, carefully obeyed Hok Lee's directions, and was duly cured by the dwarfs. Then another and another came to Hok Lee to beg his secret, and from each he extracted a vow of secrecy and a large sum of money. This went on for some years, so that at length Hok Lee became a very wealthy man, and ended his days in peace and prosperity.

From the Chinese.

THE STORY OF THE THREE BEARS

Once upon a time there were Three Bears, who lived together in a house of their own in a wood. One of them was a Little, Small, Wee Bear; and one was a Middle-sized Bear, and the other was a Great, Huge Bear. They had each a pot for their porridge, a little pot for the Little, Small, Wee Bear; and a middle-sized pot for the Middle Bear; and a great pot for the Great, Huge Bear. And they had each a chair to sit in; a little chair for the Little, Small, Wee Bear; and a middle-sized chair for the Middle Bear; and a great chair for the Great, Huge Bear. And they had each a bed to sleep in; a little bed for the Little, Small, Wee Bear; and a middle-sized bed for the Middle Bear; and a great bed for the Great, Huge Bear.

One day, after they had made the porridge for their breakfast, and poured it into their porridge-pots, they walked out into the wood while the porridge was cooling, that they might not burn their mouths by beginning too soon to eat it. And while they were walking, a little old woman came to the house. She could not have been a good, honest old woman; for, first, she looked in at the window, and then she peeped in at the keyhole; and, seeing nobody in the house, she lifted the latch. The door was not fastened, because the bears were good bears, who did nobody any harm, and never suspected that anybody would harm them. So the little old woman opened the door and went in; and well pleased she was when she saw the porridge on the table. If she had been a good little old woman she would have waited till the bears came home, and then, perhaps, they would have asked her to breakfast; for they were good bears—a little rough or so, as the manner of bears is, but for all that very good-natured and hospitable. But she was an impudent, bad old woman, and set about helping herself.

So first she tasted the porridge of the Great, Huge Bear, and that was too hot for her; and she said a bad word about that. And then she tasted the porridge of the Middle Bear; and that was too cold for her; and she said a bad word about that too. And then she went to the porridge of the Little, Small, Wee Bear, and tasted that; and that was neither too hot nor too cold, but just right; and she liked it so well, that she ate it all up: but the naughty old woman said a bad word about the little porridge-pot, because it did not hold enough for her.

Then the little old woman sate down in the chair of the Great, Huge Bear, and that was too hard for her. And then she sate down in the chair of the Middle Bear, and that was too soft for her. And then she sate down in the chair of the Little, Small, Wee Bear, and that was neither too hard nor too soft, but just right. So she seated herself in it, and there she sate till the bottom of the chair came out, and down came she, plump upon the ground. And the naughty old woman said a wicked word about that too.

Then the little old woman went up stairs into the bed-chamber in which the three bears slept. And first she lay down upon the bed of the Great, Huge Bear; but that was too high at the head for her. And next she lay down upon the bed of the Middle Bear; and that was too high at the foot for her. And then she lay down upon the bed of the Little, Small, Wee Bear; and that was neither too high at the head, nor at the foot, but just right. So she covered herself up comfortably, and lay there till she fell fast asleep.

By this time the three bears thought their porridge would be cool enough; so they came home to breakfast. Now the little old woman had left the spoon of the Great, Huge Bear, standing in his porridge.

'SOMEBODY HAS BEEN AT MY PORRIDGE!'

said the Great, Huge Bear, in his great gruff voice. And when the Middle Bear looked at his, he saw that the spoon was standing in it too. They were wooden spoons; if they had been silver ones, the naughty old woman would have put them in her pocket.

'Somebody Has Been At My Porridge!'

said the Middle Bear, in his middle voice.

Then the Little, Small, Wee Bear looked at his, and there was the spoon in the porridge-pot, but the porridge was all gone.

'*Somebody has been at my porridge, and has eaten it all up*!'

said the Little, Small Wee Bear, in his little, small wee voice.

Upon this the three bears, seeing that some one had entered their house, and eaten up the Little, Small, Wee Bear's breakfast, began to look about them. Now the little old woman had not put the hard cushion straight when she rose from the chair of the Great, Huge Bear.

'SOMEBODY HAS BEEN SITTING IN MY CHAIR!'

said the Great, Huge Bear, in his great, rough, gruff voice.

And the little old woman had squatted down the soft cushion of the Middle Bear.

'Somebody Has Been Sitting In My Chair!'

said the Middle Bear, in his middle voice.

And you know what the little old woman had done to the third chair.

'*Somebody has been sitting in my chair, and has sate the bottom of it out!*' said the Little, Small, Wee Bear, in his little, small, wee voice.

Then the three bears thought it necessary that they should make farther search; so they went up stairs into their bed-chamber. Now the little old woman had pulled the pillow of the Great, Huge Bear out of its place.

'SOMEBODY HAS BEEN LYING IN MY BED!'

said the Great, Huge Bear, in his great, rough, gruff voice.

And the little old woman had pulled the bolster of the Middle Bear out of its place.

'Somebody Has Been Lying In My Bed!'

said the Middle Bear in his middle voice.

And when the Little, Small, Wee Bear came to look at his bed, there was the bolster in its place, and the pillow in its place upon the bolster, and upon the pillow was the little old woman's ugly, dirty head,—which was not in its place, for she had no business there.

'*Somebody has been lying in my bed,—and here she is!*'

said the Little, Small, Wee Bear, in his little, small, wee voice.

The little old woman had heard in her sleep the great, rough, gruff voice of the Great, Huge Bear; but she was so fast asleep that it was no more to her than the roaring of wind or the rumbling of thunder. And she had heard the middle voice of the Middle Bear, but it was only as if she had heard someone speaking in a dream. But when she heard the little, small, wee voice of the Little, Small, Wee Bear, it was so sharp, and so shrill, that it awakened her at once. Up she started; and when she saw the Three Bears on one side of the bed, she tumbled herself out at the other, and ran to the window. Now the window was open, because the bears, like good, tidy bears as they were, always opened their bedchamber window when they got up in the morning. Out the little old woman jumped; and whether she broke her neck in the fall, or ran into the wood and was lost there, or found her way out of the wood and was taken up by the constable and sent to the House of Correction for a vagrant as she was, I cannot tell. But the Three Bears never saw anything more of her.

Southey.

PRINCE VIVIEN AND THE PRINCESS PLACIDA

Once upon a time there lived a King and Queen who loved one another dearly. Indeed the Queen, whose name was Santorina, was so pretty and so kind-hearted that it would have been a wonder if her husband had not been fond of her, while King Gridelin himself was a perfect bundle of good qualities, for the Fairy who presided at his christening had summoned the shades of all his ancestors, and taken something good from each of them to form his character. Unfortunately, though, she had given him rather too much kindness of heart, which is a thing that generally gets its possessor into trouble, but so far all things had prospered with King Gridelin. However, it was not to be expected such good fortune could last, and before very long the Queen had a lovely little daughter who was named Placida. Now the King, who thought that if she resembled her mother in face and mind she would need no other gift, never troubled to ask any of the Fairies to her christening, and this offended them mortally, so that they resolved to punish him severely for thus depriving them of their rights. So, to the despair of King Gridelin, the Queen first of all became very ill, and then disappeared altogether. If it had not been for the little Princess there is no saying what would have become of him, he was so miserable, but there she was to be brought up, and luckily the good Fairy Lolotte, in spite of all that had passed, was willing to come and take charge of her, and of her little cousin Prince Vivien, who was an orphan and had been placed under the care of his uncle, King Gridelin, when he was quite a baby. Although she neglected nothing that could possibly have been done for them, their characters, as they grew up, plainly proved that education only softens down natural defects, but cannot entirely do away with them; for Placida, who was perfectly lovely, and with a capacity and intelligence which enabled her to learn and understand anything that presented itself, was at the same time as lazy and indifferent as it is possible for anyone to be, while Vivien on the contrary was only too lively, and was for ever taking up some new thing and as promptly tiring of it, and flying off to something else which held his fickle fancy an equally short time. As these two children would possibly inherit the kingdom, it was natural that their people should take a great interest in them, and it fell out that all the tranquil and peace-loving citizens desired that Placida should one day be their Queen, while the rash and quarrelsome hoped great things for Vivien. Such a division of ideas seemed to promise civil wars and all kinds of troubles to the State, and even in the Palace the two parties frequently came into collision. As for the children themselves, though they were too well brought up to quarrel, still the difference in all their tastes and feelings made it impossible for them to like one another, so there seemed no chance of their ever consenting to be married, which was a pity, since that was the only thing that would have satisfied both parties. Prince Vivien was fully aware of the feeling in his favour, but being too honourable to wish to injure his pretty cousin, and perhaps too impatient and volatile to care to think seriously about anything, he suddenly took it into his head that he would go off by himself in search of adventure. Luckily this idea occurred to him when he was on horseback, for he would certainly have set out on foot rather than lose an instant. As it was, he simply turned his horse's head, without another thought than that of getting out of the kingdom as soon as possible. This abrupt departure was a great blow to the State, especially as no one had any idea what had become of the Prince. Even King Gridelin, who had never cared for anything since the disappearance of Queen Santorina, was roused by this new loss, and though he could not so much as look at the Princess Placida without shedding floods of tears, he resolved to see for himself what talents and capabilities she showed. He very soon found out that in addition to her natural indolence, she was being as much indulged and spoilt day by day as if the Fairy had been her grandmother, and was obliged to remonstrate very seriously upon the subject. Lolotte took his reproaches meekly, and promised faithfully that she would not encourage the Princess in her idleness and indifference any more. From this moment poor Placida's troubles began! She was actually expected to choose her own dresses, to take care of her jewels, and to find her own amusements; but rather than take so much trouble she wore the same old frock from morning till night, and never appeared in public if she could possibly avoid it. However, this was not all, King Gridelin insisted that the affairs of the kingdom should be explained to her, and that she should attend all the councils and give her opinion upon the matter in hand whenever it was asked of her, and this made her life such a burden to her that she implored Lolotte to take her away from a country where too much was required of an unhappy Princess.

  The Fairy refused at first with a great show of firmness, but who could resist the tears and entreaties of anyone so pretty as Placida? It came to this in the end, that she transported the Princess just as she was, cosily tucked up upon her favourite couch, to her own Grotto, and this new disappearance left all the people in despair, and Gridelin went about looking more distracted than ever. But now let us return to Prince Vivien, and see what his restless spirit has brought him to. Though Placida's kingdom was a large one; his horse had carried him gallantly to the limit of it, but it could go no further, and the Prince was obliged to dismount and continue his journey on foot, though this slow mode of progress tired his patience severely.

After what seemed to him a very long time, he found himself all alone in a vast forest, so dark and gloomy that he secretly shuddered; however, he chose the most promising looking path he could find, and marched along it courageously at his best speed, but in spite of all his efforts, night fell before he reached the edge of the wood.

For some time he stumbled along, keeping to the path as well as he could in the darkness, and just as he was almost wearied out he saw before him a gleam of light.

This sight revived his drooping spirits, and he made sure that he was now close to the shelter and supper he needed so much, but the more he walked towards the light the further away it seemed; sometimes he even lost sight of it altogether, and you may imagine how provoked and impatient he was by the time he finally arrived at the miserable cottage from which the light proceeded. He gave a loud knock at the door, and an old woman's voice answered from within, but as she did not seem to be hurrying herself to open it he redoubled his blows, and demanded to be let in imperiously, quite forgetting that he was no longer in his own kingdom. But all this had no effect upon the old woman, who only noticed all the uproar he was making by saying gently:

'You must have patience.'

He could hear that she really was coming to open the door to him, only she was so very long about it. First she chased away her cat, lest it should run away when the door was opened, then he heard her talking to herself and made out that her lamp wanted trimming, that she might see better who it was that knocked, and then that it lacked fresh oil, and she must refill it. So what with one thing and another she was an immense time trotting to and fro, and all the while she now and again bade the Prince have patience. When at last he stood within the little hut he saw with despair that it was a picture of poverty, and that not a crumb of anything eatable was to be seen, and when he explained to the old woman that he was dying of hunger and fatigue she only answered tranquilly that he must have patience. However, she presently showed him a bundle of straw on which he could sleep.

'But what can I have to eat?' cried Prince Vivien sharply.

'Wait a little, wait a little,' she replied. 'If you will only have patience I am just going out into the garden to gather some peas: we will shell them at our leisure, then I will light a fire and cook them, and when they are thoroughly done, we can enjoy them peaceably; there is no hurry.'

'I shall have died of starvation by the time all that is done,' said the Prince ruefully.

'Patience, patience,' said the old woman looking at him with her slow gentle smile, 'I can't be hurried. "All things come at last to him who waits;" you must have heard that often.'

Prince Vivien was wild with aggravation, but there was nothing to be done.

'Come then,' said the old woman, 'you shall hold the lamp to light me while I pick the peas.'

The Prince in his haste snatched it up so quickly that it went out, and it took him a long time to light it again with two little bits of glowing charcoal which he had to dig out from the pile of ashes upon the hearth. However, at last the peas were gathered and shelled, and the fire lighted, but then they had to be carefully counted, since the old woman declared that she would cook fifty-four, and no more. In vain did the Prince represent to her that he was famished—that fifty-four peas would go no way towards satisfying his hunger—that a few peas, more or less, surely could not matter. It was quite useless, in the end he had to count out the fifty-four, and worse than that, because he dropped one or two in his hurry, he had to begin again from the very first, to be sure the number was complete. As soon as they were cooked the old dame took a pair of scales and a morsel of bread from the cupboard, and was just about to divide it when Prince Vivien, who really could wait no longer, seized the whole piece and ate it up, saying in his turn, 'Patience.'

'You mean that for a joke,' said the old woman, as gently as ever, 'but that is really my name, and some day you will know more about me.'

Then they each ate their twenty-seven peas, and the Prince was surprised to find that he wanted nothing more, and he slept as sweetly upon his bed of straw as he had ever done in his palace.

In the morning the old woman gave him milk and bread for his breakfast, which he ate contentedly, rejoicing that there was nothing to be gathered, or counted, or cooked, and when he had finished he begged her to tell him who she was.

'That I will, with pleasure,' she replied. 'But it will be a long story.'

'Oh! if it's long, I can't listen,' cried the Prince.

'But,' said she, 'at your age, you should attend to what old people say, and learn to have patience.'

'But, but,' said the Prince, in his most impatient tone, 'old people should not be so long-winded! Tell me what country I have got into, and nothing else.'

'With all my heart,' said she. 'You are in the Forest of the Black Bird; it is here that he utters his oracles.'

'An Oracle,' cried the Prince. 'Oh! I must go and consult him.' Thereupon he drew a handful of gold from his pocket, and offered it to the old woman, and when she would not take it, he threw it down upon the table and was off like a flash of lightning, without even staying to ask the way. He took the first path that presented itself and followed it at the top of his speed, often losing his way, or stumbling over some stone, or running up against a tree, and leaving behind him without regret the cottage which had been as little to his taste as the character of its possessor. After some time he saw in the distance a huge black castle which commanded a view of the whole forest. The Prince felt certain that this must be the abode of the Oracle, and just as the sun was setting he reached its outermost gates. The whole castle was surrounded by a deep moat, and the drawbridge and the gates, and even the water in the moat, were all of the same sombre hue as the walls and towers. Upon the gate hung a huge bell, upon which was written in red letters:

'Mortal, if thou art curious to know thy fate, strike this bell, and submit to what shall befall thee.'

The Prince, without the smallest hesitation, snatched up a great stone, and hammered vigorously upon the bell, which gave forth a deep and terrible sound, the gate flew open, and closed again with a thundering clang the moment the Prince had passed through it, while from every tower and battlement rose a wheeling, screaming crowd of bats which darkened the whole sky with their multitudes. Anyone but Prince Vivien would have been terrified by such an uncanny sight, but he strode stoutly forward till he reached the second gate, which was opened to him by sixty black slaves covered from head to foot in long mantles.

He wished to speak to them, but soon discovered that they spoke an utterly unknown language, and did not seem to understand a word he said. This was a great aggravation to the Prince, who was not accustomed to keep his ideas to himself, and he positively found himself wishing for his old friend Patience. However, he had to follow his guides in silence, and they led him into a magnificent hall; the floor was of ebony, the walls of jet, and all the hangings were of black velvet, but the Prince looked round it in vain for something to eat, and then made signs that he was hungry. In the same manner he was respectfully given to understand that he must wait, and after several hours the sixty hooded and shrouded figures re-appeared, and conducted him with great ceremony, and also very very slowly, to a banqueting hall, where they all placed themselves at a long table. The dishes were arranged down the centre of it, and with his usual impetuosity the Prince seized the one that stood in front of him to draw it nearer, but soon found that it was firmly fixed in its place. Then he looked at his solemn and lugubrious neighbours, and saw that each one was supplied with a long hollow reed through which he slowly sucked up his portion, and the Prince was obliged to do the same, though he found it a frightfully tedious process. After supper, they returned as they had come to the ebony room, where he was compelled to look on while his companions played interminable games of chess, and not until he was nearly dying of weariness did they, slowly and ceremoniously as before, conduct him to his sleeping apartment. The hope of consulting the Oracle woke him very early the next morning, and his first demand was to be allowed to present himself before it, but, without replying, his attendants conducted him to a huge marble bath, very shallow at one end, and quite deep at the other, and gave him to understand that he was to go into it. The Prince, nothing loth, was for springing at once into deep water, but he was gently but forcibly held back and only allowed to stand where it was about an inch deep, and he was nearly wild with impatience when he found that this process was to be repeated every day in spite of all he could say or do, the water rising higher and higher by inches, so that for sixty days he had to live in perpetual silence, ceremoniously conducted to and fro, supping all his meals through the long reed, and looking on at innumerable games of chess, the game of all others which he detested most. But at last the water rose as high as his chin, and his bath was complete. And that day the slaves in their black robes, and each having a large bat perched upon his head, marched in slow procession with the Prince in their midst, chanting a melancholy song, to the iron gate that led into a kind of Temple. At the sound of their chanting, another band of slaves appeared, and took possession of the unhappy Vivien.

They looked to him exactly like the ones he had left, except that they moved more slowly still, and each one held a raven upon his wrist, and their harsh croakings re-echoed through the dismal place. Holding the Prince by the arms, not so much to do him honour as to restrain his impatience, they proceeded by slow degrees up the steps of the Temple, and when they at last reached the top he thought his long waiting must be at an end. But on the contrary, after slowly enshrouding him in a long black robe like their own, they led him into the Temple itself, where he was forced to witness numbers of lengthy rites and ceremonies. By this time Vivien's active impatience had subsided into passive weariness, his yawns were continual and scandalous, but nobody heeded him, he stared hopelessly at the thick black curtain which hung down straight in front of him, and could hardly believe his eyes when it presently began to slide back, and he saw before him the Black Bird. It was of enormous size, and was perched upon a thick bar of iron which ran across from one side of the Temple to the other. At the sight of it all the slaves fell upon their knees and hid their faces, and when it had three times flapped its mighty wings it uttered distinctly in Prince Vivien's own language the words:

'Prince, your only chance of happiness depends upon that which is most opposed to your own nature.'

Then the curtain fell before it once more, and the Prince, after many ceremonies, was presented with a raven which perched upon his wrist, and was conducted slowly back to the iron gate. Here the raven left him and he was handed over once more to the care of the first band of slaves, while a large bat flickered down and settled upon his head of its own accord, and so he was taken back to the marble bath, and had to go through the whole process again, only this time he began in deep water which receded daily inch by inch. When this was over the slaves escorted him to the outer gate, and took leave of him with every mark of esteem and politeness, to which it is to be feared he responded but indifferently, since the gate was no sooner opened than he took to his heels, and fled away with all his might, his one idea being to put as much space as possible between himself and the dreary place into which he had ventured so rashly, just to consult a tedious Oracle who after all had told him nothing. He actually reflected for about five seconds on his folly, and came to the conclusion that it might sometimes be advisable to think before one acted.

After wandering about for several days until he was weary and hungry, he at last succeeded in finding a way out of the forest, and soon came to a wide and rapid river, which he followed, hoping to find some means of crossing it, and it happened that as the sun rose the next morning he saw something of a dazzling whiteness moored out in the middle of the stream. Upon looking more attentively at it he found that it was one of the prettiest little ships he had ever seen, and the boat that belonged to it was made fast to the bank quite close to him. The Prince was immediately seized with the most ardent desire to go on board the ship, and shouted loudly to attract the notice of her crew, but no one answered. So he sprang into the little boat and rowed away without finding it at all hard work, for the boat was made all of white paper and was as light as a rose leaf. The ship was made of white paper too, as the Prince presently discovered when he reached it. He found not a soul on board, but there was a very cosy little bed in the cabin, and an ample supply of all sorts of good things to eat and drink, which he made up his mind to enjoy until something new happened. Having been thoroughly well brought up at the court of King Gridelin, of course he understood the art of navigation, but when once he had started, the current carried the vessel down at such a pace that before he knew where he was the Prince found himself out at sea, and a wind springing up behind him just at this moment soon drove him out of sight of land. By this time he was somewhat alarmed, and did his best to put the ship about and get back to the river, but wind and tide were too strong for him, and he began to think of the number of times, from his childhood up, that he had been warned not to meddle with water. But it was too late now to do anything but wish vainly that he had stayed on shore, and to grow heartily weary of the boat and the sea and everything connected with it. These two things, however, he did most thoroughly. To put the finishing touch to his misfortunes he presently found himself becalmed in mid-ocean, a state of affairs which would be considered trying by the most patient of men, so you may imagine how it affected Prince Vivien! He even came to wishing himself back at the Castle of the Black Bird, for there at least he saw some living beings, whereas on board the white-paper ship he was absolutely alone, and could not imagine how he was ever to get away from his wearisome prison. However, after a very long time, he did see land, and his impatience to be on shore was so great that he at once flung himself over the ship's side that he might reach it sooner by swimming. But this was quite useless, for spring as far as he might from the vessel, it was always under his feet again before he reached the water, and he had to resign himself to his fate, and wait with what patience he could muster until the winds and waves carried the ship into a kind of natural harbour which ran far into the land. After his long imprisonment at sea the Prince was delighted with the sight of the great trees which grew down to the very edge of the water, and leaping lightly on shore he speedily lost himself in the thick forest. When he had wandered a long way he stopped to rest beside a clear spring of water, but scarcely had he thrown himself down upon the mossy bank when there was a great rustling in the bushes close by, and out sprang a pretty little gazelle panting and exhausted, which fell at his feet gasping out—

'Oh! Vivien, save me!'

The Prince in great astonishment leapt to his feet, and had just time to draw his sword before he found himself face to face with a large green lion which had been hotly pursuing the poor little gazelle. Prince Vivien attacked it gallantly and a fierce combat ensued, which, however, ended before long in the Prince's dealing his adversary a terrific blow which felled him to the earth. As he fell the lion whistled loudly three times with such force that the forest rang again, and the sound must have been heard for more than two leagues round, after which having apparently nothing more to do in the world he rolled over on his side and died. The Prince without paying any further heed to him or to his whistling returned to the pretty gazelle, saying:

'Well! are you satisfied now? Since you can talk, pray tell me instantly what all this is about, and how you happen to know my name.'

'Oh, I must rest for a long time before I can talk,' she replied, 'and beside, I very much doubt if you will have leisure to listen, for the affair is by no means finished. In fact,' she continued in the same languid tone, 'you had better look behind you now.'

The Prince turned sharply round and to his horror saw a huge Giant approaching with mighty strides, crying fiercely—

'Who has made my lion whistle I should like to know?'

'I have,' replied Prince Vivien boldly, 'but I can answer for it that he will not do it again!'

At these words the Giant began to howl and lament.

'Alas, my poor Tiny, my sweet little pet,' he cried, 'but at least I can avenge thy death.'

Thereupon he rushed at the Prince, brandishing an immense serpent which was coiled about his wrist. Vivien, without losing his coolness, aimed a terrific blow at it with his sword, but no sooner did he touch the snake than it changed into a Giant and the Giant into a snake, with such rapidity that the Prince felt perfectly giddy, and this happened at least half-a-dozen times, until at last with a fortunate stroke he cut the serpent in halves, and picking up one morsel flung it with all his force at the nose of the Giant, who fell insensible on top of the lion, and in an instant a thick black cloud rolled up which hid them from view, and when it cleared away they had all disappeared.

Then the Prince, without even waiting to sheathe his sword, rushed back to the gazelle, crying:

'Now you have had plenty of time to recover your wits, and you have nothing more to fear, so tell me who you are, and what this horrible Giant, with his lion and his serpent, have to do with you and for pity's sake be quick about it.'

'I will tell you with pleasure,' she answered, 'but where is the hurry? I want you to come back with me to the Green Castle, but I don't want to walk there, it is so far, and walking is so fatiguing.'

'Let us set out at once then,' replied the Prince severely, 'or else really I shall have to leave you where you are. Surely a young and active gazelle like you ought to be ashamed of not being able to walk a few steps. The further off this castle is the faster we ought to walk, but as you don't appear to enjoy that, I will promise that we will go gently, and we can talk by the way.'

'It would be better still if you would carry me,' said she sweetly, 'but as I don't like to see people giving themselves trouble, you may carry me, and make that snail carry you.' So saying, she pointed languidly with one tiny foot at what the Prince had taken for a block of stone, but now he saw that it was a huge snail.

'What! I ride a snail!' cried the Prince; 'you are laughing at me, and beside we should not get there for a year.'

'Oh! well then don't do it,' replied the gazelle, 'I am quite willing to stay here. The grass is green, and the water clear. But if I were you I should take the advice that was given me and ride the snail.'

So, though it did not please him at all, the Prince took the gazelle in his arms, and mounted upon the back of the snail, which glided along very peaceably, entirely declining to be hurried by frequent blows from the Prince's heels. In vain did the gazelle represent to him that she was enjoying herself very much, and that this was the easiest mode of conveyance she had ever discovered. Prince Vivien was wild with impatience, and thought that the Green Castle would never be reached. However, at last, they did get there, and everyone who was in it ran to see the Prince dismount from his singular steed.

But what was his surprise, when having at her request set the gazelle gently down upon the steps which led up to the castle, he saw her suddenly change into a charming Princess, and recognized in her his pretty cousin Placida, who greeted him with her usual tranquil sweetness. His delight knew no bounds, and he followed her eagerly up into the castle, impatient to know what strange events had brought her there. But after all he had to wait for the Princess's story, for the inhabitants of the Green Lands, hearing that the Giant was dead, ran to offer the kingdom to his vanquisher, and Prince Vivien had to listen to various complimentary harangues, which took a great deal of time, though he cut them as short as politeness allowed—if not shorter. But at last he was free to rejoin Placida, who at once began the story of her adventures.

'After you had gone away,' said she, 'they tried to make me learn how to govern the kingdom, which wearied me to death, so that I begged and prayed Lolotte to take me away with her, and this she presently did, but very reluctantly. However, having been transported to her grotto upon my favourite couch, I spent several delicious days, soothed by the soft green light, which was like a beech wood in the spring, and by the murmuring of bees and the tinkle of falling water. But alas! Lolotte was forced to go away to a general assembly of the Fairies, and she came back in great dismay, telling me that her indulgence to me had cost her dear, for she had been severely reprimanded and ordered to hand me over to the Fairy Mirlifiche, who was already taking charge of you, and who had been much commended for her management of you.'

'Fine management, indeed,' interrupted the Prince, 'if it is to her I owe all the adventures I have met with! But go on with your story, my cousin. I can tell you all about my doings afterwards, and then you can judge for yourself.'

'At first I was grieved to see Lolotte cry,' resumed the Princess, 'but I soon found that grieving was very troublesome, so I thought it better to be calm, and very soon afterwards I saw the Fairy Mirlifiche arrive, mounted upon her great unicorn. She stopped before the grotto and bade Lolotte bring me out to her, at which she cried worse than ever, and kissed me a dozen times, but she dared not refuse. I was lifted up on to the unicorn, behind Mirlifiche, who said to me—

'"Hold on tight, little girl, if you don't want to break your neck."

'And, indeed, I had to hold on with all my might, for her horrible steed trotted so violently that it positively took my breath away. However, at last we stopped at a large farm, and the farmer and his wife ran out as soon as they saw the Fairy, and helped us to dismount.

'I knew that they were really a King and Queen, whom the Fairies were punishing for their ignorance and idleness. You may imagine that I was by this time half dead with fatigue, but Mirlifiche insisted upon my feeding her unicorn before I did anything else. To accomplish this I had to climb up a long ladder into the hayloft, and bring down, one after another, twenty-four handfuls of hay. Never, never before, did I have such a wearisome task! It makes me shudder to think of it now, and that was not all. In the same way I had to carry the twenty-four handfuls of hay to the stable, and then it was supper time, and I had to wait upon all the others. After that I really thought I should be allowed to go peaceably to my little bed, but, oh dear no! First of all I had to make it, for it was all in confusion, and then I had to make one for the Fairy, and tuck her in, and draw the curtains round her, beside rendering her a dozen little services which I was not at all accustomed to. Finally, when I was perfectly exhausted by all this toil, I was free to go to bed myself, but as I had never before undressed myself, and really did not know how to begin, I lay down as I was. Unfortunately, the Fairy found this out, and just as I was falling into a sweet slumber, she made me get up once more, but even then I managed to escape her vigilance, and only took off my upper robe. Indeed, I may tell you in confidence, that I always find disobedience answer very well. One is often scolded, it is true, but then one has been saved some trouble.

'At the earliest dawn of day Mirlifiche woke me, and made me take many journeys to the stable to bring her word how her unicorn had slept, and how much hay he had eaten, and then to find out what time it was, and if it was a fine day. I was so slow, and did my errands so badly, that before she left she called the King and Queen and said to them:

'"I am much more pleased with you this year. Continue to make the best of your farm, if you wish to get back to your kingdom, and also take care of this little Princess for me, and teach her to be useful, that when I come I may find her cured of her faults. If she is not—"

'Here she broke off with a significant look, and mounting my enemy the unicorn, speedily disappeared.

'Then the King and Queen, turning to me, asked me what I could do.

'"Nothing at all, I assure you," I replied in a tone which really ought to have convinced them, but they went on to describe various employments, and tried to discover which of them would be most to my taste. However, at last I persuaded them that to do nothing whatever would be the only thing that would suit me, and that if they really wanted to be kind to me, they would let me go to bed and to sleep, and not tease me about doing anything. To my great joy, they not only permitted this, but actually, when they had their own meals, the Queen brought my portion up to me. But early the next morning she appeared at my bedside, saying, with an apologetic air:

'"My pretty child, I am afraid you must really make up your mind to get up to-day. I know quite well how delightful it is to be thoroughly idle, for when my husband and I were King and Queen we did nothing at all from morning to night, and I sincerely hope that it will not be long before those happy days will come again for us. But at present we have not reached them, nor have you, and you know from what the Fairy said that perhaps worse things may happen to us if she is not obeyed. Make haste, I beg of you, and come down to breakfast, for I have put by some delicious cream for you."

'It was really very tiresome, but as there was no help for it I went down!

'But the instant breakfast was over they began again their cuckoo-cry of "What will you do?" In vain did I answer—

'"Nothing at all, if it please you, madam."

'The Queen at last gave me a spindle and about four pounds of hemp upon a distaff, and sent me out to keep the sheep, assuring me that there could not be a pleasanter occupation, and that I could take my ease as much as I pleased. I was forced to set out, very unwillingly, as you may imagine, but I had not walked far before I came to a shady bank in what seemed to me a charming place. I stretched myself cosily upon the soft grass, and with the bundle of hemp for a pillow slept as tranquilly as if there were no such things as sheep in the world, while they for their part wandered hither and thither at their own sweet will, as if there were no such thing as a shepherdess, invading every field, and browsing upon every kind of forbidden dainty, until the peasants, alarmed by the havoc they were making, raised a clamour, which at last reached the ears of the King and Queen, who ran out, and seeing the cause of the commotion, hastily collected their flock. And, indeed, the sooner the better, since they had to pay for all the damage they had done. As for me I lay still and watched them run, for I was very comfortable, and there I might be still if they had not come up, all panting and breathless, and compelled me to get up and follow them; they also reproached me bitterly, but I need hardly tell you that they did not again entrust me with the flock.

'But whatever they found for me to do it was always the same thing, I spoilt and mismanaged it all, and was so successful in provoking even the most patient people, that one day I ran away from the farm, for I was really afraid the Queen would be obliged to beat me. When I came to the little river in which the King used to fish, I found the boat tied to a tree, and stepping in I unfastened it, and floated gently down with the current. The gliding of the boat was so soothing that I did not trouble myself in the least when the Queen caught sight of me and ran along the bank, crying—

'"My boat, my boat! Husband, come and catch the little Princess who is running away with my boat!"

'The current soon carried me out of hearing of her cries, and I dreamed to the song of the ripples and the whisper of the trees, until the boat suddenly stopped, and I found it was stuck fast beside a fresh green meadow, and that the sun was rising. In the distance I saw some little houses which seemed to be built in a most singular fashion, but as I was by this time very hungry I set out towards them, but before I had walked many steps, I saw that the air was full of shining objects which seemed to be fixed, and yet I could not see what they hung from.

'I went nearer, and saw a silken cord hanging down to the ground, and pulled it just because it was so close to my hand. Instantly the whole meadow resounded to the melodious chiming of a peal of silver bells, and they sounded so pretty that I sat down to listen, and to watch them as they swung shining in the sunbeams. Before they ceased to sound, came a great flight of birds, and each one perching upon a bell added its charming song to the concert. As they ended, I looked up and saw a tall and stately dame advancing towards me, surrounded and followed by a vast flock of every kind of bird.

'"Who are you, little girl," said she, "who dares to come where I allow no mortal to live, lest my birds should be disturbed? Still, if you are clever at anything," she added, "I might be able to put up with your presence."

'"Madam," I answered, rising, "you may be very sure that I shall not do anything to alarm your birds. I only beg you, for pity's sake, to give me something to eat."

'"I will do that," she replied, "before I send you where you deserve to go."

'And thereupon she despatched six jays, who were her pages, to fetch me all sorts of biscuits, while some of the other birds brought ripe fruits. In fact, I had a delicious breakfast, though I do not like to be waited upon so quickly. It is so disagreeable to be hurried. I began to think I should like very well to stay in this pleasant country, and I said so to the stately lady, but she answered with the greatest disdain:

'"Do you think I would keep you here? *You*! Why what do you suppose would be the good of you in this country, where everybody is wide-awake and busy? No, no, I have shown you all the hospitality you will get from me."

'With these words she turned and gave a vigorous pull to the silken rope which I mentioned before, but instead of a melodious chime, there arose a hideous clanging which quite terrified me, and in an instant a huge Black Bird appeared, which alighted at the Fairy's feet, saying in a frightful voice—

'"What do you want of me, my sister?"

'"I wish you to take this little Princess to my cousin, the Giant of the Green Castle, at once," she replied, "and beg him from me to make her work day and night upon his beautiful tapestry."

'At these words the great Bird snatched me up, regardless of my cries, and flew off at a terrific pace—'

'Oh! you are joking, cousin,' interrupted Prince Vivien; 'you mean as slowly as possible. I know that horrible Black Bird, and the lengthiness of all his proceedings and surroundings.'

'Have it your own way,' replied Placida, tranquilly. 'I cannot bear arguing. Perhaps, this was not even the same bird. At any rate, he carried me off at a prodigious speed, and set me gently down in this very castle of which you are now the master. We entered by one of the windows, and when the Bird had handed me over to the Giant from whom you have been good enough to deliver me, and given the Fairy's message, it departed.

'Then the Giant turned to me, saying,

'"So you are an idler! Ah! well, we must teach you to work. You won't be the first we have cured of laziness. See how busy all my guests are."

'I looked up as he spoke, and saw that an immense gallery ran all round the hall, in which were tapestry frames, spindles, skeins of wool, patterns, and all necessary things. Before each frame about a dozen people were sitting, hard at work, at which terrible sight I fainted away, and as soon as I recovered they began to ask me what I could do.

'It was in vain that I replied as before, and with the strongest desire to be taken at my word, "Nothing at all."

'The Giant only said,

'"Then you must learn to do something; in this world there is enough work for everybody."

'It appeared that they were working into the tapestry all the stories the Fairies liked best, and they began to try and teach me to help them, but from the first class, where they tried me to begin with, I sank lower and lower, and not even the most simple stitches could I learn.

'In vain they punished me by all the usual methods. In vain the Giant showed me his menagerie, which was entirely composed of children who would not work! Nothing did me any good, and at last I was reduced to drawing water for the dyeing of the wools, and even over that I was so slow that this morning the Giant flew into a rage and changed me into a gazelle. He was just putting me into the menagerie when I happened to catch sight of a dog, and was seized with such terror that I fled away at my utmost speed, and escaped through the outer court of the castle. The Giant, fearing that I should be lost altogether, sent his green lion after me, with orders to bring me back, cost what it might, and I should certainly have let myself be caught, or eaten up, or anything, rather than run any further, if I had not luckily met you by the fountain. And oh!' concluded the Princess, 'how delightful it is once more to be able to sit still in peace. I was so tired of trying to learn things.'

Prince Vivien said that, for his part, he had been kept a great deal too still, and had not found it at all amusing, and then he recounted all his adventures with breathless rapidity. How he had taken shelter with Dame Patience, and consulted the Oracle, and voyaged in the paper ship. Then they went hand in hand to release all the prisoners in the castle, and all the Princes and Princesses who were in cages in the menagerie, for the instant the Green Giant was dead they had resumed their natural forms. As you may imagine, they were all very grateful, and Princess Placida entreated them never, never to do another stitch of work so long as they lived, and they promptly made a great bonfire in the courtyard, and solemnly burnt all the embroidery frames and spinning wheels. Then the Princess gave them splendid presents, or rather sat by while Prince Vivien gave them, and there were great rejoicings in the Green Castle, and everyone did his best to please the Prince and Princess. But with all their good intentions, they often made mistakes, for Vivien and Placida were never of one mind about their plans, so it was very confusing, and they frequently found themselves obeying the Prince's orders, very, very slowly, and rushing off with lightning speed to do something that the Princess did not wish to have done at all, until, by-and-by, the two cousins took to consulting with, and consoling one another in all these little vexations, and at last came to be so fond of each other that for Placida's sake Vivien became quite patient, and for Vivien's sake Placida made the most unheard-of exertions. But now the Fairies who had been watching all these proceedings with interest, thought it was time to interfere, and ascertain by further trials if this improvement was likely to continue, and if they really loved one another. So they caused Placida to seem to have a violent fever, and Vivien to languish and grow dull, and made each of them very uneasy about the other, and then, finding a moment when they were apart, the Fairy Mirlifiche suddenly appeared to Placida, and said—

'I have just seen Prince Vivien, and he seemed to me to be very ill.'

'Alas! yes, madam,' she answered, 'and if you will but cure him, you may take me back to the farm, or bring the Green Giant to life again, and you shall see how obedient I will be.'

'If you really wish him to recover,' said the Fairy, 'you have only to catch the Trotting Mouse and the Chaffinch-on-the-Wing and bring them to me. Only remember that time presses!'

She had hardly finished speaking before the Princess was rushing headlong out of the castle gate, and the Fairy after watching her till she was lost to sight, gave a little chuckle and went in search of the Prince, who begged her earnestly to send him back to the Black Castle, or to the paper boat if she would but save Placida's life. The Fairy shook her head, and looked very grave. She quite agreed with him, the Princess was in a bad way—'But,' said she, 'if you can find the Rosy Mole, and give him to her she will recover.' So now it was the Prince's turn to set off in a vast hurry, only as soon as he left the Castle he happened to go in exactly the opposite direction to the one Placida had taken. Now you can imagine these two devoted lovers hunting night and day. The Princess in the woods, always running, always listening, pursuing hotly after two creatures which seemed to her very hard to catch, which she yet never ceased from pursuing. The Prince on the other hand wandering continually across the meadows, his eyes fixed upon the ground, attentive to every movement among the moles. He was forced to walk slowly—slowly upon tip-toe, hardly venturing to breathe. Often he stood for hours motionless as a statue, and if the desire to succeed could have helped him he would soon have possessed the Rosy Mole. But alas! all that he caught were black and ordinary, though strange to say he never grew impatient, but always seemed ready to begin the tedious hunt again. But this changing of character is one of the most ordinary miracles which love works. Neither the Prince nor the Princess gave a thought to anything but their quest. It never even occurred to them to wonder what country they had reached. So you may guess how astonished they were one day, when having at last been successful after their long and weary chase, they cried aloud at the same instant: 'At last I have saved my beloved,' and then recognising each other's voice looked up, and rushed to meet one another with the wildest joy. Surprise kept them silent while for one delicious moment they gazed into each other's eyes, and just then who should come up but King Gridelin, for it was into his kingdom they had accidentally strayed. He recognized them in his turn and greeted them joyfully, but when they turned afterwards to look for the Rosy Mole, the Chaffinch, and the Trotting-Mouse, they had vanished, and in their places stood a lovely lady whom they did not know, the Black Bird, and the Green Giant. King Gridelin had no sooner set eyes upon the lady than with a cry of joy he clasped her in his arms, for it was no other than his long-lost wife, Santorina, about whose imprisonment in Fairyland you may perhaps read some day.

Then the Black Bird and the Green Giant resumed their natural form, for they were enchanters, and up flew Lolotte and Mirlifiche in their chariots, and then there was a great kissing and congratulating, for everybody had regained someone he loved, including the enchanters, who loved their natural forms dearly. After this they repaired to the Palace, and the wedding of Prince Vivien and Princess Placida was held at once with all the splendour imaginable.

King Gridelin and Queen Santorina, after all their experiences had no further desire to reign, so they retired happily to a peaceful place, leaving their kingdom to the Prince and Princess, who were beloved by all their subjects, and found their greatest happiness all their lives long in making other people happy.

Nonchalante et Papillon

LITTLE ONE-EYE, LITTLE TWO-EYES, AND LITTLE THREE-EYES

There was once a woman who had three daughters, of whom the eldest was called Little One-eye, because she had only one eye in the middle of her forehead; and the second, Little Two-eyes, because she had two eyes like other people; and the youngest, Little Three-eyes, because she had three eyes, and *her* third eye was also in the middle of her forehead. But because Little Two-eyes did not look any different from other children, her sisters and mother could not bear her. They would say to her, 'You with your two eyes are no better than common folk; you don't belong to us.' They pushed her here, and threw her wretched clothes there, and gave her to eat only what they left, and they were as unkind to her as ever they could be.

It happened one day that Little Two-eyes had to go out into the fields to take care of the goat, but she was still quite hungry because her sisters had given her so little to eat. So she sat down in the meadow and began to cry, and she cried so much that two little brooks ran out of her eyes. But when she looked up once in her grief there stood a woman beside her who asked, 'Little Two-eyes, what are you crying for?' Little Two-eyes answered, 'Have I not reason to cry? Because I have two eyes like other people, my sisters and my mother cannot bear me; they push me out of one corner into another, and give me nothing to eat except what they leave. To-day they have given me so little that I am still quite hungry.' Then the wise woman said, 'Little Two-eyes, dry your eyes, and I will tell you something so that you need never be hungry again. Only say to your goat,

"Little goat, bleat, Little table, appear,"

and a beautifully spread table will stand before you, with the most delicious food on it, so that you can eat as much as you want. And when you have had enough and don't want the little table any more, you have only to say,

"Little goat, bleat, Little table, away,"

and then it will vanish.' Then the wise woman went away.

But Little Two-eyes thought, 'I must try at once if what she has told me is true, for I am more hungry than ever'; and she said,

'Little goat, bleat, Little table appear,'

and scarcely had she uttered the words, when there stood a little table before her covered with a white cloth, on which were arranged a plate, with a knife and fork and a silver spoon, and the most beautiful dishes, which were smoking hot, as if they had just come out of the kitchen. Then Little Two-eyes said the shortest grace she knew, and set to work and made a good dinner. And when she had had enough, she said, as the wise woman had told her,

'Little goat, bleat, Little table, away,'

and immediately the table and all that was on it disappeared again. 'That is a splendid way of housekeeping,' thought Little Two-eyes, and she was quite happy and contented.

In the evening, when she went home with her goat, she found a little earthenware dish with the food that her sisters had thrown to her, but she did not touch it. The next day she went out again with her goat, and left the few scraps which were given her. The first and second times her sisters did not notice this, but when it happened continually, they remarked it and said, 'Something is the matter with Little Two-eyes, for she always leaves her food now, and she used to gobble up all that was given her. She must have found other means of getting food.' So in order to get at the truth, Little One-eye was told to go out with Little Two-eyes when she drove the goat to pasture, and to notice particularly what she got there, and whether anyone brought her food and drink.

Now when Little Two-eyes was setting out, Little One-eye came up to her and said, 'I will go into the field with you and see if you take good care of the goat, and if you drive him properly to get grass.' But Little Two-eyes saw what Little One-eye had in her mind, and she drove the goat into the long grass and said, 'Come, Little One-eye, we will sit down here, and I will sing you something.'

Little One-eye sat down, and as she was very much tired by the long walk to which she was not used, and by the hot day, and as Little Two-eyes went on singing.

'Little One-eye, are you awake? Little One-eye, are you asleep?'

she shut her one eye and fell asleep. When Little Two-eyes saw that Little One-eye was asleep and could find out nothing, she said,

'Little goat, bleat, Little table, appear,'

and sat down at her table and ate and drank as much as she wanted. Then she said again,

'Little goat, bleat, Little table, away.'

and in the twinkling of an eye all had vanished.

Little Two-eyes then woke Little One-eye and said, 'Little One-eye, you meant to watch, and, instead, you went to sleep; in the meantime the goat might have run far and wide. Come, we will go home.' So they went home, and Little Two-eyes again left her little dish untouched, and Little One-eye could not tell her mother why she would not eat, and said as an excuse, 'I was so sleepy out-of-doors.'

The next day the mother said to Little Three-eyes, 'This time you shall go with Little Two-eyes and watch whether she eats anything out in the fields, and whether anyone brings her food and drink, for eat and drink she must secretly.' So Little Three-eyes went to Little Two-eyes and said, 'I will go with you and see if you take good care of the goat, and if you drive him properly to get grass.' But little Two-eyes knew what Little Three-eyes had in her mind, and she drove the goat out into the tall grass and said, 'We will sit down here, Little Three-eyes, and I will sing you something.' Little Three-eyes sat down; she was tired by the walk and the hot day, and Little Two-eyes sang the same little song again:

'Little Three eyes, are you awake?'

but instead of singing as she ought to have done,

'Little Three-eyes, are you asleep?'

she sang, without thinking,

'Little *Two-eyes*, are you asleep?'

She went on singing,

'Little Three-eyes, are you awake? Little *Two-eyes*, are you asleep?'

so that the two eyes of Little Three-eyes fell asleep, but the third, which was not spoken to in the little rhyme, did not fall asleep. Of course Little Three-eyes shut that eye also out of cunning, to look as if she were asleep, but it was blinking and could see everything quite well.

And when Little Two-eyes thought that Little Three-eyes was sound asleep, she said her rhyme,

'Little goat, bleat, Little table, appear,'

and ate and drank to her heart's content, and then made the table go away again, by saying,

'Little goat, bleat, Little table, away.'

But Little Three-eyes had seen everything. Then Little Two-eyes came to her, and woke her and said, 'Well, Little Three-eyes, have you been asleep? You watch well! Come, we will go home.' When they reached home, Little Two-eyes did not eat again, and Little Three-eyes said to the mother, 'I know now why that proud thing eats nothing. When she says to the goat in the field,

"Little goat, bleat, Little table, appear,"

a table stands before her, spread with the best food, much better than we have; and when she has had enough, she says,

"Little goat, bleat, Little table, away,"

and everything disappears again. I saw it all exactly. She made two of my eyes go to sleep with a little rhyme, but the one in my forehead remained awake, luckily!'

Then the envious mother cried out, 'Will you fare better than we do? you shall not have the chance to do so again!' and she fetched a knife, and killed the goat.

When Little Two-eyes saw this, she went out full of grief, and sat down in the meadow and wept bitter tears. Then again the wise woman stood before her, and said, 'Little Two-eyes, what are you crying for?' 'Have I not reason to cry?' she answered, 'the goat, which when I said the little rhyme, spread the table so beautifully, my mother has killed, and now I must suffer hunger and want again.' The wise woman said, 'Little Two-eyes, I will give you a good piece of advice. Ask your sisters to give you the heart of the dead goat, and bury it in the earth before the house-door; that will bring you good luck.' Then she disappeared, and Little Two-eyes went home, and said to her sisters, 'Dear sisters, do give me something of my goat; I ask nothing better than its heart.' Then they laughed and said, 'You can have that if you want nothing more.' And Little Two-eyes took the heart and buried it in the evening when all was quiet, as the wise woman had told her, before the house-door. The next morning when they all awoke and came to the house-door, there stood a most wonderful tree, which had leaves of silver and fruit of gold growing on it—you never saw anything more lovely and gorgeous in your life! But they did not know how the tree had grown up in the night; only Little Two-eyes knew that it had sprung from the heart of the goat, for it was standing just where she had buried it in the ground. Then the mother said to Little One-eye, 'Climb up, my child, and break us off the fruit from the tree.' Little One-eye climbed up, but just when she was going to take hold of one of the golden apples the bough sprang out of her hands; and this happened every time, so that she could not break off a single apple, however hard she tried. Then the mother said, 'Little Three-eyes, do you climb up; you with your three eyes can see round better than Little One-eye.' So Little One-eye slid down, and Little Three-eyes climbed up; but she was not any more successful; look round as she might, the golden apples bent themselves back. At last the mother got impatient and climbed up herself, but she was even less successful than Little One-eye and Little Three-eyes in catching hold of the fruit, and only grasped at the empty air. Then Little Two-eyes said, 'I will just try once, perhaps I shall succeed better.' The sisters called out, 'You with your two eyes will no doubt succeed!' But Little Two-eyes climbed up, and the golden apples did not jump away from her, but behaved quite properly, so that she could pluck them off, one after the other, and brought a whole apron-full down with her. The mother took them from her, and, instead of behaving better to poor Little Two-eyes, as they ought to have done, they were jealous that she only could reach the fruit and behaved still more unkindly to her.

It happened one day that when they were all standing together by the tree that a young knight came riding along. 'Be quick, Little Two-eyes,' cried the two sisters, 'creep under this, so that you shall not disgrace us,' and they put over poor Little Two-eyes as quickly as possible an empty cask, which was standing close to the tree, and they pushed the golden apples which she had broken off under with her. When the knight, who was a very handsome young man, rode up, he wondered to see the marvellous tree of gold and silver, and said to the two sisters, 'Whose is this beautiful tree? Whoever will give me a twig of it shall have whatever she wants.' Then Little One-eye and Little Three-eyes answered that the tree belonged to them, and that they would certainly break him off a twig. They gave themselves a great deal of trouble, but in vain; the twigs and fruit bent back every time from their hands. Then the knight said, 'It is very strange that the tree should belong to you, and yet that you have not the power to break anything from it!' But they would have that the tree was theirs; and while they were saying this, Little Two-eyes rolled a couple of golden apples from under the cask, so that they lay at the knight's feet, for she was angry with Little One-eye and Little Three-eyes for not speaking the truth. When the knight saw the apples he was astonished, and asked where they came from. Little One-eye and Little Three-eyes answered that they had another sister, but she could not be seen because she had only two eyes, like ordinary people. But the knight demanded to see her, and called out, 'Little Two-eyes, come forth.' Then Little Two-eyes came out from under the cask quite happily, and the knight was astonished at her great beauty, and said, 'Little Two-eyes, I am sure you can break me off a twig from the tree.' 'Yes,' answered Little Two-eyes, 'I can, for the tree is mine.' So she climbed up and broke off a small branch with its silver leaves and golden fruit without any trouble, and gave it to the knight. Then he said, 'Little Two-eyes, what shall I give you for this?' 'Ah,' answered Little Two-eyes, 'I suffer hunger and thirst, want and sorrow, from early morning till late in the evening; if you would take me with you, and free me from this, I should be happy!' Then the knight lifted Little Two-eyes on his horse, and took her home to his father's castle. There he gave her beautiful clothes, and food and drink, and because he loved her so much he married her, and the wedding was celebrated with great joy.

When the handsome knight carried Little Two-eyes away with him, the two sisters envied her good luck at first. 'But the wonderful tree is still with us, after all,' they thought, 'and although we cannot break any fruit from it, everyone will stop and look at it, and will come to us and praise it; who knows whether *we* may not reap a harvest from it?' But the next morning the tree had flown, and their hopes with it; and when Little Two-eyes looked out of her window there it stood underneath, to her great delight. Little Two-eyes lived happily for a long time. Once two poor women came to the castle to beg alms. Then Little Two-eyes looked at then and recognised both her sisters, Little One-eye and Little Three-eyes, who had become so poor that they came to beg bread at her door. But Little Two-eyes bade them welcome, and was so good to them that they both repented from their hearts of having been so unkind to their sister.

Grimm.

JORINDE AND JORINGEL

There was once upon a time a castle in the middle of a thick wood where lived an old woman quite alone, for she was an enchantress. In the day-time she changed herself into a cat or a night-owl, but in the evening she became like an ordinary woman again. She could entice animals and birds to come to her, and then she would kill and cook them. If any youth came within a hundred paces of the castle, he was obliged to stand still, and could not stir from the spot till she set him free; but if a pretty girl came within this boundary, the old enchantress changed her into a bird, and shut her up in a wicker cage, which she put in one of the rooms in the castle. She had quite seven thousand of such cages in the castle with very rare birds in them.

Now, there was once a maiden called Jorinde, who was more beautiful than other maidens. She and a youth named Joringel, who was just as good-looking as she was, were betrothed to one another. Their greatest delight was to be together, and so that they might get a good long talk, they went one evening for a walk in the wood. 'Take care,' said Joringel, 'not to come too close to the castle.' It was a beautiful evening; the sun shone brightly between the stems of the trees among the dark green leaves of the forest, and the turtle-dove sang clearly on the old maybushes.

Jorinde wept from time to time, and she sat herself down in the sunshine and lamented, and Joringel lamented too. They felt as sad as if they had been condemned to die; they looked round and got quite confused, and did not remember which was their way home. Half the sun was still above the mountain and half was behind it when Joringel looked through the trees and saw the old wall of the castle quite near them. He was terrified and half dead with fright. Jorinde sang:

'My little bird with throat so red Sings sorrow, sorrow, sorrow; He sings to the little dove that's dead, Sings sorrow, sor—jug, jug, jug.'

Joringel looked up at Jorinde. She had been changed into a nightingale, who was singing 'jug, jug.' A night-owl with glowing eyes flew three times round her, and screeched three times 'tu-whit, tu-whit, tu-whoo.' Joringel could not stir; he stood there like a stone; he could not weep, or speak, or move hand or foot. Now the sun set; the owl flew into a bush, and immediately an old, bent woman came out of it; she was yellow-skinned and thin, and had large red eyes and a hooked nose, which met her chin.

She muttered to herself, caught the nightingale, and carried her away in her hand. Joringel could say nothing; he could not move from the spot, and the nightingale was gone. At last the woman came back again, and said in a gruff voice, 'Good evening, Zachiel; when the young moon shines in the basket, you are freed early, Zachiel.' Then Joringel was free. He fell on his knees before the old woman and implored her to give him back his Jorinde, but she said he should never have her again, and then went away. He called after her, he wept and lamented, but all in vain. 'What is to become of me!' he thought. Then he went away, and came at last to a strange village, where he kept sheep for a long time. He often went round the castle while he was there, but never too close. At last he dreamt one night that he had found a blood-red flower, which had in its centre a beautiful large pearl. He plucked this flower and went with it to the castle; and there everything which he touched with the flower was freed from the enchantment, and he got his Jorinde back again through it. When he awoke in the morning he began to seek mountain and valley to find such a flower. He sought it for eight days, and on the ninth early in the morning he found the blood-red flower. In its centre was a large dew-drop, as big as the most lovely pearl. He travelled day and night with this flower till he arrived at the castle. When he came within a hundred paces of it he did not cease to be able to move, but he went on till he reached the gate. He was delighted at his success, touched the great gate with the flower, and it sprung open. He entered, passed through the courtyard, and then stopped to listen for the singing of the birds; at last he heard it. He went in and found the hall in which was the enchantress, and with her seven thousand birds in their wicker cages. When she saw Joringel she was furious, and breathed out poison and gall at him, but she could not move a step towards him. He took no notice of her, and went and looked over the cages of birds; but there were many hundred nightingales, and how was he to find his Jorinde from among them? Whilst he was considering, he observed the old witch take up a cage secretly and go with it towards the door. Instantly he sprang after her, touched the cage with the flower, and the old woman as well. Now she could no longer work enchantments, and there stood Jorinde before him, with her arms round his neck, and more beautiful than ever. Then he turned all the other birds again into maidens, and he went home with his Jorinde, and they lived a long and happy life.

Grimm.

ALLERLEIRAUH; OR, THE MANY-FURRED CREATURE

There was once upon a time a King who had a wife with golden hair, and she was so beautiful that you couldn't find anyone like her in the world. It happened that she fell ill, and when she felt that she must soon die, she sent for the King, and said, 'If you want to marry after my death, make no one queen unless she is just as beautiful as I am, and has just such golden hair as I have. Promise me this.' After the King had promised her this, she closed her eyes and died.

For a long time the King was not to be comforted, and he did not even think of taking a second wife. At last his councillors said, 'The King *must* marry again, so that we may have a queen.' So messengers were sent far and wide to seek for a bride equal to the late Queen in beauty. But there was no one in the wide world, and if there had been she could not have had such golden hair. Then the messengers came home again, not having been able to find a queen.

Now, the King had a daughter, who was just as beautiful as her dead mother, and had just such golden hair. One day when she had grown up, her father looked at her, and saw that she was exactly like her mother, so he said to his councillors, 'I will marry my daughter to one of you, and she shall be queen, for she is exactly like her dead mother, and when I die her husband shall be king.' But when the Princess heard of her father's decision, she was not at all pleased, and said to him, 'Before I do your bidding, I must have three dresses; one as golden as the sun, one as silver as the moon, and one as shining as the stars. Besides these, I want a cloak made of a thousand different kinds of skin; every animal in your kingdom must give a bit of his skin to it.' But she thought to herself, 'This will be quite impossible, and I shall not have to marry someone I do not care for.' The King, however, was not to be turned from his purpose, and he commanded the most skilled maidens in his kingdom to weave the three dresses, one as golden as the sun, and one as silver as the moon, and one as shining as the stars; and he gave orders to all his huntsmen to catch one of every kind of beast in the kingdom, and to get a bit of its skin to make the cloak of a thousand pieces of fur. At last, when all was ready, the King commanded the cloak to be brought to him, and he spread it out before the Princess, and said, 'Tomorrow shall be your wedding-day.' When the Princess saw that there was no more hope of changing her father's resolution, she determined to flee away. In the night, when everyone else was sleeping, she got up and took three things from her treasures, a gold ring, a little gold spinning-wheel, and a gold reel; she put the sun, moon, and star dresses in a nut-shell, drew on the cloak of many skins, and made her face and hands black with soot. Then she commended herself to God, and went out and travelled the whole night till she came to a large forest. And as she was very much tired she sat down inside a hollow tree and fell asleep.

The sun rose and she still slept on and on, although it was nearly noon. Now, it happened that the king to whom this wood belonged was hunting in it. When his dogs came to the tree, they sniffed, and ran round and round it, barking. The King said to the huntsmen, 'See what sort of a wild beast is in there.' The huntsmen went in, and then came back and said, 'In the hollow tree there lies a wonderful animal that we don't know, and we have never seen one like it; its skin is made of a thousand pieces of fur; but it is lying down asleep.' The King said, 'See if you can catch it alive, and then fasten it to the cart, and we will take it with us.' When the huntsmen seized the maiden, she awoke and was frightened, and cried out to them, 'I am a poor child, forsaken by father and mother; take pity on me, and let me go with you.' Then they said to her, 'Many-furred Creature, you can work in the kitchen; come with us and sweep the ashes together.' So they put her in the cart and they went back to the palace. There they showed her a tiny room under the stairs, where no daylight came, and said to her, 'Many-furred Creature, you can live and sleep here.' Then she was sent into the kitchen, where she carried wood and water, poked the fire, washed vegetables, plucked fowls, swept up the ashes, and did all the dirty work.

So the Many-furred Creature lived for a long time in great poverty. Ah, beautiful King's daughter, what is going to befall you now?

It happened once when a great feast was being held in the palace, that she said to the cook, 'Can I go upstairs for a little bit and look on? I will stand outside the doors.' The cook replied, 'Yes, you can go up, but in half-an-hour you must be back here to sweep up the ashes.' Then she took her little oil-lamp, and went into her little room, drew off her fur cloak, and washed off the soot from her face and hands, so that her beauty shone forth, and it was as if one sunbeam after another were coming out of a black cloud. Then she opened the nut, and took out the dress as golden as the sun. And when she had done this, she went up to the feast, and everyone stepped out of her way, for nobody knew her, and they thought she must be a King's daughter. But the King came towards her and gave her his hand, and danced with her, thinking to himself, 'My eyes have never beheld anyone so fair!' When the dance was ended, she curtseyed to him, and when the King looked round she had disappeared, no one knew whither. The guards who were standing before the palace were called and questioned, but no one had seen her.

She had run to her little room and had quickly taken off her dress, made her face and hands black, put on the fur cloak, and was once more the Many-furred Creature. When she came into the kitchen and was setting about her work of sweeping the ashes together, the cook said to her, 'Let that wait till to-morrow, and just cook the King's soup for me; I want to have a little peep at the company upstairs; but be sure that you do not let a hair fall into it, otherwise you will get nothing to eat in future!' So the cook went away, and the Many-furred Creature cooked the soup for the King. She made a bread-soup as well as she possibly could, and when it was done, she fetched her gold ring from her little room, and laid it in the tureen in which the soup was to be served up.

When the dance was ended, the King had his soup brought to him and ate it, and it was so good that he thought he had never tasted such soup in his life. But when he came to the bottom of the dish he saw a gold ring lying there, and he could not imagine how it got in. Then he commanded the cook to be brought before him. The cook was terrified when he heard the command, and said to the Many-furred Creature, 'You must have let a hair fall into the soup, and if you have you deserve a good beating!' When he came before the King, the King asked who had cooked the soup. The cook answered, 'I cooked it.' But the King said, 'That's not true, for it was quite different and much better soup than you have ever cooked.' Then the cook said, 'I must confess; *I* did not cook the soup; the Many-furred Creature did.' 'Let her be brought before me,' said the King. When the Many-furred Creature came, the King asked her who she was. 'I am a poor child without father or mother.' Then he asked her, 'What do you do in my palace?' 'I am of no use except to have boots thrown at my head.' 'How did you get the ring which was in the soup?' he asked. 'I know nothing at all about the ring,' she answered. So the King could find out nothing, and was obliged to send her away.

After a time there was another feast, and the Many-furred Creature begged the cook as at the last one to let her go and look on. He answered, 'Yes, but come back again in half-an-hour and cook the King the bread-soup that he likes so much.' So she ran away to her little room, washed herself quickly, took out of the nut the dress as silver as the moon and put it on. Then she went upstairs looking just like a King's daughter, and the King came towards her, delighted to see her again, and as the dance had just begun, they danced together. But when the dance was ended, she disappeared again so quickly that the King could not see which way she went. She ran to her little room and changed herself once more into the Many-furred Creature, and went into the kitchen to cook the bread-soup. When the cook was upstairs, she fetched the golden spinning-wheel and put it in the dish so that the soup was poured over it. It was brought to the King, who ate it, and liked it as much as the last time. He had the cook sent to him, and again he had to confess that the Many-furred Creature had cooked the soup. Then the Many-furred Creature came before the King, but she said again that she was of no use except to have boots thrown at her head, and that she knew nothing at all of the golden spinning-wheel.

When the King had a feast for the third time, things did not turn out quite the same as at the other two. The cook said, 'You must be a witch, Many-furred Creature, for you always put something in the soup, so that it is much better and tastes nicer to the King than any that I cook.' But because she begged hard, he let her go up for the usual time. Now she put on the dress as shining as the stars, and stepped into the hall in it.

The King danced again with the beautiful maiden, and thought she had never looked so beautiful. And while he was dancing, he put a gold ring on her finger without her seeing it, and he commanded that the dance should last longer than usual. When it was finished he wanted to keep her hands in his, but she broke from him, and sprang so quickly away among the people that she vanished from his sight. She ran as fast as she could to her little room under the stairs, but because she had stayed too long beyond the half-hour, she could not stop to take off the beautiful dress, but only threw the fur cloak over it, and in her haste she did not make herself quite black with the soot, one finger remaining white. The Many-furred Creature now ran into the kitchen, cooked the King's bread-soup, and when the cook had gone, she laid the gold reel in the dish. When the King found the reel at the bottom, he had the Many-furred Creature brought to him, and then he saw the white finger, and the ring which he had put on her hand in the dance. Then he took her hand and held her tightly, and as she was trying to get away, she undid the fur-cloak a little bit and the star-dress shone out. The King seized the cloak and tore it off her. Her golden hair came down, and she stood there in her full splendour, and could not hide herself away any more. And when the soot and ashes had been washed from her face, she looked more beautiful than anyone in the world. But the King said, 'You are my dear bride, and we will never be separated from one another.' So the wedding was celebrated and they lived happily ever after.

Grimm.

THE TWELVE HUNTSMEN

Once upon a time there was a King's son who was engaged to a Princess whom he dearly loved. One day as he sat by her side feeling very happy, he received news that his father was lying at the point of death, and desired to see him before his end. So he said to his love: 'Alas! I must go off and leave you, but take this ring and wear it as a remembrance of me, and when I am King I will return and fetch you home.'

Then he rode off, and when he reached his father he found him mortally ill and very near death.

The King said: 'Dearest son, I have desired to see you again before my end. Promise me, I beg of you, that you will marry according to my wishes'; and he then named the daughter of a neighbouring King who he was anxious should be his son's wife. The Prince was so overwhelmed with grief that he could think of nothing but his father, and exclaimed: 'Yes, yes, dear father, whatever you desire shall be done.' Thereupon the King closed his eyes and died.

After the Prince had been proclaimed King, and the usual time of mourning had elapsed, he felt that he must keep the promise he had made to his father, so he sent to ask for the hand of the King's daughter, which was granted to him at once.

Now, his first love heard of this, and the thought of her lover's desertion grieved her so sadly that she pined away and nearly died. Her father said to her: 'My dearest child, why are you so unhappy? If there is anything you wish for, say so, and you shall have it.'

His daughter reflected for a moment, and then said: 'Dear father, I wish for eleven girls as nearly as possible of the same height, age, and appearance as myself.'

Said the King: 'If the thing is possible your wish shall be fulfilled'; and he had his kingdom searched till he found eleven maidens of the same height, size, and appearance as his daughter.

Then the Princess desired twelve complete huntsmen's suits to be made, all exactly alike, and the eleven maidens had to dress themselves in eleven of the suits, while she herself put on the twelfth. After this she took leave of her father, and rode off with her girls to the court of her former lover.

Here she enquired whether the King did not want some huntsmen, and if he would not take them all into his service. The King saw her but did not recognize her, and as he thought them very good-looking young people, he said, 'Yes, he would gladly engage them all.' So they became the twelve royal huntsmen.

Now, the King had a most remarkable Lion, for it knew every hidden or secret thing.

One evening the Lion said to the King: 'So you think you have got twelve huntsmen, do you?'

'Yes, certainly,' said the King, 'they *are* twelve huntsmen.'

'There you are mistaken,' said the Lion; 'they are twelve maidens.'

'That cannot possibly be,' replied the King; 'how do you mean to prove that?'

'Just have a number of peas strewed over the floor of your ante-chamber,' said the Lion, 'and you will soon see. Men have a strong, firm tread, so that if they happen to walk over peas not one will stir, but girls trip, and slip, and slide, so that the peas roll all about.'

The King was pleased with the Lion's advice, and ordered the peas to be strewn in his ante-room.

Fortunately one of the King's servants had become very partial to the young huntsmen, and hearing of the trial they were to be put to, he went to them and said: 'The Lion wants to persuade the King that you are only girls'; and then told them all the plot.

The King's daughter thanked him for the hint, and after he was gone she said to her maidens: 'Now make every effort to tread firmly on the peas.'

Next morning, when the King sent for his twelve huntsmen, and they passed through the ante-room which was plentifully strewn with peas, they trod so firmly and walked with such a steady, strong step that not a single pea rolled away or even so much as stirred. After they were gone the King said to the Lion: 'There now—you have been telling lies—you see yourself they walk like men.'

'Because they knew they were being put to the test,' answered the Lion; 'and so they made an effort; but just have a dozen spinning-wheels placed in the ante-room. When they pass through you'll see how pleased they will be, quite unlike any man.'

The King was pleased with the advice, and desired twelve spinning-wheels to be placed in his ante-chamber.

But the good-natured servant went to the huntsmen and told them all about this fresh plot. Then, as soon as the King's daughter was alone with her maidens, she exclaimed: 'Now, pray make a great effort and don't even *look* at those spinning-wheels.'

When the King sent for his twelve huntsmen next morning they walked through the ante-room without even casting a glance at the spinning-wheels.

Then the King said once more to the Lion: 'You have deceived me again; they *are* men, for they never once looked at the spinning-wheels.'

The Lion replied: 'They knew they were being tried, and they did violence to their feelings.' But the King declined to believe in the Lion any longer.

So the twelve huntsmen continued to follow the King, and he grew daily fonder of them. One day whilst they were all out hunting it so happened that news was brought that the King's intended bride was on her way and might soon be expected. When the true bride heard of this she felt as though a knife had pierced her heart, and she fell fainting to the ground. The King, fearing something had happened to his dear huntsman, ran up to help, and began drawing off his gloves. Then he saw the ring which he had given to his first love, and as he gazed into her face he knew her again, and his heart was so touched that he kissed her, and as she opened her eyes, he cried: 'I am thine and thou art mine, and no power on earth can alter that.'

To the other Princess he despatched a messenger to beg her to return to her own kingdom with all speed. 'For,' said he, 'I have got a wife, and he who finds an old key again does not require a new one.'

Thereupon the wedding was celebrated with great pomp, and the Lion was restored to the royal favour, for after all he had told the truth.

Grimm.

SPINDLE, SHUTTLE, AND NEEDLE

Once upon a time there lived a girl who lost her father and mother when she was quite a tiny child. Her godmother lived all alone in a little cottage at the far end of the village, and there she earned her living by spinning, weaving, and sewing. The old woman took the little orphan home with her and brought her up in good, pious, industrious habits.

When the girl was fifteen years old, her godmother fell ill, and, calling the child to her bedside, she said: 'My dear daughter, I feel that my end is near. I leave you my cottage, which will, at least, shelter you, and also my spindle, my weaver's shuttle, and my needle, with which to earn your bread.'

Then she laid her hands on the girl's head, blessed her, and added: 'Mind and be good, and then all will go well with you.' With that she closed her eyes for the last time, and when she was carried to her grave the girl walked behind her coffin weeping bitterly, and paid her all the last honours.

After this the girl lived all alone in the little cottage. She worked hard, spinning, weaving, and sewing, and her old godmother's blessing seemed to prosper all she did. The flax seemed to spread and increase; and when she wove a carpet or a piece of linen, or made a shirt, she was sure to find a customer who paid her well, so that not only did she feel no want herself, but she was able to help those who did.

Now, it happened that about this time the King's son was making a tour through the entire country to look out for a bride. He could not marry a poor woman, and he did not wish for a rich one.

'She shall be my wife,' said he, 'who is at once the poorest and the richest.'

When he reached the village where the girl lived, he inquired who was the richest and who the poorest woman in it. The richest was named first; the poorest, he was told, was a young girl who lived alone in a little cottage at the far end of the village.

The rich girl sat at her door dressed out in all her best clothes, and when the King's son came near she got up, went to meet him, and made him a low curtsey. He looked well at her, said nothing, but rode on further.

When he reached the poor girl's house he did not find her at her door, for she was at work in her room. The Prince reined in his horse, looked in at the window through which the sun was shining brightly, and saw the girl sitting at her wheel busily spinning away.

She looked up, and when she saw the King's son gazing in at her, she blushed red all over, cast down her eyes and span on. Whether the thread was quite as even as usual I really cannot say, but she went on spinning till the King's son had ridden off. Then she stepped to the window and opened the lattice, saying, 'The room is so hot,' but she looked after him as long as she could see the white plumes in his hat.

Then she sat down to her work once more and span on, and as she did so an old saying which, she had often heard her godmother repeat whilst at work, came into her head, and she began to sing:

'Spindle, spindle, go and see, If my love will come to me.'

Lo, and behold! the spindle leapt from her hand and rushed out of the room, and when she had sufficiently recovered from her surprise to look after it she saw it dancing merrily through the fields, dragging a long golden thread after it, and soon it was lost to sight.

The girl, having lost her spindle, took up the shuttle and, seating herself at her loom, began to weave. Meantime the spindle danced on and on, and just as it had come to the end of the golden thread, it reached the King's son.

'What do I see?' he cried; 'this spindle seems to wish to point out the way to me.' So he turned his horses head and rode back beside the golden thread.

Meantime the girl sat weaving, and sang:

'Shuttle, weave both web and woof, Bring my love beneath my roof.'

The shuttle instantly escaped from her hand, and with one bound was out at the door. On the threshold it began weaving the loveliest carpet that was ever seen. Roses and lilies bloomed on both sides, and in the centre a thicket seemed to grow with rabbits and hares running through it, stags and fawns peeping through the branches, whilst on the topmost boughs sat birds of brilliant plumage and so life-like one almost expected to hear them sing. The shuttle flew from side to side and the carpet seemed almost to grow of itself.

As the shuttle had run away the girl sat down to sew. She took her needle and sang:

'Needle, needle, stitch away, Make my chamber bright and gay,' and the needle promptly slipped from her fingers and flew about the room like lightning. You would have thought invisible spirits were at work, for in next to no time the table and benches were covered with green cloth, the chairs with velvet, and elegant silk curtains hung before the windows. The needle had barely put in its last stitch when the girl, glancing at the window, spied the white plumed hat of the King's son who was being led back by the spindle with the golden thread.

He dismounted and walked over the carpet into the house, and when he entered the room there stood the girl blushing like any rose. 'You are the poorest and yet the richest,' said he: 'come with me, you shall be my bride.'

She said nothing, but she held out her hand. Then he kissed her, and led her out, lifted her on his horse and took her to his royal palace, where the wedding was celebrated with great rejoicings.

The spindle, the shuttle, and the needle were carefully placed in the treasury, and were always held in the very highest honour.

Grimm.

THE CRYSTAL COFFIN

Now let no one say that a poor tailor can't get on in the world, and, indeed, even attain to very high honour. Nothing is required but to set the right way to work, but of course the really important thing is to succeed.

A very bright active young tailor once set off on his travels, which led him into a wood, and as he did not know the way he soon lost himself. Night came on, and there seemed to be nothing for it but to seek out the best resting-place he could find. He could have made himself quite comfortable with a bed of soft moss, but the fear of wild beasts disturbed his mind, and at last he determined to spend the night in a tree.

He sought out a tall oak tree, climbed up to the top, and felt devoutly thankful that his big smoothing-iron was in his pocket, for the wind in the tree-tops was so high that he might easily have been blown away altogether.

After passing some hours of the night, not without considerable fear and trembling, he noticed a light shining at a little distance, and hoping it might proceed from some house where he could find a better shelter than in the top of the tree, he cautiously descended and went towards the light. It led him to a little hut all woven together of reeds and rushes. He knocked bravely at the door, which opened, and by the light which shone from within he saw an old gray-haired man dressed in a coat made of bright-coloured patches. 'Who are you, and what do you want?' asked the old man roughly.

'I am a poor tailor,' replied the youth. 'I have been benighted in the forest, and I entreat you to let me take shelter in your hut till morning.'

'Go your way,' said the old man in a sulky tone, 'I'll have nothing to do with tramps. You must just go elsewhere.'

With these words he tried to slip back into his house, but the tailor laid hold of his coat-tails, and begged so hard to be allowed to stay that the old fellow, who was by no means as cross as he appeared, was at length touched by his entreaties, let him come in, and after giving him some food, showed him quite a nice bed in one corner of the room. The weary tailor required no rocking to rest, but slept sound till early morning, when he was roused from his slumbers by a tremendous noise. Loud screams and shouts pierced the thin walls of the little hut. The tailor, with new-born courage, sprang up, threw on his clothes with all speed and hurried out. There he saw a huge black bull engaged in a terrible fight with a fine large stag. They rushed at each other with such fury that the ground seemed to tremble under them and the whole air to be filled with their cries. For some time it appeared quite uncertain which would be the victor, but at length the stag drove his antlers with such force into his opponent's body that the bull fell to the ground with a terrific roar, and a few more strokes finished him.

The tailor, who had been watching the fight with amazement, was still standing motionless when the stag bounded up to him, and before he had time to escape forked him up with its great antlers, and set off at full gallop over hedges and ditches, hill and dale, through wood and water. The tailor could do nothing but hold on tight with both hands to the stag's horns and resign himself to his fate. He felt as if he were flying along. At length the stag paused before a steep rock and gently let the tailor down to the ground.

Feeling more dead than alive, he paused for a while to collect his scattered senses, but when he seemed somewhat restored the stag struck such a blow on a door in the rock that it flew open. Flames of fire rushed forth, and such clouds of steam followed that the stag had to avert its eyes. The tailor could not think what to do or which way to turn to get away from this awful wilderness, and to find his way back amongst human beings once more.

As he stood hesitating, a voice from the rock cried to him: 'Step in without fear, no harm shall befall you.'

He still lingered, but some mysterious power seemed to impel him, and passing through the door he found himself in a spacious hall, whose ceiling, walls, and floor were covered with polished tiles carved all over with unknown figures. He gazed about, full of wonder, and was just preparing to walk out again when the same voice bade him: 'Tread on the stone in the middle of the hall, and good luck will attend you.'

By this time he had grown so courageous that he did not hesitate to obey the order, and hardly had he stepped on the stone than it began to sink gently with him into the depths below. On reaching firm ground he found himself in a hall of much the same size as the upper one, but with much more in it to wonder at and admire. Round the walls were several niches, in each of which stood glass vessels filled with some bright-coloured spirit or bluish smoke. On the floor stood two large crystal boxes opposite each other, and these attracted his curiosity at once.

Stepping up to one of them, he saw within it what looked like a model in miniature of a fine castle surrounded by farms, barns, stables, and a number of other buildings. Everything was quite tiny, but so beautifully and carefully finished that it might have been the work of an accomplished artist. He would have continued gazing much longer at this remarkable curiosity had not the voice desired him to turn round and look at the crystal coffin which stood opposite.

What was his amazement at seeing a girl of surpassing loveliness lying in it! She lay as though sleeping, and her long, fair hair seemed to wrap her round like some costly mantle. Her eyes were closed, but the bright colour in her face, and the movement of a ribbon, which rose and fell with her breath, left no doubt as to her being alive.

As the tailor stood gazing at her with a beating heart, the maiden suddenly opened her eyes, and started with delighted surprise.

'Great heavens!' she cried, 'my deliverance approaches! Quick, quick, help me out of my prison; only push back the bolt of this coffin and I am free.'

The tailor promptly obeyed, when she quickly pushed back the crystal lid, stepped out of the coffin and hurried to a corner of the hall, when she proceeded to wrap herself in a large cloak. Then she sat down on a stone, desired the young man to come near, and, giving him an affectionate kiss, she said, 'My long-hoped-for deliverer, kind heaven has led you to me, and has at length put an end to all my sufferings. You are my destined husband, and, beloved by me, and endowed with every kind of riches and power, you shall spend the remainder of your life in peace and happiness. Now sit down and hear my story. I am the daughter of a wealthy nobleman. My parents died when I was very young, and they left me to the care of my eldest brother, by whom I was carefully educated. We loved each other so tenderly, and our tastes and interests were so much alike that we determined never to marry, but to spend our entire lives together. There was no lack of society at our home. Friends and neighbours paid us frequent visits, and we kept open house for all. Thus it happened that one evening a stranger rode up to the castle and asked for hospitality, as he could not reach the nearest town that night. We granted his request with ready courtesy, and during supper he entertained us with most agreeable conversation, mingled with amusing anecdotes. My brother took such a fancy to him that he pressed him to spend a couple of days with us, which, after a little hesitation, the stranger consented to do. We rose late from table, and whilst my brother was showing our guest to his room I hurried to mine, for I was very tired and longed to get to bed. I had hardly dropped off to sleep when I was roused by the sound of some soft and charming music. Wondering whence it could come, I was about to call to my maid who slept in the room next mine, when, to my surprise, I felt as if some heavy weight on my chest had taken all power from me, and I lay there unable to utter the slightest sound.

Meantime, by the light of the night lamp, I saw the stranger enter my room, though the double doors had been securely locked. He drew near and told me that through the power of his magic arts he had caused the soft music to waken me, and had made his way through bolts and bars to offer me his hand and heart. My repugnance to his magic was so great that I would not condescend to give any answer. He waited motionless for some time, hoping no doubt for a favourable reply, but as I continued silent he angrily declared that he would find means to punish my pride, and therewith he left the room in a rage.

'I spent the night in the greatest agitation, and only fell into a doze towards morning. As soon as I awoke I jumped up, and hurried to tell my brother all that had happened, but he had left his room, and his servant told me that he had gone out at daybreak to hunt with the stranger.

'My mind misgave me. I dressed in all haste, had my palfrey saddled, and rode of at full gallop towards the forest, attended by one servant only. I pushed on without pausing, and ere long I saw the stranger coming towards me, and leading a fine stag. I asked him where he had left my brother, and how he had got the stag, whose great eyes were overflowing with tears. Instead of answering he began to laugh, and I flew into such a rage that I drew a pistol and fired at him; but the bullet rebounded from his breast and struck my horse in the forehead. I fell to the ground, and the stranger muttered some words, which robbed me of my senses.

'When I came to myself I was lying in a crystal coffin in this subterranean vault. The Magician appeared again, and told me that he had transformed my brother into a stag, had reduced our castle and all its defences to miniature and locked them up in a glass box, and after turning all our household into different vapours had banished them into glass phials. If I would only yield to his wishes he could easily open these vessels, and all would then resume their former shapes.

'I would not say a word more than I had done previously, and he vanished, leaving me in my prison, where a deep sleep soon fell on me. Amongst the many dreams which floated through my brain was a cheering one of a young man who was to come and release me, and to-day, when I opened my eyes, I recognised you and saw that my dream was fulfilled. Now help me to carry out the rest of my vision. The first thing is to place the glass box which contains my castle on this large stone.'

As soon as this was done the stone gently rose through the air and transported them into the upper hall, whence they easily carried the box into the outer air. The lady then removed the lid, and it was marvellous to watch the castle, houses, and farmyards begin to grow and spread themselves till they had regained their proper size. Then the young couple returned by means of the movable stone, and brought up all the glass vessels filled with smoke. No sooner were they uncorked than the blue vapours poured out and became transformed to living people, in whom the lady joyfully recognised her many servants and attendants.

Her delight was complete when her brother (who had killed the Magician under the form of a bull) was seen coming from the forest in his proper shape, and that very day, according to her promise, she gave her hand in marriage to the happy young tailor.

Grimm.

THE THREE SNAKE-LEAVES

There was once a poor man who could no longer afford to keep his only son at home. So the son said to him, 'Dear father, you are so poor that I am only a burden to you; I would rather go out into the world and see if I can earn my own living.' The father gave him his blessing and took leave of him with much sorrow. About this time the King of a very powerful kingdom was carrying on a war; the youth therefore took service under him and went on the campaign. When they came before the enemy, a battle took place, there was some hot fighting, and it rained bullets so thickly that his comrades fell around him on all sides. And when their leader fell too the rest wished to take to flight; but the youth stepped forward and encouraged them and called out, 'We must not let our country be ruined!' Then others followed him, and he pressed on and defeated the enemy. When the King heard that he had to thank him alone for the victory, he raised him higher than anyone else in rank, gave him great treasures and made him the first in the kingdom.

The King had a daughter who was very beautiful, but she was also very capricious. She had made a vow to marry no one who would not promise her that if she died first, he would allow himself to be buried alive with her. 'If he loves me truly,' she used to say, 'what use would life be to him then?' At the same time she was willing to do the same, and if he died first to be buried with him. This curious vow had up to this time frightened away all suitors, but the young man was so captivated by her beauty, that he hesitated at nothing and asked her hand of her father. 'Do you know,' asked the King, 'what you have to promise?' 'I shall have to go into her grave with her,' he answered, 'if I outlive her, but my love is so great that I do not think of the risk.' So the King consented, and the wedding was celebrated with great splendour.

Now, they lived for a long time very happily with one another, but then it came to pass that the young Queen fell seriously ill, and no doctor could save her. And when she lay dead, the young King remembered what he had promised, and it made him shudder to think of lying in her grave alive, but there was no escape. The King had set guards before all the gates, and it was not possible to avoid his fate.

When the day arrived on which the corpse was to be laid in the royal vault, he was led thither, then the entrance was bolted and closed up.

Near the coffin stood a table on which were placed four candles, four loaves of bread, and four bottles of wine. As soon as this provision came to an end he would have to die. So he sat there full of grief and misery, eating every day only a tiny bit of bread, and drinking only a mouthful of ovine, and he watched death creeping nearer and nearer to him. One day as he was sitting staring moodily in front of him, he saw a snake creep out of the corner towards the corpse. Thinking it was going to touch it, he drew his sword and saying, 'As long as I am alive you shall not harm her,' he cut it in three pieces. After a little time a second snake crept out of the corner, but when it saw the first one lying dead and in pieces it went back and came again soon, holding three green leaves in its mouth. Then it took the three bits of the snake and laid them in order, and put one of the leaves on each wound. Immediately the pieces joined together, the snake moved itself and became alive and then both hurried away. The leaves remained lying on the ground, and it suddenly occurred to the unfortunate man who had seen everything, that the wonderful power of the leaves might also be exercised upon a human being.

So he picked up the leaves and laid one of them on the mouth and the other two on the eyes of the dead woman. And scarcely had he done this, before the blood began to circulate in her veins, then it mounted and brought colour back to her white face. Then she drew her breath, opened her eyes, and said, 'Ah! where am I?' 'You are with me, dear lady,' he answered, and told her all that had happened, and how he had brought her to life again. He then gave her some wine and bread, and when all her strength had returned she got up, and they went to the door and knocked and called so loudly that the guards heard them, and told the King. The King came himself to open the door, and there he found both happy and well, and he rejoiced with them that now all trouble was over. But the young King gave the three snake-leaves to a servant, saying to him, 'Keep them carefully for me, and always carry them with you; who knows but that they may help us in a time of need!'

It seemed, however, as if a change had come over the young Queen after she had been restored to life, and as if all her love for her husband had faded from her heart. Some time afterwards, when he wanted to take a journey over the sea to his old father, and they were on board the ship, she forgot the great love and faithfulness he had shown her and how he had saved her from death, and fell in love with the captain. And one day when the young King was lying asleep, she called the captain to her, and seized the head of the sleeping King and made him take his feet, and together they threw him into the sea. When they had done this wicked deed, she said to him, 'Now let us go home and say that he died on the journey. I will praise you so much to my father that he will marry me to you and make you the heir to the throne.' But the faithful servant, who had seen everything, let down a little boat into the sea, unobserved by them, and rowed after his master while the traitors sailed on. He took the drowned man out of the water, and with the help of the three snake-leaves which he carried with him, placing them on his mouth and eyes, he brought him to life again.

They both rowed as hard as they could night and day, and their little boat went so quickly that they reached the old King before the other two did. He was much astonished to see them come back alone, and asked what had happened to them. When he heard the wickedness of his daughter, he said, 'I cannot believe that she has acted so wrongly, but the truth will soon come to light.' He made them both go into a secret chamber, and let no one see them.

Soon after this the large ship came in, and the wicked lady appeared before her father with a very sad face. He said to her, 'Why have you come back alone? Where is your husband?'

'Ah, dear father,' she replied, 'I have come home in great grief; my husband fell ill on the voyage quite suddenly, and died, and if the good captain had not given me help, I should have died too. He was at his death-bed and can tell you everything.'

The King said, 'I will bring the dead to life again,' and he opened the door of the room and called them both out. The lady was as if thunderstruck when she caught sight of her husband; she fell on her knees and begged for mercy. But the King said, 'You shall have no mercy. He was ready to die with you, and restored you to life again; but you killed him when he was sleeping, and shall receive your deserts.'

So she and her accomplice were put in a ship which was bored through with holes, and were drawn out into the sea, where they soon perished in the waves.

Grimm.

THE RIDDLE

A King's son once had a great desire to travel through the world, so he started off, taking no one with him but one trusty servant. One day he came to a great forest, and as evening drew on he could find no shelter, and could not think where to spend the night. All of a sudden he saw a girl going towards a little house, and as he drew nearer he remarked that she was both young and pretty. He spoke to her, and said, 'Dear child, could I and my servant spend the night in this house?'

'Oh yes,' said the girl in a sad tone, 'you can if you like, but I should not advise you to do so. Better not go in.'

'Why not?' asked the King's son.

The girl sighed and answered, 'My stepmother deals in black arts, and she is not very friendly to strangers.'

The Prince guessed easily that he had fallen on a witch's house, but as by this time it was quite dark and he could go no further, and as moreover he was not at all afraid, he stepped in.

An old woman sat in an armchair near the fire, and as the strangers entered she turned her red eyes on them. 'Good evening,' she muttered, and pretending to be quite friendly. 'Won't you sit down?'

She blew up the fire on which she was cooking something in a little pot, and her daughter secretly warned the travellers to be very careful not to eat or drink anything, as the old woman's brews were apt to be dangerous.

They went to bed, and slept soundly till morning. When they were ready to start and the King's son had already mounted his horse the old woman said: 'Wait a minute, I must give you a stirrup cup.' Whilst she went to fetch it the King's son rode off, and the servant who had waited to tighten his saddle-girths was alone when the witch returned.

'Take that to your master,' she said; but as she spoke the glass cracked and the poison spurted over the horse, and it was so powerful that the poor creature sank down dead. The servant ran after his master and told him what had happened, and then, not wishing to lose the saddle as well as the horse, he went back to fetch it. When he got to the spot he saw that a raven had perched on the carcase and was pecking at it. 'Who knows whether we shall get anything better to eat to-day!' said the servant, and he shot the raven and carried it off.

Then they rode on all day through the forest without coming to the end. At nightfall they reached an inn, which they entered, and the servant gave the landlord the raven to dress for their supper. Now, as it happened, this inn was a regular resort of a band of murderers, and the old witch too was in the habit of frequenting it.

As soon as it was dark twelve murderers arrived, with the full intention of killing and robbing the strangers. Before they set to work, however, they sat down to table, and the landlord and the old witch joined them, and they all ate some broth in which the flesh of the raven had been stewed down. They had hardly taken a couple of spoonfuls when they all fell down dead, for the poison had passed from the horse to the raven and so into the broth. So there was no one left belonging to the house but the landlord's daughter, who was a good, well-meaning girl, and had taken no part in all the evil doings.

She opened all the doors, and showed the strangers the treasures the robbers had gathered together; but the Prince bade her keep them all for herself, as he wanted none of them, and so he rode further with his servant.

After travelling about for some length of time they reached a town where lived a lovely but most arrogant Princess. She had given out that anyone who asked her a riddle which she found herself unable to guess should be her husband, but should she guess it he must forfeit his head. She claimed three days in which to think over the riddles, but she was so very clever that she invariably guessed them in a much shorter time. Nine suitors had already lost their lives when the King's son arrived, and, dazzled by her beauty, determined to risk his life in hopes of winning her.

So he came before her and propounded his riddle. 'What is this?' he asked. 'One slew none and yet killed twelve.'

She could not think what it was! She thought, and thought, and looked through all her books of riddles and puzzles, but she found nothing to help her, and could not guess; in fact, she was at her wits' end. As she could think of no way to guess the riddle, she ordered her maid to steal at night into the Prince's bedroom and to listen, for she thought that he might perhaps talk aloud in his dreams and so betray the secret. But the clever servant had taken his master's place, and when the maid came he tore off the cloak she had wrapped herself in and hunted her off with a whip.

On the second night the Princess sent her lady-in-waiting, hoping that she might succeed better, but the servant took away her mantle and chased her away also.

On the third night the King's son thought he really might feel safe, so he went to bed. But in the middle of the night the Princess came herself, all huddled up in a misty grey mantle, and sat down near him. When she thought he was fast asleep, she spoke to him, hoping he would answer in the midst of his dreams, as many people do; but he was wide awake all the time, and heard and understood everything very well.

Then she asked: 'One slew none—what is that?' and he answered: 'A raven which fed on the carcase of a poisoned horse.'

She went on: 'And yet killed twelve—what is that?' 'Those are twelve murderers who ate the raven and died of it.'

As soon as she knew the riddle she tried to slip away, but he held her mantle so tightly that she was obliged to leave it behind.

Next morning the Princess announced that she had guessed the riddle, and sent for the twelve judges, before whom she declared it. But the young man begged to be heard, too, and said: 'She came by night to question me, otherwise she never could have guessed it.'

The judges said: 'Bring us some proof.' So the servant brought out the three cloaks, and when the judges saw the grey one, which the Princess was in the habit of wearing, they said: 'Let it be embroidered with gold and silver; it shall be your wedding mantle.'

Grimm.

JACK MY HEDGEHOG

There was once a farmer who lived in great comfort. He had both lands and money, but, though he was so well off, one thing was wanting to complete his happiness; he had no children. Many and many a time, when he met other farmers at the nearest market town, they would teaze him, asking how it came about that he was childless. At length he grew so angry that he exclaimed: 'I must and will have a child of some sort or kind, even should it only be a hedgehog!'

Not long after this his wife gave birth to a child, but though the lower half of the little creature was a fine boy, from the waist upwards it was a hedgehog, so that when his mother first saw him she was quite frightened, and said to her husband, 'There now, you have cursed the child yourself.' The farmer said, 'What's the use of making a fuss? I suppose the creature must be christened, but I don't see how we are to ask anyone to be sponsor to him, and what are we to call him?'

'There is nothing we can possibly call him but Jack my Hedgehog,' replied the wife.

So they took him to be christened, and the parson said: 'You'll never be able to put that child in a decent bed on account of his prickles.' Which was true, but they shook down some straw for him behind the stove, and there he lay for eight years. His father grew very tired of him and often wished him dead, but he did not die, but lay on there year after year.

Now one day there was a big fair at the market town to which the farmer meant to go, so he asked his wife what he should bring her from it. 'Some meat and a couple of big loaves for the house,' said she. Then he asked the maid what she wanted, and she said a pair of slippers and some stockings. Lastly he said, 'Well, Jack my Hedgehog, and what shall I bring you?'

'Daddy,' said he, 'do bring me a bagpipe.' When the farmer came home he gave his wife and the maid the things they had asked for, and then he went behind the stove and gave Jack my Hedgehog the bagpipes.

When Jack had got his bagpipes he said, 'Daddy, do go to the smithy and have the house cock shod for me; then I'll ride off and trouble you no more.' His father, who was delighted at the prospect of getting rid of him, had the cock shod, and when it was ready Jack my Hedgehog mounted on its back and rode off to the forest, followed by all the pigs and asses which he had promised to look after.

Having reached the forest he made the cock fly up to the top of a very tall tree with him, and there he sat looking after his pigs and donkeys, and he sat on and on for several years till he had quite a big herd; but all this time his father knew nothing about him.

As he sat up in his tree he played away on his pipes and drew the loveliest music from them. As he was playing one day a King, who had lost his way, happened to pass close by, and hearing the music he was much surprised, and sent one of his servants to find out where it came from. The man peered about, but he could see nothing but a little creature which looked like a cock with a hedgehog sitting on it, perched up in a tree. The King desired the servant to ask the strange creature why it sat there, and if it knew the shortest way to his kingdom.

On this Jack my Hedgehog stepped down from his tree and said he would undertake to show the King his way home if the King on his part would give him his written promise to let him have whatever first met him on his return.

The King thought to himself, 'That's easy enough to promise. The creature won't understand a word about it, so I can just write what I choose.'

So he took pen and ink and wrote something, and when he had done Jack my Hedgehog pointed out the way and the King got safely home.

Now when the King's daughter saw her father returning in the distance she was so delighted that she ran to meet him and threw herself into his arms. Then the King remembered Jack my Hedgehog, and he told his daughter how he had been obliged to give a written promise to bestow whatever he first met when he got home on an extraordinary creature which had shown him the way. The creature, said he, rode on a cock as though it had been a horse, and it made lovely music, but as it certainly could not read he had just written that he would *not* give it anything at all. At this the Princess was quite pleased, and said how cleverly her father had managed, for that of course nothing would induce her to have gone off with Jack my Hedgehog.

Meantime Jack minded his asses and pigs, sat aloft in his tree, played his bagpipes, and was always merry and cheery. After a time it so happened that another King, having lost his way, passed by with his servants and escort, wondering how he could find his way home, for the forest was very vast. He too heard the music, and told one of his men to find out whence it came. The man came under the tree, and looking up to the top there he saw Jack my Hedgehog astride on the cock.

The servant asked Jack what he was doing up there. 'I'm minding my pigs and donkeys; but what do you want?' was the reply. Then the servant told him they had lost their way, and wanted some one to show it them. Down came Jack my Hedgehog with his cock, and told the old King he would show him the right way if he would solemnly promise to give him the first thing he met in front of his royal castle.

The King said 'Yes,' and gave Jack a written promise to that effect.

Then Jack rode on in front pointing out the way, and the King reached his own country in safety.

Now he had an only daughter who was extremely beautiful, and who, delighted at her father's return, ran to meet him, threw her arms round his neck and kissed him heartily. Then she asked where he had been wandering so long, and he told her how he had lost his way and might never have reached home at all but for a strange creature, half-man, half-hedgehog, which rode a cock and sat up in a tree making lovely music, and which had shown him the right way. He also told her how he had been obliged to pledge his word to give the creature the first thing which met him outside his castle gate, and he felt very sad at the thought that she had been the first thing to meet him.

But the Princess comforted him, and said she should be quite willing to go with Jack my Hedgehog whenever he came to fetch her, because of the great love she bore to her dear old father.

Jack my Hedgehog continued to herd his pigs, and they increased in number till there were so many that the forest seemed full of them. So he made up his mind to live there no longer, and sent a message to his father telling him to have all the stables and outhouses in the village cleared, as he was going to bring such an enormous herd that all who would might kill what they chose. His father was much vexed at this news, for he thought Jack had died long ago. Jack my Hedgehog mounted his cock, and driving his pigs before him into the village, he let every one kill as many as they chose, and such a hacking and hewing of pork went on as you might have heard for miles off.

Then said Jack, 'Daddy, let the blacksmith shoe my cock once more; then I'll ride off, and I promise you I'll never come back again as long as I live.' So the father had the cock shod, and rejoiced at the idea of getting rid of his son.

Then Jack my Hedgehog set off for the first kingdom, and there the King had given strict orders that if anyone should be seen riding a cock and carrying a bagpipe he was to be chased away and shot at, and on no account to be allowed to enter the palace. So when Jack my Hedgehog rode up the guards charged him with their bayonets, but he put spurs to his cock, flew up over the gate right to the King's windows, let himself down on the sill, and called out that if he was not given what had been promised him, both the King and his daughter should pay for it with their lives. Then the King coaxed and entreated his daughter to go with Jack and so save both their lives.

The Princess dressed herself all in white, and her father gave her a coach with six horses and servants in gorgeous liveries and quantities of money. She stepped into the coach, and Jack my Hedgehog with his cock and pipes took his place beside her. They both took leave, and the King fully expected never to set eyes on them again. But matters turned out very differently from what he had expected, for when they had got a certain distance from the town Jack tore all the Princess's smart clothes off her, and pricked her all over with his bristles, saying: 'That's what you get for treachery. Now go back, I'll have no more to say to you.' And with that he hunted her home, and she felt she had been disgraced and put to shame till her life's end.

Then Jack my Hedgehog rode on with his cock and bagpipes to the country of the second King to whom he had shown the way. Now this King had given orders that, in the event of Jack's coming the guards were to present arms, the people to cheer, and he was to be conducted in triumph to the royal palace.

When the King's daughter saw Jack my Hedgehog, she was a good deal startled, for he certainly was very peculiar looking; but after all she considered that she had given her word and it couldn't be helped. So she made Jack welcome and they were betrothed to each other, and at dinner he sat next her at the royal table, and they ate and drank together.

When they retired to rest the Princess feared lest Jack should kiss her because of his prickles, but he told her not to be alarmed as no harm should befall her. Then he begged the old King to place a watch of four men just outside his bedroom door, and to desire them to make a big fire. When he was about to lie down in bed he would creep out of his hedgehog skin, and leave it lying at the bedside; then the men must rush in, throw the skin into the fire, and stand by till it was entirely burnt up.

And so it was, for when it struck eleven, Jack my Hedgehog went to his room, took off his skin and left it at the foot of the bed. The men rushed in, quickly seized the skin and threw it on the fire, and directly it was all burnt

Jack was released from his enchantment and lay in his bed a man from head to foot, but quite black as though he had been severely scorched.

The King sent off for his physician in ordinary, who washed Jack all over with various essences and salves, so that he became white and was a remarkably handsome young man. When the King's daughter saw him she was greatly pleased, and next day the marriage ceremony was performed, and the old King bestowed his kingdom on Jack my Hedgehog.

After some years Jack and his wife went to visit his father, but the farmer did not recognize him, and declared he had no son; he had had one, but that one was born with bristles like a hedgehog, and had gone off into the wide world. Then Jack told his story, and his old father rejoiced and returned to live with him in his kingdom.

Grimm.

THE GOLDEN LADS

A poor man and his wife lived in a little cottage, where they supported themselves by catching fish in the nearest river, and got on as best they could, living from hand to mouth. One day it happened that when the fisherman drew in his net he found in it a remarkable fish, for it was entirely of gold. As he was inspecting it with some surprise, the fish opened its mouth and said: 'Listen to me, fisher; if you will just throw me back into the water I'll turn your poor little cottage into a splendid castle.'

The fisher replied: 'What good, pray, will a castle be to me if I have nothing to eat in it?'

'Oh,' said the gold fish, 'I'll take care of that. There will be a cupboard in the castle, in which you will find dishes of every kind of food you can wish for most.'

'If that's the case,' said the man, 'I've no objection to oblige you.'

'Yes,' observed the fish, 'but there is one condition attached to my offer, and that is that you are not to reveal to a soul where your good fortune comes from. If you say a word about it, it will all vanish.'

The man threw the fish back into the water, and went home. But on the spot where his cottage used to stand he found a spacious castle. He opened his eyes wide, went in and found his wife dressed out in smart clothes, sitting in a splendidly furnished drawing-room. She was in high spirits, and cried out: 'Oh husband! how can this all have happened? I am so pleased!'

'Yes,' said her husband, 'so am I pleased; but I'm uncommonly hungry, and I want something to eat at once.'

Said his wife, 'I've got nothing, and I don't know where anything is in this new house.'

'Never mind,' replied the man. 'I see a big cupboard there. Suppose you unlock it.'

When the cupboard was opened they found meat, cakes, fruit, and wine, all spread out in the most tempting fashions. The wife clapped her hands with joy, and cried: 'Dear heart! what more can one wish for?' and they sat down and ate and drank.

When they had finished the wife asked, 'But husband, where do all these riches come from?'

'Ah!' said he, 'don't ask me. I dare not tell you. If I reveal the secret to anyone, it will be all up with us.'

'Very well,' she replied, 'if I'm not to be told, of course I don't want to know anything about it.'

But she was not really in earnest, for her curiosity never left her a moment's peace by day or night, and she teazed and worried her husband to such a pitch, that at length he quite lost patience and blurted out that it all came from a wonderful golden fish which he had caught and set free again. Hardly were the words well out of his mouth, when castle, cupboard, and all vanished, and there they were sitting in their poor little fishing hut once more.

The man had to betake himself to his former trade, and set to fishing again. As luck would have it, he caught the golden fish a second time.

'Now listen,' said the fish, 'if you'll throw me back into the water, I'll give you back the castle and the cupboard with all its good things; but now take care, and don't for your life betray where you got them, or you'll just lose them again.'

'I'll be very careful,' promised the fisher, and threw the fish back into the water. When he went home he found all their former splendour restored, and his wife overjoyed at their good fortune. But her curiosity still continued to torment her, and after restraining it with a great effort for a couple of days, she began questioning her husband again, as to what had happened, and how he had managed.

The man kept silence for some time, but at last she irritated him so much that he burst out with the secret, and in one moment the castle was gone, and they sat once more in their wretched old hut.

'There!' exclaimed the man, 'you *would* have it—now we may just go on short commons.'

'Ah!' said his wife, 'after all I'd rather not have all the riches in the world if I can't know where they come from—I shall not have a moment's peace.'

The man took to his fishing again, and one day fate brought the gold fish into his net for the third time. 'Well,' said the fish, 'I see that I am evidently destined to fall into your hands. Now take me home, and cut me into six pieces. Give two bits to your wife to eat, two to your horse, and plant the remaining two in your garden, and they will bring you a blessing.'

The man carried the fish home, and did exactly as he had been told. After a time, it came to pass that from the two pieces he had planted in the garden two golden lilies grew up, and that his horse had two golden foals, whilst his wife gave birth to twin boys who were all golden.

The children grew up both tall and handsome, and the foals and the lilies grew with them.

One day the children came to their father and said, 'Father, we want to mount on golden steeds, and ride forth to see the world.'

Their father answered sadly, 'How can I bear it if, when you are far away, I know nothing about you?' and they said, 'The golden lilies will tell you all about us if you look at them. If they seem to droop, you will know we are ill, and if they fall down and fade away, it will be a sign we are dead.'

So off they rode, and came to an inn where were a number of people who, as soon as they saw the two golden lads, began to laugh and jeer at them. When one of them heard this, his heart failed him, and he thought he would go no further into the world, so he turned back and rode home to his father, but his brother rode on till he reached the outskirts of a huge forest. Here he was told, 'It will never do for you to ride through the forest, it is full of robbers, and you're sure to come to grief, especially when they see that you and your horse are golden. They will certainly fall on you and kill you.' However, he was not to be intimidated, but said, 'I must and will ride on.'

So he procured some bears' skins, and covered himself and his horse with them, so that not a particle of gold could be seen, and then rode bravely on into the heart of the forest.

When he had got some way he heard a rustling through the bushes and presently a sound of voices. Someone whispered on one side of him: 'There goes someone,' and was answered from the other side: 'Oh, let him pass. He's only a bear-keeper, and as poor as any church mouse.' So golden lad rode through the forest and no harm befell him.

One day he came to a village, where he saw a girl who struck him as being the loveliest creature in the whole world, and as he felt a great love for her, he went up to her and said: 'I love you with all my heart; will you be my wife?' And the girl liked him so much that she put her hand in his and replied: 'Yes, I will be your wife, and will be true to you as long as I live.'

So they were married, and in the middle of all the festivities and rejoicings the bride's father came home and was not a little surprised at finding his daughter celebrating her wedding. He enquired: 'And who is the bridegroom?'

Then someone pointed out to him the golden lad, who was still wrapped up in the bear's skin, and the father exclaimed angrily: 'Never shall a mere bear-keeper have my daughter,' and tried to rush at him and kill him. But the bride did all she could to pacify him, and begged hard, saying: 'After all he is my husband, and I love him with all my heart,' so that at length he gave in.

However, he could not dismiss the thought from his mind, and next morning he rose very early, for he felt he must go and look at his daughter's husband and see whether he really was nothing better than a mere ragged beggar. So he went to his son-in-law's room, and who should he see lying in the bed but a splendid golden man, and the rough bearskin thrown on the ground close by. Then he slipped quietly away, and thought to himself, 'How lucky that I managed to control my rage! I should certainly have committed a great crime.'

Meantime the golden lad dreamt that he was out hunting and was giving chase to a noble stag, and when he woke he said to his bride: 'I must go off and hunt.' She felt very anxious, and begged he would stay at home, adding: 'Some mishap might so easily befall you,' but he answered, 'I must and will go.'

So he went off into the forest, and before long a fine stag, such as he had seen in his dream, stopped just in front of him. He took aim, and was about to fire when the stag bounded away. Then he started off in pursuit, making his way through bushes and briars, and never stopped all day; but in the evening the stag entirely disappeared, and when golden lad came to look about him he found himself just opposite a hut in which lived a witch. He knocked at the door, which was opened by a little old woman who asked, 'What do you want at this late hour in the midst of this great forest?'

He said, 'Haven't you seen a stag about here?'

'Yes,' said she, 'I know the stag well,' and as she spoke a little dog ran out of the house and began barking and snapping at the stranger.

'Be quiet, you little toad,' he cried, 'or I'll shoot you dead.'

Then the witch flew into a great rage, and screamed out, 'What! you'll kill my dog, will you?' and the next moment he was turned to stone and lay there immovable, whilst his bride waited for him in vain and thought to herself, 'Alas! no doubt the evil I feared, and which has made my heart so heavy, has befallen him.'

Meantime, the other brother was standing near the golden lilies at home, when suddenly one of them bent over and fell to the ground. 'Good heavens!' cried he, 'some great misfortune has befallen my brother. I must set off at once; perhaps I may still be in time to save him.'

His father entreated him, 'Stay at home. If I should lose you too, what would become of me?'

But his son replied, 'I must and will go.'

Then he mounted his golden horse, and rode off till he reached the forest where his brother lay transformed to stone. The old witch came out of her house and called to him, for she would gladly have cast her spells on him too, but he took care not to go near her, and called out: 'Restore my brother to life at once, or I'll shoot you down on the spot.'

Reluctantly she touched the stone with her finger, and in a moment it resumed its human shape. The two golden lads fell into each other's arms and kissed each other with joy, and then rode off together to the edge of the forest, where they parted, one to return to his old father, and the other to his bride.

When the former got home his father said, 'I knew you had delivered your brother, for all of a sudden the golden lily reared itself up and burst into blossom.'

Then they all lived happily to their lives' ends, and all things went well with them.

Grimm.

THE WHITE SNAKE

Not very long ago there lived a King, the fame of whose wisdom was spread far and wide. Nothing appeared to be unknown to him, and it really seemed as if tidings of the most secret matters must be borne to him by the winds. He had one very peculiar habit. Every day, after the dinner table had been cleared, and everyone had retired, a confidential servant brought in a dish. It was covered, and neither the servant nor anyone else had any idea what was on it, for the King never removed the cover or partook of the dish, till he was quite alone.

This went on for some time till, one day, the servant who removed the dish was so overcome with curiosity, that he could not resist carrying it off to his own room. After carefully locking the door, he lifted the cover, and there he saw a white snake lying on the dish. On seeing it he could not restrain his desire to taste it, so he cut off a small piece and put it in his mouth.

Hardly had it touched his tongue than he heard a strange sort of whispering of tiny voices outside his window. He stepped to the casement to listen, and found that the sound proceeded from the sparrows, who were talking together and telling each other all they had seen in the fields and woods. The piece of the white snake which he had eaten had enabled him to understand the language of animals.

Now on this particular day, it so happened that the Queen lost her favourite ring, and suspicion fell on the confidential servant who had access to all parts of the palace. The King sent for him, and threatened him angrily, saying that if he had not found the thief by the next day, he should himself be taken up and tried.

It was useless to assert his innocence; he was dismissed without ceremony. In his agitation and distress, he went down to the yard to think over what he could do in this trouble. Here were a number of ducks resting near a little stream, and pluming, themselves with their bills, whilst they kept up an animated conversation amongst themselves. The servant stood still listening to them. They were talking of where they had been waddling about all the morning, and of the good food they had found, but one of them remarked rather sadly, 'There's something lying very heavy on my stomach, for in my haste I've swallowed a ring, which was lying just under the Queen's window.'

No sooner did the servant hear this than he seized the duck by the neck, carried it off to the kitchen, and said to the cook, 'Suppose you kill this duck; you see she's nice and fat.'

'Yes, indeed,' said the cook, weighing the duck in his hand, 'she certainly has spared no pains to stuff herself well, and must have been waiting for the spit for some time.' So he chopped off her head, and when she was opened there was the Queen's ring in her stomach.

It was easy enough now for the servant to prove his innocence, and the King, feeling he had done him an injustice, and anxious to make some amends, desired him to ask any favour he chose, and promised to give him the highest post at Court he could wish for.

The servant, however, declined everything, and only begged for a horse and some money to enable him to travel, as he was anxious to see something of the world.

When his request was granted, he set off on his journey, and in the course of it he one day came to a large pond, on the edge of which he noticed three fishes which had got entangled in the reeds and were gasping for water. Though fish are generally supposed to be quite mute, he heard them grieving aloud at the prospect of dying in this wretched manner. Having a very kind heart he dismounted and soon set the prisoners free, and in the water once more. They flapped with joy, and stretching up their heads cried to him: 'We will remember, and reward you for saving us.'

He rode further, and after a while he thought he heard a voice in the sand under his feet. He paused to listen, and heard the King of the Ants complaining: 'If only men with their awkward beasts would keep clear of us! That stupid horse is crushing my people mercilessly to death with his great hoofs.' The servant at once turned into a side path, and the Ant-King called after him, 'We'll remember and reward you.'

The road next led through a wood, where he saw a father and a mother raven standing by their nest and throwing out their young: 'Away with you, you young rascals!' they cried, 'we can't feed you any longer. You are quite big enough to support yourselves now.' The poor little birds lay on the ground flapping and beating their wings, and shrieked, 'We poor helpless children, feed ourselves indeed! Why, we can't even fly yet; what can we do but die of hunger?' Then the kind youth dismounted, drew his sword, and killing his horse left it there as food for the young ravens. They hopped up, satisfied their hunger, and piped: 'We'll remember, and reward you!'

He was now obliged to trust to his own legs, and after walking a long way he reached a big town. Here he found a great crowd and much commotion in the streets, and a herald rode about announcing, 'The King's daughter seeks a husband, but whoever would woo her must first execute a difficult task, and if he does not succeed he must be content to forfeit his life.' Many had risked their lives, but in vain. When the youth saw the King's daughter, he was so dazzled by her beauty, that he forgot all idea of danger, and went to the King to announce himself a suitor.

On this he was led out to a large lake, and a gold ring was thrown into it before his eyes. The King desired him to dive after it, adding, 'If you return without it you will be thrown back into the lake time after time, till you are drowned in its depths.'

Everyone felt sorry for the handsome young fellow and left him alone on the shore. There he stood thinking and wondering what he could do, when all of a sudden he saw three fishes swimming along, and recognised them as the very same whose lives he had saved. The middle fish held a mussel in its mouth, which it laid at the young man's feet, and when he picked it up and opened it, there was the golden ring inside.

Full of delight he brought it to the King's daughter, expecting to receive his promised reward. The haughty Princess, however, on hearing that he was not her equal by birth despised him, and exacted the fulfilment of a second task.

She went into the garden, and with her own hands she strewed ten sacks full of millet all over the grass. 'He must pick all that up to-morrow morning before sunrise,' she said; 'not a grain must be lost.'

The youth sat down in the garden and wondered how it would be possible for him to accomplish such a task, but he could think of no expedient, and sat there sadly expecting to meet his death at daybreak.

But when the first rays of the rising sun fell on the garden, he saw the ten sacks all completely filled, standing there in a row, and not a single grain missing. The Ant-King, with his thousands and thousands of followers, had come during the night, and the grateful creatures had industriously gathered all the millet together and put it in the sacks.

The King's daughter came down to the garden herself, and saw to her amazement that her suitor had accomplished the task she had given him. But even now she could not bend her proud heart, and she said, 'Though he has executed these two tasks, yet he shall not be my husband till he brings me an apple from the tree of life.'

The young man did not even know where the tree of life grew, but he set off, determined to walk as far as his legs would carry him, though he had no hope of ever finding it.

After journeying through three different kingdoms he reached a wood one night, and lying down under a tree prepared to go to sleep there. Suddenly he heard a sound in the boughs, and a golden apple fell right into his hand. At the same moment three ravens flew down to him, perched on his knee and said, 'We are the three young ravens whom you saved from starvation. When we grew up and heard you were searching for the golden apple, we flew far away over the seas to the end of the world, where the tree of life grows, and fetched the golden apple for you.'

Full of joy the young man started on his way back and brought the golden apple to the lovely Princess, whose objections were now entirely silenced. They divided the apple of life and ate it together, and her heart grew full of love for him, so they lived together to a great age in undisturbed happiness.

Grimm.

THE STORY OF A CLEVER TAILOR

Once upon a time there lived an exceedingly proud Princess. If any suitor for her hand ventured to present himself, she would give him some riddle or conundrum to guess, and if he failed to do so, he was hunted out of the town with scorn and derision. She gave out publicly that all comers were welcome to try their skill, and that whoever could solve her riddle should be her husband.

Now it happened that three tailors had met together, and the two elder thought, that after having successfully put in so many fine and strong stitches with never a wrong one amongst them, they were certain to do the right thing here too. The third tailor was a lazy young scamp who did not even know his own trade properly, but who thought that surely luck would stand by him now, just for once, for, if not, what *was* to become of him?

The two others said to him, 'You just stay at home, you'll never get on much with your small allowance of brains.' But the little tailor was not to be daunted, and said he had set his mind on it and meant to shift for himself, so off he started as though the whole world belonged to him.

The three tailors arrived at Court, where they had themselves duly presented to the Princess, and begged she would propound her riddles, 'for,' said they, 'here were the right men at last, with wits so sharp and so fine you might almost thread a needle with them.'

Then said the Princess, 'I have on my head two different kinds of hair. Of what colours are they?'

'If that's all,' said the first tailor, 'they are most likely black and white, like the kind of cloth we call pepper-and-salt.'

'Wrong,' said the Princess.

'Then,' said the second tailor, 'if they are not black and white, no doubt they are red and brown, like my father's Sunday coat.'

'Wrong again,' said the Princess; 'now let the third speak. I see he thinks he knows all about it.'

Then the young tailor stepped boldly to the front and said, 'The Princess has one silver and one golden hair on her head, and those are the two colours.'

When the Princess heard this she turned quite pale, and almost fainted away with fear, for the little tailor had hit the mark, and she had firmly believed that not a soul could guess it. When she had recovered herself she said, 'Don't fancy you have won me yet, there is something else you must do first. Below in the stable is a bear with whom you must spend the night, and if when I get up in the morning I find you still alive you shall marry me.'

She quite expected to rid herself of the tailor in this way, for the bear had never left anyone alive who had once come within reach of his claws. The tailor, however, had no notion of being scared, but said cheerily, 'Bravely dared is half won.'

When evening came on he was taken to the stable. The bear tried to get at him at once and to give him a warm welcome with his great paws. 'Gently, gently,' said the tailor, 'I'll soon teach you to be quiet,' and he coolly drew a handful of walnuts from his pocket and began cracking and eating them as though he had not a care or anxiety in the world. When the bear saw this he began to long for some nuts himself. The tailor dived into his pocket and gave him a handful, but they were pebbles, not nuts. The bear thrust them into his mouth, but try as he might he could not manage to crack them. 'Dear me,' thought he, 'what a stupid fool I must be—can't even crack a nut,' and he said to the tailor, 'I say, crack my nuts for me, will you?'

'You're a nice sort of fellow,' said the tailor; 'the idea of having those great jaws and not being able even to crack a walnut!' So he took the stone, quickly changed it for a nut, and crack! it split open in a moment.

'Let me try again,' said the bear; 'when I see the thing done it looks so easy I fancy I *must* be able to manage it myself.'

So the tailor gave him some more pebbles, and the bear bit and gnawed away as hard as he could, but I need hardly say that he did not succeed in cracking one of them.

Presently the tailor took out a little fiddle and began playing on it. When the bear heard the music he could not help dancing, and after he had danced some time he was so pleased that he said to the tailor, 'I say, is fiddling difficult?' 'Mere child's play,' replied the tailor; 'look here! you press the strings with the fingers of the left hand, and with the right, you draw the bow across them, so—then it goes as easily as possible, up and down, tra la la la la—'

'Oh,' cried the bear, 'I do wish I could play like that, then I could dance whenever the fancy took me. What do you think? Would you give me some lessons?'

'With all my heart,' said the tailor, 'if you are sharp about it. But just let me look at your paws. Dear me, your nails are terribly long; I must really cut them first.' Then he fetched a pair of stocks, and the bear laid his paws on them, and the tailor screwed them up tight. 'Now just wait whilst I fetch my scissors,' said he, and left the bear growling away to his heart's content, whilst he lay down in a corner and fell fast asleep.

When the Princess heard the bear growling so loud that night, she made sure he was roaring with delight as he worried the tailor.

Next morning she rose feeling quite cheerful and free from care, but when she looked across towards the stables, there stood the tailor in front of the door looking as fresh and lively as a fish in the water.

After this it was impossible to break the promise she had made so publicly, so the King ordered out the state coach to take her and the tailor to church to be married.

As they were starting, the two bad-hearted other tailors, who were envious of the younger one's happiness, went to the stable and unscrewed the bear. Off he tore after the carriage, foaming with rage. The Princess heard his puffing and roaring, and growing frightened she cried: 'Oh dear! the bear is after us and will certainly catch us up!' The tailor remained quite unmoved. He quietly stood on his head, stuck his legs out at the carriage window and called out to the bear, 'Do you see my stocks? If you don't go home this minute I'll screw you tight into them.'

When the bear saw and heard this he turned right round and ran off as fast as his legs would carry him. The tailor drove on unmolested to church, where he and the Princess were married, and he lived with her many years as happy and merry as a lark. Whoever does not believe this story must pay a dollar.

Grimm.

THE GOLDEN MERMAID

A powerful king had, among many other treasures, a wonderful tree in his garden, which bore every year beautiful golden apples. But the King was never able to enjoy his treasure, for he might watch and guard them as he liked, as soon as they began to get ripe they were always stolen. At last, in despair, he sent for his three sons, and said to the two eldest, 'Get yourselves ready for a journey. Take gold and silver with you, and a large retinue of servants, as beseems two noble princes, and go through the world till you find out who it is that steals my golden apples, and, if possible, bring the thief to me that I may punish him as he deserves.' His sons were delighted at this proposal, for they had long wished to see something of the world, so they got ready for their journey with all haste, bade their father farewell, and left the town.

The youngest Prince was much disappointed that he too was not sent out on his travels; but his father wouldn't hear of his going, for he had always been looked upon as the stupid one of the family, and the King was afraid of something happening to him. But the Prince begged and implored so long, that at last his father consented to let him go, and furnished him with gold and silver as he had done his brothers. But he gave him the most wretched horse in his stable, because the foolish youth hadn't asked for a better. So he too set out on his journey to secure the thief, amid the jeers and laughter of the whole court and town.

His path led him first through a wood, and he hadn't gone very far when he met a lean-looking wolf who stood still as he approached. The Prince asked him if he were hungry, and when the wolf said he was, he got down from his horse and said, 'If you are really as you say and look, you may take my horse and eat it.'

The wolf didn't wait to have the offer repeated, but set to work, and soon made an end of the poor beast. When the Prince saw how different the wolf looked when he had finished his meal, he said to him, 'Now, my friend, since you have eaten up my horse, and I have such a long way to go, that, with the best will in the world, I couldn't manage it on foot, the least you can do for me is to act as my horse and to take me on your back.'

'Most certainly,' said the wolf, and, letting the Prince mount him, he trotted gaily through the wood. After they had gone a little way he turned round and asked his rider where he wanted to go to, and the Prince proceeded to tell him the whole story of the golden apples that had been stolen out of the King's garden, and how his other two brothers had set forth with many followers to find the thief. When he had finished his story, the wolf, who was in reality no wolf but a mighty magician, said he thought he could tell him who the thief was, and could help him to secure him. 'There lives,' he said, 'in a neighbouring country, a mighty emperor who has a beautiful golden bird in a cage, and this is the creature who steals the golden apples, but it flies so fast that it is impossible to catch it at its theft. You must slip into the Emperor's palace by night and steal the bird with the cage; but be very careful not to touch the walls as you go out.'

The following night the Prince stole into the Emperor's palace, and found the bird in its cage as the wolf had told him he would. He took hold of it carefully, but in spite of all his caution he touched the wall in trying to pass by some sleeping watchmen. They awoke at once, and, seizing him, beat him and put him into chains. Next day he was led before the Emperor, who at once condemned him to death and to be thrown into a dark dungeon till the day of his execution arrived.

The wolf, who, of course, knew by his magic arts all that had happened to the Prince, turned himself at once into a mighty monarch with a large train of followers, and proceeded to the Court of the Emperor, where he was received with every show of honour. The Emperor and he conversed on many subjects, and, among other things, the stranger asked his host if he had many slaves. The Emperor told him he had more than he knew what to do with, and that a new one had been captured that very night for trying to steal his magic bird, but that as he had already more than enough to feed and support, he was going to have this last captive hanged next morning.

'He must have been a most daring thief,' said the King, 'to try and steal the magic bird, for depend upon it the creature must have been well guarded. I would really like to see this bold rascal.' 'By all means,' said the Emperor; and he himself led his guest down to the dungeon where the unfortunate Prince was kept prisoner. When the Emperor stepped out of the cell with the King, the latter turned to him and said, 'Most mighty Emperor, I have been much disappointed. I had thought to find a powerful robber, and instead of that I have seen the most miserable creature I can imagine. Hanging is far too good for him. If I had to sentence him I should make him perform some very difficult task, under pain of death. If he did it so much the better for you, and if he didn't, matters would just be as they are now and he could still be hanged.' 'Your counsel,' said the Emperor, 'is excellent, and, as it happens, I've got the very thing for him to do. My nearest neighbour, who is also a mighty Emperor, possesses a golden horse which he guards most carefully. The prisoner shall be told to steal this horse and bring it to me.'

The Prince was then let out of his dungeon, and told his life would be spared if he succeeded in bringing the golden horse to the Emperor. He did not feel very elated at this announcement, for he did not know how in the world he was to set about the task, and he started on his way weeping bitterly, and wondering what had made him leave his father's house and kingdom. But before he had gone far his friend the wolf stood before him and said, 'Dear Prince, why are you so cast down? It is true you didn't succeed in catching the bird; but don't let that discourage you, for this time you will be all the more careful, and will doubtless catch the horse.' With these and like words the wolf comforted the Prince, and warned him specially not to touch the wall or let the horse touch it as he led it out, or he would fail in the same way as he had done with the bird.

After a somewhat lengthy journey the Prince and the wolf came to the kingdom ruled over by the Emperor who possessed the golden horse. One evening late they reached the capital, and the wolf advised the Prince to set to work at once, before their presence in the city had aroused the watchfulness of the guards. They slipped unnoticed into the Emperor's stables and into the very place where there were the most guards, for there the wolf rightly surmised they would find the horse. When they came to a certain inner door the wolf told the Prince to remain outside, while he went in. In a short time he returned and said, 'My dear Prince, the horse is most securely watched, but I have bewitched all the guards, and if you will only be careful not to touch the wall yourself, or let the horse touch it as you go out, there is no danger and the game is yours. The Prince, who had made up his mind to be more than cautious this time, went cheerfully to work. He found all the guards fast asleep, and, slipping into the horse's stall, he seized it by the bridle and led it out; but, unfortunately, before they had got quite clear of the stables a gadfly stung the horse and caused it to switch its tail, whereby it touched the wall. In a moment all the guards awoke, seized the Prince and beat him mercilessly with their horse-whips, after which they bound him with chains, and flung him into a dungeon. Next morning they brought him before the Emperor, who treated him exactly as the King with the golden bird had done, and commanded him to be beheaded on the following day.

When the wolf-magician saw that the Prince had failed this time too, he transformed himself again into a mighty king, and proceeded with an even more gorgeous retinue than the first time to the Court of the Emperor. He was courteously received and entertained, and once more after dinner he led the conversation on to the subject of slaves, and in the course of it again requested to be allowed to see the bold robber who had dared to break into the Emperor's stable to steal his most valuable possession. The Emperor consented, and all happened exactly as it had done at the court of the Emperor with the golden bird; the prisoner's life was to be spared only on condition that within three days he should obtain possession of the golden mermaid, whom hitherto no mortal had ever approached.

Very depressed by his dangerous and difficult task, the Prince left his gloomy prison; but, to his great joy, he met his friend the wolf before he had gone many miles on his journey. The cunning creature pretended he knew nothing of what had happened to the Prince, and asked him how he had fared with the horse. The Prince told him all about his misadventure, and the condition on which the Emperor had promised to spare his life. Then the wolf reminded him that he had twice got him out of prison, and that if he would only trust in him, and do exactly as he told him, he would certainly succeed in this last undertaking. Thereupon they bent their steps towards the sea, which stretched out before them, as far as their eyes could see, all the waves dancing and glittering in the bright sunshine. 'Now,' continued the wolf, 'I am going to turn myself into a boat full of the most beautiful silken merchandise, and you must jump boldly into the boat, and steer with my tail in your hand right out into the open sea. You will soon come upon the golden mermaid. Whatever you do, don't follow her if she calls you, but on the contrary say to her, "The buyer comes to the seller, not the seller to the buyer." After which you must steer towards the land, and she will follow you, for she won't be able to resist the beautiful wares you have on board your ship.'

The Prince promised faithfully to do all he had been told, whereupon the wolf changed himself into a ship full of most exquisite silks, of every shade and colour imaginable. The astonished Prince stepped into the boat, and, holding the wolf's tail in his hand, he steered boldly out into the open sea, where the sun was gilding the blue waves with its golden rays. Soon he saw the golden mermaid swimming near the ship, beckoning and calling to him to follow her; but, mindful of the wolf's warning, he told her in a loud voice that if she wished to buy anything she must come to him. With these words he turned his magic ship round and steered back towards the land. The mermaid called out to him to stand still, but he refused to listen to her and never paused till he reached the sand of the shore. Here he stopped and waited for the mermaid, who had swum after him. When she drew near the boat he saw that she was far more beautiful than any mortal he had ever beheld. She swam round the ship for some time, and then swung herself gracefully on board, in order to examine the beautiful silken stuffs more closely. Then the Prince seized her in his arms, and kissing her tenderly on the cheeks and lips, he told her she was his for ever; at the same moment the boat turned into a wolf again, which so terrified the mermaid that she clung to the Prince for protection.

So the golden mermaid was successfully caught, and she soon felt quite happy in her new life when she saw she had nothing to fear either from the Prince or the wolf—she rode on the back of the latter, and the Prince rode behind her. When they reached the country ruled over by the Emperor with the golden horse, the Prince jumped down, and, helping the mermaid to alight, he led her before the Emperor. At the sight of the beautiful mermaid and of the grim wolf, who stuck close to the Prince this time, the guards all made respectful obeisance, and soon the three stood before his Imperial Majesty. When the Emperor heard from the Prince how he had gained possession of his fair prize, he at once recognized that he had been helped by some magic art, and on the spot gave up all claim to the beautiful mermaid. 'Dear youth,' he said, 'forgive me for my shameful conduct to you, and, as a sign that you pardon me, accept the golden horse as a present. I acknowledge your power to be greater even than I can understand, for you have succeeded in gaining possession of the golden mermaid, whom hitherto no mortal has ever been able to approach.' Then they all sat down to a huge feast, and the Prince had to relate his adventures all over again, to the wonder and astonishment of the whole company.

But the Prince was wearying now to return to his own kingdom, so as soon as the feast was over he took farewell of the Emperor, and set out on his homeward way. He lifted the mermaid on to the golden horse, and swung himself up behind her—and so they rode on merrily, with the wolf trotting behind, till they came to the country of the Emperor with the golden bird. The renown of the Prince and his adventure had gone before him, and the Emperor sat on his throne awaiting the arrival of the Prince and his companions. When the three rode into the courtyard of the palace, they were surprised and delighted to find everything festively illuminated and decorated for their reception. When the Prince and the golden mermaid, with the wolf behind them, mounted the steps of the palace, the Emperor came forward to meet them, and led them to the throne room. At the same moment a servant appeared with the golden bird in its golden cage, and the Emperor begged the Prince to accept it with his love, and to forgive him the indignity he had suffered at his hands. Then the Emperor bent low before the beautiful mermaid, and, offering her his arm, he led her into dinner, closely followed by the Prince and her friend the wolf; the latter seating himself at table, not the least embarrassed that no one had invited him to do so.

As soon as the sumptuous meal was over, the Prince and his mermaid took leave of the Emperor, and, seating themselves on the golden horse, continued their homeward journey. On the way the wolf turned to the Prince and said, 'Dear friends, I must now bid you farewell, but I leave you under such happy circumstances that I cannot feel our parting to be a sad one.' The Prince was very unhappy when he heard these words, and begged the wolf to stay with them always; but this the good creature refused to do, though he thanked the Prince kindly for his invitation, and called out as he disappeared into the thicket, 'Should any evil befall you, dear Prince, at any time, you may rely on my friendship and gratitude.' These were the wolf's parting words, and the Prince could not restrain his tears when he saw his friend vanishing in the distance; but one glance at his beloved mermaid soon cheered him up again, and they continued on their journey merrily.

The news of his son's adventures had already reached his father's Court, and everyone was more than astonished at the success of the once despised Prince. His elder brothers, who had in vain gone in pursuit of the thief of the golden apples, were furious over their younger brother's good fortune, and plotted and planned how they were to kill him. They hid themselves in the wood through which the Prince had to pass on his way to the palace, and there fell on him, and, having beaten him to death, they carried off the golden horse and the golden bird. But nothing they could do would persuade the golden mermaid to go with them or move from the spot, for ever since she had left the sea, she had so attached herself to her Prince that she asked nothing else than to live or die with him.

For many weeks the poor mermaid sat and watched over the dead body of her lover, weeping salt tears over his loss, when suddenly one day their old friend the wolf appeared and said, 'Cover the Prince's body with all the leaves and flowers you can find in the wood.' The maiden did as he told her, and then the wolf breathed over the flowery grave, and, lo and behold! the Prince lay there sleeping as peacefully as a child. 'Now you may wake him if you like,' said the wolf, and the mermaid bent over him and gently kissed the wounds his brothers had made on his forehead, and the Prince awoke, and you may imagine how delighted he was to find his beautiful mermaid beside him, though he felt a little depressed when he thought of the loss of the golden bird and the golden horse. After a time the wolf, who had likewise fallen on the Prince's neck, advised them to continue their journey, and once more the Prince and his lovely bride mounted on the faithful beast's back.

The King's joy was great when he embraced his youngest son, for he had long since despaired of his return. He received the wolf and the beautiful golden mermaid most cordially too, and the Prince was made to tell his adventures all over from the beginning. The poor old father grew very sad when he heard of the shameful conduct of his elder sons, and had them called before him. They turned as white as death when they saw their brother, whom they thought they had murdered, standing beside them alive and well, and so startled were they that when the King asked them why they had behaved so wickedly to their brother they could think of no lie, but confessed at once that they had slain the young Prince in order to obtain possession of the golden horse and the golden bird. Their father's wrath knew no bounds, and he ordered them both to be banished, but he could not do enough to honour his youngest son, and his marriage with the beautiful mermaid was celebrated with much pomp and magnificence. When the festivities were over, the wolf bade them all farewell, and returned once more to his life in the woods, much to the regret of the old King and the young Prince and his bride.

And so ended the adventures of the Prince with his friend the wolf.

Grimm.

THE WAR OF THE WOLF AND THE FOX

There was once upon a time a man and his wife who had an old cat and an old dog. One day the man, whose name was Simon, said to his wife, whose name was Susan, 'Why should we keep our old cat any longer? She never catches any mice now-a-days, and is so useless that I have made up my mind to drown her.'

But his wife replied, 'Don't do that, for I'm sure she could still catch mice.'

'Rubbish,' said Simon. 'The mice might dance on her and she would never catch one. I've quite made up my mind that the next time I see her, I shall put her in the water.'

Susan was very unhappy when she heard this, and so was the cat, who had been listening to the conversation behind the stove. When Simon went off to his work, the poor cat miawed so pitifully, and looked up so pathetically into Susan's face, that the woman quickly opened the door and said, 'Fly for your life, my poor little beast, and get well away from here before your master returns.'

The cat took her advice, and ran as quickly as her poor old legs would carry her into the wood, and when Simon came home, his wife told him that the cat had vanished.

'So much the better for her,' said Simon. 'And now we have got rid of her, we must consider what we are to do with the old dog. He is quite deaf and blind, and invariably barks when there is no need, and makes no sound when there is. I think the best thing I can do with him is to hang him.'

But soft-hearted Susan replied, 'Please don't do so; he's surely not so useless as all that.'

'Don't be foolish,' said her husband. 'The courtyard might be full of thieves and he'd never discover it. No, the first time I see him, it's all up with him, I can tell you.'

Susan was very unhappy at his words, and so was the dog, who was lying in the corner of the room and had heard everything. As soon as Simon had gone to his work, he stood up and howled so touchingly that Susan quickly opened the door, and said 'Fly for your life, poor beast, before your master gets home.' And the dog ran into the wood with his tail between his legs.

When her husband returned, his wife told him that the dog had disappeared.

'That's lucky for him,' said Simon, but Susan sighed, for she had been very fond of the poor creature.

Now it happened that the cat and dog met each other on their travels, and though they had not been the best of friends at home, they were quite glad to meet among strangers. They sat down under a holly tree and both poured forth their woes.

Presently a fox passed by, and seeing the pair sitting together in a disconsolate fashion, he asked them why they sat there, and what they were grumbling about.

The cat replied, 'I have caught many a mouse in my day, but now that I am old and past work, my master wants to drown me.'

And the dog said, 'Many a night have I watched and guarded my master's house, and now that I am old and deaf, he wants to hang me.'

The fox answered, 'That's the way of the world. But I'll help you to get back into your master's favour, only you must first help me in my own troubles.'

They promised to do their best, and the fox continued, 'The wolf has declared war against me, and is at this moment marching to meet me in company with the bear and the wild boar, and to-morrow there will be a fierce battle between us.'

'All right,' said the dog and the cat, 'we will stand by you, and if we are killed, it is at any rate better to die on the field of battle than to perish ignobly at home,' and they shook paws and concluded the bargain. The fox sent word to the wolf to meet him at a certain place, and the three set forth to encounter him and his friends.

The wolf, the bear, and the wild boar arrived on the spot first, and when they had waited some time for the fox, the dog, and the cat, the bear said, 'I'll climb up into the oak tree, and look if I can see them coming.'

The first time he looked round he said, 'I can see nothing,' and the second time he looked round he said, 'I can still see nothing.' But the third time he said, 'I see a mighty army in the distance, and one of the warriors has the biggest lance you ever saw!'

This was the cat, who was marching along with her tail erect.

And so they laughed and jeered, and it was so hot that the bear said, 'The enemy won't be here at this rate for many hours to come, so I'll just curl myself up in the fork of the tree and have a little sleep.'

And the wolf lay down under the oak, and the wild boar buried himself in some straw, so that nothing was seen of him but one ear.

And while they were lying there, the fox, the cat and the dog arrived. When the cat saw the wild boar's ear, she pounced upon it, thinking it was a mouse in the straw.

The wild boar got up in a dreadful fright, gave one loud grunt and disappeared into the wood. But the cat was even more startled than the boar, and, spitting with terror, she scrambled up into the fork of the tree, and as it happened right into the bear's face. Now it was the bear's turn to be alarmed, and with a mighty growl he jumped down from the oak and fell right on the top of the wolf and killed him as dead as a stone.

On their way home from the war the fox caught score of mice, and when they reached Simon's cottage he put them all on the stove and said to the cat, 'Now go and fetch one mouse after the other, and lay them down before your master.'

'All right,' said the cat, and did exactly as the fox told her.

When Susan saw this she said to her husband, 'Just look, here is our old cat back again, and see what a lot of mice she has caught.'

'Wonders will never cease,' cried Simon. 'I certainly never thought the old cat would ever catch another mouse.'

But Susan answered, 'There, you see, I always said our cat was a most excellent creature—but you men always think you know best.'

In the meantime the fox said to the dog, 'Our friend Simon has just killed a pig; when it gets a little darker, you must go into the courtyard and bark with all your might.'

'All right,' said the dog, and as soon as it grew dusk he began to bark loudly.

Susan, who heard him first, said to her husband, 'Our dog must have come back, for I hear him barking lustily. Do go out and see what's the matter; perhaps thieves may be stealing our sausages.'

But Simon answered, 'The foolish brute is as deaf as a post and is always barking at nothing,' and he refused to get up.

The next morning Susan got up early to go to church at the neighbouring town, and she thought she would take some sausages to her aunt who lived there. But when she went to her larder, she found all the sausages gone, and a great hole in the floor. She called out to her husband, 'I was perfectly right. Thieves have been here last night, and they have not left a single sausage. Oh! if you had only got up when I asked you to!'

Then Simon scratched his head and said, 'I can't understand it at all. I certainly never believed the old dog was so quick at hearing.'

But Susan replied, 'I always told you our old dog was the best dog in the world—but as usual you thought you knew so much better. Men are the same all the world over.'

And the fox scored a point too, for he had carried away the sausages himself!

Grimm.

THE STORY OF THE FISHERMAN AND HIS WIFE

There was once a fisherman and his wife who lived together in a little hut close to the sea, and the fisherman used to go down every day to fish; and he would fish and fish. So he used to sit with his rod and gaze into the shining water; and he would gaze and gaze.

Now, once the line was pulled deep under the water, and when he hauled it up he hauled a large flounder with it. The flounder said to him, 'Listen, fisherman. I pray you to let me go; I am not a real flounder, I am an enchanted Prince. What good will it do you if you kill me—I shall not taste nice? Put me back into the water and let me swim away.'

'Well,' said the man, 'you need not make so much noise about it; I am sure I had much better let a flounder that can talk swim away.' With these words he put him back again into the shining water, and the flounder sank to the bottom, leaving a long streak of blood behind. Then the fisherman got up, and went home to his wife in the hut.

'Husband,' said his wife, 'have you caught nothing to-day?'

'No,' said the man. 'I caught a flounder who said he was an enchanted prince, so I let him swim away again.'

'Did you wish nothing from him?' said his wife.

'No,' said the man; 'what should I have wished from him?'

'Ah!' said the woman, 'it's dreadful to have to live all one's life in this hut that is so small and dirty; you ought to have wished for a cottage. Go now and call him; say to him that we choose to have a cottage, and he will certainly give it you.'

'Alas!' said the man, 'why should I go down there again?'

'Why,' said his wife, 'you caught him, and then let him go again, so he is sure to give you what you ask. Go down quickly.'

The man did not like going at all, but as his wife was not to be persuaded, he went down to the sea.

When he came there the sea was quite green and yellow, and was no longer shining. So he stood on the shore and said:

'Once a prince, but changed you be Into a flounder in the sea. Come! for my wife, Ilsebel, Wishes what I dare not tell.'

Then the flounder came swimming up and said, 'Well, what does she want?'

'Alas!' said the man, 'my wife says I ought to have kept you and wished something from you. She does not want to live any longer in the hut; she would like a cottage.'

'Go home, then,' said the flounder; 'she has it.'

So the man went home, and there was his wife no longer in the hut, but in its place was a beautiful cottage, and his wife was sitting in front of the door on a bench. She took him by the hand and said to him, 'Come inside, and see if this is not much better.' They went in, and inside the cottage was a tiny hall, and a beautiful sitting-room, and a bedroom in which stood a bed, a kitchen and a dining-room all furnished with the best of everything, and fitted up with every kind of tin and copper utensil. And outside was a little yard in which were chickens and ducks, and also a little garden with vegetables and fruit trees.

'See,' said the wife, 'isn't this nice?'

'Yes,' answered her husband; 'here we shall remain and live very happily.'

'We will think about that,' said his wife.

With these words they had their supper and went to bed. All went well for a week or a fortnight, then the wife said:

'Listen, husband; the cottage is much too small, and so is the yard and the garden; the flounder might just as well have sent us a larger house. I should like to live in a great stone castle. Go down to the flounder, and tell him to send us a castle.'

'Ah, wife!' said the fisherman, 'the cottage is quite good enough; why do we choose to live in a castle?'

'Why?' said the wife. 'You go down; the flounder can quite well do that.'

'No, wife,' said the man; 'the flounder gave us the cottage. I do not like to go to him again; he might take it amiss.'

'Go,' said his wife. 'He can certainly give it us, and ought to do so willingly. Go at once.'

The fisherman's heart was very heavy, and he did not like going. He said to himself, 'It is not right.' Still, he went down.

When he came to the sea, the water was all violet and dark-blue, and dull and thick, and no longer green and yellow, but it was still smooth.

So he stood there and said:

'Once a prince, but changed you be Into a flounder in the sea. Come! for my wife, Ilsebel, Wishes what I dare not tell.'

'What does she want now?' said the flounder.

'Ah!' said the fisherman, half-ashamed, 'she wants to live in a great stone castle.'

'Go home; she is standing before the door,' said the flounder.

The fisherman went home and thought he would find no house. When he came near, there stood a great stone palace, and his wife was standing on the steps, about to enter. She took him by the hand and said, 'Come inside.'

Then he went with her, and inside the castle was a large hall with a marble floor, and there were heaps of servants who threw open the great doors, and the walls were covered with beautiful tapestry, and in the apartments were gilded chairs and tables, and crystal chandeliers hung from the ceiling, and all the rooms were beautifully carpeted. The best of food and drink also was set before them when they wished to dine. And outside the house was a large courtyard with horse and cow stables and a coach-house—all fine buildings; and a splendid garden with most beautiful flowers and fruit, and in a park quite a league long were deer and roe and hares, and everything one could wish for.

'Now,' said the wife, 'isn't this beautiful?'

'Yes, indeed,' said the fisherman. 'Now we will stay here and live in this beautiful castle, and be very happy.'

'We will consider the matter,' said his wife, and they went to bed.

The next morning the wife woke up first at daybreak, and looked out of the bed at the beautiful country stretched before her. Her husband was still sleeping, so she dug her elbows into his side and said:

'Husband, get up and look out of the window. Could we not become the king of all this land? Go down to the flounder and tell him we choose to be king.'

'Ah, wife!' replied her husband, 'why should we be king? I don't want to be king.'

'Well,' said his wife, 'if you don't want to be king, I will be king. Go down to the flounder; I will be king.'

'Alas! wife,' said the fisherman, 'why do you want to be king? I can't ask him that.'

'And why not?' said his wife. 'Go down at once. I must be king.'

So the fisherman went, though much vexed that his wife wanted to be king. 'It is not right! It is not right,' he thought. He did not wish to go, yet he went.

When he came to the sea, the water was a dark-grey colour, and it was heaving against the shore. So he stood and said:

'Once a prince, but changed you be Into a flounder in the sea. Come! for my wife, Ilsebel, Wishes what I dare not tell.'

'What does she want now?' asked the flounder.

'Alas!' said the fisherman, 'she wants to be king.'

'Go home; she is that already,' said the flounder.

The fisherman went home, and when he came near the palace he saw that it had become much larger, and that it had great towers and splendid ornamental carving on it. A sentinel was standing before the gate, and there were numbers of soldiers with kettledrums and trumpets. And when he went into the palace, he found everything was of pure marble and gold, and the curtains of damask with tassels of gold. Then the doors of the hall flew open, and there stood the whole Court round his wife, who was sitting on a high throne of gold and diamonds; she wore a great golden crown, and had a sceptre of gold and precious stones in her hand, and by her on either side stood six pages in a row, each one a head taller than the other. Then he went before her and said:

'Ah, wife! are you king now?'

'Yes,' said his wife; 'now I am king.'

He stood looking at her, and when he had looked for some time, he said:

'Let that be enough, wife, now that you are king! Now we have nothing more to wish for.'

'Nay, husband,' said his wife restlessly, 'my wishing powers are boundless; I cannot restrain them any longer. Go down to the flounder; king I am, now I must be emperor.'

'Alas! wife,' said the fisherman, 'why do you want to be emperor?'

'Husband,' said she, 'go to the flounder; I will be emperor.'

'Ah, wife,' he said, 'he cannot make you emperor; I don't like to ask him that. There is only one emperor in the kingdom. Indeed and indeed he cannot make you emperor.'

'What!' said his wife. 'I am king, and you are my husband. Will you go at once? Go! If he can make king he can make emperor, and emperor I must and will be. Go!'

So he had to go. But as he went, he felt quite frightened, and he thought to himself, 'This can't be right; to be emperor is too ambitious; the flounder will be tired out at last.'

Thinking this he came to the shore. The sea was quite black and thick, and it was breaking high on the beach; the foam was flying about, and the wind was blowing; everything looked bleak. The fisherman was chilled with fear. He stood and said:

'Once a prince, but changed you be Into a flounder in the sea. Come! for my wife, Ilsebel, Wishes what I dare not tell.'

'What does she want now?' asked flounder.

'Alas! flounder,' he said, 'my wife wants to be emperor.'

'Go home,' said the flounder; 'she is that already.'

So the fisherman went home, and when he came there he saw the whole castle was made of polished marble, ornamented with alabaster statues and gold. Before the gate soldiers were marching, blowing trumpets and beating drums. Inside the palace were walking barons, counts, and dukes, acting as servants; they opened the door, which was of beaten gold. And when he entered, he saw his wife upon a throne which was made out of a single block of gold, and which was quite six cubits high. She had on a great golden crown which was three yards high and set with brilliants and sparkling gems. In one hand she held a sceptre, and in the other the imperial globe, and on either side of her stood two rows of halberdiers, each smaller than the other, from a seven-foot giant to the tiniest little dwarf no higher than my little finger. Many princes and dukes were standing before her. The fisherman went up to her quietly and said:

'Wife, are you emperor now?'

'Yes,' she said, 'I am emperor.'

He stood looking at her magnificence, and when he had watched her for some time, said:

'Ah, wife, let that be enough, now that you are emperor.'

'Husband,' said she, 'why are you standing there? I am emperor now, and I want to be pope too; go down to the flounder.'

'Alas! wife,' said the fisherman, 'what more do you want? You cannot be pope; there is only one pope in Christendom, and he cannot make you that.'

'Husband,' she said, 'I will be pope. Go down quickly; I must be pope to-day.'

'No, wife,' said the fisherman; 'I can't ask him that. It is not right; it is too much. The flounder cannot make you pope.'

'Husband, what nonsense!' said his wife. 'If he can make emperor, he can make, pope too. Go down this instant; I am emperor and you are my husband. Will you be off at once?'

So he was frightened and went out; but he felt quite faint, and trembled and shook, and his knees and legs began to give way under him. The wind was blowing fiercely across the land, and the clouds flying across the sky looked as gloomy as if it were night; the leaves were being blown from the trees; the water was foaming and seething and dashing upon the shore, and in the distance he saw the ships in great distress, dancing and tossing on the waves. Still the sky was very blue in the middle, although at the sides it was an angry red as in a great storm. So he stood shuddering in anxiety, and said:

'Once a prince, but changed you be Into a flounder in the sea. Come! for my wife, Ilsebel, Wishes what I dare not tell.'

'Well, what does she want now?' asked the flounder.

'Alas!' said the fisherman, 'she wants to be pope.'

'Go home, then; she is that already,' said the flounder.

Then he went home, and when he came there he saw, as it were, a large church surrounded by palaces. He pushed his way through the people. The interior was lit up with thousands and thousands of candles, and his wife was dressed in cloth of gold and was sitting on a much higher throne, and she wore three great golden crowns. Round her were numbers of Church dignitaries, and on either side were standing two rows of tapers, the largest of them as tall as a steeple, and the smallest as tiny as a Christmas-tree candle. All the emperors and kings were on their knees before her, and were kissing her foot.

'Wife,' said the fisherman looking at her, 'are you pope now?'

'Yes,' said she; 'I am pope.'

So he stood staring at her, and it was as if he were looking at the bright sun. When he had watched her for some time he said:

'Ah, wife, let it be enough now that you are pope.'

But she sat as straight as a tree, and did not move or bend the least bit. He said again:

'Wife, be content now that you are pope. You cannot become anything more.'

'We will think about that,' said his wife.

With these words they went to bed. But the woman was not content; her greed would not allow her to sleep, and she kept on thinking and thinking what she could still become. The fisherman slept well and soundly, for he had done a great deal that day, but his wife could not sleep at all, and turned from one side to another the whole night long, and thought, till she could think no longer, what more she could become. Then the sun began to rise, and when she saw the red dawn she went to the end of the bed and looked at it, and as she was watching the sun rise, out of the window, she thought, 'Ha! could I not make the sun and man rise?'

'Husband,' said she, poking him in the ribs with her elbows, 'wake up. Go down to the flounder; I will be a god.'

The fisherman was still half asleep, yet he was so frightened that he fell out of bed. He thought he had not heard aright, and opened his eyes wide and said:

'What did you say, wife?'

'Husband,' she said, 'if I cannot make the sun and man rise when I appear I cannot rest. I shall never have a quiet moment till I can make the sun and man rise.'

He looked at her in horror, and a shudder ran over him.

'Go down at once; I will be a god.'

'Alas! wife,' said the fisherman, falling on his knees before her, 'the flounder cannot do that. Emperor and pope he can make you. I implore you, be content and remain pope.'

Then she flew into a passion, her hair hung wildly about her face, she pushed him with her foot and screamed:

'I am not contented, and I shall not be contented! Will you go?'

So he hurried on his clothes as fast as possible, and ran away as if he were mad.

But the storm was raging so fiercely that he could scarcely stand. Houses and trees were being blown down, the mountains were being shaken, and pieces of rock were rolling in the sea. The sky was as black as ink, it was thundering and lightening, and the sea was tossing in great waves as high as church towers and mountains, and each had a white crest of foam.

So he shouted, not able to hear his own voice:

'Once a prince, but changed you be Into a flounder in the sea. Come! for my wife, Ilsebel, Wishes what I dare not tell.'

'Well, what does she want now?' asked the flounder.

'Alas!' said he, 'she wants to be a god.'

'Go home, then; she is sitting again in the hut.'

And there they are sitting to this day.

Grimm.

THE THREE MUSICIANS

Once upon a time three musicians left their home and set out on their travels. They had all learnt music from the same master, and they determined to stick together and to seek their fortune in foreign lands. They wandered merrily from place to place and made quite a good living, and were much appreciated by everyone who heard them play. One evening they came to a village where they delighted all the company with their beautiful music. At last they ceased playing, and began to eat and drink and listen to the talk that was going on around them. They heard all the gossip of the place, and many wonderful things were related and discussed. At last the conversation fell on a castle in the neighbourhood, about which many strange and marvellous things were told. One person said that hidden treasure was to be found there; another that the richest food was always to be had there, although the castle was uninhabited; and a third, that an evil spirit dwelt within the walls, so terrible, that anyone who forced his way into the castle came out of it more dead than alive.

As soon as the three musicians were alone in their bedroom they agreed to go and examine the mysterious castle, and, if possible, to find and carry away the hidden treasure. They determined, too, to make the attempt separately, one after the other, according to age, and they settled that a whole day was to be given to each adventurer in which to try his luck.

The fiddler was the first to set out on his adventures, and did so in the best of spirits and full of courage. When he reached the castle he found the outer gate open, quite as if he were an expected guest, but no sooner had he stepped across the entry than the heavy door closed behind him with a bang, and was bolted with a huge iron bar, exactly as if a sentinel were doing his office and keeping watch, but no human being was to be seen anywhere. An awful terror overcame the fiddler; but it was hopeless to think of turning back or of standing still, and the hopes of finding gold and other treasures gave him strength and courage to force his way further into the castle. Upstairs and downstairs he wandered, through lofty halls, splendid rooms, and lovely little boudoirs, everything beautifully arranged, and all kept in the most perfect order. But the silence of death reigned everywhere, and no living thing, not even a fly, was to be seen. Notwithstanding, the youth felt his spirits return to him when he entered the lower regions of the castle, for in the kitchen the most tempting and delicious food was spread out, the cellars were full of the most costly wine, and the store-room crammed with pots of every sort of jam you can imagine. A cheerful fire was burning in the kitchen, before which a roast was being basted by unseen hands, and all kinds of vegetables and other dainty dishes were being prepared in like manner. Before the fiddler had time to think, he was ushered into a little room by invisible hands, and there a table was spread for him with all the delicious food he had seen cooking in the kitchen.

The youth first seized his fiddle and played a beautiful air on it which echoed through the silent halls, and then he fell to and began to eat a hearty meal. Before long, however, the door opened and a tiny man stepped into the room, not more than three feet high, clothed in a dressing-gown, and with a small wrinkled face, and a grey beard which reached down to the silver buckles of his shoes. And the little man sat down beside the fiddler and shared his meal. When they got to the game course the fiddler handed the dwarf a knife and fork, and begged him to help himself first, and then to pass the dish on. The little creature nodded, but helped himself so clumsily that he dropped the piece of meat he had carved on to the floor.

The good-natured fiddler bent down to pick it up, but in the twinkling of an eye the little man had jumped on to his back, and beat him till he was black and blue all over his head and body. At last, when the fiddler was nearly dead, the little wretch left off, and shoved the poor fellow out of the iron gate which he had entered in such good spirits a few hours before. The fresh air revived him a little, and in a short time he was able to stagger with aching limbs back to the inn where his companions were staying. It was night when he reached the place, and the other two musicians were fast asleep. The next morning they were much astonished at finding the fiddler in bed beside them, and overwhelmed him with questions; but their friend hid his back and face, and answered them very shortly, saying, 'Go there yourselves, and see what's to be seen! It is a ticklish matter, that I can assure you.'

The second musician, who was a trumpeter, now made his way to the castle, and everything happened to him exactly as it had to the fiddler. He was just as hospitably entertained at first, and then just as cruelly beaten and belaboured, so that next morning he too lay in his bed like a wounded hare, assuring his friends that the task of getting into the haunted castle was no enviable one. Notwithstanding the warning of his companions, the third musician, who played the flute, was still determined to try his luck, and, full of courage and daring, he set out, resolved, if possible, to find and secure the hidden treasure.

Fearlessly he wandered the whole castle, and as he roamed through the splendid empty apartments he thought to himself how nice it would be to live there always, especially with a full larder and cellar at his disposal. A table was spread for him too, and when he had wandered about for some time, singing and playing the flute, he sat down as his companions had done, prepared to enjoy the delicious food that was spread out in front of him. Then the little man with the beard entered as before and seated himself beside the flute-player, who wasn't the least startled at his appearance, but chatted away to him as if he had known him all his life. But he didn't find his companion very communicative. At last they came to the game, and, as usual, the little man let his piece fall on the ground. The flute-player was good-naturedly just going to pick it up, when he perceived that the little dwarf was in the act of springing on his back. Then he turned round sharply, and, seizing the little creature by his beard, he gave him such a shaking that he tore his beard out, and the dwarf sank groaning to the ground.

But as soon as the youth had the beard in his hands he felt so strong that he was fit for anything, and he perceived all sorts of things in the castle that he had not noticed before, but, on the other hand, all strength seemed to have gone from the little man. He whined and sobbed out: 'Give, oh give me my beard again, and I will instruct you in all the magic art that surrounds this castle, and will help you to carry off the hidden treasure, which will make you rich and happy for ever.'

But the cunning flute-player replied: 'I will give you back your beard, but you must first help me as you have promised to do. Till you have done so, I don't let your beard out of my hands.'

Then the old man found himself obliged to fulfil his promise, though he had had no intention of doing so, and had only desired to get his beard back. He made the youth follow him through dark secret passages, underground vaults, and grey rocks till at last they came to an open field, which looked as if it belonged to a more beautiful world than ours. Then they came to a stream of rushing water; but the little man drew out a wand and touched the waves, whereupon the waters parted and stood still, and the two crossed the river with dry feet. And how beautiful everything on the other side was! lovely green paths leading through woods and fields covered with flowers, birds with gold and silver feathers singing on the trees, lovely butterflies and glittering beetles fluttered and crawled about, and dear little beasts hid in the bushes and hedges. The sky above them was not blue, but like rays of pure gold, and the stars looked twice their usual size, and far more brilliant than on our earth.

The youth grew more and more astonished when the little grey man led him into a castle far bigger and more splendid than the one they had left. Here, too, the deepest silence reigned. They wandered all through the castle, and came at last to a room in the middle of which stood a bed hung all round with heavy curtains. Over the bed hung a bird's cage, and the bird inside it was singing beautiful songs into the silent space. The little grey man lifted the curtains from the bed and beckoned the youth to approach. On the rich silk cushions embroidered with gold a lovely maiden lay sleeping. She was as beautiful as an angel, with golden hair which fell in curls over her marble shoulders, and a diamond crown sparkled on her forehead. But a sleep as of death held her in its spell, and no noise seemed able to waken the sleeper.

Then the little man turned to the wondering youth and said: 'See, here is the sleeping child! She is a mighty Princess. This splendid castle and this enchanted land are hers, but for hundreds of years she has slept this magic sleep, and during all that time no human being has been able to find their way here. I alone have kept guard over her, and have gone daily to my own castle to get food and to beat the greedy gold-seekers who forced their way into my dwelling. I have watched over the Princess carefully all these years and saw that no stranger came near her, but all my magic power lay in my beard, and now that you have taken it away I am helpless, and can no longer hold the beautiful Princess in her enchanted sleep, but am forced to reveal my treasured secret to you. So set to work and do as I tell you. Take the bird which hangs over the Princess's head, and which by its song sang her into this enchanted sleep—a song which it has had to continue ever since; take it and kill it, and cut its little heart out and burn it to a powder, and then put it into the Princess's mouth; then she will instantly awaken, and will bestow on you her heart and hand, her kingdom and castle, and all her treasures.

The little dwarf paused, quite worn out, and the youth did not wait long to do his bidding. He did all he was told carefully and promptly, and having cut the little bird's heart out he proceeded to make it into a powder. No sooner had he placed it in the Princess's mouth than she opened her lovely eyes, and, looking up into the happy youth's face, she kissed him tenderly, thanked him for freeing her from her magic sleep, and promised to be his wife. At the same moment a sound as of thunder was heard all over the castle, and on all the staircases and in every room sounds were to be heard. Then a troop of servants, male and female, flocked into the apartment where the happy couple sat, and after wishing the Princess and her bridegroom joy, they dispersed all over the castle to their different occupations.

But the little grey dwarf began now to demand his beard again from the youth, for in his wicked heart he was determined to make an end of all their happiness; he knew that if only his beard were once more on his chin, he would be able to do what he liked with them all. But the clever flute-player was quite a match for the little man in cunning, and said: 'All right, you needn't be afraid, you shall get your beard back before we part; but you must allow my bride and me to accompany you a bit on your homeward way.'

The dwarf could not refuse this request, and so they all went together through the beautiful green paths and flowery meadows, and came at last to the river which flowed for miles round the Princess's land and formed the boundary of her kingdom. There was no bridge or ferryboat to be seen anywhere, and it was impossible to get over to the other side, for the boldest swimmer would not have dared to brave the fierce current and roaring waters. Then the youth said to the dwarf: 'Give me your wand in order that I may part the waves.'

And the dwarf was forced to do as he was told because the youth still kept his beard from him; but the wicked little creature chuckled with joy and thought to himself: 'The foolish youth will hand me my beard as soon as we have crossed the river, and then my power will return, and I will seize my wand and prevent them both ever returning to their beautiful country.'

But the dwarf's wicked intentions were doomed to disappointment. The happy youth struck the water with his wand, and the waves at once parted and stood still, and the dwarf went on in front and crossed the stream. No sooner had he done so than the waters closed behind him, and the youth and his lovely bride stood safe on the other side. Then they threw his beard to the old man across the river, but they kept his wand, so that the wicked dwarf could never again enter their kingdom. So the happy couple returned to their castle, and lived there in peace and plenty for ever after. But the other two musicians waited in vain for the return of their companion; and when he never came they said: 'Ah, he's gone to play the flute,' till the saying passed into a proverb, and was always said of anyone who set out to perform a task from which he never returned.

Grimm.

THE THREE DOGS

There was once upon a time a shepherd who had two children, a son and a daughter. When he was on his death-bed he turned to them and said, 'I have nothing to leave you but three sheep and a small house; divide them between you, as you like, but don't quarrel over them whatever you do.'

When the shepherd was dead, the brother asked his sister which she would like best, the sheep or the little house; and when she had chosen the house he said, 'Then I'll take the sheep and go out to seek my fortune in the wide world. I don't see why I shouldn't be as lucky as many another who has set out on the same search, and it wasn't for nothing that I was born on a Sunday.'

And so he started on his travels, driving his three sheep in front of him, and for a long time it seemed as if fortune didn't mean to favour him at all. One day he was sitting disconsolately at a cross road, when a man suddenly appeared before him with three black dogs, each one bigger than the other.

'Hullo, my fine fellow,' said the man, 'I see you have three fat sheep. I'll tell you what; if you'll give them to me, I'll give you my three dogs.'

In spite of his sadness, the youth smiled and replied, 'What would I do with your dogs? My sheep at least feed themselves, but I should have to find food for the dogs.'

'My dogs are not like other dogs,' said the stranger; 'they will feed you instead of you them, and will make your fortune. The smallest one is called "Salt," and will bring you food whenever you wish; the second is called "Pepper," and will tear anyone to pieces who offers to hurt you; and the great big strong one is called "Mustard," and is so powerful that it will break iron or steel with its teeth.'

The shepherd at last let himself be persuaded, and gave the stranger his sheep. In order to test the truth of his statement about the dogs, he said at once, 'Salt, I am hungry,' and before the words were out of his mouth the dog had disappeared, and returned in a few minutes with a large basket full of the most delicious food. Then the youth congratulated himself on the bargain he had made, and continued his journey in the best of spirits.

One day he met a carriage and pair, all draped in black; even the horses were covered with black trappings, and the coachman was clothed in crape from top to toe. Inside the carriage sat a beautiful girl in a black dress crying bitterly. The horses advanced slowly and mournfully, with their heads bent on the ground.

'Coachman, what's the meaning of all this grief?' asked the shepherd.

At first the coachman wouldn't say anything, but when the youth pressed him he told him that a huge dragon dwelt in the neighbourhood, and required yearly the sacrifice of a beautiful maiden. This year the lot had fallen on the King's daughter, and the whole country was filled with woe and lamentation in consequence.

The shepherd felt very sorry for the lovely maiden, and determined to follow the carriage. In a little it halted at the foot of a high mountain. The girl got out, and walked slowly and sadly to meet her terrible fate. The coachman perceived that the shepherd wished to follow her, and warned him not to do so if he valued his life; but the shepherd wouldn't listen to his advice. When they had climbed about half-way up the hill they saw a terrible-looking monster with the body of a snake, and with huge wings and claws, coming towards them, breathing forth flames of fire, and preparing to seize its victim. Then the shepherd called, 'Pepper, come to the rescue,' and the second dog set upon the dragon, and after a fierce struggle bit it so sharply in the neck that the monster rolled over, and in a few moments breathed its last. Then the dog ate up the body, all except its two front teeth, which the shepherd picked up and put in his pocket.

The Princess was quite overcome with terror and joy, and fell fainting at the feet of her deliverer. When she recovered her consciousness she begged the shepherd to return with her to her father, who would reward him richly. But the youth answered that he wanted to see something of the world, and that he would return again in three years, and nothing would make him change this resolve. The Princess seated herself once more in her carriage, and, bidding each other farewell, she and the shepherd separated, she to return home, and he to see the world.

But while the Princess was driving over a bridge the carriage suddenly stood still, and the coachman turned round to her and said, 'Your deliverer has gone, and doesn't thank you for your gratitude. It would be nice of you to make a poor fellow happy; therefore you may tell your father that it was I who slew the dragon, and if you refuse to, I will throw you into the river, and no one will be any the wiser, for they will think the dragon has devoured you.'

The maiden was in a dreadful state when she heard these words; but there was nothing for her to do but to swear that she would give out the coachman as her deliverer, and not to divulge the secret to anyone. So they returned to the capital, and everyone was delighted when they saw the Princess had returned unharmed; the black flags were taken down from all the palace towers, and gay-coloured ones put up in their place, and the King embraced his daughter and her supposed rescuer with tears of joy, and, turning to the coachman, he said, 'You have not only saved the life of my child, but you have also freed the country from a terrible scourge; therefore, it is only fitting that you should be richly rewarded. Take, therefore, my daughter for your wife; but as she is still so young, do not let the marriage be celebrated for another year.'

The coachman thanked the King for his graciousness, and was then led away to be richly dressed and instructed in all the arts and graces that befitted his new position. But the poor Princess wept bitterly, though she did not dare to confide her grief to anyone. When the year was over, she begged so hard for another year's respite that it was granted to her. But this year passed also, and she threw herself at her father's feet, and begged so piteously for one more year that the King's heart was melted, and he yielded to her request, much to the Princess's joy, for she knew that her real deliverer would appear at the end of the third year. And so the year passed away like the other two, and the wedding-day was fixed, and all the people were prepared to feast and make merry.

But on the wedding-day it happened that a stranger came to the town with three black dogs. He asked what the meaning of all the feasting and fuss was, and they told him that the King's daughter was just going to be married to the man who had slain the terrible dragon. The stranger at once denounced the coachman as a liar; but no one would listen to him, and he was seized and thrown into a cell with iron doors.

While he was lying on his straw pallet, pondering mournfully on his fate, he thought he heard the low whining of his dogs outside; then an idea dawned on him, and he called out as loudly as he could, 'Mustard, come to my help,' and in a second he saw the paws of his biggest dog at the window of his cell, and before he could count two the creature had bitten through the iron bars and stood beside him. Then they both let themselves out of the prison by the window, and the poor youth was free once more, though he felt very sad when he thought that another was to enjoy the reward that rightfully belonged to him. He felt hungry too, so he called his dog 'Salt,' and asked him to bring home some food. The faithful creature trotted off, and soon returned with a table-napkin full of the most delicious food, and the napkin itself was embroidered with a kingly crown.

The King had just seated himself at the wedding-feast with all his Court, when the dog appeared and licked the Princess's hand in an appealing manner. With a joyful start she recognised the beast, and bound her own table-napkin round his neck. Then she plucked up her courage and told her father the whole story. The King at once sent a servant to follow the dog, and in a short time the stranger was led into the Kings presence. The former coachman grew as white as a sheet when he saw the shepherd, and, falling on his knees, begged for mercy and pardon. The Princess recognized her deliverer at once, and did not need the proof of the two dragon's teeth which he drew from his pocket. The coachman was thrown into a dark dungeon, and the shepherd took his place at the Princess's side, and this time, you may be sure, she did not beg for the wedding to be put off.

The young couple lived for some time in great peace and happiness, when suddenly one day the former shepherd bethought himself of his poor sister and expressed a wish to see her again, and to let her share in his good fortune. So they sent a carriage to fetch her, and soon she arrived at the court, and found herself once more in her brother's arms. Then one of the dogs spoke and said, 'Our task is done; you have no more need of us. We only waited to see that you did not forget your sister in your prosperity.' And with these words the three dogs became three birds and flew away into the heavens.

Grimm.